Poet, journalist, lover of freedom, Walt Whitman was born near Huntington, Long Island, New York, on May 31, 1819. His father—a farmer and later a carpenter—moved his wife and nine children to Brooklyn in 1823. Walt attended public school until the age of twelve. Then for two decades he worked alternately as printer and journalist, except for two years of teaching on Long Island. In 1848, his "free soil" political beliefs lost him the editorship of the conservative Brooklyn *Eagle,* and he left the East, traveling South to New Orleans where he had contracted to write for the *Crescent.* Fascinated by the city, Whitman spent three months there; he then returned home to Brooklyn by way of St. Louis, Chicago, the Great Lakes, Niagara Falls, Albany, and the Hudson. In 1855, Whitman published his great tribute to America, the volume of poems which was to become his life's work, *Leaves of Grass.* Although praised by Emerson, it met with a disappointing reception, and Whitman continued, thereafter, to revise and expand it. In all, between 1855 and 1892, he published nine editions. During the Civil War and for some years after, Whitman worked as a war correspondent and government clerk, devoting much of his time to caring for the sick and wounded in the hospitals around Washington. His reactions to and interpretations of the struggle for freedom are to be found in *The Wound Dresser, Drum-Taps,* and in the Civil War section of *Specimen Days.* First published in 1882, this book contains Whitman's great themes; and it presents "specimen" events in the author's life and in the life of nineteenth-century America. Stricken with paralysis in 1873, the poet retired to Camden, New Jersey, where he lived until his death on March 26, 1892.

Walt Whitman

Leaves of Grass

With an Introduction by Gay Wilson Allen

Ⓒ

A SIGNET CLASSIC from
NEW AMERICAN LIBRARY
TIMES MIRROR
New York and Scarborough, Ontario
The New English Library Limited, London

INTRODUCTION COPYRIGHT © 1955, 1958,
BY GAY WILSON ALLEN

Library of Congress Catalog Card No. 54-10986

SIGNET CLASSIC TRADEMARK REG. U.S. PAT. OFF. AND FOREIGN COUNTRIES
REGISTERED TRADEMARK—MARCA REGISTRADA
HECHO EN CHICAGO, U.S.A.

SIGNET, SIGNET CLASSICS, MENTOR, PLUME AND MERIDIAN BOOKS
are published *in the United States* by
The New American Library, Inc.,
1301 Avenue of the Americas, New York, New York 10019,
in Canada by The New American Library of Canada Limited,
81 Mack Avenue, Scarborough, Ontario M1L 1M8,
in the United Kingdom by The New English Library Limited,
Barnard's Inn, Holborn, London, EC1N 2JR, England

18 19 20 21 22 23 24

PRINTED IN THE UNITED STATES OF AMERICA

INTRODUCTION

1. The Book and Its Author

Today Walt Whitman's *Leaves of Grass* is almost universally recognized as one of the masterpieces of world literature, but it did not have an impressive beginning.

Early in July, 1855, a thin quarto volume of ninety-five pages, bound in green cloth ornately stamped with roots, leaves, buds, and small flowers, was placed on sale in several bookstores in New York and Brooklyn. Although it was distributed and advertised by Fowler & Wells, publishers of books and magazines on phrenology, *Leaves of Grass* had been printed at the author's own expense by his friends the Rome Brothers in Brooklyn. Fewer than eight hundred copies were printed, and of these only two hundred were immediately bound.

Whitman withheld his name from the title page, but displayed himself in shirt sleeves and a nonchalant pose in a frontispiece photograph. Doubtless he intended thus to emphasize the personal nature of his poems and their informal style, a guess corroborated by a passage in his longest poem, then untitled but later called "Song of Myself," in which he stated his name and his supposed attributes:

> Walt Whitman, a kosmos, of Manhattan the son,
> Turbulent, fleshy, sensual, eating, drinking and breeding,
> No sentimentalist, no stander above men and women or
>   apart from them,
> No more modest than immodest.

But this eccentric manner of signing his book made Ralph Waldo Emerson, to whom Whitman sent a complimentary copy, doubtful of the real name of the poet. On July 21, 1855, he wrote: "I did not know until I, last night, saw the book advertised in a newspaper, that I could trust the name as real and available for a post office."

Emerson was one of the few literary men to see merit in this strange book—indeed, one of the few persons to read it at all, though there were more than the poet knew about at the time. In his first unrestrained enthusiasm the older poet wrote the younger: "I greet you at the beginning of a great career, which yet must have had a long foreground somewhere, for such a start. I rubbed my eyes a little to see if this

v

sunbeam were no illusion; but the solid sense of the book is a sober certainty. . . . " Whitman was naturally delighted, as well he might have been, with such warm praise from the famous New England poet. It fortified him against the abuse of less perceptive critics, and he was soon to receive enough abuse to overwhelm a sensitive young poet. But Walt Whitman was abundantly endowed with courage and determination, and he immediately began the preparation of a second edition to be published the following year.

There were a few other readers who recognized the importance of the first *Leaves of Grass,* but Emerson alone sensed its "long foreground." Indeed, it has taken critics and scholars nearly a century to discover the truth of Emerson's sure insight. Not even Whitman's intimate friends and associates—in fact, they least of all—were aware of the vast intellectual preparation and effort that went into the 1855 *Leaves of Grass.* His formal education had been scanty, being limited to five or six years of attending public school in the village of Brooklyn, N. Y. He was born May 31, 1819, at West Hills, a little farming community on Long Island, three miles south of Huntington. His father had learned the carpenter's trade, and is said to have been a competent and meticulous workman, but for some reason he never prospered. He was, in fact, already a failure when he moved his family to Brooklyn in 1823. He was interested in books and ideas, especially those of deistic Tom Paine, whom he knew personally, and the socialistic theories of Frances Wright. But he had received almost no formal education, and his wife, Louisa Van Velsor, daughter of a Dutch farmer on Long Island, was nearly illiterate.

Walter Whitman, Jr., was the second of nine children, and because his father was always hard pressed to feed and clothe his large family, he began at the age of eleven to work as an office boy. By his twelfth year he had quit school altogether and was apprenticed to the printing trade. For two decades he worked alternately as printer and journalist, except for two years of teaching in various country schools on Long Island. During the 1840's he wrote for popular magazines, edited several newspapers in New York City, and held the editorship of the Brooklyn *Eagle* for two years. The stories and poems he contributed to the magazines were conventional, sentimental, and undistinguished, but in journalism he was fairly competent. However, he did not prosper as an editor because practically all newspapers at that time were violently partisan and his "free soil" convictions did not agree with the political policies of the Democratic owners of the papers on which he was employed.

After he lost his editorship of the Brooklyn *Eagle,* Whitman traveled by train, stagecoach, and steamboat to New Orleans—then an arduous journey—where he worked for three months on the newly-founded *Crescent*. Returning to Brooklyn, he edited a "free soil" newspaper and took an active part in the campaign of Martin Van Buren and Charles Francis Adams on the Free Soil ticket in 1848. Whitman continued to edit his paper, the *Freeman*, for nearly a year after the defeat of the Free Soil party, but he was finally forced to give it up.

Though nominally a Democrat, Whitman now found the Democratic press virtually closed to him. His political convictions had forced him out of journalism, though he continued to contribute occasionally to the New York *Post*, edited by his friend William Cullen Bryant, the *Tribune*, edited by Horace Greeley, and the Brooklyn *Advertiser*. But he could not support himself with these fugitive pieces. It was not by accident or caprice, therefore, that he joined his father in the building trade. In a short time he became a contractor, speculating modestly in real estate and house building like his father, though with more success. In fact, in the early 1850's Brooklyn was experiencing a lively building boom, and Whitman had excellent opportunities for accumulating wealth. He might have done so, too, if he had not acquired a greater ambition.

This ambition was the writing and publishing of a volume of poems which at an early stage in his planning he had decided to call *Leaves of Grass*. For years orators, authors, and editorial writers had been calling for a native literature commensurate with American natural resources, ample geography, and political idealism. This demand for an indigenous literature had of course been profoundly influenced by European Romanticism, and yet at the same time national pride had brought about the intellectual rejection of Europe, politically and culturally. In 1837 Emerson had declared in his "American Scholar" address: "Our day of dependence, our long apprenticeship to the learning of other lands, draws to a close. . . . We have listened too long to the courtly muses of Europe."

The call for an original, native poet stirred Walt Whitman's imagination. He himself was descended from several generations of typical rural Americans, half-Dutch, half-British in origin. For his daily associates he habitually chose the mechanics, ferry-boat pilots, stage drivers, and rough, uneducated workingmen whom he had known all his life as relatives, neighbors, and companions in the saloons and on the streets of Brooklyn and New York. He shared their patriotic pride in the territorial expansion of the young nation, and looked upon the material growth of the United States as a blessing to all mankind, providing a refuge for the oppressed of every nation. He was acutely aware of his country's shortcomings, and hoped through his poems and speeches (for many years he cherished the futile ambition of becoming a great public speaker) to spread and propagate democracy. But if Walt Whitman's qualifications for becoming his nation's poetic spokesman had been no more than devout patriotism and a journalist's gift for propaganda, he would never have become a great poet.

To an educated observer Whitman would have seemed to have almost no chance at all of becoming a real poet. But appearances were deceiving. In his own way he had been acquiring exactly the training he needed. Despite his slow movements and leisurely habits, his careless dress and association with ferrymen and stage drivers, he had assiduously cultivated his mind and esthetic sensibilities. From early boyhood he had been fond of the theater, and as a young man he became a devotee of the Italian opera. In Brooklyn he had also become intimate with painters and sculptors, notably William Sidney Mount, Walter Libby, Henry Kirke Brown, and John Quincy Ward. He spent many hours in the libraries of New York City. And in the 1850's he frequented the Egyptian Museum on lower Broadway, where he acquired an interest in the history of the human race and the myths and religions of ancient peoples that broadened his intellectual horizon. In both cities he attended lectures on astronomy, which also gave him new concepts of time and man's place in the vast structure of the universe. Although largely self-taught, Walt Whitman actually read more widely, both in quantity and in variety of subjects, than many of the authors of the period who had attended famous colleges. Whenever possible, however, he obtained knowledge through talks with explorers, scientists, and learned persons, such as Dr. Henry Abbott, owner of the Egyptian Museum. Walt Whitman was indeed a paradox. He recited Shakespeare from the top of a Broadway omnibus, where he sat beside the driver; he carried translations of Homer in his pocket when he went on fishing trips or spent the day alone on Coney Island (then a lonely spot); by choice he consorted with the most ignorant men, but loved opera and was welcomed in the studios of leading painters and sculptors.

But neither experience with the world nor the reading of many books makes a poet. He must, first of all, be endowed with a poet's temperament and sensibility, and ultimately with the gift of language. This endowment defies objective analysis, but Whitman's poems testify to the acute sensitivity of his touch, hearing, sight, and smell. Most important of all in the making of a great poet is an inner compulsion demanding outlet through the symbols of poetry. Whitman experienced this compulsion to an extraordinary degree in the years immediately preceding the completion of the first *Leaves of Grass*. To one of his most intimate friends he confessed later that he had written the first *Leaves* "under great pressure,—pressure from within." He felt that he *"must* do it." This confession indicates a strong probability that the real motivating force was subconscious, as the abundance of sexual imagery in the early poems implies. Whitman rationalized his motive by contending (in an open letter to Emerson printed in the second edition of *Leaves of Grass*) that sex must be brought out of concealment into the open in order to foster a sane, healthy attitude toward this important phase of life. In the twentieth century this argument is readily acceptable; and one of Whitman's most lasting achievements was his contribution toward the breaking down of prudery and taboos against sex in literature.

But probably Whitman himself was only dimly aware of the generating power of "the pressure from within." In his early poems he exhibited a strong desire to make personal confessions. In "Song of Myself" (section 28) he feels betrayed by his senses, and complains of the "prurient provokers stiffening my limbs." This motivation has been explained by several critics as auto-eroticism, but the term is hardly adequate for the poet's complex psychology. There can no longer be any doubt that, despite their intensity, Whitman's sexual impulses were somewhat ambiguous. Every human organism, biologists tell us, has some cells of the opposite sex. In the absence of scientific data, we can only guess at the balance of the sexes in the body of Walt Whitman, but his compulsion to confess and to justify his emotions indicates at least a strong psychic disturbance. Later Whitman used the word "perturbation" for this disturbance, a term which he had encountered in the lectures on astronomy which he had heard and read. The term means, "disturbance of the regular . . . motion of a heavenly body, produced by some force additional to that which causes its regular motion." Whitman himself thought his *Drum-Taps* poems superior esthetically to *Leaves of Grass* because they had "none of the perturbations of Leaves of Grass" (the first three editions).

The process by which a poem is created in the mind of the poet is still little understood either by psychologists or literary critics, but it seems to begin with a profound emotional turbulence, probably on the subconscious level. From this turbulence not only emotional impulses but even verbal images float up into the poet's consciousness. If he writes the poem while the turbulence is still going on, he is not likely to have control over his esthetic form.

This theory illuminates the problem of esthetics in Whitman's poems. His most vivid and original imagery is found in "Song of Myself," but the emotional tone of this poem is very uneven and its structure has defied the best efforts of many critics, though some recent ones profess to find a thematic structure in it. Furthermore, there is frequently a conflict between Whitman's desire to be personal, to make intimate revelations to his reader, and his intuitions of truths about life and the meaning of existence. In writing "Crossing Brooklyn Ferry" Whitman had sufficient control over his inner turbulence to compose a poem with beautiful symmetry of imagery, rhythm, and pattern of symbols. A few years later in "Out of the Cradle Endlessly Rocking" he exhibited similar control, and the same can be said of "When Lilacs Last in the Dooryard Bloom'd," which was completed several months after the death of Lincoln—an exemplification of Wordsworth's theory of "emotion recollected in tranquility."

It is significant, too, that in these poems in which the poet has control, his poetic message is the transcending of time and achieving a philosophy of death. In the "Ferry" poem life is always fluid and souls are forever crossing from the material to the immaterial world, and back again. In the "Cradle" poem the boy becomes a poet when he vicariously gains knowledge of death. In "Lilacs" the poet joins hands with "the thought of death" (grief for a personal loss) and "the knowledge of death" (philosophical acceptance)—"Comrades mine and I in the midst"—and arrives with them, completely resigned, at the end of the coffin's journey, "in the fragrant pines and cedars dusk and dim." Here the poet submerges his own personality and thereby transcends the bounds of his finite life. He achieves the fullness of selfhood, always his poetic and philosophical goal, in his esthetic intuition of the necessity for physical dissolution in the perpetuity of life.

Of course the personal experiences that created the turbulence in Whitman's psyche profoundly affected his poetic intuitions, but the relationship between biography and artistic creation is so complex and subtle that it can not be satisfactorily explained—if ever—in a few sentences, though some hints can be given. Whitman's reading of Lucretius may account for his intellectual acceptance, in his first two editions, of death as a part of the cycle of nature. At first he was anxious about his personal "identity," but he was consoled, as "Song of the Open Road" shows, by belief in "the progress of the souls of men and women along the grand roads of the universe." In this period his poetic faculties were exhilaratingly stimulated by his psychic turmoils; they did not affect him in an unhealthy manner.

But the failure of Whitman's first two editions, lack of success in his editorship of the Brooklyn Times in 1857–59, and his inability to find rewarding love and friendship, brought him to almost tragic despair around 1859. Early in 1860 he was elated by the offer of a young Boston publishing house, Thayer and Eldridge, to bring out a new, expanded edition of Leaves of Grass. A few months later, however, the firm went into bankruptcy as a result of the Civil War. Though discouraged by the bankruptcy, the poet was beneficially stimulated by the war. "Beat! Beat! Drums!" witnesses his surging patriotism. He did not enlist because he was forty-two and the main support of his mother and feeble-minded brother, Edward, but a year and a half later he went down to the battlefield in Virginia to find his wounded brother George, whose wound proved not to be serious, and stayed on in Washington to help alleviate suffering in the army hospitals. "The Wound Dresser" shows the compassion that the hospital scenes aroused in him. Now he had seen death itself, not merely thought and dreamed of it.

After the war Whitman remained in Washington as a government clerk until a paralytic stroke in 1873 forced him to depart; he then went to live with George in Camden, N. J. His mother also died in that year, and during the winter of 1873–74 Whitman was so lonely and depressed that he longed for death, but "Prayer of Columbus" reveals the religious faith that saved him. Although he never recovered his health, his last two decades in Camden were relieved by increasing recognition abroad, especially in England, and he was able to draw spiritual strength and emotional solace from the philosophy which he had spent a lifetime cultivating. He died March 26, 1892, wracked by half a dozen diseases, but calm and cheerful to the last. He had become the "great poet" he had envisioned in 1855.

2. Literary Theory and Practice

In his 1855 Preface Whitman declared, "The poetic quality is not marshalled in rhyme or uniformity or abstract addresses to things nor in melancholy complaints or good precepts, but is the life of these and much else and is in the soul." For this reason "the greatest poet brings the spirit of any or all events and passions and scenes and persons . . . to bear on your individual character as you hear or read." Thus Whitman wanted his "expression" to be "transcendent and new. It is to be indirect and not direct or descriptive or epic."

But Whitman's esthetics was no " art for art's sake" theory. In fact, he professed scorn for beauty alone, and searched always for some profound truth residing in or emanating from external form, surface appearance, or "show," to use his favorite term (usually in the plural). Whitman believed poetry to be a variety of knowledge, and he exercised his poetic faculties not to create beauty but to recover and propagate wisdom— "recover" because he held the Platonic notion that truth is eternal and existed before the world was created. "The poets of the kosmos advance through all interpositions and coverings and turmoils and stratagems to first principles," he says in his 1855 Preface, and elaborates in "Song of Myself" as "truth" (sections 20 and 30):

> To me the converging objects of the universe perpetually flow,

All are written to me, and I must get what the writing means.

. . . .

All truths wait in all things, . . .

In "Song of the Rolling Earth" this becomes "the unspoken meanings of the earth," and in the same year (1856) the poet calls it "wisdom" in "Song of the Open Road" (section 6).

Whitman accepted unreservedly the Romantic philosophy that the natural world is a vast analogue of the spiritual. With the pantheists he believed that God incarnated Himself in His creation, and that to understand God man has only to commune with visible Nature. Thus in "A Song for Occupations" Whitman declares that "Objects gross and the unseen soul are one"; asserts in "Crossing Brooklyn Ferry" (1856 version) that "We realize the soul only by you, you faithful solids and fluids"; and asks and answers in "Starting from Paumanok" (section 13) the question of the soul's appearance:

Was somebody asking to see the soul?
See, your own shape and countenance, persons, sub-
    stances, beasts, the trees, the running rivers, the
    rocks and sands.

. . . .

Behold, the body includes and is the meaning, the main
    concern, and includes and is the soul;
Whoever you are, how superb and how divine is your
    body, or any part of it!

Here the poet uses "soul" and not "God," but he declares in section 48 of "Song of Myself" that he hears and beholds "God in every object," sees Him "In the faces of men and women," and finds "letters from God dropt in the street, and every one is sign'd by God's name." Yet he is "not curious about God," because God is everywhere, and because he worships not God but the Divinity innate in each individual self. In section 24 he even declares himself to be "Divine . . . inside and out." This pride and arrogance of selfhood shocked many of Whitman's contemporaries, but it was not so much man as his potentialities that the poet worshipped. Belief in the spirituality of the innate self became the core of Whitman's religion, and the source of his faith that death is no more to be feared than birth, because both are merely stages in the never-ending transmutations of body and soul.

Consequently, Whitman's poems are filled with symbols of resurrection, from fish-eggs to sprouting grass and Adam propagating the human race—for example, section 31 of "Song of Myself":

> I believe a leaf of grass is no less than the journey-work of the stars,
> And the pismire is equally perfect, and a grain of sand, and the egg of the wren,
> And the tree-toad is a chef-d'œuvre for the highest,
> And the running blackberry would adorn the parlors of heaven . . .

Whitman worships the human body not only because every man or woman is the son or daughter of God (a basic tenet of his "new religion") but also because it ferries the seeds of life, so that each person bridges (potentially at least) past and future generations. The act of procreation he describes ("Song of Myself," section 29) as:

> Parting track'd by arriving, perpetual payment of perpetual loan,
> Rich showering rain, and recompense richer afterward.
>
> Sprouts take and accumulate, stand by the curb prolific and vital,
> Landscapes projected masculine, full-sized and golden.

The poet, too, is a propagator, and Whitman often uses sexual imagery to describe his function, begetting a new race on mothers fit for conception. And this is not inconsistent with his role as cultural time-binder, conserving the knowledge and experience of past generations and by his imaginative intuition drawing upon his vision of the future, thereby making both past and future become present and available to his readers. As he says in the 1855 Preface,

> Without effort and without exposing in the least how it is done the greatest poet brings the spirit of any or all events and passions and scenes and persons some more and some less to bear on your individual character as you hear or read. To do this well is to compete with the laws that pursue and follow time. What is the purpose must surely be there and the clue of it must be there . . . and the faintest indication is the indication of the best and then becomes the clearest indication. Past and present and future are not disjoined but joined. The greatest poet forms the consistence of what is to be from what has been and is. He drags the dead out of their coffins and stands them again on their feet . . . he says to the past, Rise and walk before me that I may realize

you. He learns the lesson . . . he places himself where the future becomes present.

For a poet to be capable of performing these miracles he would have to be "great" indeed, and Whitman calls him not only a poet of the cosmos but himself a "kosmos" (his preferred spelling), that is, a symbolic microcosm of the macrocosm. By the magic of sympathetic identification, the symbolic "I" in his poems can range back and forth in time and space. Whitman's poems are suffused with cosmic emotion when he images the evolutionary processes which have culminated in his own birth and personal identity in the physical world (section 44 of "Song of Myself"):

> All forces have been steadily employ'd to complete and delight me.
> Now on this spot I stand with my robust soul.

Here Whitman draws simultaneously upon both mysticism and contemporary science. As a mystic he finds "the kelson of the universe" to be love, and he trusts the "Faithful and friendly . . . arms" of nature that have carried and guided him to the present moment of human existence. But scientific theory (in astronomy, as mentioned earlier, and biology and geology, all of which he studied in books, lectures, and journalistic popularizations) enables him to visualize his evolutionary origin ("Song of Myself," section 44):

> My feet strike an apex of the apices of the stairs,
> On every step bunches of ages, and larger bunches between the steps,
> All below duly travel'd, and still I mount and mount.

Thus through the lyric "I" of "Song of Myself," speaking for the human race from its first faint inception to its future culmination, Whitman can prophesy (section 51):

> The past and present wilt—I have fill'd them, emptied them,
> And proceed to fill my next fold of the future.

The cosmic poet and the national poet would seem logically to be at opposite ends of the literary spectrum, but Whitman was more successful in fusing the two than might be expected. And he was aided, of course, by the sanguine nationalism of the American people in the mid-nineteenth century. From the Puritans the young nation had inherited the belief that God had ordained a special, fortunate destiny for it. The Puritans had intended the Theocratic State of Massachusetts to be God's Own Government on earth. And the successes of the American people in their two wars with England had increased their confidence in a Providential destiny. After the acquisition of the vast territories in the regions of Oregon and California just nine years before Whitman published his first *Leaves of Grass*, the possibilities for future growth and development seemed fairly to stagger the imagination of most Americans. They shared William Cullen Bryant's vision of the "Mother of a Mighty Race," whom her "elder dames" across the sea hated in their pride and jealousy:

> There's freedom at thy gates and rest
> For Earth's down-trodden and opprest,
> A shelter for the hunted head,
> For the starved laborer toil and bread,
>   Power, at thy bounds,
> Stops and calls back his baffled hounds.

Despite the fact that slavery still existed in the United States, Whitman continued to harbor this national dream, this idealistic hope. The man who had sacrificed his journalistic career in the cause of "free soil" was, of course, fully aware of the evil of slavery. In 1856 in a political tract called "The Eighteenth Presidency!" he admitted that, "At present, the personnel of the government of these thirty millions, in executives and elsewhere, is drawn from limber-tongued lawyers, very fluent but empty feeble old men, professional politicians," and rarely from "the solid body of the people." In this tract Whitman even predicted a civil war if the slaveowners continued to dominate the national legislature and the judiciary. Yet he still had faith in the innate goodness of human nature and the common people.

When he wrote his 1855 Preface Whitman was not narrowly provincial or chauvinistic. Although he believed that all previous nations had failed to provide a society worthy of humanity, he did not reject or undervalue their contributions: "America does not repel the past or what it has produced under its forms or amid other politics or the idea of castes or the old religions." . . . Each age and nation, he thought, had made its contribution. America must now build upon these past achievements and surpass them. But he was never complacent about present conditions; his ideal nation was always something to be attained in the future. He did say in the 1855 Preface, "Here at last is something in the doings of man that corresponds with the broadcast doings of the day and night." But in the same paragraph he showed that what he meant was that nature had made unprecedented development possible: "One sees it must indeed own the riches of the summer and winter, and need never be bankrupt while corn grows from the ground or the orchards drop apples or the bays contain fish or men beget children upon women." Two paragraphs later Whitman stated his main theme: "The largeness of nature or the nation were monstrous without a corresponding largeness and generosity of the spirit of the citizen."

As late as 1874, in "Song of the Redwood-Tree," (section 3), Whitman reasserted his belief that on the North American continent, with its abundant and inexhaustible natural resources, a new society could arise "proportionate to Nature." But it was not material prosperity, mere wealth or power, or world-domination, that he expected:

> But more in you than these, lands of the Western shore,
> (These but the means, the implements, the standing-
> ground,)
> I see in you, certain to come, the promise of thousands of
> years, till now deferr'd.
> Promis'd to be fulfill'd, our common kind, the race.

Such prophecy as this Whitman always conceived to be the highest function of the poet, and he did not confine his "prophecy" to his own nation. In "Passage to India" (1868–71), he set forth the role of the poet as that of humanizing the discoveries and inventions of science and technology:

> Then not your deeds only O voyagers, O scientists and
> inventors, shall be justified,
> All these hearts as of fretted children shall be sooth'd,
> All affection shall be fully responded to, the secret shall
> be told,
> All these separations and gaps shall be taken up and
> hook'd and link'd together,
> The whole earth, this cold, impassive, voiceless earth, shall
> be completely justified,
> Trinitas divine shall be gloriously accomplish'd and com-
> pacted by the true son of God, the poet,
> (He shall indeed pass the straits and conquer the moun-
> tains,
> He shall double the Cape of Good Hope to some pur-
> pose,)
> Nature and Man shall be disjoin'd and diffused no more,
> The true son of God shall absolutely fuse them.

Walt Whitman must be given credit for being truly prophetic, in every sense of the word, in foreseeing the importance of humanizing science. In the twentieth century this is the great problem facing the human race, and the poet who could restore perfect harmony between man and nature would be "the true son of God" indeed. But can the poet— or any artist—accomplish such a miracle? During the European Renaissance poets not only believed that they could influence the conduct of men and politics but felt keenly their moral responsibility to do so. Milton, too, wrote his *Paradise Lost* to "justify" (significantly one of Whitman's key words in "Passage to India") the ways of God to men, though his poem has lived for other reasons. Shelley, closer to Whitman in theory as well as time, regarded poetry as "at once the centre and circumference of knowledge; it is that which comprehends all science, and that to which all science must be referred." In the twentieth century, however, the poet's function has been generally relegated to esthetics: the creation of pleasing combinations of sounds, images, and symbols—the latter often esoteric. T. S. Eliot, the most influential poet and critic of the first half of the century, objected to the "New Humanists" of the 1930's because they wanted literature to take over the function of religion, which they saw everywhere in decay.

This is not an argument that can be settled by the critic of Walt Whitman. In fact, only time can settle it. During the past two decades literary theory has traveled away from Whitman's position, and this trend has mitigated his influence, at least in England and the United States. This trend has also obscured Whitman's genuine esthetic achievements, for he wrote some poems of great literary merit, no matter what one may think of his doctrines. To mention Eliot again, he has declared that, "When Whitman speaks of the lilacs or the mocking-bird, his theories and beliefs drop away like a needless pretext. . . . " However, though some readers may admire the music of "When Lilacs Last in the Dooryard Bloom'd," or the imagery of plants and birds and planets in these poems, without sharing the poet's ideas and sentiments, their esthetic structure exemplifies the poet's moral and psychological purposes.

In practically all Whitman's poems the basic prosodic form is parallelism, or "thought rhythm," as in ancient Hebraic verse, though he may not have got it directly from the Bible. Here the unit of structure is not fundamentally either accentual or temporal, though Whitman had a good ear for both time and accent. In his verse the line is the unit (notice the usual comma at the end of each line). The second line balances the first, completing or supplementing its meaning. This is truly an equalitarian structure, in harmony with Whitman's pluralistic philosophy that "There can be any number of supremes" ("By Blue Ontario's Shore," section 3).

Similarly, Whitman's imagery is panoramic, unending, flowing, expanding. Perhaps a better term for it is *montage*. Viewed philosophically, this is Whitman's means of visualizing his belief that all parts of the universe are closely joined and interdependent, and that his "soul" is a part of the World-Soul. Thus the "I" of "Song of Myself" soars like a Greek god through time and space (section 33):

My ties and ballasts leave me, my elbows rest in sea-gaps,
I skirt sierras, my palms cover continents,
I am afoot with my vision.

In his vision, as Whitman says in "Salut au Monde!" (section 2), "latitude widens, longitude lengthens." This vicarious desire to embrace the physical world explains his fondness for enumeration, for "catalogues," as they have been called. Sometimes they are tiresome lists, but they can be charged with the poet's enthusiasm for the never-ceasing miracle of existence. And under the roving eye of the poet the panorama is always changing, one scene flowing into another.

Whitman evolved his prosodic techniques at a time when Americans were particularly space-conscious. The Oregon and California territories had been acquired as recently as 1846, and everyone was trying to grasp the significance of the continental expanse of the new nation. Whitman expresses this space-consciousness both in his imagery and in his long lines, each with its own organic rhythm. In an individual passage he can capture, for example, the actual sound and motion of the ocean, as in "Out of the Cradle Endlessly Rocking," or marching feet turned westward in "Pioneers! O Pioneers!" Even in syntactical structure he can convey the empathy of space and movement. A brilliant example is the first sentence (extending through twenty-two lines) of "Out of the Cradle," which suggests both the sound of the water and the sensation of walking in deceptive moonlight across uncultivated fields down to the wave-lapped shore. In "Lilacs" both syntax and patterns of accents carry the reader with the coffin on its long, circuitous journey, day and night, through towns and woods and fields, awakening to new life in springtime. Or in a short poem like "A Noiseless Patient Spider" he can evoke the loneliness of the human soul "surrounded, detached, in measureless oceans of space." Thus, writing in the nineteenth century, Walt Whitman anticipated some of the most vital poetic techniques and psychological problems of the twentieth century.

3. Editions of *Leaves of Grass*

The book usually known as *Leaves of Grass* is the final edition, printed a few months before Whitman's death, and often referred to by his friends as the "Death-Bed Edition." The text of this Signet Classic edition is that of the "Death-Bed" book. Between 1855 and 1892 Whitman published or had printed at his own expense no fewer than nine separate editions of his *Leaves of Grass*, all different in contents and arrangements of the poems until 1881 (eighth edition), when he adopted a permanent grouping of his poems. After 1881 he continued to add poems to his book, but he simply tacked these on as annexes (see pp. 384–416) and left the text of 1881 undisturbed.

Whitman spent nearly four decades trying to produce a book that would satisfy him, and he finally died content with his effort. In 1891 he wrote this note for his executors: ". . . I place upon you the injunction that whatever may be added to the *Leaves* shall be supplementary [he left some poems in manuscript], avowed as such, leaving the book complete as I left it, consecutive to the point I left off. . . . In the long run the world will do as it pleases with the book. I am determined to have the world know what I was pleased to do." His dying wish has been granted, and the world knows him best by what he "was pleased to do."

Nevertheless, the reader will understand the "authorized" *Leaves of Grass* better by knowing something of its growth or transmutation. In some ways the last is superior to all previous editions, but it did not grow naturally like the rings of a tree, as Whitman and his first biographers liked to think. It did not, in other words, grow by accretion, by accumulating layer on layer of new tissue. This final version might better be compared to a house built out of the materials salvaged from the wreck of former houses, with new materials used for the annexes.

Each edition of *Leaves of Grass* reveals, if studied with sufficient care, a great deal of the poet's life, his moods, emotional crises, ambitions, and ripening philosophy. But most of the individual poems, especially the longer ones, cannot be relied upon entirely for these details. If Whitman had preserved each poem more or less as he first published it, and had arranged his poems in the chronology of their composition, we would have in the final collection a record of his inner life—not strictly autobiography, but a record of his spiritual and poetic development. To some extent his major poems do give us intimations of such development. "Song of Myself" is characteristic of the first edition (1855), "Crossing Brooklyn Ferry" of the second (1856), "Out of the Cradle Endlessly Rocking" of the third (1860), "When Lilacs Last in the Dooryard Bloom'd" of the fourth (1867), "Passage to India" of the fifth (1872), "Prayer of Columbus" and "Song of the Redwood-Tree" of the sixth (1876); but here the major poems end. Perhaps the new group titles, "Birds of Passage," "Sea-Drift," "By the Roadside," and "Autumn Rivulets," might be said to characterize the seventh edition (1881), and certainly the permanent arrangement of the poems marks a final stage in the evolution of the book. The ninth edition (1892) merely reprinted the eighth edition, with the addition of the two annexes 'Sands at Seventy" and "Good-Bye My Fancy." But Whitman complicated the history by his repeated tinkering with his poems and reshuffling of them.

Whitman's main intention in grouping his poems was obviously thematic, and in nearly every group his first poem, or sometimes first two or three poems, aptly fits the title, though this is not true of all poems in a given group. The order of the groups also reveals a plan. "Inscriptions" serve as prologue, or poems stating the "program" of the whole book; "Children of Adam" is concerned, at least theoretically, with procreation; the "Calamus" poems with male friendship, though again not consistently. After "Calamus" come twelve poems, some of them major, without a group title; apparently the poet found them too diversified to classify. But then we have "Birds of Passage" and "Sea-Drift," containing some of the poet's best work, especially in "Sea-Drift," written near the height of his power. Most of these group titles are highly connotative and symbolical, and in general the sequence of poems suggests an allegory of life: birth, manhood, middle age, old age, and death. More accurately, the sequence of the group titles suggests this allegory; the sequence of the poems themselves is not consistent, and some motifs are repeated. For example, Whitman ended his 1860 edition with "So Long!" and throughout the remaining editions he was always bidding his readers farewell. Several times he expected his latest edition to be his last, especially in 1872, 1876, and 1881. Of course, these forebodings were strongly influenced by the state of his health; he was not well in 1872, and in 1873 suffered a paralytic stroke from which he never entirely recovered, though he survived for nineteen years.

One of Whitman's fondest desires was to establish an intimate rapport with each reader of his poems, and his final edition, even in its illogicalities, reveals the man more intimately than the earlier editions. The farewell-motif of the previous editions is found here in the last poem in each of the last four groups: "A Clear Midnight," "So Long!", "After the Supper and Talk," and "Good-Bye My Fancy!" But the old poet is humanly "loth, O so loth to depart!", and "Garrulous to the very last." Even his ultimate "Good-Bye My Fancy!" is not, however, really "good-bye," but "hail!" It is appropriate that the poet who had written so many poems on the natural goodness of death and the certainty of resurrection does not lose faith in the immortality of his poetic faculty, his "Fancy," and believes that it will survive with his soul. Such faith nourishes the hardy perennial, *Leaves of Grass,* and keeps it green for each new generation of readers. Above all else it is a book of faith: faith in the self, faith in Nature, faith in human nature, faith in the Creator of man and nature, and faith always in the regenerative power of poetry, the antiseptic of the soul.

GAY WILSON ALLEN
Professor of English
New York University

CONTENTS

INTRODUCTION by Gay Wilson Allen, v

INSCRIPTIONS
    One's-Self I Sing, 31
    As I Ponder'd in Silence, 31
    In Cabin'd Ships at Sea, 31
    To Foreign Lands, 32
    To a Historian, 32
    To Thee Old Cause, 33
    Eidólons, 33
    For Him I Sing, 35
    When I Read the Book, 35
    Beginning My Studies, 36
    Beginners, 36
    To the States, 36
    On Journeys through the States, 36
    To a Certain Cantatrice, 37
    Me Imperturbe, 37
    Savantism, 37
    The Ship Starting, 38
    I Hear America Singing, 38
    What Place Is Besieged? 38
    Still Though the One I Sing, 38
    Shut Not Your Doors, 38
    Poets to Come, 39
    To You, 39
    Thou Reader, 39

Starting from Paumanok, 39
Song of Myself, 49

CHILDREN OF ADAM
    To the Garden the World, 96
    From Pent-up Aching Rivers, 97
    I Sing the Body Electric, 98
    A Woman Waits for Me, 105
    Spontaneous Me, 106
    One Hour to Madness and Joy, 108
    Out of the Rolling Ocean the Crowd, 109
    Ages and Ages Returning at Intervals, 109
    We Two, How Long We were Fool'd, 109
    O Hymen! O Hymenee! 110
    I am He That Aches with Love, 110
    Native Moments, 110
    Once I Pass'd through a Populous City, 111
    I Heard You Solemn-Sweet Pipes of the Organ, 111
    Facing West from California's Shores, 111
    As Adam Early in the Morning, 112

CALAMUS

In Paths Untrodden, 112
Scented Herbage of My Breast, 112
Whoever You are Holding Me Now in Hand, 114
For You O Democracy, 115
These I Singing in Spring, 116
Not Heaving from my Ribb'd Breast Only, 117
Of the Terrible Doubt of Appearances, 117
The Base of All Metaphysics, 118
Recorders Ages Hence, 118
When I Heard at the Close of the Day, 119
Are You the New Person Drawn toward Me? 119
Roots and Leaves Themselves Alone, 120
Not Heat Flames up and Consumes, 120
Trickle Drops, 121
City of Orgies, 121
Behold This Swarthy Face, 121
I Saw in Louisiana a Live-Oak Growing, 121
To a Stranger, 122
This Moment Yearning and Thoughtful, 122
I Hear It Was Charged against Me, 123
The Prairie-Grass Dividing, 123
When I Peruse the Conquer'd Fame, 123
We Two Boys Together Clinging, 124
A Promise to California, 124
Here the Frailest Leaves of Me, 124
No Labor-Saving Machine, 124
A Glimpse, 124
A Leaf for Hand in Hand, 125
Earth My Likeness, 125
I Dream'd in a Dream, 125
What Think You I Take My Pen in Hand? 125
To the East and to the West, 126
Sometimes with One I Love, 126
To a Western Boy, 126
Fast-Anchor'd Eternal O Love, 126
Among the Multitude, 126
O You Whom I Often and Silently Come, 127
That Shadow My Likeness, 127
Full of Life Now, 127

Salut au Monde! 127
Song of the Open Road, 136
Crossing Brooklyn Ferry, 144
Song of the Answerer, 149
Our Old Feuillage, 153
A Song of Joys, 158
Song of the Broad-Axe, 163
Song of the Exposition, 172
Song of the Redwood-Tree, 180
A Song for Occupations, 183
A Song of the Rolling Earth, 190
Youth, Day, Old Age, and Night, 194

BIRDS OF PASSAGE
>Song of the Universal, 195
Pioneers! O Pioneers! 196
To You, 200
France the 18th Year of These States, 202
Myself and Mine, 203
Year of Meteors (1859-60), 204
With Antecedents, 205

A Broadway Pageant, 206

SEA-DRIFT
>Out of the Cradle Endlessly Rocking, 209
As I Ebb'd with the Ocean of Life, 214
Tears, 217
To the Man-of-War-Bird, 217
Aboard at a Ship's Helm, 218
On the Beach at Night, 218
The World Below the Brine, 219
On the Beach at Night Alone, 219
Song for All Seas, All Ships, 220
Patroling Barnegat, 221
After the Sea-Ship, 221

BY THE ROADSIDE
>A Boston Ballad—1854, 222
Europe the 72d and 73d Years of These States, 223
A Hand-Mirror, 225
Gods, 225
Germs, 226
Thoughts, 226
When I Heard the Learn'd Astronomer, 226
Perfections, 227
O Me! O Life! 227
To a President, 227
I Sit and Look Out, 227
To Rich Givers, 228
The Dalliance of the Eagles, 228
Roaming in Thought, 228
A Farm Picture, 229
A Child's Amaze, 229
The Runner, 229
Beautiful Women, 229
Mother and Babe, 229
Thought, 229
Visor'd 229
Thought, 229
Gliding O'er All, 230
Hast Never Come to Thee an Hour, 230
Thought, 230
To Old Age, 230
Locations and Times, 230
Offerings, 230
To the States, To Identify the 16th, 17th or 18th
    Presidentiad, 230

DRUM-TAPS

First O Songs for a Prelude, 231
Eighteen Sixty-One, 233
Beat! Beat! Drums! 233
From Paumanok Starting I Fly like a Bird, 234
Song of the Banner at Daybreak, 235
Rise O Days from Your Fathomless Deeps, 240
Virginia—the West, 241
City of Ships, 242
The Centenarian's Story, 242
Cavalry Crossing a Ford, 246
Bivouac on a Mountain Side, 246
An Army Corps on the March, 247
By the Bivouac's Fitful Flame, 247
Come Up from the Fields Father, 247
Vigil Strange I Kept on the Field One Night, 249
A March in the Ranks Hard-Prest, 250
A Sight in Camp in the Daybreak Gray and Dim, 251
As Toilsome I Wander'd Virginia's Woods, 251
Not the Pilot, 252
Year That Trembled and Reel'd Beneath Me, 252
The Wound-Dresser, 252
Long, Too Long America, 254
Give Me the Splendid Silent Sun, 255
Dirge for Two Veterans, 256
Over the Carnage Rose Prophetic a Voice, 257
I saw Old General at Bay, 258
The Artilleryman's Vision, 258
Ethiopia Saluting the Colors, 259
Not Youth Pertains to Me, 259
Race of Veterans, 260
World Take Good Notice, 260
O Tan-Faced Prairie-Boy, 260
Look Down Fair Moon, 260
Reconciliation, 260
How Solemn as One by One, 261
As I Lay with My Head in Your Lap
    Camerado, 261
Delicate Cluster, 262
To a Certain Civilian, 262
Lo, Victress on the Peaks, 262
Spirit whose Work is Done, 262
Adieu to a Soldier, 263
Turn O Libertad, 264
To the Leaven'd Soil They Trod, 264

MEMORIES OF PRESIDENT LINCOLN

When Lilacs Last in the Dooryard
    Bloom'd, 265
O Captain! My Captain! 271
Hush'd Be the Camps To-day, 272
This Dust Was Once the Man, 272

By Blue Ontario's Shore, 273
Reversals, 285

AUTUMN RIVULETS

As Consequent, *Etc.*, 285
The Return of the Heroes, 286
There Was a Child Went Forth, 290
Old Ireland, 292
The City Dead-House, 292
This Compost, 293
To a Foil'd European Revolutionaire, 295
Unnamed Lands, 296
Song of Prudence, 297
The Singer in the Prison, 299
Warble for Lilac Time, 301
Outlines for a Tomb, 302
Out from Behind This Mask, 303
Vocalism, 304
To Him That was Crucified, 305
You Felons on Trial in Courts, 305
Laws for Creations, 306
To a Common Prostitute, 306
I Was Looking a Long While, 307
Thought, 307
Miracles, 307
Sparkles from the Wheel, 308
To a Pupil, 309
Unfolded Out of the Folds, 309
What Am I After All, 310
Kosmos, 310
Others May Praise What They Like, 310
Who Learns My Lesson Complete, 311
Tests, 312
The Torch, 312
O Star of France (1870-71), 312
The Ox Tamer, 313
An Old Man's Thought of School, 314
Wandering at Morn, 315
Italian Music in Dakota, 315
With All Thy Gifts, 315
My Picture-Gallery, 316
The Prairie States, 316

Proud Music of the Storm, 316
Passage to India, 321
Prayer of Columbus, 328
The Sleepers, 330
Transpositions, 337
To Think of Time, 337

WHISPERS OF HEAVENLY DEATH

Darest Thou Now O Soul, 342
Whispers of Heavenly Death, 343
Chanting the Square Deific, 343
Of Him I Love Day and Night, 345
Yet, Yet, Ye Downcast Hours, 345
As If a Phantom Caress'd Me, 346
Assurances, 346
Quicksand Years, 347
That Music Always Round Me, 347

What Ship Puzzled at Sea, 347
A Noiseless Patient Spider, 347
O Living Always, Always Dying, 348
To One Shortly to Die, 348
Night on the Prairies, 348
Thought, 349
The Last Invocation, 350
As I Watch'd the Ploughman Ploughing, 350
Pensive and Faltering, 350

Thou Mother with Thy Equal Brood, 350
A Paumanok Picture, 355

FROM NOON TO STARRY NIGHT

Thou Orb Aloft Full-Dazzling, 355
Faces, 356
The Mystic Trumpeter, 359
To a Locomotive in Winter, 362
O Magnet-South, 362
Mannahatta, 364
All is Truth, 364
A Riddle Song, 365
Excelsior, 366
Ah Poverties, Wincings and Sulky Retreats, 367
Thoughts, 367
Mediums, 368
Weave In, My Hardy Life, 368
Spain, 1873-74, 368
By Broad Potomac's Shore, 369
From Far Dakota's Cañons (June 25, 1876), 369
Old War-Dreams, 370
Thick-Sprinkled Bunting, 370
What Best I See in Thee, 371
Spirit That Form'd This Scene, 371
As I Walk These Broad Majestic Days, 371
A Clear Midnight, 372

SONGS OF PARTING

As the Time Draws Nigh, 372
Years of the Modern, 373
Ashes of Soldiers, 374
Thoughts, 375
Song at Sunset, 377
As at Thy Portals Also Death, 378
My Legacy, 379
Pensive on Her Dead Gazing, 379
Camps of Green, 380
The Sobbing of the Bells, 381
As They Draw to a Close, 381
Joy, Shipmate, Joy, 381
The Untold Want, 381
Portals, 381
These Carols, 382
Now Finalè to the Shore, 382
So Long! 382

FIRST ANNEX: SANDS AT SEVENTY

Mannahatta, 384
Paumanok, 385
From Montauk Point, 385
To Those Who've Fail'd, 385
A Carol Closing Sixty-Nine, 385
The Bravest Soldiers, 385
A Font of Type, 386
As I Sit Writing Here, 386
My Canary Bird, 386
Queries to My Seventieth Year, 386
The Wallabout Martyrs, 386
The First Dandelion, 387
America, 387
Memories, 387
To-day and Thee, 387
After the Dazzle of Day, 387
Abraham Lincoln, Born Feb. 12, 1809, 387
Out of May's Shows Selected, 387
Halcyon Days, 388
Fancies at Navesink, 388
    (*The Pilot in the Mist—Had I the Choice—*
       You Tides With Ceaseless Swell—Last of
       Ebb, and Daylight Waning—And Yet Not
       You Alone—Proudly the Flood Comes In
       —By That Long Scan of Waves—Then
       Last of All.)
Election Day, November, 1884, 390
With Husky-Haughty Lips, O Sea, 391
Death of General Grant, 392
Red Jacket (from Aloft), 392
Washington's Monument, February, 1885, 392
Of That Blithe Throat of Thine, 393
Broadway, 393
To Get the Final Lilt of Songs, 394
Old Salt Kossabone, 394
The Dead Tenor, 394
Continuities, 395
Yonnondio, 395
Life, 396
"Going Somewhere", 396
Small the Theme of My Chant, 396
True Conquerors, 397
The United States to Old World Critics, 397
The Calming Thought of All, 397
Thanks in Old Age, 397
Life and Death, 398
The Voice of the Rain, 398
Soon Shall the Winter's Foil Be Here, 398
While Not the Past Forgetting, 399
The Dying Veteran, 399
Stronger Lessons, 399
A Prairie Sunset, 400
Twenty Years, 400
Orange Buds by Mail From Florida, 400
Twilight, 401
You Lingering Sparse Leaves of Me, 401

Not Meagre, Latent Boughs Alone,   401
The Dead Emperor,   401
As the Greek's Signal Flame,   401
The Dismantled Ship,   402
Now Precedent Songs, Farewell,   402
An Evening Lull,   402
Old Age's Lambent Peaks,   403
After the Supper and Talk,   403

SECOND ANNEX: GOOD-BYE MY FANCY

Sail Out for Good, Eidólon Yacht,   403
Lingering Last Drops,   404
Good-Bye My Fancy,   404
On, On the Same, Ye Jocund Twain,   404
My 71st Year,   405
Apparitions,   405
The Pallid Wreath,   405
An Ended Day,   406
Old Age's Ship & Crafty Death's,   406
To the Pending Year,   406
Shakspere-Bacon's Cipher,   407
Long, Long Hence,   407
Bravo, Paris Exposition,   407
Interpolation Sounds,   407
To the Sunset Breeze,   408
Old Chants,   409
A Christmas Greeting,   409
Sounds of the Winter,   410
A Twilight Song,   410
When the Full-Grown Poet Came,   411
Osceola,   411
A Voice from Death,   411
A Persian Lesson,   413
The Commonplace,   413
"The Rounded Catalogue Divine Complete",   414
Mirages,   414
L. of G.'s Purport,   415
The Unexpress'd,   415
Grand is the Seen,   415
Unseen Buds,   416
Good-Bye My Fancy!   416

INDEX OF TITLES,   417

Come, said my Soul,
Such verses for my Body let us write, (for we are one,)
That should I after death invisibly return,
Or, long, long hence, in other spheres,
There to some group of mates the chants resuming,
(Tallying Earth's soil, trees, winds, tumultuous waves,)
Ever with pleas'd smile I may keep on,
Ever and ever yet the verses owning—as, first, I here and now
Signing for Soul and Body, set to them my name,

Walt Whitman

Author's Note from 1891–92 Edition

As there are now several editions of L. of G., different text and dates, I wish to say that I prefer and recommend this present one, complete, for future printing, if there should be any; a copy and fac-simile, indeed, of the text of these 438 pages. The subsequent adjusting interval which is so important to form'd and launch'd work, books especially, has pass'd; and waiting till fully after that, I have given my concluding words.

W. W.

INSCRIPTIONS

ONE'S-SELF I SING

One's-self I sing, a simple separate person,
Yet utter the word Democratic, the word En-Masse.

Of physiology from top to toe I sing,
Not physiognomy alone nor brain alone is worthy for the
    Muse,
        I say the Form complete is worthier far,
The Female equally with the Male I sing.

Of Life immense in passion, pulse, and power,
Cheerful, for freest action form'd under the laws divine,
The Modern Man I sing.

AS I PONDER'D IN SILENCE

As I ponder'd in silence,
Returning upon my poems, considering, lingering long,
A Phantom arose before me with distrustful aspect,
Terrible in beauty, age, and power,
The genius of poets of old lands,
As to me directing like flame its eyes,
With finger pointing to many immortal songs,
And menacing voice, *What singest thou?* it said,
Know'st thou not there is but one theme for ever-enduring
         bards?
And that is the theme of War, the fortune of battles,
The making of perfect soldiers.
Be it so, then I answer'd,
I too haughty Shade also sing war, and a longer and greater one
         than any,
Waged in my book with varying fortune, with flight, advance
         and retreat, victory deferr'd and wavering,
(Yet methinks certain, or as good as certain, at the last,) the
         field the world,
For life and death, for the Body and for the eternal Soul,
Lo, I too am come, chanting the chant of battles,
I above all promote brave soldiers.

IN CABIN'D SHIPS AT SEA

In cabin'd ships at sea,
The boundless blue on every side expanding,
With whistling winds and music of the waves, the large im-
         perious waves,

31

Or some lone bark buoy'd on the dense marine,
Where joyous full of faith, spreading white sails,
She cleaves the ether mid the sparkle and the foam of day, or
          under many a star at night,
By sailors young and old haply will I, a reminiscence of the
          land, be read,
In full rapport at last.

Here are our thoughts, voyagers' thoughts.
Here not the land, firm land, alone appears, may then by them
          be said,
The sky o'erarches here, we feel the undulating deck beneath
          our feet,
We feel the long pulsation, ebb and flow of endless motion,
The tones of unseen mystery, the vague and vast suggestions of
          the briny world, the liquid-flowing syllables,
The perfume, the faint creaking of the cordage, the melancholy
          rhythm,
The boundless vista and the horizon far and dim are all here,
And this is ocean's poem.

Then falter not O book, fulfil your destiny,
You not a reminiscence of the land alone,
You too as a lone bark cleaving the ether, purpos'd I know not
          whither, yet ever full of faith,
Consort to every ship that sails, sail you!
Bear forth to them folded my love, (dear mariners, for you
          I fold it here in every leaf;)
Speed on my book! spread your white sails my little bark
          athwart the imperious waves,
Chant on, sail on, bear o'er the boundless blue from me to
          every sea,
This song for mariners and all their ships.

TO FOREIGN LANDS

I heard that you ask'd for something to prove this puzzle the
          New World,
And to define America, her athletic Democracy,
Therefore I send you my poems that you behold in them what
          you wanted.

TO A HISTORIAN

You who celebrate bygones,
Who have explored the outward, the surfaces of the races,
          the life that has exhibited itself,
Who have treated of man as the creature of politics, aggre-
          gates, rulers and priests,
I, habitan of the Alleghanies, treating of him as he is in him-
          self in his own rights,

Pressing the pulse of the life that has seldom exhibited itself,
 (the great pride of man in himself,)
Chanter of Personality, outlining what is yet to be,
I project the history of the future.

TO THEE OLD CAUSE

To thee old cause!
Thou peerless, passionate, good cause,
Thou stern, remorseless, sweet idea,
Deathless throughout the ages, races, lands,
After a strange sad war, great war for thee,
(I think all war through time was really fought, and ever will
 be really fought, for thee,)
These chants for thee, the eternal march of thee.

(A war O soldiers not for itself alone,
Far, far more stood silently waiting behind, now to advance
 in this book.)

Thou orb of many orbs!
Thou seething principle! thou well-kept, latent germ! thou
 centre!
Around the idea of thee the war revolving,
With all its angry and vehement play of causes,
(With vast results to come for thrice a thousand years,)
These recitatives for thee,—my book and the war are one,
Merged in its spirit I and mine, as the contest hinged on thee,
As a wheel on its axis turns, this book unwitting to itself,
Around the idea of thee.

EIDÓLONS

I met a seer,
Passing the hues and objects of the world,
The fields of art and learning, pleasure, sense,
 To glean eidólons.

Put in thy chants said he,
No more the puzzling hour nor day, nor segments, parts,
 put in,
Put first before the rest as light for all and entrance-song of all,
 That of eidólons.

Ever the dim beginning,
Ever the growth, the rounding of the circle,
Ever the summit and the merge at last, (to surely start again,)
 Eidólons! eidólons!

Ever the mutable,
Ever materials, changing, crumbling, re-cohering,

Ever the ateliers, the factories divine,
   Issuing eidólons.

Lo, I or you,
Or woman, man, or state, known or unknown,
We seeming solid wealth, strength, beauty build,
   But really build eidólons.

The ostent evanescent,
The substance of an artist's mood or savan's studies long,
Or warrior's, martyr's, hero's toils,
   To fashion his eidólon.

Of every human life,
(The units gather'd, posted, not a thought, emotion, deed, left
    out,)
The whole or large or small summ'd, added up,
   In its eidólon.

The old, old urge,
Based on the ancient pinnacles, lo, newer, higher pinnacles,
From science and the modern still impell'd,
   The old, old urge, eidólons.

The present now and here,
America's busy, teeming, intricate whirl,
Of aggregate and segregate for only thence releasing,
   To-day's eidólons.

These with the past,
Of vanish'd lands, of all the reigns of kings across the sea,
Old conquerors, old campaigns, old sailors' voyages,
   Joining eidólons.

Densities, growth, façades,
Strata of mountains, soils, rocks, giant trees,
Far-born, far-dying, living long, to leave,
   Eidólons everlasting.

Exaltè, rapt, ecstatic,
The visible but their womb of birth,
Of orbic tendencies to shape and shape and shape,
   The mighty earth-eidólon.

All space, all time,
(The stars, the terrible perturbations of the suns,
Swelling, collapsing, ending, serving their longer, shorter use,)
   Fill'd with eidólons only.

The noiseless myriads,
The infinite oceans where the rivers empty,
The separate countless free identities, like eyesight,
   The true realities, eidólons.

Not this the world,
Nor these the universes, they the universes,
Purport and end, ever the permanent life of life,
    Eidólons, eidólons,

Beyond thy lectures learn'd professor,
Beyond thy telescope or spectroscope observer keen, beyond
    all mathematics,
Beyond the doctor's surgery, anatomy, beyond the chemist
    with his chemistry,
    The entities of entities, eidólons.

Unfix'd yet fix'd,
Ever shall be, ever have been and are,
Sweeping the present to the infinite future,
    Eidólons, eidólons, eidólons.

The prophet and the bard,
Shall yet maintain themselves, in higher stages yet,
Shall mediate to the Modern, to Democracy, interpret yet to
    them,
    God and eidólons.

And thee my soul,
Joys, ceaseless exercises, exaltations,
Thy yearning amply fed at last, prepared to meet,
    Thy mates, eidólons.

Thy body permanent,
The body lurking there within thy body,
The only purport of the form thou art, the real I myself,
    An image, an eidólon.

Thy very songs not in thy songs,
No special strains to sing, none for itself,
But from the whole resulting, rising at last and floating,
    A round full-orb'd eidólon.

FOR HIM I SING

For him I sing,
I raise the present on the past,
(As some perennial tree out of its roots, the present on the
    past,)
With time and space I him dilate and fuse the immortal laws,
To make himself by them the law unto himself.

WHEN I READ THE BOOK

When I read the book, the biography famous,
And is this then (said I) what the author calls a man's life?
And so will some one when I am dead and gone write my life?

(As if any man really knew aught of my life,
Why even I myself I often think know little or nothing of my
    real life,
Only a few hints, a few diffused faint clews and indirections
I seek for my own use to trace out here.)

BEGINNING MY STUDIES

Beginning my studies the first step pleas'd me so much,
The mere fact consciousness, these forms, the power of
    motion,
The least insect or animal, the senses, eyesight, love,
The first step I say awed me and pleas'd me so much,
I have hardly gone and hardly wish'd to go any farther,
But stop and loiter all the time to sing it in ecstatic songs.

BEGINNERS

How they are provided for upon the earth, (appearing at
    intervals,)
How dear and dreadful they are to the earth,
How they inure to themselves as much as to any—what a
    paradox appears their age,
How people respond to them, yet know them not,
How there is something relentless in their fate all times,
How all times mischoose the objects of their adulation and
    reward,
And how the same inexorable price must still be paid for the
    same great purchase.

TO THE STATES

To the States or any one of them, or any city of the States,
    Resist much, obey little,
Once unquestioning obedience, once fully enslaved,
Once fully enslaved, no nation, state, city, of this earth, ever
    afterward resumes its liberty.

ON JOURNEYS THROUGH THE STATES

On journeys through the States we start,
(Ay through the world, urged by these songs,
Sailing henceforth to every land, to every sea,)
We willing learners of all, teachers of all, and lovers of all.

We have watch'd the seasons dispensing themselves and pass-
    ing on,
And have said, Why should not a man or woman do as much
    as the seasons, and effuse as much?

We dwell a while in every city and town,

We pass through Kanada, the North-east, the vast valley of
          the Mississippi, and the Southern States,
We confer on equal terms with each of the States,
We make trial of ourselves and invite men and women to
          hear,
We say to ourselves, Remember, fear not, be candid, promulge
          the body and the soul,
Dwell a while and pass on, be copious, temperate, chaste,
          magnetic,
And what you effuse may then return as the seasons return,
And may be just as much as the seasons.

TO A CERTAIN CANTATRICE

Here, take this gift,
I was reserving it for some hero, speaker, or general,
One who should serve the good old cause, the great idea, the
          progress and freedom of the race,
Some brave confronter of despots, some daring rebel;
But I see that what I was reserving belongs to you just as much
          as to any.

ME IMPERTURBE

Me imperturbe, standing at ease in Nature,
Master of all or mistress of all, aplomb in the midst of irra-
          tional things,
Imbued as they, passive, receptive, silent as they,
Finding my occupation, poverty, notoriety, foibles, crimes,
          less important than I thought,
Me toward the Mexican sea, or in the Mannahatta or the
          Tennessee, or far north or inland,
A river man, or a man of the woods or of any farm-life of
          these States or of the coast, or the lakes or
          Kanada,
Me wherever my life is lived, O to be self-balanced for con-
          tingencies,
To confront night, storms, hunger, ridicule, accidents, rebuffs,
          as the trees and animals do.

SAVANTISM

Thither as I look I see each result and glory retracing itself
          and nestling close, always obligated,
Thither hours, months, years—thither trades, compacts, estab-
          lishments, even the most minute,
Thither every-day life, speech, utensils, politics, persons, es-
          tates;
Thither we also, I with my leaves and songs, trustful, admirant,
As a father to his father going takes his children along with
          him.

THE SHIP STARTING

Lo, the unbounded sea,
On its breast a ship starting, spreading all sails, carrying even
        her moonsails,
The pennant is flying aloft as she speeds she speeds so stately
        —below emulous waves press forward,
They surround the ship with shining curving motions and
        foam.

I HEAR AMERICA SINGING

I hear America singing, the varied carols I hear,
Those of mechanics, each one singing his as it should be
        blithe and strong,
The carpenter singing his as he measures his plank or beam,
The mason singing his as he makes ready for work, or leaves
        off work,
The boatman singing what belongs to him in his boat, the
        deck-hand singing on the steamboat deck,
The shoemaker singing as he sits on his bench, the hatter
        singing as he stands,
The wood-cutter's song, the ploughboy's on his way in the
        morning, or at noon intermission or at sun-
        down,
The delicious singing of the mother, or of the young wife at
        work, or of the girl sewing or washing,
Each singing what belongs to him or her and to none else,
The day what belongs to the day—at night the party of young
        fellows, robust, friendly,
Singing with open mouths their strong melodious songs.

WHAT PLACE IS BESIEGED?

What place is besieged, and vainly tries to raise the siege?
Lo, I send to that place a commander, swift, brave, immortal,
And with him horse and foot, and parks of artillery,
And artillery-men, the deadliest that ever fired gun.

STILL THOUGH THE ONE I SING

Still though the one I sing,
(One, yet of contradictions made,) I dedicate to Nationality,
I leave in him revolt, (O latent right of insurrection! O quench-
        less, indispensable fire!)

SHUT NOT YOUR DOORS

Shut not your doors to me proud libraries,
For that which was lacking on all your well-fill'd shelves, yet
        needed most, I bring,
Forth from the war emerging, a book I have made,

The words of my book nothing, the drift of it every thing,
A book separate, not link'd with the rest nor felt by the
    intellect,
But you ye untold latencies will thrill to every page.

POETS TO COME

Poets to come! orators, singers, musicians to come!
Not to-day is to justify me and answer what I am for,
But you, a new brood, native, athletic, continental, greater than
    before known,
Arouse! For you must justify me.

I myself but write one or two indicative words for the future,
I but advance a moment only to wheel and hurry back in the
    darkness.

I am a man who, sauntering along without fully stopping, turns
    a casual look upon you and then averts his
    face,
Leaving it to you to prove and define it,
Expecting the main things from you.

TO YOU

Stranger, if you passing meet me and desire to speak to me, why
    should you not speak to me?
And why should I not speak to you?

THOU READER

Thou reader throbbest life and pride and love the same as I,
Therefore for thee the following chants.

STARTING FROM PAUMANOK

1

Starting from fish-shape Paumanok where I was born,
Well-begotten, and rais'd by a perfect mother,
After roaming many lands, lover of populous pavements,
Dweller in Mannahatta my city, or on southern savannas,
Or a soldier camp'd or carrying my knapsack and gun, or a
    miner in California,
Or rude in my home in Dakota's woods, my diet meat, my
    drink from the spring,
Or withdrawn to muse and meditate in some deep recess,
Far from the clank of crowds intervals passing rapt and happy,
Aware of the fresh free giver the flowing Missouri, aware of
    mighty Niagara,
Aware of the buffalo herds grazing the plains, the hirsute and
    strong-breasted bull,

Of earth, rocks, Fifth-month flowers experienced, stars, rain,
      snow, my amaze,
Having studied the mocking-bird's tones and the flight of the
      mountain-hawk,
And heard at dawn the unrivall'd one, the hermit thrush from
      the swamp-cedars,
Solitary, singing in the West, I strike up for a New World.

2

Victory, union, faith, identity, time,
The indissoluble compacts, riches, mystery,
Eternal progress, the kosmos, and the modern reports.

This then is life,
Here is what has come to the surface after so many throes
      and convulsions.

How curious! how real!
Underfoot the divine soil, overhead the sun.

See revolving globe,
The ancestor-continents away group'd together,
The present and future continents north and south, with the
      isthmus between.

See, vast trackless spaces,
As in a dream they change, they swiftly fill,
Countless masses debouch upon them,
They are now cover'd with the foremost people, arts, institu-
      tions, known.

See, projected through time,
For me an audience interminable.
With firm and regular step they wend, they never stop,
Successions of men, Americanos, a hundred millions,
One generation playing its part and passing on,
Another generation playing its part and passing on in its turn,
With faces turn'd sideways or backward towards me to listen,
With eyes retrospective towards me.

3

Americanos! conquerors! marches humanitarian!
Foremost! century marches! Libertad! masses!
For you a programme of chants.

Chants of the prairies,
Chants of the long-running Mississippi, and down to the Mexi-
      can sea,
Chants of Ohio, Indiana, Illinois, Iowa, Wisconsin and Minne-
      sota,

Chants going forth from the centre from Kansas, and thence
     equidistant,
Shooting in pulses of fire ceaseless to vivify all.

4

Take my leaves America, take them South and take them
     North,
Make welcome for them everywhere, for they are your own
     offspring,
Surround them East and West, for they would surround you,
And you precedents, connect lovingly with them, for they
     connect lovingly with you.

I conn'd old times,
I sat studying at the feet of the great masters,
Now if eligible O that the great masters might return and
     study me.

In the name of these States shall I scorn the antique?
Why these are the children of the antique to justify it.

5

Dead poets, philosophs, priests,
Martyrs, artists, inventors, governments long since,
Language-shapers on other shores,
Nations once powerful, now reduced, withdrawn, or desolate,
I dare not proceed till I respectfully credit what you have
     left wafted hither,
I have perused it, own it is admirable, (moving awhile among
     it,)
Think nothing can ever be greater, nothing can ever deserve
     more than it deserves,
Regarding it all intently a long while, then dismissing it,
I stand in my place with my own day here.

Here lands female and male,
Here the heir-ship and heiress-ship of the world, here the
     flame of materials,
Here spirituality the translatress, the openly-avow'd,
The ever-tending, the finalè of visible forms,
The satisfier, after due long-waiting now advancing,
Yes here comes my mistress the soul.

6

The soul,
Forever and forever—longer than soil is brown and solid—
     longer than water ebbs and flows.

I will make the poems of materials, for I think they are to
     be the most spiritual poems,

And I will make the poems of my body and of mortality,
For I think I shall then supply myself with the poems of my
        soul and of immortality.

I will make a song for these States that no one State may
        under any circumstances be subjected to
        another State,
And I will make a song that there shall be comity by day and
        by night between all the States, and between
        any two of them,
And I will make a song for the ears of the President, full of
        weapons with menacing points,
And behind the weapons countless dissatisfied faces;
And a song make I of the One form'd out of all,
The fang'd and glittering One whose head is over all,
Resolute warlike One including and over all,
(However high the head of any else that head is over all.)

I will acknowledge contemporary lands,
I will trail the whole geography of the globe and salute cour-
        teously every city large and small,
And employments! I will put in my poems that with you is
        heroism upon land and sea,
And I will report all heroism from an American point of
        view.

I will sing the song of companionship,
I will show what alone must finally compact these,
I believe these are to found their own ideal of manly love,
        indicating it in me,
I will therefore let flame from me the burning fires that were
        threatening to consume me,
I will lift what has too long kept down those smouldering
        fires,
I will give them complete abandonment,
I will write the evangel-poem of comrades and of love,
For who but I should understand love with all its sorrow and
        joy?
And who but I should be the poet of comrades?

7

I am the credulous man of qualities, ages, races,
I advance from the people in their own spirit,
Here is what sings unrestricted faith.

Omnes! omnes! let others ignore what they may,
I make the poem of evil also, I commemorate that part also,
I am myself just as much evil as good, and my nation is—and
        I say there is in fact no evil,

(Or if there is I say it is just as important to you, to the land
or to me, as any thing else.)

I too, following many and follow'd by many, inaugurate a
religion, I descend into the arena,
(It may be I am destin'd to utter the loudest cries there, the
winner's pealing shouts,
Who knows? they may rise from me yet, and soar above
every thing.)

Each is not for its own sake,
I say the whole earth and all the stars in the sky are for
religion's sake.
I say no man has ever yet been half devout enough,
None has ever yet adored or worship'd half enough,
None has begun to think how divine he himself is, and how
certain the future is.

I say that the real and permanent grandeur of these States
must be their religion,
Otherwise there is no real and permanent grandeur;
(Nor character nor life worthy the name without religion,
Nor land nor man or woman without religion.)

8

What are you doing young man?
Are you so earnest, so given up to literature, science, art,
amours?
These ostensible realities, politics, points?
Your ambition or business whatever it may be?

It is well—against such I say not a word, I am their poet also,
But behold! such swiftly subside, burnt up for religion's sake,
For not all matter is fuel to heat, impalpable flame, the essen-
tial life of the earth,
Any more than such are to religion.

9

What do you seek so pensive and silent?
What do you need camerado?
Dear son do you think it is love?

Listen dear son—listen America, daughter or son,
It is a painful thing to love a man or woman to excess, and yet
it satisfies, it is great,
But there is something else very great, it makes the whole
coincide,
It, magnificent, beyond materials, with continuous hands
sweeps and provides for all.

10

Know you, solely to drop in the earth the germs of a greater
religion,
The following chants each for its kind I sing.
My comrade!
For you to share with me two greatnesses, and a third one
rising inclusive and more resplendent,
The greatness of Love and Democracy, and the greatness of
Religion.

Melange mine own, the unseen and the seen,
Mysterious ocean where the streams empty,
Prophetic spirit of materials shifting and flickering around me,
Living beings, identities now doubtless near us in the air that
we know not of,
Contact daily and hourly that will not release me,
These selecting, these in hints demanded of me.

Not he with a daily kiss onward from childhood kissing me,
Has winded and twisted around me that which holds me to
him,
Any more than I am held to the heavens and all the spiritual
world,
After what they have done to me, suggesting themes.

O such themes—equalities! O divine average!
Warblings under the sun, usher'd as now, or at noon, or set-
ting,
Strains musical flowing through ages, now reaching hither,
I take to your reckless and composite chords, add to them,
and cheerfully pass them forward.

11

As I have walk'd in Alabama my morning walk,
I have seen where the she-bird the mocking-bird sat on her
nest in the briers hatching her brood.
I have seen the he-bird also,
I have paus'd to hear him near at hand inflating his throat
and joyfully singing.

And while I paus'd it came to me that what he really sang for
was not there only,
Nor for his mate nor himself only, nor all sent back by the
echoes,
But subtle, clandestine, away beyond,
A charge transmitted and gift occult for those being born.

12

Democracy! near at hand to you a throat is now inflating itself
and joyfully singing.

Ma femme! for the brood beyond us and of us,
For those who belong here and those to come,
I exultant to be ready for them will now shake out carols
          stronger and haughtier than have ever yet
          been heard upon earth.

I will make the songs of passion to give them their way,
And your songs outlaw'd offenders, for I scan you with kin-
          dred eyes, and carry you with me the same
          as any.

I will make the true poem of riches,
To earn for the body and the mind whatever adheres and goes
          forward and is not dropt by death;
I will effuse egotism and show it underlying all, and I will be
          the bard of personality,
And I will show of male and female that either is but the
          equal of the other,
And sexual organs and acts! do you concentrate in me, for I
          am determin'd to tell you with courageous
          clear voice to prove you illustrious,
And I will show that there is no imperfection in the present,
          and can be none in the future,
And I will show that whatever happens to anybody it may
          be turn'd to beautiful results,
And I will show that nothing can happen more beautiful
          than death,
And I will thread a thread through my poems that time and
          events are compact,
And that all the things of the universe are perfect miracles,
          each as profound as any.

I will not make poems with reference to parts,
But I will make poems, songs, thoughts, with reference to
          ensemble,
And I will not sing with reference to a day, but with refer-
          ence to all days,
And I will not make a poem nor the least part of a poem but
          has reference to the soul,
Because having look'd at the objects of the universe, I find
          there is no one nor any particle of one but
          has reference to the soul.

13

Was somebody asking to see the soul?
See, your own shape and countenance, persons, substances,
          beasts, the trees, the running rivers, the rocks
          and sands.

All hold spiritual joys and afterwards loosen them;
How can the real body ever die and be buried?

Of your real body and any man's or woman's real body,
Item for item it will elude the hands of the corpse-cleaners
          and pass to fitting spheres,
Carrying what has accrued to it from the moment of birth
          to the moment of death.

Not the types set up by the printer return their impression, the
          meaning, the main concern,
Any more than a man's substance and life or a woman's sub-
          stance and life return in the body and the
          soul,
Indifferently before death and after death.

Behold, the body includes and is the meaning, the main con-
          cern, and includes and is the soul;
Whoever you are, how superb and how divine is your body,
          or any part of it!

14

Whoever you are, to you endless announcements!

Daughter of the lands did you wait for your poet?
Did you wait for one with a flowing mouth and indicative
          hand?

Toward the male of the States, and toward the female of the
          States,
Exulting words, words to Democracy's lands.

Interlink'd, food-yielding lands!
Land of coal and iron! land of gold! land of cotton, sugar,
          rice!
Land of wheat, beef, pork! land of wool and hemp! land of
          the apple and the grape!
Land of the pastoral plains, the grass-fields of the world!
          land of those sweet-air'd interminable pla-
          teaus!
Land of the herd, the garden, the healthy house of adobie!
Lands where the north-west Columbia winds, and where the
          south-west Colorado winds!
Land of the eastern Chesapeake! land of the Delaware!
Land of Ontario, Erie, Huron, Michigan!
Land of the Old Thirteen! Massachusetts land! land of Ver-
          mont and Connecticut!
Land of the ocean shores! land of sierras and peaks!
Land of boatmen and sailors! fishermen's land!
Inextricable lands! the clutch'd together! the passionate ones!
The side by side! the elder and younger brothers! the bony-
          limb'd!

The great women's land! the feminine! the experienced sisters
    and the inexperienced sisters!
Far breath'd land! Arctic braced! Mexican breez'd! the di-
    verse! the compact!
The Pennsylvanian! the Virginian! the double Carolinian!
O all and each well-loved by me! my intrepid nations! O I
    at any rate include you all with perfect love!
I cannot be discharged from you! not from one any sooner
    than another!
O death! O for all that, I am yet of you unseen this hour with
    irrepressible love,
Walking New England, a friend, a traveler,
Splashing my bare feet in the edge of the summer ripples on
    Paumanok's sands,
Crossing the prairies, dwelling again in Chicago, dwelling in
    every town,
Observing shows, births, improvements, structures, arts,
Listening to orators and oratresses in public halls,
Of and through the States as during life, each man and woman
    my neighbor,
The Louisianian, the Georgian, as near to me, and I as near
    to him and her,
The Mississippian and Arkansian yet with me, and I yet with
    any of them,
Yet upon the plains west of the spinal river, yet in my house
    of adobie,
Yet returning eastward, yet in the Seaside State or in Mary-
    land,
Yet Kanadian cheerily braving the winter, the snow and ice
    welcome to me,
Yet a true son either of Maine or of the Granite State, or
    the Narragansett Bay State, or the Empire
    State,
Yet sailing to other shores to annex the same, yet welcoming
    every new brother,
Hereby applying these leaves to the new ones from the hour
    they unite with the old ones,
Coming among the new ones myself to be their companion
    and equal, coming personally to you now,
Enjoining you to acts, characters, spectacles, with me.

15

With me with firm holding, yet haste, haste on.

For your life adhere to me,
(I may have to be persuaded many times before I consent to
    give myself really to you, but what of that?
Must not Nature be persuaded many times?)

No dainty dolce affettuoso I,
Bearded, sun-burnt, gray-neck'd, forbidding, I have arrived,
To be wrestled with as I pass for the solid prizes of the universe,
For such I afford whoever can persevere to win them.

16

On my way a moment I pause,
Here for you! and here for America!
Still the present I raise aloft, still the future of the States I harbinge glad and sublime,
And for the past I pronounce what the air holds of the red aborigines.

The red aborigines,
Leaving natural breaths, sounds of rain and winds, calls as of birds and animals in the woods, syllabled to us for names,
Okonee, Koosa, Ottawa, Monongahela, Sauk, Natchez, Chattahoochee, Kaqueta, Oronoco,
Wabash, Miami, Saginaw, Chippewa, Oshkosh, Walla-Walla,
Leaving such to the States they melt, they depart, charging the water and the land with names.

17

Expanding and swift, henceforth,
Elements, breeds, adjustments, turbulent, quick and audacious,
A world primal again, vistas of glory incessant and branching,
A new race dominating previous ones and grander far, with new contests,
New politics, new literatures and religions, new inventions and arts.

These, my voice announcing—I will sleep no more but arise,
You oceans that have been calm within me! how I feel you, fathomless, stirring, preparing unprecedented waves and storms.

18

See, steamers steaming through my poems,
See, in my poems immigrants continually coming and landing,
See, in arriere, the wigwam, the trail, the hunter's hut, the flatboat, the maize-leaf, the claim, the rude fence, and the backwoods village,
See, on the one side the Western Sea and on the other the Eastern Sea, how they advance and retreat upon my poems as upon their own shores,
See, pastures and forests in my poems—see, animals wild and tame—see, beyond the Kaw, countless herds

of buffalo feeding on short curly grass,
See, in my poems, cities, solid, vast, inland, with paved streets,
      with iron and stone edifices, ceaseless ve-
      hicles, and commerce,
See, the many-cylinder'd steam printing-press—see, the elec-
      tric telegraph stretching across the continent,
See, through Atlantica's depths pulses American Europe
      reaching, pulses of Europe duly return'd,
See, the strong and quick locomotive as it departs, panting,
      blowing the steam-whistle,
See, ploughmen ploughing farms—see, miners digging mines
      —see, the numberless factories,
See, mechanics busy at their benches with tools—see from
      among them superior judges, philosophs,
      Presidents, emerge, drest in working
      dresses,
See, lounging through the shops and fields of the States, me
      well-belov'd, close-held by day and night,
Hear the loud echoes of my songs here—read the hints come
      at last.

19

O camerado close! O you and me at last, and us two only.
O a word to clear one's path ahead endlessly!
O something ecstatic and undemonstrable! O music wild!
O now I triumph—-and you shall also;
O hand in hand—O wholesome pleasure—O one more de-
      sirer and lover!
O to haste firm holding—to haste, haste on with me.

SONG OF MYSELF

1

I celebrate myself, and sing myself,
And what I assume you shall assume,
For every atom belonging to me as good belongs to you.

I loafe and invite my soul,
I lean and loafe at my ease observing a spear of summer
      grass.

My tongue, every atom of my blood, form'd from this soil,
      this air,
Born here of parents born here from parents the same, and
      their parents the same,
I, now thirty-seven years old in perfect health begin,
Hoping to cease not till death.

Creeds and schools in abeyance,
Retiring back a while sufficed at what they are, but never
      forgotten,

I harbor for good or bad, I permit to speak at every hazard,
Nature without check with original energy.

2

Houses and rooms are full of perfumes, the shelves are
    crowded with perfumes,
I breathe the fragrance myself and know it and like it,
The distillation would intoxicate me also, but I shall not let it.

The atmosphere is not a perfume, it has no taste of the dis-
    tillation, it is odorless,
It is for my mouth forever, I am in love with it,
I will go to the bank by the wood and become undisguised
    and naked,
I am mad for it to be in contact with me.

The smoke of my own breath,
Echoes, ripples, buzz'd whispers, love-root, silk-thread, crotch
    and vine,
My respiration and inspiration, the beating of my heart, the
    passing of blood and air through my lungs,
The sniff of green leaves and dry leaves, and of the shore and
    dark-color'd sea-rocks, and of hay in the
    barn,
The sound of the belch'd words of my voice loos'd to the
    eddies of the wind,
A few light kisses, a few embraces, a reaching around of
    arms,
The play of shine and shade on the trees as the supple boughs
    wag,
The delight alone or in the rush of the streets, or along the
    fields and hill-sides,
The feeling of health, the full-noon trill, the song of me rising
    from bed and meeting the sun.

Have you reckon'd a thousand acres much? have you reckon'd
    the earth much?
Have you practis'd so long to learn to read?
Have you felt so proud to get at the meaning of poems?

Stop this day and night with me and you shall possess the
    origin of all poems,
You shall possess the good of the earth and sun, (there are
    millions of suns left,)
You shall no longer take things at second or third hand, nor
    look through the eyes of the dead, nor feed
    on the spectres in books,
You shall not look through my eyes either, nor take things
    from me,
You shall listen to all sides and filter them from your self.

3

I have heard what the talkers were talking, the talk of the
    beginning and the end,
But I do not talk of the beginning or the end.

There was never any more inception than there is now,
Nor any more youth or age than there is now,
And will never be any more perfection than there is now,
Nor any more heaven or hell than there is now.

Urge and urge and urge,
Always the procreant urge of the world.
Out of the dimness opposite equals advance, always substance
    and increase, always sex,
Always a knit of identity, always distinction, always a breed
    of life.

To elaborate is no avail, learn'd and unlearn'd feel that it is so.

Sure as the most certain sure, plumb in the uprights, well
    entretied, braced in the beams,
Stout as a horse, affectionate, haughty, electrical,
I and this mystery here we stand.

Clear and sweet is my soul, and clear and sweet is all that
    is not my soul.

Lack one lacks both, and the unseen is proved by the seen,
Till that becomes unseen and receives proof in its turn.

Showing the best and dividing it from the worst age vexes age,
Knowing the perfect fitness and equanimity of things, while
    they discuss I am silent, and go bathe and
    admire myself.

Welcome is every organ and attribute of me, and of any man
    hearty and clean,
Not an inch nor a particle of an inch is vile, and none shall be
    less familiar than the rest.

I am satisfied—I see, dance, laugh, sing;
As the hugging and loving bed-fellow sleeps at my side
    through the night, and withdraws at the peep
    of the day with stealthy tread,
Leaving me baskets cover'd with white towels swelling the
    house with their plenty,
Shall I postpone my acceptation and realization and scream
    at my eyes,
That they turn from gazing after and down the road,
And forthwith cipher and show me to a cent,
Exactly the value of one and exactly the value of two, and
    which is ahead?

4

Trippers and askers surround me,
People I meet, the effect upon me of my early life or the ward
and city I live in, or the nation,
The latest dates, discoveries, inventions, societies, authors old
and new,
My dinner, dress, associates, looks, compliments, dues,
The real or fancied indifference of some man or woman I
love,
The sickness of one of my folks or of myself, or ill-doing
or loss or lack of money, or depressions or
exaltations,
Battles, the horrors of fratricidal war, the fever of doubtful
news, the fitful events;
These come to me days and nights and go from me again,
But they are not the Me myself.

Apart from the pulling and hauling stands what I am,
Stands amused, complacent, compassionating, idle, unitary,
Looks down, is erect, or bends an arm on an impalpable cer-
tain rest,
Looking with side-curved head curious what will come next,
Both in and out of the game and watching and wondering at it.

Backward I see in my own days where I sweated through fog
with linguists and contenders,
I have no mockings or arguments, I witness and wait.

5

I believe in you my soul, the other I am must not abase itself
to you,
And you must not be abased to the other.

Loafe with me on the grass, loose the stop from your throat,
Not words, not music or rhyme I want, not custom or lecture,
not even the best,
Only the lull I like, the hum of your valvèd voice.

I mind how once we lay such a transparent summer morning,
How you settled your head athwart my hips and gently turn'd
over upon me,
And parted the shirt from my bosom-bone, and plunged your
tongue to my bare-stript heart,
And reach'd till you felt my beard, and reach'd till you held
my feet.

Swiftly arose and spread around me the peace and knowledge
that pass all the argument of the earth,
And I know that the hand of God is the promise of my own,
And I know that the spirit of God is the brother of my own,

And that all the men ever born are also my brothers, and the
   women my sisters and lovers,
And that a kelson of the creation is love,
And limitless are leaves stiff or drooping in the fields,
And brown ants in the little wells beneath them,
And mossy scabs of the worm fence, heap'd stones, elder,
   mullein and poke-weed.

6

A child said *What is the grass?* fetching it to me with full
   hands,
How could I answer the child? I do not know what it is any
   more than he.

I guess it must be the flag of my disposition, out of hopeful
   green stuff woven.

Or I guess it is the handkerchief of the Lord,
A scented gift and remembrancer designedly dropt,
Bearing the owner's name someway in the corners, that we may
   see and remark, and say *Whose?*

Or I guess the grass is itself a child, the produced babe of the
   vegetation.

Or I guess it is a uniform hieroglyphic,
And it means, Sprouting alike in broad zones and narrow
   zones,
Growing among black folks as among white,
Kanuck, Tuckahoe, Congressman, Cuff, I give them the same,
   I receive them the same.

And now it seems to me the beautiful uncut hair of graves.

Tenderly will I use you curling grass,
It may be you transpire from the breasts of young men,
It may be if I had known them I would have loved them,
It may be you are from old people, or from offspring taken
   soon out of their mothers' laps,
And here you are the mothers' laps.

This grass is very dark to be from the white heads of old
   mothers,
Darker than the colorless beards of old men,
Dark to come from under the faint red roofs of mouths.
O I perceive after all so many uttering tongues,
And I perceive they do not come from the roofs of mouths for
   nothing.

I wish I could translate the hints about the dead young men
   and women,

And the hints about old men and mothers, and the offspring
      taken soon out of their laps.

What do you think has become of the young and old men?
And what do you think has become of the women and
      children?

They are alive and well somewhere,
The smallest sprout shows there is really no death,
And if ever there was it led forward life, and does not wait at
      the end to arrest it,
And ceas'd the moment life appear'd.

All goes onward and outward, nothing collapses,
And to die is different from what any one supposed, and
      luckier.

7

Has any one supposed it lucky to be born?
I hasten to inform him or her it is just as lucky to die, and I
      know it.

I pass death with the dying and birth with the new-wash'd
      babe, and am not contain'd between my hat
      and boots,
And peruse manifold objects, no two alike and everyone good,
The earth good and the stars good, and their adjuncts all good.

I am not an earth nor an adjunct of an earth,
I am the mate and companion of people, all just as immortal
      and fathomless as myself,
(They do not know how immortal, but I know.)

Every kind for itself and its own, for me mine male and female,
For me those that have been boys and that love women,
For me the man that is proud and feels how it stings to be
      slighted,
For me the sweet-heart and the old maid, for me mothers and
      the mothers of mothers,
For me lips that have smiled, eyes that have shed tears,
For me children and the begetters of children.

Undrape! you are not guilty to me, nor stale nor discarded,
I see through the broadcloth and gingham whether or no,
And am around, tenacious, acquisitive, tireless, and cannot be
      shaken away.

8

The little one sleeps in its cradle,
I lift the gauze and look a long time, and silently brush away
      flies with my hand.

The youngster and the red-faced girl turn aside up the bushy
    hill,
I peeringly view them from the top.

The suicide sprawls on the bloody floor of the bedroom,
I witness the corpse with its dabbled hair, I note where the
    pistol has fallen.

The blab of the pave, tires of carts, sluff of boot-soles, talk of
    the promenaders,
The heavy omnibus, the driver with his interrogating thumb,
    the clank of the shod horses on the granite
    floor,
The snow-sleighs, clinkink, shouted jokes, pelts of snow-balls,
The hurrahs for popular favorites, the fury of rous'd mobs,
The flap of the curtain'd litter, a sick man inside borne to the
    hospital,
The meeting of enemies, the sudden oath, the blows and fall,
The excited crowd, the policeman with his star quickly work-
    ing his passage to the centre of the crowd,
The impassive stones that receive and return so many echoes,
What groans of over-fed or half-starv'd who fall sunstruck or
    in fits,
What exclamations of women taken suddenly who hurry home
    and give birth to babes,
What living and buried speech is always vibrating here, what
    howls restrain'd by decorum,
Arrests of criminals, slights, adulterous offers made, accept-
    ances, rejections with convex lips,
I mind them or the show or resonance of them—I come and
    I depart.

9

The big doors of the country barn stand open and ready,
The dried grass of the harvest-time loads the slow-drawn
    wagon,
The clear light plays on the brown gray and green intertinged,
The armfuls are pack'd to the sagging mow.

I am there, I help, I came stretch'd atop of the load,
I felt its soft jolts, one leg reclined on the other,
I jump from the cross-beams and seize the clover and timothy,
And roll head over heels and tangle my hair full of wisps.

10

Alone far in the wilds and mountains I hunt,
Wandering amazed at my own lightness and glee,
In the late afternoon choosing a safe spot to pass the night,
Kindling a fire and broiling the fresh-kill'd game,

Falling asleep on the gather'd leaves with my dog and gun by
       my side.

The Yankee clipper is under her sky-sails, she cuts the sparkle
       and scud,
My eyes settle the land, I bend at her prow or shout joyously
       from the deck.

The boatmen and clam-diggers arose early and stopt for me,
I tuck'd my trowser-ends in my boots and went and had a good
       time;
You should have been with us that day round the chowder-
       kettle.

I saw the marriage of the trapper in the open air in the far
       west, the bride was a red girl,
Her father and his friends sat near cross-legged and dumbly
       smoking, they had moccasins to their feet
       and large thick blankets hanging from their
       shoulders,
On a bank lounged the trapper, he was drest mostly in skins,
       his luxuriant beard and curls protected his
       neck, he held his bride by the hand,
She had long eyelashes, her head was bare, her coarse straight
       locks descended upon her voluptuous limbs
       and reach'd to her feet.

The runaway slave came to my house and stopt outside,
I heard his motions crackling the twigs of the woodpile,
Through the swung half-door of the kitchen I saw him limpsy
       and weak,
And went where he sat on a log and led him in and assured
       him,
And brought water and fill'd a tub for his sweated body and
       bruis'd feet,
And gave him a room that enter'd from my own, and gave him
       some coarse clean clothes,
And remember perfectly well his revolving eyes and his awk-
       wardness,
And remember putting plasters on the galls of his neck and
       ankles;
He staid with me a week before he was recuperated and pass'd
       north,
I had him sit next me at table, my fire-lock lean'd in the corner.

11

Twenty-eight young men bathe by the shore,
Twenty-eight young men and all so friendly;
Twenty-eight years of womanly life and all so lonesome.
She owns the fine house by the rise of the bank,

She hides handsome and richly drest aft the blinds of the
    window.

Which of the young men does ᶥhe like the best?
Ah the homeliest of them is beautiful to her.

Where are you off to, lady? for I see you,
You splash in the water there, yet stay stock still in your room.

Dancing and laughing along the beach came the twenty-ninth
    bather,
The rest did not see her, but she saw them and loved them.

The beards of the young men glisten'd with wet, it ran from
    their long hair,
Little streams pass'd all over their bodies.

An unseen hand also pass'd over their bodies,
It descended tremblingly from their temples and ribs.

The young men float on their backs, their white bellies bulge to
    the sun, they do not ask who seizes fast to
    them,
They do not know who puffs and declines with pendant and
    bending arch,
They do not think whom they souse with spray.

12

The butcher-boy puts off his killing-clothes, or sharpens his
    knife at the stall in the market,
I loiter enjoying his repartee and his shuffle and break-down.

Blacksmiths with grimed and hairy chests environ the anvil,
Each has his main-sledge, they are all out, there is a great heat
    in the fire.

From the cinder-strew'd threshold I follow their movements,
The lithe sheer of their waists plays even with their massive
    arms,
Overhand the hammers swing, overhand so slow, overhand so
    sure,
They do not hasten, each man hits in his place.

13

The negro holds firmly the reins of his four horses, the block
    swags underneath on its tied-over chain,
The negro that drives the long dray of the stone-yard, steady
    and tall he stands pois'd on one leg on the
    string-piece,
His blue shirt exposes his ample neck and breast and loosens
    over his hip-band,

His glance is calm and commanding, he tosses the slouch of his
        hat away from his forehead,
The sun falls on his crispy hair and mustache, falls on the black
        of his polish'd and perfect limbs.

I behold the picturesque giant and love him, and I do not stop
        there,
I go with the team also.

In me the caresser of life wherever moving, backward as well
        as forward sluing,
To niches aside and junior bending, not a person or object
        missing,
Absorbing all to myself and for this song.

Oxen that rattle the yoke and chain or halt in the leafy shade,
        what is that you express in your eyes?
It seems to me more than all the print I have read in my life.

My tread scares the wood-drake and wood-duck on my distant
        and day-long ramble,
They rise together, they slowly circle around.

I believe in those wing'd purposes,
And acknowledge red, yellow, white, playing within me,
And consider green and violet and the tufted crown inten-
        tional,
And do not call the tortoise unworthy because she is not some-
        thing else,
And the jay in the woods never studied the gamut, yet trills
        pretty well to me,
And the look of the bay mare shames silliness out of me.

14

The wild gander leads his flock through the cool night,
Ya-honk he says, and sounds it down to me like an invitation,
The pert may suppose it meaningless, but I listening close,
Find its purpose and place up there toward the wintry sky.

The sharp-hoof'd moose of the north, the cat on the house-sill,
        the chickadee, the prairie-dog,
The litter of the grunting sow as they tug at her teats,
The brood of the turkey-hen and she with her half-spread
        wings,
I see in them and myself the same old law.

The press of my foot to the earth springs a hundred affections,
They scorn the best I can do to relate them.

I am enamour'd of growing out-doors,
Of men that live among cattle or taste of the ocean or woods,

Of the builders and steerers of ships and the wielders of axes
        and mauls, and the drivers of horses,
I can eat and sleep with them week in and week out.

What is commonest, cheapest, nearest, easiest, is Me,
Me going in for my chances, spending for vast returns,
Adorning myself to bestow myself on the first that will take me,
Not asking the sky to come down to my good will,
Scattering it freely forever.

15

The pure contralto sings in the organ loft,
The carpenter dresses his plank, the tongue of his foreplane
        whistles its wild ascending lisp,
The married and unmarried children ride home to their
        Thanksgiving dinner,
The pilot seizes the king-pin, he heaves down with a strong
        arm,
The mate stands braced in the whale-boat, lance and harpoon
        are ready,
The duck-shooter walks by silent and cautious stretches,
The deacons are ordain'd with cross'd hands at the altar,
The spinning-girl retreats and advances to the hum of the big
        wheel,
The farmer stops by the bars as he walks on a First-day loafe
        and looks at the oats and rye,
The lunatic is carried at last to the asylum a confirm'd case,
(He will never sleep any more as he did in the cot in his moth-
        er's bedroom;)
The jour printer with gray head and gaunt jaws works at his
        case,
He turns his quid of tobacco while his eyes blurr with the
        manuscript;
The malform'd limbs are tied to the surgeon's table,
What is removed drops horribly in a pail;
The quadroon girl is sold at the auction-stand, the drunkard
        nods by the bar-room stove,
The machinist rolls up his sleeves, the policeman travels his
        beat, the gate-keeper marks who pass,
The young fellow drives the express-wagon, (I love him,
        though I do not know him;)
The half-breed straps on his light boots to compete in the race,
The western turkey-shooting draws old and young, some lean
        on their rifles, some sit on logs,
Out from the crowd steps the marksman, takes his position,
        levels his piece;
The groups of newly-come immigrants cover the wharf or
        levee,

As the woolly-pates hoe in the sugar-field, the overseer views
    them from his saddle,
The bugle calls in the ball-room, the gentlemen run for their
    partners, the dancers bow to each other,
The youth lies awake in the cedar-roof'd garret and harks to
    the musical rain,
The Wolverine sets traps on the creek that helps fill the Huron,
The squaw wrapt in her yellow-hemm'd cloth is offering moc-
    casins and bead-bags for sale,
The connoisseur peers along the exhibition-gallery with half-
    shut eyes bent sideways,
As the deck-hands make fast the steamboat the plank is thrown
    for the shore-going passengers,
The young sister holds out the skein while the elder sister winds
    it off in a ball, and stops now and then for
    the knots,
The one-year wife is recovering and happy having a week ago
    borne her first child.
The clean-hair'd Yankee girl works with her sewing-machine
    or in the factory or mill,
The paving-man leans on his two-handed rammer, the re-
    porter's lead flies swiftly over the note-book,
    the sign-painter is lettering with blue and
    gold,
The canal boy trots on the tow-path, the book-keeper counts at
    his desk, the shoemaker waxes his thread,
The conductor beats time for the band and all the performers
    follow him,
The child is baptized, the convert is making his first profes-
    sions,
The regatta is spread on the bay, the race is begun, (how the
    white sails sparkle!)
The drover watching his drove sings out to them that would
    stray,
The pedler sweats with his pack on his back, (the purchaser
    higgling about the odd cent;)
The bride unrumples her white dress, the minute-hand of the
    clock moves slowly,
The opium-eater reclines with rigid head and just-open'd lips,
The prostitute draggles her shawl, her bonnet bobs on her tipsy
    and pimpled neck,
The crowd laugh at her blackguard oaths, the men jeer and
    wink to each other,
(Miserable! I do not laugh at your oaths nor jeer you;)
The President holding a cabinet council is surrounded by the
    great Secretaries,
On the piazza walk three matrons stately and friendly with
    twined arms,

The crew of the fish-smack pack repeated layers of halibut in
  the hold,
The Missourian crosses the plains toting his wares and his
  cattle,
As the fare-collector goes through the train he gives notice by
  the jingling of loose change,
The floor-men are laying the floor, the tinners are tinning the
  roof, the masons are calling for mortar,
In single file each shouldering his hod pass onward the labor-
  ers;
Seasons pursuing each other the indescribable crowd is gath-
  er'd, it is the fourth of Seventh-month, (what
  salutes of cannon and small arms!)
Seasons pursuing each other the plougher ploughs, the mower
  mows, and the winter-grain falls in the
  ground;
Off on the lakes the pike-fisher watches and waits by the hole
  in the frozen surface,
The stumps stand thick round the clearing, the squatter strikes
  deep with his axe,
Flatboatmen make fast towards dusk near the cotton-wood or
  pecan-trees,
Coon-seekers go through the regions of the Red river or
  through those drain'd by the Tennessee, or
  through those of the Arkansas,
Torches shine in the dark that hangs on the Chattahooche or
  Altamahaw,
Patriarchs sit at supper with sons and grandsons and great-
  grandsons around them,
In walls of adobie, in canvas tents, rest hunters and trappers
  after their day's sport,
The city sleeps and the country sleeps,
The living sleep for their time, the dead sleep for their time,
The old husband sleeps by his wife and the young husband
  sleeps by his wife;
And these tend inward to me, and I tend outward to them,
And such as it is to be of these more or less I am,
And of these one and all I weave the song of myself.

16

I am of old and young, of the foolish as much as the wise,
Regardless of others, ever regardful of others,
Maternal as well as paternal, a child as well as a man,
Stuff'd with the stuff that is coarse and stuff'd with the stuff that
  is fine,
One of the Nation of many nations, the smallest the same and
  the largest the same,
A Southerner soon as a Northerner, a planter nonchalant and
  hospitable down by the Oconee I live,

A Yankee bound my own way ready for trade, my joints the
            limberest joints on earth and the sternest
            joints on earth,
A Kentuckian walking the vale of the Elkhorn in my deer-
            skin leggings, a Louisianian or Georgian,
A boatman over lakes or bays or along coasts, a Hoosier, a
            Badger, Buckeye;
At home on Kanadian snow-shoes or up in the bush, or with
            fishermen off Newfoundland,
At home in the fleet of ice-boats, sailing with the rest and
            tacking,
At home on the hills of Vermont or in the woods of Maine,
            or the Texan ranch,
Comrade of Californians, comrade of Free North-Westerners,
            (loving their big proportions,)
Comrade of raftsmen and coalmen, comrade of all who shake
            hands and welcome to drink and meat,
A learner with the simplest, a teacher of the thoughtfullest,
A novice beginning yet experient of myriads of seasons,
Of every hue and caste am I, of every rank and religion,
A farmer, mechanic, artist, gentleman, sailor, quaker,
Prisoner, fancy-man, rowdy, lawyer, physician, priest.

I resist any thing better than my own diversity,
Breathe the air but leave plenty after me,
And am not stuck up, and am in my place.

(The moth and the fish-eggs are in their place,
The bright suns I see and the dark suns I cannot see are in their
            place,
The palpable is in its place and the impalpable is in its place.)

17

These are really the thoughts of all men in all ages and lands,
            they are not original with me,
If they are not yours as much as mine they are nothing, or
            next to nothing,
If they are not the riddle and the untying of the riddle they
            are nothing,
If they are not just as close as they are distant they are nothing.

This is the grass that grows wherever the land is and the
            water is,
This is the common air that bathes the globe.

18

With music strong I come, with my cornets and my drums,
I play not marches for accepted victors only, I play marches
            for conquer'd and slain persons.

Have you heard that it was good to gain the day?
I also say it is good to fall, battles are lost in the same spirit
in which they are won.

I beat and pound for the dead,
I blow through my embouchures my loudest and gayest for
them.

Vivas to those who have fail'd!
And to those whose war-vessels sank in the sea!
And to those themselves who sank in the sea!
And to all generals that lost engagements, and all overcome
heroes!
And the numberless unknown heroes equal to the greatest
heroes known!

19

This is the meal equally set, this the meat for natural hunger,
It is for the wicked just the same as the righteous, I make
appointments with all,
I will not have a single person slighted or left away,
The kept-woman, sponger, thief, are hereby invited,
The heavy-lipp'd slave is invited, the venerealee is invited;
There shall be no difference between them and the rest.

This is the press of a bashful hand, this the float and odor of
hair,
This the touch of my lips to yours, this the murmur of
yearning,
This the far-off depth and height reflecting my own face,
This the thoughtful merge of myself, and the outlet again.

Do you guess I have some intricate purpose?
Well I have, for the Fourth-month showers have, and the mica
on the side of a rock has.

Do you take it I would astonish?
Does the daylight astonish? does the early redstart twittering
through the woods?
Do I astonish more than they?

This hour I tell things in confidence,
I might not tell everybody, but I will tell you.

20

Who goes there? hankering, gross, mystical, nude;
How is it I extract strength from the beef I eat?

What is a man anyhow? what am I? what are you?
All I mark as my own you shall offset it with your own,
Else it were time lost listening to me.

I do not snivel that snivel the world over,
That months are vacuums and the ground but wallow and
    filth.

Whimpering and truckling fold with powders for invalids,
                conformity goes to the fourth-remov'd,
I wear my hat as I please indoors or out.

Why should I pray? why should I venerate and be ceremo-
        nious?

Having pried through the strata, analyzed to a hair, counsel'd
                with doctors and calculated close,
I find no sweeter fat than sticks to my own bones.

In all people I see myself, none more and not one a barley-
        corn less,
And the good or bad I say of myself I say of them.

I know I am solid and sound,
To me the converging objects of the universe perpetually
        flow,
All are written to me, and I must get what the writing means.

I know I am deathless,
I know this orbit of mine cannot be swept by a carpenter's
        compass,
I know I shall not pass like a child's carlacue cut with a
        burnt stick at night.

I know I am august,
I do not trouble my spirit to vindicate itself or be understood,
I see that the elementary laws never apologize,
(I reckon I behave no prouder than the level I plant my
        house by, after all.)

I exist as I am, that is enough,
If no other in the world be aware I sit content,
And if each and all be aware I sit content.

One world is aware and by far the largest to me, and that is
        myself,
And whether I come to my own to-day or in ten thousand or
        ten million years,
I can cheerfully take it now, or with equal cheerfulness I can
        wait.
My foothold is tenon'd and mortis'd in granite,
I laugh at what you call dissolution,
And I know the amplitude of time.

21

I am the poet of the Body and I am the poet of the Soul,
The pleasures of heaven are with me and the pains of hell are
    with me,
The first I graft and increase upon myself, the latter I trans-
    late into a new tongue.

I am the poet of the woman the same as the man,
And I say it is as great to be a woman as to be a man,
And I say there is nothing greater than the mother of men.

I chant the chant of dilation or pride,
We have had ducking and deprecating about enough,
I show that size is only development.

Have you outstript the rest? are you the President?
It is a trifle, they will more than arrive there every one, and
    still pass on.

I am he that walks with the tender and growing night,
I call to the earth and sea half-held by the night.

Press close bare-bosom'd night—press close magnetic nour-
    ishing night!
Night of south winds—night of the large few stars!
Still nodding night—mad naked summer night.

Smile O voluptuous cool-breath'd earth!
Earth of the slumbering and liquid trees!
Earth of departed sunset—earth of the mountains misty-
    topt!
Earth of the vitreous pour of the full moon just tinged with
    blue!
Earth of shine and dark mottling the tide of the river!
Earth of the limpid gray of clouds brighter and clearer for
    my sake!
Far-swooping elbow'd earth—rich apple-blossom'd earth!
Smile, for your lover comes.

Prodigal, you have given me love—therefore I to you give
    love!
O unspeakable passionate love.

22

You sea! I resign myself to you also—I guess what you mean,
I behold from the beach your crooked inviting fingers,
I believe you refuse to go back without feeling of me,
We must have a turn together, I undress, hurry me out of
    sight of the land,
Cushion me soft, rock me in billowy drowse,
Dash me with amorous wet, I can repay you.

Sea of stretch'd ground-swells,
Sea breathing broad and convulsive breaths,
Sea of the brine of life and of unshovell'd yet always-ready
    graves,
Howler and scooper of storms, capricious and dainty sea,
I am integral with you, I too am of one phase and of all
    phases.

Partaker of influx and efflux I, extoller of hate and concilia-
    tion,
Extoller of amies and those that sleep in each others' arms,

I am he attesting sympathy,
(Shall I make my list of things in the house and skip the house
    that supports them?)

I am not the poet of goodness only, I do not decline to be the
    poet of wickedness also.

What blurt is this about virtue and about vice?
Evil propels me and reform of evil propels me, I stand in-
    different,
My gait is no fault-finder's or rejectors gait;
I moisten the roots of all that has grown.

Did you fear some scrofula out of the unflagging pregnancy?
Did you guess the celestial laws are yet to be work'd over and
    rectified?

I find one side a balance and the antipodal side a balance,
Soft doctrine as steady help as stable doctrine,
Thoughts and deeds of the present our rouse and early start.

This minute that comes to me over the past decillions,
There is no better than it and now.

What behaved well in the past or behaves well to-day is not
    such a wonder,
The wonder is always and always how there can be a mean
    man or an infidel.

23

Endless unfolding of words of ages!
And mine a word of the modern, the word En-Masse.

A word of the faith that never balks,
Here or henceforward it is all the same to me, I accept Time
    absolutely.

It alone is without flaw, it alone rounds and completes all,
That mystic baffling wonder alone completes all.

I accept Reality and dare not question it,
Materialism first and last imbuing.

Hurrah for positive science! long live exact demonstration!
Fetch stonecrop mixt with cedar and branches of lilac,
This is the lexicographer, this the chemist, this made a gram-
mar of the old cartouches,
These mariners put the ship through dangerous unknown
seas,
This is the geologist, this works with the scalpel, and this is
a mathematician.

Gentlemen, to you the first honors always!
Your facts are useful, and yet they are not my dwelling,
I but enter by them to an area of my dwelling.

Less the reminders of properties told my words,
And more the reminders they of life untold, and of freedom
and extrication,
And make short account of neuters and geldings, and favor
men and women fully equipt.
And beat the gong of revolt, and stop with fugitives and
them that plot and conspire.

24

Walt Whitman, a kosmos, of Manhattan the son,
Turbulent, fleshy, sensual, eating, drinking and breeding,
No sentimentalist, no stander above men and women or apart
from them,
No more modest than immodest.

Unscrew the locks from the doors!
Unscrew the doors themselves from their jambs!

Whoever degrades another degrades me,
And whatever is done or said returns at last to me.

Through me the afflatus surging and surging, through me the
current and index.

I speak the pass-word primeval, I give the sign of democracy,
By God! I will accept nothing which all cannot have their
counterpart of on the same terms.

Through me many long dumb voices,
Voices of the interminable generations of prisoners and slaves,
Voices of the diseas'd and despairing and of thieves and
dwarfs,
Voices of cycles of preparation and accretion,
And of the threads that connect the stars, and of wombs and
of the father-stuff,
And of the rights of them the others are down upon,
Of the deform'd, trivial, flat, foolish, despised,
Fog in the air, beetles rolling balls of dung.

Through me forbidden voices,
Voices of sexes and lusts, voices veil'd and I remove the veil,
Voices indecent by me clarified and transfigur'd.

I do not press my fingers across my mouth,
I keep as delicate around the bowels as around the head and
      heart,
Copulation is no more rank to me than death is.

I believe in the flesh and the appetites,
Seeing, hearing, feeling, are miracles, and each part and tag
      of me is a miracle.

Divine am I inside and out, and I make holy whatever I touch
      or am touch'd from,
The scent of these arm-pits aroma finer than prayer,
This head more than churches, bibles, and all the creeds.

If I worship one thing more than another it shall be the spread
      of my own body, or any part of it,
Translucent mould of me it shall be you!
Shaded ledges and rests it shall be you!
Firm masculine colter it shall be you!
Whatever goes to the tilth of me it shall be you!
You my rich blood! your milky stream pale strippings of my
      life!
Breast that presses against other breasts it shall be you!
My brain it shall be your occult convolutions!
Root of wash'd sweet-flag! timorous pond-snipe! nest of
      guarded duplicate eggs! it shall be you!
Mix'd tussled hay of head, beard, brawn, it shall be you!
Trickling sap of maple, fibre of manly wheat, it shall be you!
Sun so generous it shall be you!
Vapors lighting and shading my face it shall be you!
You sweaty brooks and dews it shall be you!
Winds whose soft-tickling genitals rub against me it shall be
      you!
Broad muscular fields, branches of live oak, loving lounger in
      my winding paths, it shall be you!
Hands I have taken, face I have kiss'd, mortal I have ever
      touch'd, it shall be you.

I dote on myself, there is that lot of me and all so luscious,
Each moment and whatever happens thrills me with joy,
I cannot tell how my ankles bend, nor whence the cause of
      my faintest wish,
Nor the cause of the friendship I emit, nor the cause of the
      friendship I take again.

That I walk up my stoop, I pause to consider if it really be,
A morning-glory at my window satisfies me more than the
      metaphysics of books.

To behold the day-break!
The little light fades the immense and diaphanous shadows,
The air tastes good to my palate.

Hefts of the moving world at innocent gambols silently rising,
    freshly exuding,
Scooting obliquely high and low.

Something I cannot see puts upward libidinous prongs,
Seas of bright juice suffuse heaven.

The earth by the sky staid with, the daily close of their junc-
    tion,
The heav'd challenge from the east that moment over my
    head,
The mocking taunt, See then whether you shall be master!

25

Dazzling and tremendous how quick the sun-rise would kill
    me,
If I could not now and always send sun-rise out of me.

We also ascend dazzling and tremendous as the sun,
We found our own O my soul in the calm and cool of the
    daybreak.

My voice goes after what my eyes cannot reach,
With the twirl of my tongue I encompass worlds and volumes
    of worlds.

Speech is the twin of my vision, it is unequal to measure
    itself,
It provokes me forever, it says sarcastically,
Walt you contain enough, why don't you let it out then?

Come now I will not be tantalized, you conceive too much of
    articulation,
Do you not know O speech how the buds beneath you are
    folded?
Waiting in gloom, protected by frost,
The dirt receding before my prophetical screams,
I underlying causes to balance them at last,
My knowledge my live parts, it keeping tally with the mean-
    ing of all things,
Happiness, (which whoever hears me let him or her set out in
    search of this day.)

My final merit I refuse you, I refuse putting from me what
    I really am,
Encompass worlds, but never try to encompass me,
I crowd your sleekest and best by simply looking toward you.

Writing and talk do not prove me,
I carry the plenum of proof and every thing else in my face,
With the hush of my lips I wholly confound the skeptic.

26

Now I will do nothing but listen,
To accrue what I hear into this song, to let sounds contribute
           toward it.

I hear bravuras of birds, bustle of growing wheat, gossip of
           flames, clack of sticks cooking my meals,
I hear the sound I love, the sound of the human voice,
I hear all sounds running together, combined, fused or fol-
           lowing,
Sounds of the city and sounds out of the city, sounds of the
           day and night,
Talkative young ones to those that like them, the loud laugh
           of work-people at their meals,
The angry base of disjointed friendship, the faint tones of the
           sick,
The judge with hands tight to the desk, his pallid lips pro-
           nouncing a death-sentence,
The heave'e'yo of stevedores unloading ships by the wharves,
           the refrain of the anchor-lifters,
The ring of alarm-bells, the cry of fire, the whirr of swift-
           streaking engines and hose-carts with pre-
           monitory tinkles and color'd lights,
The steam-whistle, the solid roll of the train of approaching
           cars,
The slow march play'd at the head of the association march-
           ing two and two,
(They go to guard some corpse, the flag-tops are draped with
           black muslin.)

I hear the violoncello, ('tis the young man's heart's com-
           plaint,)
I hear the key'd cornet, it glides quickly in through my ears,
It shakes mad-sweet pangs through my belly and breast.

I hear the chorus, it is a grand opera,
Ah this indeed is music—this suits me.

A tenor large and fresh as the creation fills me,
The orbic flex of his mouth is pouring and filling me full.

I hear the train'd soprano (what work with hers is this?)
The orchestra whirls me wider than Uranus flies,
It wrenches such ardors from me I did not know I possess'd
           them,
It sails me, I dab with bare feet, they are lick'd by the indo-
           lent waves,

I am cut by bitter and angry hail, I lose my breath,
Steep'd amid honey'd morphine, my windpipe throttled in
    fakes of death,
At length let up again to feel the puzzle of puzzles,
And that we call Being.

27

To be in any form, what is that?
(Round and round we go, all of us, and ever come back
    thither,)
If nothing lay more develop'd the quahaug in its callous shell
    were enough.

Mine is no callous shell,
I have instant conductors all over me whether I pass or stop,
They seize every object and lead it harmlessly through me.

I merely stir, press, feel with my fingers, and am happy,
To touch my person to some one else's is about as much as
    I can stand.

28

Is this then a touch? quivering me to a new identity,
Flames and ether making a rush for my veins,
Treacherous tip of me reaching and crowding to help them,
My flesh and blood playing out lightning to strike what is
    hardly different from myself,
On all sides prurient provokers stiffening my limbs,
Straining the udder of my heart for its withheld drip,
Behaving licentious toward me, taking no denial,
Depriving me of my best as for a purpose,
Unbuttoning my clothes, holding me by the bare waist,
Deluding my confusion with the calm of the sunlight and
    pasture-fields,
Immodestly sliding the fellow-senses away,
They bribed to swap off with touch and go and graze at the
    edges of me,
No consideration, no regard for my draining strength or my
    anger,
Fetching the rest of the herd around to enjoy them a while,
Then all uniting to stand on a headland and worry me.
The sentries desert every other part of me,
They have left me helpless to a red marauder,
They all come to the headland to witness and assist against me.

I am given up by traitors,
I talk wildly, I have lost my wits, I and nobody else am the
    greatest traitor,
I went myself first to the headland, my own hands carried
    me there.

You villain touch! what are you doing? my breath is tight
        in its throat,
Unclench your floodgates, you are too much for me.

29

Blind loving wrestling touch, sheath'd hooded sharp-tooth'd
        touch!
Did it make you ache so, leaving me?

Parting track'd by arriving, perpetual payment of perpetual
        loan,
Rich showering rain, and recompense richer afterward.

Sprouts take and accumulate, stand by the curb prolific and
        vital,
Landscapes projected masculine, full-sized and golden.

30

All truths wait in all things,
They neither hasten their own delivery nor resist it,
They do not need the obstetric forceps of the surgeon,
The insignificant is as big to me as any,
(What is less or more than a touch?)

Logic and sermons never convince,
The damp of the night drives deeper into my soul.

(Only what proves itself to every man and woman is so,
Only what nobody denies is so.)

A minute and a drop of me settle my brain,
I believe the soggy clods shall become lovers and lamps,
And a compend of compends is the meat of a man or woman,
And a summit and flower there is the feeling they have for
        each other,
And they are to branch boundlessly out of that lesson until
        it becomes omnific,
And until one and all shall delight us, and we them.

31

I believe a leaf of grass is no less than the journey-work of
        the stars,
And the pismire is equally perfect, and a grain of sand, and
        the egg of the wren,
And the tree-toad is a chef-d'œuvre for the highest,
And the running blackberry would adorn the parlors of
        heaven,
And the narrowest hinge in my hand puts to scorn all ma-
        chinery,
And the cow crunching with depress'd head surpasses any
        statue,

And a mouse is miracle enough to stagger sextillions of
    infidels.

I find I incorporate gneiss, coal, long-threaded moss, fruits,
    grains, esculent roots,
And am stucco'd with quadrupeds and birds all over,
And have distanced what is behind me for good reasons,
But call any thing back again when I desire it.

In vain the speeding or shyness,
In vain the plutonic rocks send their old heat against my ap-
    proach,
In vain the mastodon retreats beneath its own powder'd bones,
In vain objects stand leagues off and assume manifold shapes,
In vain the ocean settling in hollows and the great monsters
    lying low,
In vain the buzzard houses herself with the sky,
In vain the snake slides through the creepers and logs,
In vain the elk takes to the inner passes of the woods,
In vain the razor-bill'd auk sails far north to Labrador,
I follow quickly, I ascend to the nest in the fissure of the cliff.

32

I think I could turn and live with animals, they are so placid
    and self-contain'd,
I stand and look at them long and long.

They do not sweat and whine about their condition,
They do not lie awake in the dark and weep for their sins,
They do not make me sick discussing their duty to God,
Not one is dissatisfied, not one is demented with the mania
    of owning things,
Not one kneels to another, nor to his kind that lived thousands
    of years ago,
Not one is respectable or unhappy over the whole earth.
So they show their relations to me and I accept them,
They bring me tokens of myself, they evince them plainly in
    their possession.

I wonder where they get those tokens,
Did I pass that way huge times ago and negligently drop them?

Myself moving forward then and now and forever,
Gathering and showing more always and with velocity,
Infinite and omnigenous, and the like of these among them,
Not too exclusive toward the reachers of my remembrancers,
Picking out here one that I love, and now go with him on
    brotherly terms.

A gigantic beauty of a stallion, fresh and responsive to my
    caresses,
Head high in the forehead, wide between the ears,

Limbs glossy and supple, tail dusting the ground,
Eyes full of sparkling wickedness, ears finely cut, flexibly
    moving.

His nostrils dilate as my heels embrace him,
His well-built limbs tremble with pleasure as we race around
    and return.
I but use you a minute, then I resign you, stallion,
Why do I need your paces when I myself out-gallop them?
Even as I stand or sit passing faster than you.

33

Space and Time! now I see it is true, what I guess'd at,
What I guess'd when I loaf'd on the grass,
What I guess'd while I lay alone in my bed,
And again as I walk'd the beach under the paling stars of the
    morning.

My ties and ballasts leave me, my elbows rest in sea-gaps,
I skirt sierras, my palms cover continents,
I am afoot with my vision.

By the city's quadrangular houses—in log huts, camping with
    lumbermen,
Along the ruts of the turnpike, along the dry gulch and rivulet
    bed,
Weeding my onion-patch or hoeing rows of carrots and pars-
    nips, crossing savannas, trailing in forests,
Prospecting, gold-digging, girdling the trees of a new pur-
    chase,
Scorch'd ankle-deep by the hot sand, hauling my boat down
    the shallow river,
Where the panther walks to and fro on a limb overhead,
    where the buck turns furiously at the hunter,
Where the rattlesnake suns his flabby length on a rock, where
    the otter is feeding on fish,
Where the alligator in his tough pimples sleeps by the bayou,
Where the black bear is searching for roots or honey, where
    the beaver pats the mud with his paddle-
    shaped tail;
Over the growing sugar, over the yellow-flower'd cotton plant,
    over the rice in its low moist field,
Over the sharp-peak'd farmhouse, with its scallop'd scum and
    slender shoots from the gutters,
Over the western persimmon, over the long-leav'd corn, over
    the delicate blue-flower flax,
Over the white and brown buckwheat, a hummer and buzzer
    there with the rest,
Over the dusky green of the rye as it ripples and shades in the
    breeze;

Scaling mountains, pulling myself cautiously up, holding on
        by low scragged limbs,
Walking the path worn in the grass and beat through the
        leaves of the brush,
Where the quail is whistling betwixt the woods and the wheat-
        lot,
Where the bat flies in the Seventh-month eve, where the great
        gold-bug drops through the dark,
Where the brook puts out of the roots of the old tree and flows
        to the meadow,
Where cattle stand and shake away flies with the tremulous
        shuddering of their hides,
Where the cheese-cloth hangs in the kitchen, where andirons
        straddle the hearth-slab, where cobwebs fall
        in festoons from the rafters;
Where trip-hammers crash, where the press is whirling its
        cylinders,
Where the human heart beats with terrible throes under its
        ribs,
Where the pear-shaped balloon is floating aloft, (floating in it
        myself and looking composedly down,)
Where the life-car is drawn on the slip-noose, where the heat
        hatches pale-green eggs in the dented sand,
Where the she-whale swims with her calf and never forsakes it,
Where the steam-ship trails hind-ways its long pennant of
        smoke,
Where the fin of the shark cuts like a black chip out of the
        water,
Where the half-burn'd brig is riding on unknown currents,
Where shells grow to her slimy deck, where the dead are cor-
        rupting below;
Where the dense-starr'd flag is borne at the head of the regi-
        ments,
Approaching Manhattan up by the long-stretching island,
Under Niagara, the cataract falling like a veil over my coun-
        tenance,
Upon a door-step, upon the horse-block of hard wood out-
        side,
Upon the race-course, or enjoying picnics or jigs or a good
        game of base-ball,
At he-festivals, with blackguard gibes, ironical license, bull-
        dances, drinking, laughter,
At the cider-mill tasting the sweets of the brown mash, sucking
        the juice through a straw,
At apple-peelings wanting kisses for all the red fruit I find,
At musters, beach-parties, friendly bees, huskings, house-
        raisings;
Where the mocking-bird sounds his delicious gurgles, cackles,
        screams, weeps,

Where the hay-rick stands in the barn-yard, where the dry-
        stalks are scatter'd, where the brood-cow
        waits in the hovel,
Where the bull advances to do his masculine work, where the
        stud to the mare, where the cock is treading
        the hen,
Where the heifers browse, where geese nip their food with
        short jerks,
Where sun-down shadows lengthen over the limitless and lone-
        some prairie,
Where herds of buffalo make a crawling spread of the square
        miles far and near,
Where the humming-bird shimmers, where the neck of the
        long-lived swan is curving and winding,
Where the laughing-gull scoots by the shore, where she laughs
        her near-human laugh,
Where bee-hives range on a gray bench in the garden half hid
        by the high weeds,
Where band-neck'd partridges roost in a ring on the ground
        with their heads out,
Where burial coaches enter the arch'd gates of a cemetery,
Where winter wolves bark amid wastes of snow and icicled
        trees,
Where the yellow-crown'd heron comes to the edge of the
        marsh at night and feeds upon small crabs,
Where the splash of swimmers and divers cools the warm
        noon,
Where the katy-did works her chromatic reed on the walnut-
        tree over the well,
Through patches of citrons and cucumbers with silver-wired
        leaves,
Through the salt-lick or orange glade, or under conical firs,
Through the gymnasium, through the curtain'd saloon,
        through the office or public hall;
Pleas'd with the native and pleas'd with the foreign, pleas'd
        with the new and old,
Pleas'd with the homely woman as well as the handsome,
Pleas'd with the quakeress as she puts off her bonnet and
        talks melodiously,
Pleas'd with the tune of the choir of the whitewash'd church,
Pleas'd with the earnest words of the sweating Methodist
        preacher, impress'd seriously at the camp-
        meeting;
Looking in at the shop-windows of Broadway the whole fore-
        noon, flatting the flesh of my nose on the
        thick plate glass,
Wandering the same afternoon with my face turn'd up to
        the clouds, or down a lane or along the
        beach,

My right and left arms round the sides of two friends, and
    I in the middle;
Coming home with the silent and dark-cheek'd bush-boy,
    (behind me he rides at the drape of the day,)
Far from the settlements studying the print of animals' feet,
    or the moccasin print,
By the cot in the hospital reaching lemonade to a feverish
    patient,
Nigh the coffin'd corpse when all is still, examining with a
    candle;
Voyaging to every port to dicker and adventure,
Hurrying with the modern crowd as eager and fickle as any,
Hot toward one I hate, ready in my madness to knife him,
Solitary at midnight in my back yard, my thoughts gone from
    me a long while,
Walking the old hills of Judæa with the beautiful gentle God
    by my side,
Speeding through space, speeding through heaven and the
    stars,
Speeding amid the seven satellites and the broad ring, and
    the diameter of eighty thousand miles,
Speeding with tail'd meteors, throwing fire-balls like the rest,
Carrying the crescent child that carries its own full mother
    in its belly,
Storming, enjoying, planning, loving, cautioning,
Backing and filling, appearing and disappearing,
I tread day and night such roads.

I visit the orchards of spheres and look at the product,
And look at quintillions ripen'd and look at quintillions green.

I fly those flights of a fluid and swallowing soul,
My course runs below the soundings of plummets.

I help myself to material and immaterial,
No guard can shut me off, no law prevent me.

I anchor my ship for a little while only,
My messengers continually cruise away or bring their returns
    to me.

I go hunting polar furs and the seal, leaping chasms with a
    pike-pointed staff, clinging to topples of brit-
    tle and blue.

I ascend to the foretruck,
I take my place late at night in the crow's-nest,
We sail the arctic sea, it is plenty light enough,
Through the clear atmosphere I stretch around on the won-
    derful beauty,

The enormous masses of ice pass me and I pass them, the
    scenery is plain in all directions,
The white-topt mountains show in the distance, I fling out
    my fancies toward them,
We are approaching some great battle-field in which we are
    soon to be engaged,
We pass the colossal outposts of the encampment, we pass
    with still feet and caution,
Or we are entering by the suburbs some vast and ruin'd city,
The blocks and fallen architecture more than all the living
    cities of the globe.

I am a free companion, I bivouac by invading watchfires,
I turn the bridegroom out of bed and stay with the bride
    myself,
I tighten her all night to my thighs and lips.

My voice is the wife's voice, the screech by the rail of the
    stairs,
They fetch my man's body up dripping and drown'd.

I understand the large hearts of heroes,
The courage of present times and all times,
How the skipper saw the crowded and rudderless wreck of
    the steamship, and Death chasing it up and
    down the storm,
How he knuckled tight and gave not back an inch, and was
    faithful of days and faithful of nights,
And chalk'd in large letters on a board, *Be of good cheer,
we will not desert you;*
How he follow'd with them and tack'd with them three days
    and would not give it up,
How he saved the drifting company at last,
How the lank loose-gown'd women look'd when boated from
    the side of their prepared graves,
How the silent old-faced infants and the lifted sick, and the
    sharp-lipp'd unshaven men;
All this I swallow, it tastes good, I like it well, it becomes
    mine,
I am the man, I suffer'd, I was there.

The disdain and calmness of martyrs,
The mother of old, condemn'd for a witch, burnt with dry
    wood, her children gazing on,
The hounded slave that flags in the race, leans by the fence,
    blowing, cover'd with sweat,
The twinges that sting like needles his legs and neck, the mur-
    derous buckshot and the bullets,
All these I feel or am.

I am the hounded slave, I wince at the bite of the dogs,

Hell and despair are upon me, crack and again crack the
    marksmen,
I clutch the rails of the fence, my gored ribs, thinn'd with
    the ooze of my skin,
I fall on the weeds and stones,
The riders spur their unwilling horses, haul close,
Taunt my dizzy ears and beat me violently over the head
    with whipstocks.

Agonies are one of my changes of garments.
I do not ask the wounded person how he feels, I myself be-
    come the wounded person,
My hurts turn livid upon me as I lean on a cane and observe.

I am the mash'd fireman with breast-bone broken,
Tumbling walls buried me in their debris,
Heat and smoke I inspired, I heard the yelling shouts of my
    comrades,
I heard the distant click of their picks and shovels,
They have clear'd the beams away, they tenderly lift me forth.

I lie in the night air in my red shirt, the pervading hush is
    for my sake,
Painless after all I lie exhausted but not so unhappy,
White and beautiful are the faces around me, the heads are
    bared of their fire-caps,
The kneeling crowd fades with the light of the torches.

Distant and dead resuscitate,
They show as the dial or move as the hands of me, I am the
    clock myself.

I am an old artillerist, I tell of my fort's bombardment,
I am there again.

Again the long roll of the drummers,
Again the attacking cannon, mortars,
Again to my listening ears the cannon responsive.

I take part, I see and hear the whole,
The cries, curses, roar, the plaudits for well-aim'd shots,
The ambulanza slowly passing trailing its red drip,
Workmen searching after damages, making indispensable
    repairs,
The fall of grenades through the rent roof, the fan-shaped
    explosion,
The whizz of limbs, heads, stone, wood, iron, high in the air.

Again gurgles the mouth of my dying general, he furiously
    waves with his hand,
He gasps through the clot *Mind not me—mind—the entrench-
    ments.*

34

Now I tell what I know in Texas in my early youth,
(I tell not the fall of Alamo,
Not one escaped to tell the fall of Alamo,
The hundred and fifty are dumb yet at Alamo,)
'Tis the tale of the murder in cold blood of four hundred and
        twelve young men.

Retreating they had form'd in a hollow square with their
        baggage for breastworks,
Nine hundred lives out of the surrounding enemy's, nine times
        their number, was the price they took in
        advance,
Their colonel was wounded and their ammunition gone,
They treated for an honorable capitulation, receiv'd writing
        and seal, gave up their arms and march'd
        back prisoners of war.

They were the glory of the race of rangers,
Matchless with horse, rifle, song, supper, courtship,
Large, turbulent, generous, handsome, proud, and affec-
        tionate,
Bearded, sunburnt, drest in the free costume of hunters,
Not a single one over thirty years of age.

The second First-day morning they were brought out in squads
        and massacred, it was beautiful early sum-
        mer,
The work commenced about five o'clock and was over by
        eight.

None obey'd the command to kneel,
Some made a mad and helpless rush, some stood stark and
        straight,
A few fell at once, shot in the temple or heart, the living and
        dead lay together,
The maim'd and mangled dug in the dirt, the new-comers saw
        them there,
Some half-kill'd attempted to crawl away,
These were despatch'd with bayonets or batter'd with the
        blunts of muskets.
A youth not seventeen years old seiz'd his assassin till two
        more came to release him,
The three were all torn and cover'd with the boy's blood.

At eleven o'clock began the burning of the bodies;
That is the tale of the murder of the four hundred and twelve
        young men.

35

Would you hear of an old-time sea-fight?
Would you learn who won by the light of the moon and stars?
List to the yarn, as my grandmother's father the sailor told
        it to me.

Our foe was no skulk in his ship I tell you, (said he,)
His was the surly English pluck, and there is no tougher or
        truer, and never was, and never will be;
Along the lower'd eve he came horribly raking us.

We closed with him, the yards entangled, the cannon touch'd,
My captain lash'd fast with his own hands.

We had receiv'd some eighteen pound shots under the water,
On our lower-gun-deck two large pieces had burst at the first
        fire, killing all around and blowing up over-
        head.

Fighting at sun-down, fighting at dark,
Ten o'clock at night, the full moon well up, our leaks on the
        gain, and five feet of water reported,
The master-at-arms loosing the prisoners confined in the
        after-hold to give them a chance for them-
        selves.

The transit to and from the magazine is now stopt by the
        sentinels,
They see so many strange faces they do not know whom to
        trust.

Our frigate takes fire,
The other asks if we demand quarter?
If our colors are struck and the fighting done?

Now I laugh content, for I hear the voice of my little captain,
We have not struck, he composedly cries, *we have just begun
        our part of the fighting.*

Only three guns are in use,
One is directed by the captain himself against the enemy's
        main-mast,
Two well serv'd with grape and canister silence his musketry
        and clear his decks.

The tops alone second the fire of this little battery, especially
        the main-top,
They hold out bravely during the whole of the action.

Not a moment's cease,
The leaks gain fast on the pumps, the fire eats toward the
        powder-magazine.

One of the pumps has been shot away, it is generally thought
we are sinking.

Serene stands the little captain,
He is not hurried, his voice is neither high nor low,
His eyes give more light to us than our battle-lanterns.

Toward twelve there in the beams of the moon they surren-
der to us.

36

Stretch'd and still lies the midnight,
Two great hulls motionless on the breast of the darkness,
Our vessel riddled and slowly sinking, preparations to pass
to the one we have conquer'd,
The captain on the quarter-deck coldly giving his orders
through a countenance white as a sheet,
Near by the corpse of the child that serv'd in the cabin,
The dead face of an old salt with long white hair and care-
fully curl'd whiskers,
The flames spite of all that can be done flickering aloft and
below,
The husky voices of the two or three officers yet fit for duty,
Formless stacks of bodies and bodies by themselves, dabs of
flesh upon the masts and spars,
Cut of cordage, dangle of rigging, slight shock of the soothe
of waves,
Black and impassive guns, litter of powder-parcels, strong
scent,
A few large stars overhead, silent and mournful shining,
Delicate sniffs of sea-breeze, smells of sedgy grass and fields
by the shore, death-messages given in charge
to survivors,
The hiss of the surgeon's knife, the gnawing teeth of his saw,
Wheeze, cluck, swash of falling blood, short wild scream,
and long, dull, tapering groan,
These so, these irretrievable.

37

You laggards there on guard! look to your arms!
In at the conquer'd doors they crowd! I am possess'd!
Embody all presences outlaw'd or suffering,
See myself in prison shaped like another man.
And feel the dull unintermitted pain,
For me the keepers of convicts shoulder their carbines and
keep watch.
It is I let out in the morning and barr'd at night.

Not a mutineer walks handcuff'd to jail but I am handcuff'd
to him and walk by his side,

(I am less the jolly one there, and more the silent one with
    sweat on my twitching lips.)

Not a youngster is taken for larceny but I go up too, and am
    tried and sentenced.

Not a cholera patient lies at the last gasp but I also lie at the
    last gasp,
My face is ash-color'd, my sinews gnarl, away from me people
    retreat.

Askers embody themselves in me and I am embodied in
    them,
I project my hat, sit shame-faced, and beg.

38

Enough! enough! enough!
Somehow I have been stunn'd. Stand back!
Give me a little time beyond my cuff'd head, slumbers, dreams,
    gaping,
I discover myself on the verge of a usual mistake.

That I could forget the mockers and insults!
That I could forget the trickling tears and the blows of the
    bludgeons and hammers!
That I could look with a separate look on my own crucifixion
    and bloody crowning!

I remember now,
I resume the overstaid fraction,
The grave of rock multiplies what has been confided to it,
    or to any graves,
Corpses rise, gashes heal, fastenings roll from me.

I troop forth replenish'd with supreme power, one of an
    average unending procession,
Inland and sea-coast we go, and pass all boundary lines,
Our swift ordinances on their way over the whole earth,
The blossoms we wear in our hats the growth of thousands
    of years.

Eleves, I salute you! come forward!
Continue your annotations, continue your questionings.

39

The friendly and flowing savage, who is he?
Is he waiting for civilization, or past it and mastering it?

Is he some Southwesterner rais'd out-doors? is he Kanadian?
Is he from the Mississippi country? Iowa, Oregon, California?
The mountains? prairie-life, bush-life? or sailor from the sea?

Wherever he goes men and women accept and desire him,
They desire he should like them, touch them, speak to them,
    stay with them.

Behavior lawless as snow-flakes, words simple as grass, un-
    comb'd head, laughter, and naivetè,
Slow-stepping feet, common features, common modes and
    emanations,
They descend in new forms from the tips of his fingers,
They are wafted with the odor of his body or breath, they fly
    out of the glance of his eyes.

40

Flaunt of the sunshine I need not your bask—lie over!
You light surfaces only, I force surfaces and depths also.

Earth! you seem to look for something at my hands,
Say, old top-knot, what do you want?

Man or woman, I might tell how I like you, but cannot,
And might tell what it is in me and what it is in you, but
    cannot,
And might tell that pining I have, that pulse of my nights and
    days.

Behold, I do not give lectures or a little charity,
When I give I give myself.

You there, impotent, loose in the knees,
Open your scarf'd chops till I blow grit within you,
Spread your palms and lift the flaps of your pockets,
I am not to be denied, I compel, I have stores plenty and to
    spare,
And any thing I have I bestow.

I do not ask who you are, that is not important to me,
You can do nothing and be nothing but what I will infold you.

To cotton-field drudge or cleaner of privies I lean,
On his right cheek I put the family kiss,
And in my soul I swear I never will deny him.

On women fit for conception I start bigger and nimbler babes,
(This day I am jetting the stuff of far more arrogant republics.)

To any one dying, thither I speed and twist the knob of the
    door,
Turn the bed-clothes toward the foot of the bed,
Let the physician and the priest go home.

I seize the descending man and raise him with resistless will,
O despairer, here is my neck,

By God, you shall not go down! hang your whole weight upon
    me.

I dilate you with tremendous breath, I buoy you up,
Every room of the house do I fill with an arm'd force,
Lovers of me, bafflers of graves.

Sleep—I and they keep guard all night,
Not doubt, not disease shall dare to lay finger upon you,
I have embraced you, and henceforth possess you to myself,
And when you rise in the morning you will find what I tell
    you is so.

41

I am he bringing help for the sick as they pant on their backs,
And for strong upright men I bring yet more needed help.

I heard what was said of the universe,
Heard it and heard it of several thousand years;
It is middling well as far as it goes—but is that all?

Magnifying and applying come I,
Outbidding at the start the old cautious hucksters,
Taking myself the exact dimensions of Jehovah,
Lithographing Kronos, Zeus his son, and Hercules his grand-
    son,
Buying drafts of Osiris, Isis, Belus, Brahma, Buddha,
In my portfolio placing Manito loose, Allah on a leaf, the
    crucifix engraved,
With Odin and the hideous-faced Mexitli and every idol and
    image,
Taking them all for what they are worth and not a cent more,
Admitting they were alive and did the work of their days,
(They bore mites as for unfledg'd birds who have now to
    rise and fly and sing for themselves,)
Accepting the rough deific sketches to fill out better in myself,
    bestowing them freely on each man and
    woman I see,
Discovering as much or more in a framer framing a house,
Putting higher claims for him there with his roll'd-up
    sleeves driving the mallet and chisel,
Not objecting to special revelations, considering a curl of
    smoke or a hair on the back of my hand just
    as curious as any revelation,
Lads ahold of fire-engines and hook-and-ladder ropes no less
    to me than the gods of the antique wars,
Minding their voices peal through the crash of destruction,
Their brawny limbs passing safe over charr'd laths, their white
    foreheads whole and unhurt out of the
    flames;

By the mechanic's wife with her babe at her nipple interceding
        for every person born,
Three scythes at harvest whizzing in a row from three lusty
        angels with shirts bagg'd out at their waists,
The snag-tooth'd hostler with red hair redeeming sins past
        and to come,
Selling all he possesses, traveling on foot to fee lawyers for
        his brother and sit by him while he is tried for
        forgery;
What was strewn in the amplest strewing the square rod about
        me, and not filling the square rod then,
The bull and the bug never worshipp'd half enough,
Dung and dirt more admirable than was dream'd,
The supernatural of no account, myself waiting my time to be
        one of the supremes,
The day getting ready for me when I shall do as much good
        as the best, and be as prodigious;
By my life-lumps! becoming already a creator,
Putting myself here and now to the ambush'd womb of the
        shadows.

42

A call in the midst of the crowd,
My own voice, orotund sweeping and final.

Come my children,
Come my boys and girls, my women, household and inti-
        mates,
Now the performer launches his nerve, he has pass'd his prel-
        ude on the reeds within.

Easily written loose-finger'd chords—I feel the thrum of your
        climax and close.

My head slues round on my neck,
Music rolls, but not from the organ,
Folks are around me, but they are no household of mine.

Ever the hard unsunk ground,
Ever the eaters and drinkers, ever the upward and downward
        sun, ever the air and the ceaseless tides,
Ever myself and my neighbors, refreshing, wicked, real,
Ever the old inexplicable query, ever that thorn'd thumb, that
        breath of itches and thirsts,
Ever the vexer's *hoot! hoot!* till we find where the sly one hides
        and bring him forth,
Ever love, ever the sobbing liquid of life,
Ever the bandage under the chin, ever the trestles of death.

Here and there with dimes on the eyes walking,
To feed the greed of the belly the brains liberally spooning,

Tickets buying, taking, selling, but in to the feast never once
    going,
Many sweating, ploughing, thrashing, and then the chaff for
    payment receiving,
A few idly owning, and they the wheat continually claiming.

This is the city and I am one of the citizens,
Whatever interests the rest interests me, politics, wars, mar-
    kets, newspapers, schools,
The mayor and councils, banks, tariffs, steamships, factories,
    stocks, stores, real estate and personal estate.

The little plentiful manikins skipping around in collars and
    tail'd coats,
I am aware who they are, (they are positively not worms or
    fleas,)
I acknowledge the duplicates of myself, the weakest and
    shallowest is deathless with me,
What I do and say the same waits for them,
Every thought that flounders in me the same flounders in them.

I know perfectly well my own egotism,
Know my omnivorous lines and must not write any less,
And would fetch you whoever you are flush with myself.

Not words of routine this song of mine,
But abruptly to question, to leap beyond yet nearer bring;
This printed and bound book—but the printer and the print-
    ing-office boy?
The well-taken photographs—but your wife or friend close
    and solid in your arms?
The black ship mail'd with iron, her mighty guns in her tur-
    rets—but the pluck of the captain and engi-
    neers?
In the houses the dishes and fare and furniture—but the host
    and hostess, and the look out of their eyes?
The sky up there—yet here or next door, or across the way?
The saints and sages in history—but you yourself?
Sermons, creeds, theology—but the fathomless human brain,
And what is reason? and what is love? and what is life?

43

I do not despise you priests, all time, the world over,
My faith is the greatest of faiths and the least of faiths,
Enclosing worship ancient and modern and all between an-
    cient and modern,
Believing I shall come again upon the earth after five thou-
    sand years,
Waiting responses from oracles, honoring the gods, saluting
    the sun,

Making a fetich of the first rock or stump, powowing with
  sticks in the circle of obis,
Helping the llama or brahmin as he trims the lamps of the
  idols,
Dancing yet through the streets in a phallic procession, rapt
  and austere in the woods a gymnosophist,
Drinking mead from the skull-cap, to Shastas and Vedas ad-
  mirant, minding the Koran,
Walking the teokallis, spotted with gore from the stone and
  knife, beating the serpent-skin drum,
Accepting the Gospels, accepting him that was crucified,
  knowing assuredly that he is divine,
To the mass kneeling or the puritan's prayer rising, or sitting
  patiently in a pew,
Ranting and frothing in my insane crisis, or waiting dead-
  like till my spirit arouses me,
Looking forth on pavement and land, or outside of pavement
  and land,
Belonging to the winders of the circuit of circuits.

One of that centripetal and centrifugal gang I turn and talk
  like a man leaving charges before a journey.

Down-hearted doubters dull and excluded,
Frivolous, sullen, moping, angry, affected, dishearten'd,
  atheistical,
I know every one of you, I know the sea of torment, doubt,
  despair and unbelief.

How the flukes splash!
How they contort rapid as lightning, with spasms and spouts
  of blood!

Be at peace bloody flukes of doubters and sullen mopers,
I take my place among you as much as among any,
The past is the push of you, me, all, precisely the same,
And what is yet untried and afterward is for you, me, all pre-
  cisely the same.

I do not know what is untried and afterward,
But I know it will in its turn prove sufficient, and cannot fail.

Each who passes is consider'd, each who stops is consider'd,
  not a single one can it fail.

It cannot fail the young man who died and was buried,
Nor the young woman who died and was put by his side,
Nor the little child that peep'd in at the door, and then drew
  back and was never seen again,
Nor the old man who has lived without purpose, and feels it
  with bitterness worse than gall,

Nor him in the poor house tubercled by rum and the bad dis-
order,
Nor the numberless slaughter'd and wreck'd, nor the brutish
koboo call'd the ordure of humanity,
Nor the sacs merely floating with open mouths for food to
slip in,
Nor any thing in the earth, or down in the oldest graves of the
earth,
Nor any thing in the myriads of spheres, nor the myriads of
myriads that inhabit them,
Nor the present, nor the least wisp that is known.

44

It is time to explain myself—let us stand up.

What is known I strip away,
I launch all men and women forward with me into the Un-
known.
The clock indicates the moment—but what does eternity indi-
cate?

We have thus far exhausted trillions of winters and summers,
There are trillions ahead, and trillions ahead of them.

Births have brought us richness and variety,
And other births will bring us richness and variety.

I do not call one greater and one smaller,
That which fills its period and place is equal to any.

Were mankind murderous or jealous upon you, my brother,
my sister?
I am sorry for you, they are not murderous or jealous upon
me,
All has been gentle with me, I keep no account with lamen-
tation,
(What have I to do with lamentation?)

I am an acme of things accomplish'd, and I an encloser of
things to be.

My feet strike an apex of the apices of the stairs,
On every step bunches of ages, and larger bunches between
the steps,
All below duly travel'd, and still I mount and mount.

Rise after rise bow the phantoms behind me,
Afar down I see the huge first Nothing, I know I was even
there,
I waited unseen and always, and slept through the lethargic
mist,

And took my time, and took no hurt from the fetid carbon.

Long I was hugg'd close—long and long.

Immense have been the preparations for me,
Faithful and friendly the arms that have help'd me.

Cycles ferried my cradle, rowing and rowing like cheerful
        boatmen,
For room to me stars kept aside in their own rings,
They sent influences to look after what was to hold me.

Before I was born out of my mother generations guided me,
My embryo has never been torpid, nothing could overlay it.

For it the nebula cohered to an orb,
The long slow strata piled to rest it on,
Vast vegetables gave it sustenance,
Monstrous sauroids transported it in their mouths and de-
        posited it with care.

All forces have been steadily employ'd to complete and delight
        me,
Now on this spot I stand with my robust soul.

45

O span of youth! ever-push'd elasticity.
O manhood, balanced, florid and full.

My lovers suffocate me,
Crowding my lips, thick in the pores of my skin,
Jostling me through streets and public halls, coming naked to
        me at night,
Crying by day *Ahoy!* from the rocks of the river, swinging
        and chirping over my head,
Calling my name from flower-beds, vines, tangled underbrush,
Lighting on every moment of my life,
Bussing my body with soft balsamic busses,
Noiselessly passing handfuls out of their hearts and giving
        them to be mine.

Old age superbly rising! O welcome, ineffable grace of dying
        days!

Every condition promulges not only itself, it promulges what
        grows after and out of itself,
And the dark hush promulges as much as any.

I open my scuttle at night and see the far-sprinkled systems,
And all I see multiplied as high as I can cipher edge but the
        rim of the farther systems.

Wider and wider they spread, expanding, always expanding,
Outward and outward and forever outward.

My sun has his sun and round him obediently wheels,
He joins with his partners a group of superior circuit,
And greater sets follow, making specks of the greatest inside
        them.

There is no stoppage and never can be stoppage,
If I, you, and the worlds, and all beneath or upon their sur-
        faces, were this moment reduced back to a
        pallid float, it would not avail in the long
        run,
We should surely bring up again where we now stand,
And surely go as much farther, and then farther and farther.

A few quadrillions of eras, a few octillions of cubic leagues,
        do not hazard the span or make it impatient,
They are but parts, any thing is but a part.

See ever so far, there is limitless space outside of that,
Count ever so much, there is limitless time around that.

My rendezvous is appointed, it is certain,
The Lord will be there and wait till I come on perfect terms,
The great Camerado, the lover true for whom I pine will be
        there.

46

I know I have the best of time and space, and was never
        measured and never will be measured.

I tramp a perpetual journey, (come listen all!)
My signs are a rain-proof coat, good shoes, and a staff cut
        from the woods,
No friend of mine takes his ease in my chair,
I have no chair, no church, no philosophy,
I lead no man to a dinner-table, library, exchange,
But each man and each woman of you I lead upon a knoll,
My left hand hooking you round the waist,
My right hand pointing to landscapes of continents and the
        public road.

Not I, not any one else can travel that road for you,
You must travel it for yourself.

It is not far, it is within reach,
Perhaps you have been on it since you were born and did not
        know,
Perhaps it is everywhere on water and on land.

Shoulder your duds dear son, and I will mine, and let us
          hasten forth,
Wonderful cities and free nations we shall fetch as we go.

If you tire, give me both burdens, and rest the chuff of your
          hand on my hip,
And in due time you shall repay the same service to me,
For after we start we never lie by again.

This day before dawn I ascended a hill and look'd at the
          crowded heaven,
And I said to my spirit *When we become the enfolders of those
          orbs, and the pleasure and knowledge of
          every thing in them, shall we be fill'd and
          satisfied then?*
And my spirit said *No, we but level that lift to pass and con-
          tinue beyond.*

You are also asking me questions and I hear you,
I answer that I cannot answer, you must find out for yourself.

Sit a while dear son,
Here are biscuits to eat and here is milk to drink,
But as soon as you sleep and renew yourself in sweet clothes,
          I kiss you with a good-by kiss and open the
          gate for your egress hence.

Long enough have you dream'd contemptible dreams,
Now I wash the gum from your eyes,
You must habit yourself to the dazzle of the light and of every
          moment of your life.

Long have you timidly waded holding a plank by the shore,
Now I will you to be a bold swimmer,
To jump off in the midst of the sea, rise again, nod to me,
          shout, and laughingly dash with your hair.

47

I am the teacher of athletes,
He that by me spreads a wider breast than my own proves
          the width of my own,
He most honors my style who learns under it to destroy the
          teacher.

The boy I love, the same becomes a man not through derived
          power, but in his own right,
Wicked rather than virtuous out of conformity or fear,
Fond of his sweetheart, relishing well his steak,
Unrequited love or a slight cutting him worse than sharp
          steel cuts,

First-rate to ride, to fight, to hit the bull's eye, to sail a skiff,
        to sing a song or play on the banjo,
Preferring scars and the beard and faces pitted with small-
        pox over all latherers,
And those well-tann'd to those that keep out of the sun.

I teach straying from me, yet who can stray from me?
I follow you whoever you are from the present hour,
My words itch at your ears till you understand them.

I do not say these things for a dollar or to fill up the time while
        I wait for a boat,
(It is you talking just as much as myself, I act as the tongue
        of you,
Tied in your mouth, in mine it begins to be loosen'd.)

I swear I will never again mention love or death inside a house,
And I swear I will never translate myself at all, only to him or
        her who privately stays with me in the open
        air.

If you would understand me go to the heights or water-shore,
The nearest gnat is an explanation, and a drop or motion of
        waves a key,
The maul, the oar, the hand-saw, second my words.

No shutter'd room or school can commune with me,
But roughs and little children better than they.

The young mechanic is closest to me, he knows me well,
The woodman that takes his axe and jug with him shall take
        me with him all day,
The farm-boy ploughing in the field feels good at the sound
        of my voice,
In vessels that sail my words sail, I go with fishermen and
        seamen and love them.

The soldier camp'd or upon the march is mine,
On the night ere the pending battle many seek me, and I do
        not fail them,
On that solemn night (it may be their last) those that know
        me seek me.

My face rubs to the hunter's face when he lies down alone in
        his blanket,
The driver thinking of me does not mind the jolt of his wagon,
The young mother and old mother comprehend me,
The girl and the wife rest the needle a moment and forget
        where they are,
They and all would resume what I have told them.

48

I have said that the soul is not more than the body,
And I have said that the body is not more than the soul,
And nothing, not God, is greater to one than one's self is,
And whoever walks a furlong without sympathy walks to his
     own funeral drest in his shroud,
And I or you pocketless of a dime may purchase the pick of
     the earth,
And to glance with an eye or show a bean in its pod confounds
     the learning of all times,
And there is no trade or employment but the young man fol-
     lowing it may become a hero,
And there is no object so soft but it makes a hub for the
     wheel'd universe,
And I say to any man or woman, Let your soul stand cool and
     composed before a million universes.

And I say to mankind, Be not curious about God,
For I who am curious about each am not curious about God.
(No array of terms can say how much I am at peace about
     God and about death.)

I hear and behold God in every object, yet understand God
     not in the least,
Nor do I understand who there can be more wonderful than
     myself.

Why should I wish to see God better than this day?
I see something of God each hour of the twenty-four, and
     each moment then,
In the faces of men and women I see God, and in my own
     face in the glass,
I find letters from God dropt in the street, and every one is
     sign'd by God's name,
And I leave them where they are, for I know that wheresoe'er
     I go
Others will punctually come for ever and ever.

49

And as to you Death, and you bitter hug of mortality, it is
     idle to try to alarm me.

To his work without flinching the accoucheur comes,
I see the elder-hand pressing receiving supporting,
I recline by the sills of the exquisite flexible doors,
And mark the outlet, and mark the relief and escape.

And as to you Corpse I think you are good manure, but that
     does not offend me,
I smell the white roses sweet-scented and growing.

I reach to the leafy lips, I reach to the polish'd breasts of
    melons.

And as to you Life I reckon you are the leavings of many
    deaths,
(No doubt I have died myself ten thousand times before.)

I hear you whispering there O stars of heaven,
O suns—O grass of graves—O perpetual transfers and pro-
    motions,
If you do not say any thing how can I say any thing?

Of the turbid pool that lies in the autumn forest,
Of the moon that descends the steeps of the soughing twi-
    light,
Toss, sparkles of day and dusk—toss on the black stems that
    decay in the muck,
Toss to the moaning gibberish of the dry limbs.

I ascend from the moon, I ascend from the night,
I perceive that the ghastly glimmer is noonday sunbeams
    reflected,
And debouch to the steady and central from the offspring
    great or small.

50

There is that in me—I do not know what it is—but I know it
    is in me.

Wrench'd and sweaty—calm and cool then my body becomes,
I sleep—I sleep long.

I do not know it—it is without name—it is a word unsaid,
It is not in any dictionary, utterance, symbol.

Something it swings on more than the earth I swing on,
To it the creation is the friend whose embracing awakes me.

Perhaps I might tell more. Outlines! I plead for my brothers
    and sisters.

Do you see O my brothers and sisters?
It is not chaos or death—it is form, union, plan—it is eternal
    life—it is Happiness.

51

The past and present wilt—I have fill'd them, emptied them,
And proceed to fill my next fold of the future.

Listener up there! what have you to confide to me?
Look in my face while I snuff the sidle of evening,
(Talk honestly, no one else hears you, and I stay only a
    minute longer.)

Do I contradict myself?
Very well then I contradict myself,
(I am large, I contain multitudes.)

I concentrate toward them that are nigh, I wait on the door-
    slab.

Who has done his day's work? who will soonest be through
    with his supper?
Who wishes to walk with me?

Will you speak before I am gone? will you prove already too
    late?

52

The spotted hawk swoops by and accuses me, he complains
    of my gab and my loitering.

I too am not a bit tamed, I too am untranslatable,
I sound my barbaric yawp over the roofs of the world.

The last scud of day holds back for me,
It flings my likeness after the rest and true as any on the
    shadow'd wilds,
It coaxes me to the vapor and the dusk.

I depart as air, I shake my white locks at the runaway sun,
I effuse my flesh in eddies, and drift it in lacy jags.

I bequeath myself to the dirt to grow from the grass I love,
If you want me again look for me under your boot-soles.

You will hardly know who I am or what I mean,
But I shall be good health to you nevertheless,
And filter and fibre your blood.

Failing to fetch me at first keep encouraged,
Missing me one place search another,
I stop somewhere waiting for you.

CHILDREN OF ADAM

TO THE GARDEN THE WORLD

To the garden the world anew ascending,
Potent mates, daughters, sons, preluding,
The love, the life of their bodies, meaning and being,
Curious here behold my resurrection after slumber,
The revolving cycles in their wide sweep having brought me
    again,

Amorous, mature, all beautiful to me, all wondrous,
My limbs and the quivering fire that ever plays through them,
        for reasons, most wondrous,
Existing I peer and penetrate still,
Content with the present, content with the past,
By my side or back of me Eve following,
Or in front, and I following her just the same.

FROM PENT-UP ACHING RIVERS

From pent-up aching rivers,
From that of myself without which I were nothing,
From what I am determin'd to make illustrious, even if I
        stand sole among men,
From my own voice resonant, singing the phallus,
Singing the song of procreation,
Singing the need of superb children and therein superb grown
        people,
Singing the muscular urge and the blending,
Singing the bedfellow's song, (O resistless yearning!
O for any and each the body correlative attracting!
O for you whoever you are your correlative body! O it, more
        than all else, you delighting!)
From the hungry gnaw that eats me night and day,
From native moments, from bashful pains, singing them,
Seeking something yet unfound though I have diligently
        sought it many a long year,
Singing the true song of the soul fitful at random,
Renascent with grossest Nature or among animals,
Of that, of them and what goes with them my poems inform-
        ing,
Of the smell of apples and lemons, of the pairing of birds,
Of the wet of woods, of the lapping of waves,
Of the mad pushes of waves upon the land, I them chanting,
The overture lightly sounding, the strain anticipating,
The welcome nearness, the sight of the perfect body,
The swimmer swimming naked in the bath, or motionless on
        his back lying and floating,
The female form approaching, I pensive, love-flesh tremulous
        aching,
The divine list for myself or you or for any one making,
The face, the limbs, the index from head to foot, and what it
        arouses,
The mystic deliria, the madness amorous, the utter abandon-
        ment,
(Hark close and still what I now whisper to you,
I love you, O you entirely possess me,
O that you and I escape from the rest and go utterly off, free
        and lawless,

Two hawks in the air, two fishes swimming in the sea not more
          lawless than we;)
The furious storm through me careering, I passionately trem-
          bling,
The oath of the inseparableness of two together, of the woman
          that loves me and whom I love more than
          my life, that oath swearing,
(O I willingly stake all for you,
O let me be lost if it must be so!
O you and I! what is it to us what the rest do or think?
What is all else to us? only that we enjoy each other and ex-
          haust each other if it must be so;)
From the master, the pilot I yield the vessel to,
The general commanding me, commanding all, from him per-
          mission taking,
From time the programme hastening, (I have loiter'd too long
          as it is,)
From sex, from the warp and from the woof,
From privacy, from frequent repinings alone,
From plenty of persons near and yet the right person not near,
From the soft sliding of hands over me and thrusting of fingers
          through my hair and beard,
From the long sustain'd kiss upon the mouth or bosom,
From the close pressure that makes me or any man drunk,
          fainting with excess,
From what the divine husband knows, from the work of
          fatherhood,
From exultation, victory and relief from the bedfellow's em-
          brace in the night,
From the act-poems of eyes, hands, hips and bosoms,
From the cling of the trembling arm,
From the bending curve and the clinch,
From side by side the pliant coverlet off-throwing,
From the one so unwilling to have me leave, and me just as
          unwilling to leave,
(Yet a moment O tender waiter, and I return,)
From the hour of shining stars and dropping dews,
From the night a moment I emerging flitting out,
Celebrate you act divine and you children prepared for,
And you stalwart loins.

I SING THE BODY ELECTRIC

1

I sing the body electric,
The armies of those I love engirth me and I engirth them,
They will not let me off till I go with them, respond to them,
And discorrupt them, and charge them full with the charge of
          the soul.

Was it doubted that those who corrupt their own bodies con-
ceal themselves?
And if those who defile the living are as bad as they who defile
the dead?
And if the body does not do fully as much as the soul?
And if the body were not the soul, what is the soul?

2

The love of the body of man or woman balks account, the body
itself balks account,
That of the male is perfect, and that of the female is perfect.

The expression of the face balks account,
But the expression of a well-made man appears not only in
his face,
It is in his limbs and joints also, it is curiously in the joints of
his hips and wrists,
It is in his walk, the carriage of his neck, the flex of his waist
and knees, dress does not hide him,
The strong sweet quality he has strikes through the cotton
and broadcloth,
To see him pass conveys as much as the best poem, perhaps
more,
You linger to see his back, and the back of his neck and shoul-
der-side.

The sprawl and fulness of babes, the bosoms and heads of
women, the folds of their dress, their style as
we pass in the street, the contour of their
shape downwards,
The swimmer naked in the swimming-bath, seen as he swims
through the transparent green-shine, or lies
with his face up and rolls silently to and fro
in the heave of the water,
The bending forward and backward of rowers in row-boats,
the horseman in his saddle,
Girls, mothers, house-keepers, in all their performances,
The group of laborers seated at noon-time with their open din-
ner kettles, and their wives waiting,
The female soothing a child, the farmer's daughter in the gar-
den or cow-yard,
The young fellow hoeing corn, the sleigh-driver driving his six
horses through the crowd,
The wrestle of wrestlers, two apprentice-boys, quite grown,
lusty, good-natured, native-born, out on the
vacant lot at sundown after work,
The coats and caps thrown down, the embrace of love and
resistance,

The upper-hold and under-hold, the hair rumpled over and
        blinding the eyes;
The march of firemen in their own costumes, the play of mas-
        culine muscle through clean-setting trowsers
        and waist-straps,
The slow return from the fire, the pause when the bell strikes
        suddenly again, and the listening on the alert,
The natural, perfect, varied attitudes, the bent head, the curv'd
        neck and the counting;
Such-like I love—I loosen myself, pass freely, am at the moth-
        er's breast with the little child,
Swim with the swimmers, wrestle with wrestlers, march in line
        with the firemen, and pause, listen, count.

3

I knew a man, a common farmer, the father of five sons,
And in them the fathers of sons, and in them the fathers of
        sons.

This man was of wonderful vigor, calmness, beauty of person,
The shape of his head, the pale yellow and white of his hair
        and beard, the immeasurable meaning of his
        black eye, the richness and breadth of his
        manners,
These I used to go and visit him to see, he was wise also,
He was six feet tall, he was over eighty years old, his sons were
        massive, clean, bearded, tan-faced, hand-
        some,
They and his daughters loved him, all who saw him loved him,
They did not love him by allowance, they loved him with per-
        sonal love,
He drank water only, the blood show'd like scarlet through the
        clear-brown skin of his face,
He was a frequent gunner and fisher, he sail'd his boat himself,
        he had a fine one presented to him by a ship-
        joiner, he had fowling-pieces presented to
        him by men that loved him,
When he went with his five sons and many grand-sons to hunt
        or fish, you would pick him out as the most
        beautiful and vigorous of the gang,
You would wish long and long to be with him, you would wish
        to sit by him in the boat that you and he
        might touch each other.

4

I have perceiv'd that to be with those I like is enough,
To stop in company with the rest at evening is enough,
To be surrounded by beautiful, curious, breathing, laughing
        flesh is enough,

To pass among them or touch any one, or rest my arm ever so
           lightly round his or her neck for a moment,
           what is this then?
I do not ask any more delight, I swim in it as in a sea.

There is something in staying close to men and women and
           looking on them, and in the contact and odor
           of them, that pleases the soul well,
All things please the soul, but these please the soul well.

5

This is the female form,
A divine nimbus exhales from it from head to foot,
It attracts with fierce undeniable attraction,
I am drawn by its breath as if I were no more than a helpless
           vapor, all falls aside but myself and it,
Books, art, religion, time, the visible and solid earth, and what
           was expected of heaven or fear'd of hell, are
           now consumed,
Mad filaments, ungovernable shoots play out of it, the response
           likewise ungovernable,
Hair, bosom, hips, bend of legs, negligent falling hands all dif-
           fused, mine too diffused,
Ebb stung by the flow and flow stung by the ebb, love-flesh
           swelling and deliciously aching,
Limitless limpid jets of love hot and enormous, quivering jelly
           of love, white-blow and delirious juice,
Bridegroom night of love working surely and softly into the
           prostrate dawn,
Undulating into the willing and yielding day,
Lost in the cleave of the clasping and sweet-flesh'd day.

This the nucleus—after the child is born of woman, man is
           born of woman,
This the bath of birth, this the merge of small and large, and
           the outlet again.

Be not ashamed women, your privilege encloses the rest, and is
           the exit of the rest,
You are the gates of the body, and you are the gates of the
           soul.

The female contains all qualities and tempers them,
She is in her place and moves with perfect balance,
She is all things duly veil'd, she is both passive and active,
She is to conceive daughters as well as sons, and sons as well
           as daughters.

As I see my soul reflected in Nature,
As I see through a mist, One with inexpressible completeness,
           sanity, beauty,

See the bent head and arms folded over the breast, the Female
    I see.

6

The male is not less the soul nor more, he too is in his place,
He too is all qualities, he is action and power,
The flush of the known universe is in him,
Scorn becomes him well, and appetite and defiance become
    him well,
The wildest largest passions, bliss that is utmost, sorrow that is
    utmost become him well, pride is for him,
The full-spread pride of man is calming and excellent to the
    soul,
Knowledge becomes him, he likes it always, he brings every
    thing to the test of himself,
Whatever the survey, whatever the sea and the sail he strikes
    soundings at last only here,
(Where else does he strike soundings except here?)

The man's body is sacred and the woman's body is sacred,
No matter who it is, it is sacred—is it the meanest one in the
    laborers' gang?
Is it one of the dull-faced immigrants just landed on the wharf?
Each belongs here or anywhere just as much as the well-off,
    just as much as you,
Each has his or her place in the procession.

(All is a procession,
The universe is a procession with measured and perfect mo-
    tion.)

Do you know so much yourself that you call the meanest
    ignorant?
Do you suppose you have a right to a good sight, and he or she
    has no right to a sight?
Do you think matter has cohered together from its diffuse float,
    and the soil is on the surface, and water runs
    and vegetation sprouts,
For you only, and not for him and her?

7

A man's body at auction,
(For before the war I often go to the slave-mart and watch
    the sale,)
I help the auctioneer, the sloven does not half know his
    business.

Gentlemen look on this wonder,
Whatever the bids of the bidders they cannot be high enough
    for it,

For it the globe lay preparing quintillions of years without one
      animal or plant,
For it the revolving cycles truly and steadily roll'd.

In this head the all-baffling brain,
In it and below it the makings of heroes.

Examine these limbs, red, black, or white, they are cunning
      in tendon and nerve,
They shall be stript that you may see them.

Exquisite senses, life-lit eyes, pluck, volition,
Flakes of breast-muscle, pliant backbone and neck, flesh not
      flabby, good-sized arms and legs,
And wonders within there yet.

Within there runs blood,
The same old blood! the same red-running blood!
There swells and jets a heart, there all passions, desires, reach-
      ings, aspirations,
(Do you think they are not there because they are not express'd
      in parlors and lecture-rooms?)

This is not only one man, this the father of those who shall be
      fathers in their turns,
In him the start of populous states and rich republics,
Of him countless immortal lives with countless embodiments
      and enjoyments.

How do you know who shall come from the offspring of his
      offspring through the centuries?
(Who might you find you have come from yourself, if you
      could trace back through the centuries?)

8

A woman's body at auction,
She too is not only herself, she is the teeming mother of moth-
      ers,
She is the bearer of them that shall grow and be mates to the
      mothers.

Have you ever loved the body of a woman?
Have you ever loved the body of a man?

Do you not see that these are exactly the same to all in all
      nations and times all over the earth?

If anything is sacred the human body is sacred,
And the glory and sweet of a man is the token of manhood
      untainted,
And in man or woman a clean, strong, firm-fibred body, is
      more beautiful than the most beautiful face.

Have you seen the fool that corrupted his own live body? or
        the fool that corrupted her own live body?
For they do not conceal themselves, and cannot conceal them-
        selves.

9

O my body! I dare not desert the likes of you in other men
        and women, nor the likes of the parts of you,
I believe the likes of you are to stand or fall with the likes
        of the soul, (and that they are the soul,)
I believe the likes of you shall stand or fall with my poems, and
        that they are my poems,
Man's, woman's, child's, youth's, wife's, husband's, mother's,
        father's, young man's, young woman's poems,
Head, neck, hair, ears, drop and tympan of the ears,
Eyes, eye-fringes, iris of the eye, eyebrows, and the waking
        or sleeping of the lids,
Mouth, tongue, lips, teeth, roof of the mouth, jaws, and the
        jaw-hinges,
Nose, nostrils of the nose, and the partition,
Cheeks, temples, forehead, chin, throat, back of the neck,
        neck-slue,
Strong shoulders, manly beard, scapula, hind-shoulders, and
        the ample side-round of the chest,
Upper-arm, armpit, elbow-socket, lower-arm, arm-sinews, arm-
        bones,
Wrist and wrist-joints, hand, palm, knuckles, thumb, fore-
        finger, finger-joints, finger-nails,
Broad breast-front, curling hair of the breast, breast-bone,
        breast-side,
Ribs, belly, backbone, joints of the backbone,
Hips, hip-sockets, hip-strength, inward and outward round,
        man-balls, man-root,
Strong set of thighs, well carrying the trunk above,
Leg-fibres, knee, knee-pan, upper-leg, under-leg,
Ankles, instep, foot-ball, toes, toe-joints, the heel;
All attitudes, all the shapeliness, all the belongings of my or
        your body or of any one's body, male or
        female,
The lung-sponges, the stomach-sac, the bowels sweet and clean,
The brain in its folds inside the skull-frame,
Sympathies, heart-valves, palate-valves, sexuality, maternity,
Womanhood and all that is a woman, and the man that comes
        from woman,
The womb, the teats, nipples, breast-milk, tears, laughter,
        weeping, love-looks, love-perturbations and
        risings,
The voice, articulation, language, whispering, shouting aloud,
Food, drink, pulse, digestion, sweat, sleep, walking, swimming,

Poise on the hips, leaping, reclining, embracing, arm-curving
        and tightening,
The continual changes of the flex of the mouth, and around the
        eyes,
The skin, the sunburnt shade, freckles, hair,
The curious sympathy one feels when feeling with the hand
        the naked meat of the body,
The circling rivers the breath, and breathing it in and out,
The beauty of the waist, and thence of the hips, and thence
        downward toward the knees,
The thin red jellies within you or within me, the bones and
        the marrow in the bones,
The exquisite realization of health;
O I say these are not the parts and poems of the body only, but
        of the soul,
O I say now these are the soul!

A WOMAN WAITS FOR ME

A woman waits for me, she contains all, nothing is lacking,
Yet all were lacking if sex were lacking, or if the moisture of
        the right man were lacking.

Sex contains all, bodies, souls,
Meanings, proofs, purities, delicacies, results, promulgations,
Songs, commands, health, pride, the maternal mystery, the
        seminal milk,
All hopes, benefactions, bestowals, all the passions, loves,
        beauties, delights of the earth,
All the governments, judges, gods, follow'd persons of the
        earth,
These are contain'd in sex as parts of itself and justifications of
        itself.

Without shame the man I like knows and avows the delicious-
        ness of his sex,
Without shame the woman I like knows and avows hers.

Now I will dismiss myself from impassive women,
I will go stay with her who waits for me, and with those women
        that are warm-blooded and sufficient for me,
I see that they understand me and do not deny me,
I see that they are worthy of me, I will be the robust husband
        of those women.

They are not one jot less than I am,
They are tann'd in the face by shining suns and blowing winds,
Their flesh has the old divine suppleness and strength,
They know how to swim, row, ride, wrestle, shoot, run, strike,
        retreat, advance, resist, defend themselves,
They are ultimate in their own right—they are calm, clear,
        well-possess'd of themselves.

I draw you close to me, you women,
I cannot let you go, I would do you good,
I am for you, and you are for me, not only for our own sake,
      but for others' sakes,
Envelop'd in you sleep greater heroes and bards,
They refuse to awake at the touch of any man but me.

It is I, you women, I make my way,
I am stern, acrid, large, undissuadable, but I love you,
I do not hurt you any more than is necessary for you,
I pour the stuff to start sons and daughters fit for these States,
      I press with slow rude muscle,
I brace myself effectually, I listen to no entreaties,
I dare not withdraw till I deposit what has so long accumulated
      within me.

Through you I drain the pent-up rivers of myself,
In you I wrap a thousand onward years,
On you I graft the grafts of the best-beloved of me and Amer-
      ica,
The drops I distil upon you shall grow fierce and athletic girls,
      new artists, musicians, and singers,
The babes I beget upon you are to beget babes in their turn,
I shall demand perfect men and women out of my love-spend-
      ings,
I shall expect them to interpenetrate with others, as I and you
      interpenetrate now,
I shall count on the fruits of the gushing showers of them, as
      I count on the fruits of the gushing showers
      I give now,
I shall look for loving crops from the birth, life, death, immor-
      tality, I plant so lovingly now.

SPONTANEOUS ME

Spontaneous me, Nature,
The loving day, the mounting sun, the friend I am happy with,
The arm of my friend hanging idly over my shoulder,
The hillside whiten'd with blossoms of the mountain ash,
The same late in autumn, the hues of red, yellow, drab, pur-
      ple, and light and dark green,
The rich coverlet of the grass, animals and birds, the private
      untrimm'd bank, the primitive apples, the
      pebble-stones,
Beautiful dripping fragments, the negligent list of one after
      another as I happen to call them to me or
      think of them,
The real poems, (what we call poems being merely pictures,)
The poems of the privacy of the night, and of men like me,

This poem drooping shy and unseen that I always carry, and
   that all men carry,
(Know once for all, avow'd on purpose, wherever are men like
   me, are our lusty lurking masculine poems,)
Love-thoughts, love-juice, love-odor, love-yielding, love-climb-
   ers, and the climbing sap,
Arms and hands of love, lips of love, phallic thumb of love,
   breasts of love, bellies press'd and glued to-
   gether with love,
Earth of chaste love, life that is only life after love,
The body of my love, the body of the woman I love, the body
   of the man, the body of the earth,
Soft forenoon airs that blow from the south-west,
The hairy wild-bee that murmurs and hankers up and down,
   that grips the full-grown lady-flower, curves
   upon her with amorous firm legs, takes his
   will of her, and holds himself tremulous and
   tight till he is satisfied;
The wet of woods through the early hours,
Two sleepers at night lying close together as they sleep, one
   with an arm slanting down across and below
   the waist of the other,
The smell of apples, aromas from crush'd sage-plant, mint,
   birch-bark,
The boy's longings, the glow and pressure as he confides to
   me what he was dreaming,
The dead leaf whirling its spiral whirl and falling still and con-
   tent to the ground,
The no-form'd stings that sights, people, objects, sting me with,
The hubb'd sting of myself, stinging me as much as it ever can
   any one,
The sensitive, orbic, underlapp'd brothers, that only privileged
   feelers may be intimate where they are,
The curious roamer the hand roaming all over the body, the
   bashful withdrawing of flesh where the fingers
   soothingly pause and edge themselves,
The limpid liquid within the young man,
The vex'd corrosion so pensive and so painful,
The torment, the irritable tide that will not be at rest,
The like of the same I feel, the like of the same in others,
The young man that flushes and flushes, and the young woman
   that flushes and flushes,
The young man that wakes deep at night, the hot hand seeking
   to repress what would master him,
The mystic amorous night, the strange half-welcome pangs,
   visions, sweats,
The pulse pounding through palms and trembling encircling
   fingers, the young man all color'd, red,
   ashamed, angry;

The souse upon me of my lover the sea, as I lie willing and
      naked,
The merriment of the twin babes that crawl over the grass in
      the sun, the mother never turning her vigilant
      eyes from them,
The walnut-trunk, the walnut-husks, and the ripening or
      ripen'd long-round walnuts,
The continence of vegetables, birds, animals,
The consequent meanness of me should I skulk or find myself
      indecent, while birds and animals never once
      skulk or find themselves indecent,
The great chastity of paternity to match the great chastity of
      maternity,
The oath of procreation I have sworn, my Adamic and fresh
      daughters,
The greed that eats me day and night with hungry gnaw, till I
      saturate what shall produce boys to fill my
      place when I am through,
The wholesome relief, repose, content,
And this bunch pluck'd at random from myself,
It has done its work—I toss it carelessly to fall where it may.

ONE HOUR TO MADNESS AND JOY

One hour to madness and joy! O furious! O confine me not!
(What is this that frees me so in storms?
What do my shouts amid lightnings and raging winds mean?)

O to drink the mystic deliria deeper than any other man!
O savage and tender achings! (I bequeath them to you, my
      children,
I tell them to you, for reasons, O bridegroom and bride.)

O to be yielded to you whoever you are, and you to be yielded
      to me in defiance of the world!
O to return to Paradise! O bashful and feminine!
O to draw you to me, to plant on you for the first time the lips
      of a determin'd man.

O the puzzle, the thrice-tied knot, the deep and dark pool, all
      untied and illumin'd!
O to speed where there is space enough and air enough at last!
To be absolv'd from previous ties and conventions, I from
      mine and you from yours!
To find a new unthought-of nonchalance with the best of Na-
      ture!
To have the gag remov'd from one's mouth!
To have the feeling to-day or any day I am sufficient as I am.

O something unprov'd! something in a trance!
To escape utterly from others' anchors and holds!

To drive free! to love free! to dash reckless and dangerous!
To court destruction with taunts, with invitations!
To ascend, to leap to the heavens of the love indicated to me!
To rise thither with my inebriate soul!

To be lost if it must be so!
To feed the remainder of life with one hour of fulness and
        freedom!
With one brief hour of madness and joy.

OUT OF THE ROLLING OCEAN THE CROWD

Out of the rolling ocean the crowd came a drop gently to me,
Whispering *I love you, before long I die,*
I have travel'd a long way merely to look on you to touch you,
For I could not die till I once look'd on you,
For I fear'd I might afterward lose you.

Now we have met, we have look'd, we are safe,
Return in peace to the ocean my love,
I too am part of that ocean my love, we are not so much
        separated,
Behold the great rondure, the cohesion of all, how perfect!
But as for me, for you, the irresistible sea is to separate us,
As for an hour carrying us diverse, yet cannot carry us diverse
        forever;
Be not impatient—a little space—know you I salute the air,
        the ocean and the land,
Every day at sundown for your dear sake my love.

AGES AND AGES RETURNING AT INTERVALS

Ages and ages returning at intervals,
Undestroy'd, wandering immortal,
Lusty, phallic, with the potent original loins, perfectly sweet,
I, chanter of Adamic songs,
Through the new garden the West, the great cities calling,
Deliriate, thus prelude what is generated, offering these, offer-
        ing myself,
Bathing myself, bathing my songs in Sex,
Offspring of my loins.

WE TWO, HOW LONG WE WERE FOOL'D

We two, how long we were fool'd,
Now transmuted, we swiftly escape as Nature escapes,
We are Nature, long have we been absent, but now we return,
We become plants, trunks, foliage, roots, bark,
We are bedded in the ground, we are rocks,
We are oaks, we grow in the openings side by side,

We browse, we are two among the wild herds spontaneous as
    any,
We are two fishes swimming in the sea together,
We are what locust blossoms are, we drop scent around lanes
    mornings and evenings,
We are also the coarse smut of beasts, vegetables, minerals,
We are two predatory hawks, we soar above and look down,
We are two resplendent suns, we it is who balance ourselves
    orbic and stellar, we are as two comets,
We prowl fang'd and four-footed in the woods, we spring on
    prey,
We are two clouds forenoons and afternoons driving over-
    head,
We are seas mingling, we are two of those cheerful waves roll-
    ing over each other and interwetting each
    other,
We are what the atmosphere is, transparent, receptive, per-
    vious, impervious,
We are snow, rain, cold, darkness, we are each product and
    influence of the globe,
We have circled and circled till we have arrived home again,
    we too,
We have voided all but freedom and all but our own joy.

O HYMEN! O HYMENEE!

O hymen! O hymenee! why do you tantalize me thus?
O why sting me for a swift moment only?
Why can you not continue? O why do you now cease?
Is it because if you continued beyond the swift moment you
    would soon certainly kill me?

I AM HE THAT ACHES WITH LOVE

I am he that aches with amorous love;
Does the earth gravitate; does not all matter, aching, attract
    all matter?
So the body of me to all I meet or know.

NATIVE MOMENTS

Native moments—when you come upon me—ah you are here
    now,
Give me now libidinous joys only,
Give me the drench of my passions, give me life coarse and
    rank,
To-day I go consort with Nature's darlings, to-night too,
I am for those who believe in loose delights, I share the mid-
    night orgies of young men,
I dance with the dancers and drink with the drinkers,

The echoes ring with our indecent calls, I pick out some low
        person for my dearest friend,
He shall be lawless, rude, illiterate, he shall be one condemned
        by others for deeds done,
I will play a part no longer, why should I exile myself from
        my companions?
O you shunn'd persons, I at least do not shun you,
I come forthwith in your midst, I will be your poet,
I will be more to you than to any of the rest.

ONCE I PASS'D THROUGH A POPULOUS CITY

Once I pass'd through a populous city imprinting my brain
        for future use with its shows, architecture,
        customs, traditions,
Yet now of all that city I remember only a woman I casually
        met there who detain'd me for love of me,
Day by day and night by night we were together—all else has
        long been forgotten by me,
I remember I say only that woman who passionately clung
        to me,
Again we wander, we love, we separate again,
Again she holds me by the hand, I must not go,
I see her close beside me with silent lips sad and tremulous.

I HEARD YOU SOLEMN-SWEET PIPES OF THE ORGAN

I heard you solemn-sweet pipes of the organ as last Sunday
        morn I pass'd the church,
Winds of autumn, as I walk'd the woods at dusk I heard your
        long-stretch'd sighs up above so mournful,
I heard the perfect Italian tenor singing at the opera, I heard
        the soprano in the midst of the quartet sing-
        ing;
Heart of my love! you too I heard murmuring low through
        one of the wrists around my head,
Heard the pulse of you when all was still ringing little bells
        last night under my ear.

FACING WEST FROM CALIFORNIA'S SHORES

Facing west from California's shores,
Inquiring, tireless, seeking what is yet unfound,
I, a child, very old, over waves, towards the house of mater-
        nity, the land of migrations, look afar,
Look off the shores of my Western sea, the circle almost cir-
        cled;
For starting westward from Hindustan, from the vales of Kash-
        mere,

From Asia, from the north, from the God, the sage, and the
       hero,
From the south, from the flowery peninsulas and the spice
       islands,
Long having wander'd since, round the earth having wander'd,
Now I face home again, very pleas'd and joyous,
(But where is what I started for so long ago?
And why is it yet unfound?)

AS ADAM EARLY IN THE MORNING

As Adam early in the morning,
Walking forth from the bower refresh'd with sleep,
Behold me where I pass, hear my voice, approach,
Touch me, touch the palm of your hand to my body as I pass,
Be not afraid of my body.

CALAMUS

IN PATHS UNTRODDEN

In paths untrodden,
In the growth by margins of pond-waters,
Escaped from the life that exhibits itself,
From all the standards hitherto publish'd, from the pleasures,
       profits, conformities,
Which too long I was offering to feed my soul,
Clear to me now standards not yet publish'd, clear to me that
       my soul,
That the soul of the man I speak for rejoices in comrades,
Here by myself away from the clank of the world,
Tallying and talk'd to here by tongues aromatic,
No longer abash'd, (for in this secluded spot I can respond as
       I would not dare elsewhere,)
Strong upon me the life that does not exhibit itself, yet con-
       tains all the rest,
Resolv'd to sing no songs to-day but those of manly attachment,
Projecting them along that substantial life,
Bequeathing hence types of athletic love,
Afternoon this delicious Ninth-month in my forty-first year,
I proceed for all who are or have been young men,
To tell the secret of my nights and days,
To celebrate the need of comrades.

SCENTED HERBAGE OF MY BREAST

Scented herbage of my breast,
Leaves from you I glean, I write, to be perused best afterwards,

Tomb-leaves, body-leaves growing up above me above death,
Perennial roots, tall leaves, O the winter shall not freeze you
　　　　　delicate leaves,
Every year shall you bloom again, out from where you retired
　　　　　you shall emerge again;
O I do not know whether many passing by will discover you
　　　　　or inhale your faint odor, but I believe a few
　　　　　will;
O slender leaves! O blossoms of my blood! I permit you to tell
　　　　　in your own way of the heart that is under
　　　　　you,
O I do not know what you mean there underneath yourselves,
　　　　　you are not happiness,
You are often more bitter than I can bear, you burn and sting
　　　　　me,
Yet you are beautiful to me you faint-tinged roots, you make
　　　　　me think of death,
Death is beautiful from you, (what indeed is finally beautiful
　　　　　except death and love?)
O I think it is not for life I am chanting here my chant of
　　　　　lovers, I think it must be for death,
For how calm, how solemn it grows to ascend to the atmos-
　　　　　phere of lovers,
Death or life I am then indifferent, my soul declines to prefer,
(I am not sure but the high soul of lovers welcomes death
　　　　　most,)
Indeed O death, I think now these leaves mean precisely the
　　　　　same as you mean,
Grow up taller sweet leaves that I may see! grow up out of
　　　　　my breast!
Spring away from the conceal'd heart there!
Do not fold yourself so in your pink-tinged roots timid leaves!
Do not remain down there so ashamed, herbage of my breast!
Come I am determin'd to unbare this broad breast of mine, I
　　　　　have long enough stifled and choked;
Emblematic and capricious blades I leave you, now you serve
　　　　　me not,
I will say what I have to say by itself,
I will sound myself and comrades only, I will never again utter
　　　　　a call only their call,
I will raise with it immortal reverberations through the States,
I will give an example to lovers to take permanent shape and
　　　　　will through the States,
Through me shall the words be said to make death exhilarating.
Give me your tone therefore O death, that I may accord with
　　　　　it,
Give me yourself, for I see that you belong to me now above
　　　　　all, and are folded inseparably together, you
　　　　　love and death are,

Nor will I allow you to balk me any more with what I was
        calling life,
For now it is convey'd to me that you are the purports essen-
        tial,
That you hide in these shifting forms of life, for reasons, and
        that they are mainly for you,
That you beyond them come forth to remain, the real reality,
That behind the mask of materials you patiently wait, no mat-
        ter how long,
That you will one day perhaps take control of all,
That you will perhaps dissipate this entire show of appearance,
That may-be you are what it is all for, but it does not last so
        very long,
But you will last very long.

WHOEVER YOU ARE HOLDING ME NOW IN HAND

Whoever you are holding me now in hand,
Without one thing all will be useless,
I give you fair warning before you attempt me further,
I am not what you supposed, but far different.

Who is he that would become my follower?
Who would sign himself a candidate for my affections?

The way is suspicious, the result uncertain, perhaps destructive,
You would have to give up all else, I alone would expect to be
        your sole and exclusive standard,
Your novitiate would even then be long and exhausting,
The whole past theory of your life and all conformity to the
        lives around you would have to be aban-
        don'd,
Therefore release me now before troubling yourself any fur-
        ther, let go your hand from my shoulders,
Put me down and depart on your way.

Or else by stealth in some wood for trial,
Or back of a rock in the open air,
(For in any roof'd room of a house I emerge not, nor in com-
        pany,
And in libraries I lie as one dumb, a gawk, or unborn, or
        dead,)
But just possibly with you on a high hill, first watching lest any
        person for miles around approach unawares,
Or possibly with you sailing at sea, or on the beach of the sea
        or some quiet island,
Here to put your lips upon mine I permit you,
With the comrade's long-dwelling kiss or the new husband's
        kiss,
For I am the new husband and I am the comrade.

Or if you will, thrusting me beneath your clothing,
Where I may feel the throbs of your heart or rest upon your
      hip,
Carry me when you go forth over land or sea;
For thus merely touching you is enough, is best,
And thus touching you would I silently sleep and be carried
      eternally.

But these leaves conning you con at peril,
For these leaves and me you will not understand,
They will elude you at first and still more afterward, I will
      certainly elude you,
Even while you should think you had unquestionably caught
      me, behold!
Already you see I have escaped from you.

For it is not what I have put into it that I have written this
      book,
Nor is it by reading it you will acquire it,
Nor do those know me best who admire me and vauntingly
      praise me,
Nor will the candidates for my love (unless at most a very
      few) prove victorious,
Nor will my poems do good only, they will do just as much
      evil, perhaps more,
For all is useless without that which you may guess at many
      times and not hit, that which I hinted at;
Therefore release me and depart on your way.

FOR YOU O DEMOCRACY

Come, I will make the continent indissoluble,
I will make the most splendid race the sun ever shone upon,
I will make divine magnetic lands,
      With the love of comrades,
      With the life-long love of comrades.

I will plant companionship thick as trees along all the rivers
      of America, and along the shores of the great
      lakes, and all over the prairies,
I will make inseparable cities with their arms about each other's
      necks,
      By the love of comrades,
      By the manly love of comrades,

For you these from me, O Democracy, to serve you ma femme!
For you, for you I am trilling these songs.

THESE I SINGING IN SPRING

These I singing in spring collect for lovers,
(For who but I should understand lovers and all their sorrow
        and joy?
And who but I should be the poet of comrades?)
Collecting I traverse the garden the world, but soon I pass the
        gates,
Now along the pond-side, now wading in a little, fearing not
        the wet,
Now by the post-and-rail fences where the old stones thrown
        there, pick'd from the fields, have accumu-
        lated,
(Wild-flowers and vines and weeds come up through the stones
        and partly cover them, beyond these I pass,)
Far, far in the forest, or sauntering later in summer, before I
        think where I go,
Solitary, smelling the earthy smell, stopping now and then in
        the silence,
Alone I had thought, yet soon a troop gathers around me,
Some walk by my side and some behind, and some embrace
        my arms or neck,
They the spirits of dear friends dead or alive, thicker they
        come, a great crowd, and I in the middle,
Collecting, dispensing, singing, there I wander with them,
Plucking something for tokens, tossing toward whoever is near
        me,
Here, lilac, with a branch of pine,
Here, out of my pocket, some moss which I pull'd off a live-oak
        in Florida as it hung trailing down,
Here, some pinks and laurel leaves, and a handful of sage,
And here what I now draw from the water, wading in the
        pond-side,
(O here I last saw him that tenderly loves me, and returns
        again never to separate from me,
And this, O this shall henceforth be the token of comrades,
        this calamus-root shall,
Interchange it youths with each other! let none render it back!)
And twigs of maple and a bunch of wild orange and chestnut,
And stems of currants and plum-blows, and the aromatic
        cedar,
These I compass'd around by a thick cloud of spirits,
Wandering, point to or touch as I pass, or throw them loosely
        from me,
Indicating to each one what he shall have, giving something
        to each;
But what I drew from the water by the pond-side, that I reserve,
I will give of it, but only to them that love as I myself am
        capable of loving.

NOT HEAVING FROM MY RIBB'D BREAST ONLY

Not heaving from my ribb'd breast only,
Not in sighs at night in rage dissatisfied with myself,
Not in those long-drawn, ill-supprest sighs,
Not in many an oath and promise broken,
Not in my wilful and savage soul's volition,
Not in the subtle nourishment of the air,
Not in this beating and pounding at my temples and wrists,
Not in the curious systole and diastole within which will one
      day cease,
Not in many a hungry wish told to the skies only,
Not in cries, laughter, defiances, thrown from me when alone
      far in the wilds,
Not in husky pantings through clinch'd teeth,
Not in sounded and resounded words, chattering words, echoes,
      dead words,
Not in the murmurs of my dreams while I sleep,
Nor the other murmurs of these incredible dreams of every
      day,
Nor in the limbs and senses of my body that take you and
      dismiss you continually—not there,
Not in any or all of them O adhesiveness! O pulse of my life!
Need I that you exist and show yourself any more than in these
      songs.

OF THE TERRIBLE DOUBT OF APPEARANCES

Of the terrible doubt of appearances,
Of the uncertainty after all, that we may be deluded,
That may-be reliance and hope are but speculations after all,
That may-be identity beyond the grave is a beautiful fable only,
May-be the things I perceive, the animals, plants, men, hills,
      shining and flowing waters,
The skies of day and night, colors, densities, forms, may-be
      these are (as doubtless they are) only appa-
      ritions, and the real something has yet to be
      known,
(How often they dart out of themselves as if to confound me
      and mock me!
How often I think neither I know, nor any man knows, aught
      of them,)
May-be seeming to me what they are (as doubtless they in-
      indeed but seem) as from my present point
      of view, and might prove (as of course they
      would) nought of what they appear, or
      nought anyhow, from entirely changed points
      of view;

To me these and the like of these are curiously answer'd by my
      lovers, my dear friends,
When he whom I love travels with me or sits a long while
      holding me by the hand,
When the subtle air, the impalpable, the sense that words and
      reason hold not, surround us and pervade us,
Then I am charged with untold and untellable wisdom, I am
      silent, I require nothing further,
I cannot answer the question of appearances or that of identity
      beyond the grave,
But I walk or sit indifferent, I am satisfied,
He ahold of my hand has completely satisfied me.

THE BASE OF ALL METAPHYSICS

And now gentlemen,
A word I give to remain in your memories and minds,
As base and finalè too for all metaphysics.

(So to the students the old professor,
At the close of his crowded course.)

Having studied the new and antique, the Greek and Germanic
      systems,
Kant having studied and stated, Fichte and Schelling and
      Hegel,
Stated the lore of Plato, and Socrates greater than Plato,
And greater than Socrates sought and stated, Christ divine
      having studied long,
I see reminiscent to-day those Greek and Germanic systems,
See the philosophies all, Christian churches and tenets see,
Yet underneath Socrates clearly see, and underneath Christ
      the divine I see,
The dear love of man for his comrade, the attraction of friend
      to friend,
Of the well-married husband and wife, of children and parents,
Of city for city and land for land.

RECORDERS AGES HENCE

Recorders ages hence,
Come, I will take you down underneath this impassive ex-
      terior, I will tell you what to say of me,
Publish my name and hang up my picture as that of the ten-
      derest lover,
The friend the lover's portrait, of whom his friend his lover
      was fondest,
Who was not proud of his songs, but of the measureless ocean
      of love within him, and freely pour'd it forth,
Who often walk'd lonesome walks thinking of his dear friends,
      his lovers,

Who pensive away from one he lov'd often lay sleepless and
           dissatisfied at night,
Who knew too well the sick, sick dread lest the one he lov'd
           might secretly be indifferent to him,
Whose happiest days were far away through fields, in woods,
           on hills, he and another wandering hand in
           hand, they twain apart from other men,
Who oft as he saunter'd the streets curv'd with his arm the
           shoulder of his friend, while the arm of his
           friend rested upon him also.

WHEN I HEARD AT THE CLOSE OF THE DAY

When I heard at the close of the day how my name had been
           receiv'd with plaudits in the capitol, still it
           was not a happy night for me that follow'd,
And else when I carous'd, or when my plans were accom-
           plish'd, still I was not happy,
But the day when I rose at dawn from the bed of perfect health,
           refresh'd, singing, inhaling the ripe breath
           of autumn,
When I saw the full moon in the west grow pale and disappear
           in the morning light,
When I wander'd alone over the beach, and undressing bathed,
           laughing with the cool waters, and saw the
           sun rise,
And when I thought how my dear friend my lover was on his
           way coming, O then I was happy,
O then each breath tasted sweeter, and all that day my food
           nourish'd me more, and the beautiful day
           pass'd well,
And the next came with equal joy, and with the next at evening
           came my friend,
And that night while all was still I heard the waters roll slowly
           continually up the shores,
I heard the hissing rustle of the liquid and sands as directed to
           me whispering to congratulate me,
For the one I love most lay sleeping by me under the same
           cover in the cool night,
In the stillness in the autumn moonbeams his face was inclined
           toward me,
And his arm lay lightly around my breast—and that night I
           was happy.

ARE YOU THE NEW PERSON DRAWN
TOWARD ME?

Are you the new person drawn toward me?
To begin with take warning, I am surely far different from
           what you suppose;

Do you suppose you will find in me your ideal?
Do you think it is so easy to have me become your lover?
Do you think the friendship of me would be unalloy'd satis-
        faction?
Do you think I am trusty and faithful?
Do you see no further than this façade, this smooth and toler-
        ant manner of me?
Do you suppose yourself advancing on real ground toward a
        real heroic man?
Have you no thought O dreamer that it may be all maya,
        illusion?

ROOTS AND LEAVES THEMSELVES ALONE

Roots and leaves themselves alone are these,
Scents brought to men and women from the wild woods and
        pond-side,
Breast-sorrel and pinks of love, fingers that wind around tighter
        than vines,
Gushes from the throats of birds hid in the foliage of trees as
        the sun is risen,
Breezes of land and love sent from living shores to you on the
        living sea, to you O sailors!
Frost-mellow'd berries and Third-month twigs offer'd fresh
        to young persons wandering out in the fields
        when the winter breaks up,
Love-buds put before you and within you whoever you are,
Buds to be unfolded on the old terms,
If you bring the warmth of the sun to them they will open and
        bring form, color, perfume, to you,
If you become the aliment and the wet they will become flow-
        ers, fruits, tall branches and trees.

NOT HEAT FLAMES UP AND CONSUMES

Not heat flames up and consumes,
Not sea-waves hurry in and out,
Not the air delicious and dry, the air of ripe summer, bears
        lightly along white down-balls of myriads of
        seeds,
Wafted, sailing gracefully, to drop where they may;
Not these, O none of these more than the flames of me, con-
        suming, burning for his love whom I love,
O none more than I hurrying in and out;
Does the tide hurry, seeking something, and never give up?
        O I the same,
O nor down-balls nor perfumes, nor the high rain-emitting
        clouds, are borne through the open air,
Any more than my soul is borne through the open air,
Wafted in all directions O love, for friendship, for you.

TRICKLE DROPS

Trickle drops! my blue veins leaving!
O drops of me! trickle, slow drops,
Candid from me falling, drip, bleeding drops,
From wounds made to free you whence you were prison'd,
From my face, from my forehead and lips,
From my breast, from within where I was conceal'd, press
      forth red drops, confession drops,
Stain every page, stain every song I sing, every word I say,
      bloody drops,
Let them know your scarlet heat, let them glisten,
Saturate them with yourself all ashamed and wet,
Glow upon all I have written or shall write, bleeding drops,
Let it all be seen in your light, blushing drops.

CITY OF ORGIES

City of orgies, walks and joys,
City whom that I have lived and sung in your midst will one
      day make you illustrious,
Not the pageants of you, not your shifting tableaus, your spec-
      tacles, repay me,
Not the interminable rows of your houses, nor the ships at the
      wharves,
Nor the processions in the streets, nor the bright windows with
      goods in them,
Nor to converse with learn'd persons, or bear my share in the
      soiree or feast;
Not those, but as I pass O Manhattan, your frequent and swift
      flash of eyes offering me love,
Offering response to my own—these repay me,
Lovers, continual lovers, only repay me.

BEHOLD THIS SWARTHY FACE

Behold this swarthy face, these gray eyes,
This beard, the white wool unclipt upon my neck,
My brown hands and the silent manner of me without charm;
Yet comes one a Manhattanese and ever at parting kisses me
      lightly on the lips with robust love,
And I on the crossing of the street or on the ship's deck give a
      kiss in return,
We observe that salute of American comrades land and sea,
We are those two natural and nonchalant persons.

I SAW IN LOUISIANA A LIVE-OAK GROWING

I saw in Louisiana a live-oak growing,
All alone stood it and the moss hung down from the branches,

Without any companion it grew there uttering joyous leaves of
        dark green,
And its look, rude, unbending, lusty, made me think of myself,
But I wonder'd how it could utter joyous leaves standing alone
        there without its friend near, for I knew I
        could not,
And I broke off a twig with a certain number of leaves upon
        it, and twined around it a little moss,
And brought it away, and I have placed it in sight in my room,
It is not needed to remind me as of my own dear friends,
(For I believe lately I think of little else than of them,)
Yet it remains to me a curious token, it makes me think of
        manly love;
For all that, and though the live-oak glistens there in Louisiana
        solitary in a wide flat space,
Uttering joyous leaves all its life without a friend a lover near,
I know very well I could not.

TO A STRANGER

Passing stranger! you do not know how longingly I look upon
        you,
You must be he I was seeking, or she I was seeking, (it comes
        to me as of a dream,)
I have somewhere surely lived a life of joy with you,
All is recall'd as we flit by each other, fluid, affectionate, chaste,
        matured,
You grew up with me, were a boy with me or a girl with me,
I ate with you and slept with you, your body has become not
        yours only nor left my body mine only,
You give me the pleasure of your eyes, face, flesh, as we pass,
        you take of my beard, breast, hands, in re-
        turn,
I am not to speak to you, I am to think of you when I sit alone
        or wake at night alone,
I am to wait, I do not doubt I am to meet you again,
I am to see to it that I do not lose you.

THIS MOMENT YEARNING AND THOUGHTFUL

This moment yearning and thoughtful sitting alone,
It seems to me there are other men in other lands yearning and
        thoughtful,
It seems to me I can look over and behold them in Germany,
        Italy, France, Spain,
Or far, far away, in China, or in Russia or Japan, talking
        other dialects,
And it seems to me if I could know those men I should become
        attached to them as I do to men in my own
        lands,

O I know we should be brethren and lovers,
I know I should be happy with them.

I HEAR IT WAS CHARGED AGAINST ME

I hear it was charged against me that I sought to destroy insti-
tutions,
But really I am neither for nor against institutions,
(What indeed have I in common with them? or what with the
destruction of them?)
Only I will establish in the Mannahatta and in every city of
these States inland and seaboard,
And in the fields and woods, and above every keel little or
large that dents the water,
Without edifices or rules or trustees or any argument,
The institution of the dear love of comrades.

THE PRAIRIE-GRASS DIVIDING

The prairie-grass dividing, its special odor breathing,
I demand of it the spiritual corresponding,
Demand the most copious and close companionship of men,
Demand the blades to rise of words, acts, beings,
Those of the open atmosphere, coarse, sunlit, fresh, nutritious,
Those that go their own gait, erect, stepping with freedom and
command, leading not following,
Those with a never-quell'd audacity, those with sweet and
lusty flesh clear of taint,
Those that look carelessly in the faces of Presidents and gover-
nors, as to say *Who are you?*
Those of earth-born passion, simple, never constrain'd, never
obedient,
Those of inland America.

WHEN I PERUSE THE CONQUER'D FAME

When I peruse the conquer'd fame of heroes and the victories
of mighty generals, I do not envy the gen-
erals,
Nor the President in his Presidency, nor the rich in his great
house,
But when I hear of the brotherhood of lovers, how it was with
them,
How together through life, through dangers, odium, unchang-
ing, long and long,
Through youth and through middle and old age, how unfalter-
ing, how affectionate and faithful they were,
Then I am pensive—I hastily walk away fill'd with the bitterest
envy.

WE TWO BOYS TOGETHER CLINGING

We two boys together clinging,
One the other never leaving,
Up and down the roads going, North and South excursions
   making,
Power enjoying, elbows stretching, fingers clutching,
Arm'd and fearless, eating, drinking, sleeping, loving,
No law less than ourselves owning, sailing, soldiering, thieving,
   threatening,
Misers, menials, priests alarming, air breathing, water drink-
   ing, on the turf or the sea-beach dancing,
Cities wrenching, ease scorning, statues mocking, feebleness
   chasing,
Fulfilling our foray.

A PROMISE TO CALIFORNIA

A promise to California,
Or inland to the great pastoral Plains, and on to Puget sound
   and Oregon;
Sojourning east a while longer, soon I travel toward you, to
   remain, to teach robust American love,
For I know very well that I and robust love belong among you,
   inland, and along the Western sea;
For these States tend inland and toward the Western sea, and
   I will also.

HERE THE FRAILEST LEAVES OF ME

Here the frailest leaves of me and yet my strongest lasting,
Here I shade and hide my thoughts, I myself do not expose
   them,
And yet they expose me more than all my other poems.

NO LABOR-SAVING MACHINE

No labor-saving machine,
Nor discovery have I made,
Nor will I be able to leave behind me any wealthy bequest to
   found a hospital or library,
Nor reminiscence of any deed of courage for America,
Nor literary success nor intellect, nor book for the book-shelf,
But a few carols vibrating through the air I leave,
For comrades and lovers.

A GLIMPSE

A glimpse through an interstice caught,
Of a crowd of workmen and drivers in a bar-room around the
   stove late of a winter night, and I unremark'd
   seated in a corner,

Of a youth who loves me and whom I love, silently approach-
   ing and seating himself near, that he may
   hold me by the hand,
A long while amid the noises of coming and going, of drinking
   and oath and smutty jest,
There we two, content, happy in being together, speaking little,
   perhaps not a word.

A LEAF FOR HAND IN HAND

A leaf for hand in hand;
You natural persons old and young!
You on the Mississippi and on all the branches and bayous of
   the Mississippi!
You friendly boatmen and mechanics! you roughs!
You twain! and all processions moving along the streets!
I wish to infuse myself among you till I see it common for
   you to walk hand in hand.

EARTH, MY LIKENESS

Earth, my likeness,
Though you look so impassive, ample and spheric there,
I now suspect that is not all;
I now suspect there is something fierce in you eligible to burst
   forth,
For an athlete is enamour'd of me, and I of him,
But toward him there is something fierce and terrible in me
   eligible to burst forth,
I dare not tell it in words, not even in these songs.

I DREAM'D IN A DREAM

I dream'd in a dream I saw a city invincible to the attacks of
   the whole of the rest of the earth,
I dream'd that was the new city of Friends,
Nothing was greater there than the quality of robust love, it
   led the rest,
It was seen every hour in the actions of the men of that city,
And in all their looks and words.

WHAT THINK YOU I TAKE MY PEN IN HAND?

What think you I take my pen in hand to record?
The battle-ship, perfect-model'd, majestic, that I saw pass the
   offing to-day under full sail?
The splendors of the past day? or the splendor of the night that
   envelops me?
Or the vaunted glory and growth of the great city spread
   around me?—no;
But merely of two simple men I saw to-day on the pier in the

midst of the crowd, parting the parting of
dear friends,
The one to remain hung on the other's neck and passionately
kiss'd him,
While the one to depart tightly prest the one to remain in his
arms.

TO THE EAST AND TO THE WEST

To the East and to the West,
To the man of the Seaside State and of Pennsylvania,
To the Kanadian of the north, to the Southerner I love,
These with perfect trust to depict you as myself, the germs are
in all men,
I believe the main purport of these States is to found a superb
friendship, exaltè, previously unknown,
Because I perceive it waits, and has been always waiting,
latent in all men.

SOMETIMES WITH ONE I LOVE

Sometimes with one I love I fill myself with rage for fear I
effuse unreturn'd love,
But now I think there is no unreturn'd love, the pay is certain
one way or another,
(I loved a certain person ardently and my love was not re-
turn'd,
Yet out of that I have written these songs.)

TO A WESTERN BOY

Many things to absorb I teach to help you become eleve of
mine;
Yet if blood like mine circle not in your veins,
If you be not silently selected by lovers and do not silently
select lovers,
Of what use is it that you seek to become eleve of mine?

FAST-ANCHOR'D ETERNAL O LOVE!

Fast-anchor'd eternal O love! O woman I love!
O bride! O wife! more resistless than I can tell, the thought
of you!
Then separate, as disembodied or another born,
Ethereal, the last athletic reality, my consolation,
I ascend, I float in the regions of your love O man,
O sharer of my roving life.

AMONG THE MULTITUDE

Among the men and women the multitude,
I perceive one picking me out by secret and divine signs,

Acknowledging none else, not parent, wife, husband, brother,
              child, any nearer than I am,
Some are baffled, but that one is not—that one knows me.

Ah lover and perfect equal,
I meant that you should discover me so by faint indirections,
And I when I meet you mean to discover you by the like in you.

O YOU WHOM I OFTEN AND SILENTLY COME

O you whom I often and silently come where you are that I
              may be with you,
As I walk by your side or sit near, or remain in the same room
              with you,
Little you know the subtle electric fire that for your sake is
              playing within me.

THAT SHADOW MY LIKENESS

That shadow my likeness that goes to and fro seeking a liveli-
              hood, chattering, chaffering,
How often I find myself standing and looking at it where it
              flits,
How often I question and doubt whether that is really me;
But among my lovers and caroling these songs,
O I never doubt whether that is really me.

FULL OF LIFE NOW

Full of life now, compact, visible,
I, forty years old the eighty-third year of the States,
To one a century hence or any number of centuries hence,
To you yet unborn these, seeking you.

When you read these I that was visible am become invisible,
Now it is you, compact, visible, realizing my poems, seeking
              me,
Fancying how happy you were if I could be with you and
              become your comrade;
Be it as if I were with you. (Be not too certain but I am now
              with you.)

SALUT AU MONDE!

1

O take my hand Walt Whitman!
Such gliding wonders! such sights and sounds!
Such join'd unended links, each hook'd to the next,
Each answering all, each sharing the earth with all.
What widens within you Walt Whitman?
What waves and soils exuding?

What climes? what persons and cities are here?
Who are the infants, some playing, some slumbering?
Who are the girls? who are the married women?
Who are the groups of old men going slowly with their arms
            about each other's necks?
What rivers are these? what forests and fruits are these?
What are the mountains call'd that rise so high in the mists?
What myriads of dwellings are they fill'd with dwellers?

2

Within me latitude widens, longitude lengthens,
Asia, Africa, Europe, are to the east—America is provided
            for in the west,
Banding the bulge of the earth winds the hot equator,
Curiously north and south turn the axis-ends,
Within me is the longest day, the sun wheels in slanting rings,
            it does not set for months,
Stretch'd in due time within me the midnight sun just rises
            above the horizon and sinks again,
Within me zones, seas, cataracts, forests, volcanoes, groups,
Malaysia, Polynesia, and the great West Indian islands.

3

What do you hear Walt Whitman?

I hear the workman singing and the farmer's wife singing,
I hear in the distance the sounds of children and of animals
            early in the day,
I hear emulous shouts of Australians pursuing the wild horse,
I hear the Spanish dance with castanets in the chestnut shade,
            to the rebeck and guitar,
I hear continual echoes from the Thames,
I hear fierce French liberty songs,
I hear of the Italian boat-sculler the musical recitative of old
            poems,
I hear the locusts in Syria as they strike the grain and grass
            with the showers of their terrible clouds,
I hear the Coptic refrain toward sundown, pensively falling
            on the breast of the black venerable vast
            mother the Nile,
I hear the chirp of the Mexican muleteer, and the bells of the
            mule,
I hear the Arab muezzin calling from the top of the mosque,
I hear the Christian priests at the altars of their churches, I
            hear the responsive base and soprano,
I hear the cry of the Cossack, and the sailor's voice putting to
            sea at Okotsk,
I hear the wheeze of the slave-coffle as the slaves march on,
            as the husky gangs pass on by twos and

threes, fasten'd together with wrist-chains
and ankle-chains,
I hear the Hebrew reading his records and psalms,
I hear the rhythmic myths of the Greeks, and the strong
legends of the Romans,
I hear the tale of the divine life and bloody death of the
beautiful God the Christ,
I hear the Hindoo teaching his favorite pupil the loves, wars,
adages, transmitted safely to this day from
poets who wrote three thousand years ago.

4

What do you see Walt Whitman?
Who are they you salute, and that one after another salute you?

I see a great round wonder rolling through space,
I see diminute farms, hamlets, ruins, graveyards, jails, fac-
tories, palaces, hovels, huts of barbarians,
tents of nomads upon the surface,
I see the shaded part on one side where the sleepers are sleep-
ing, and the sunlit part on the other side,
I see the curious rapid change of the light and shade,
I see distant lands, as real and near to the inhabitants of them
as my land is to me.

I see plenteous waters,
I see mountain peaks, I see the sierras of Andes where they
range,
I see plainly the Himalayas, Chian Shahs, Altays, Ghauts,
I see the giant pinnacles of Elbruz, Kazbek, Bazardjusi,
I see the Styrian Alps, and the Karnac Alps,
I see the Pyrenees, Balks, Carpathians, and to the north the
Dofrafields, and off at sea mount Hecla,
I see Vesuvius and Etna, the mountains of the Moon, and the
Red mountains of Madagascar,
I see the Lybian, Arabian, and Asiatic deserts,
I see huge dreadful Arctic and Antarctic icebergs,
I see the superior oceans and the inferior ones, the Atlantic
and Pacific, the sea of Mexico, the Brazilian
sea, and the sea of Peru,
The waters of Hindustan, the China Sea, and the gulf of
Guinea,
The Japan waters, the beautiful bay of Nagasaki land-lock'd
in its mountains,
The spread of the Baltic, Caspian, Bothnia, the British shores,
and the bay of Biscay,
The clear-sunn'd Mediterranean, and from one to another of
its islands,
The White sea, and the sea around Greenland.

I behold the mariners of the world,
Some are in storms, some in the night with the watch on the
    lookout,
Some drifting helplessly, some with contagious diseases.

I behold the sail and steamships of the world, some in clusters
    in port, some on their voyages,
Some double the cape of Storms, some cape Verde, others
    capes Guardafui, Bon, or Bajadore,
Others Dondra head, others pass the straits of Sunda, others
    cape Lopatka, others Behring's straits,
Others cape Horn, others sail the gulf of Mexico or along
    Cuba or Hayti, others Hudson's bay or
    Baffin's bay,
Others pass the straits of Dover, others enter the Wash, others
    the firth of Solway, others round cape Clear,
    others the Land's End,
Others traverse the Zuyder Zee or the Scheld,
Others as comers and goers at Gibraltar or the Dardanelles,
Others sternly push their way through the northern winter-
    packs,
Others descend or ascend the Obi or the Lena,
Others the Niger or the Congo, others the Indus, the Buram-
    pooter and Cambodia,
Others wait steam'd up ready to start in the ports of Australia,
Wait at Liverpool, Glasgow, Dublin, Marseilles, Lisbon,
    Naples, Hamburg, Bremen, Bordeaux, the
    Hague, Copenhagen,
Wait at Valparaiso, Rio Janeiro, Panama.

5

I see the tracks of the railroads of the earth,
I see them in Great Britain, I see them in Europe,
I see them in Asia and in Africa.

I see the electric telegraphs of the earth,
I see the filaments of the news of the wars, deaths, losses, gains,
    passions, of my race.

I see the long river-stripes of the earth,
I see the Amazon and the Paraguay,
I see the four great rivers of China, the Amour, the Yellow
    River, the Yiang-tse, and the Pearl,
I see where the Seine flows, and where the Danube, the Loire,
    the Rhone, and the Guadalquiver flow,
I see the windings of the Volga, the Dneiper, the Oder,
I see the Tuscan going down the Arno, and the Venetian
    along the Po,
I see the Greek seaman sailing out of Egina bay.

6

I see the site of the old empire of Assyria, and that of Persia,
  and that of India,
I see the falling of the Ganges over the high rim of Saukara.
I see the place of the idea of the Deity incarnated by avatars in
  human forms,
I see the spots of the successions of priests on the earth,
  oracles, sacrificers, brahmins, sabians, llamas,
  monks, muftis, exhorters,
I see where druids walk'd the groves of Mona, I see the mis-
  tletoe and vervain,
I see the temples of the deaths of the bodies of Gods, I see the
  old signifiers.

I see Christ eating the bread of his last supper in the midst of
  youths and old persons,
I see where the strong divine young man the Hercules toil'd
  faithfully and long and then died,
I see the place of the innocent rich life and hapless fate of the
  beautiful nocturnal son, the full-limb'd Bac-
  chus,
I see Kneph, blooming, drest in blue, with the crown of
  feathers on his head,
I see Hermes unsuspected, dying, well-belov'd, saying to the
  people *Do not weep for me,*
*This is not my true country, I have lived banish'd from my true
  country, I now go back there,*
I return to the celestial sphere where every one goes in his turn.

7

I see the battle-fields of the earth, grass grows upon them and
  blossoms and corn,
I see the tracks of ancient and modern expeditions.

I see the nameless masonries, venerable messages of the un-
  known events, heroes, records of the earth.

I see the places of the sagas,
I see pine-trees and fir-trees torn by northern blasts,
I see granite bowlders and cliffs, I see green meadows and
  lakes,
I see the burial-cairns of Scandinavian warriors,
I see them raised high with stones by the marge of restless
  oceans, that the dead men's spirits when they
  wearied of their quiet graves might rise up
  through the mounds and gaze on the tossing
  billows, and be refresh'd by storms, immen-
  sity, liberty, action.

I see the steppes of Asia,
I see the tumuli of Mongolia, I see the tents of Kalmucks and
        Baskirs,
I see the nomadic tribes with herds of oxen and cows,
I see the table-lands notch'd with ravines, I see the jungles and
        deserts,
I see the camel, the wild steed, the bustard, the fat-tail'd sheep,
        the antelope, and the burrowing wolf.

I see the highlands of Abyssinia,
I see flocks of goats feeding, and see the fig-tree, tamarind,
        date,
And see fields of teff-wheat and places of verdure and gold.
I see the Brazilian vaquero,
I see the Bolivian ascending mount Sorata,
I see the Wacho crossing the plains, I see the incomparable
        rider of horses with his lasso on his arm,
I see over the pampas the pursuit of wild cattle for their hides.

8

I see the regions of snow and ice,
I see the sharp-eyed Samoiede and the Finn,
I see the seal-seeker in his boat poising his lance,
I see the Siberian on his slight-built sledge drawn by dogs,
I see the porpoise-hunters, I see the whale-crews of the south
        Pacific and the north Atlantic,
I see the cliffs, glaciers, torrents, valleys, of Switzerland—I
        mark the long winters and the isolation.

9

I see the cities of the earth and make myself at random a part
        of them,
I am a real Parisian,
I am a habitan of Vienna, St. Petersburg, Berlin, Constanti-
        nople,
I am of Adelaide, Sidney, Melbourne,
I am of London, Manchester, Bristol, Edinburgh, Limerick,
I am of Madrid, Cadiz, Barcelona, Oporto, Lyons, Brussels,
        Berne, Frankfort, Stuttgart, Turin, Florence,
I belong in Moscow, Cracow, Warsaw, or northward in Chris-
        tiana or Stockholm, or in Siberian Irkutsk, or
        in some street in Iceland,
I descend upon all those cities, and rise from them again.

10

I see vapors exhaling from unexplored countries,
I see the savage types, the bow and arrow, the poison'd splint,
        the fetich, and the obi.

I see African and Asiatic towns,
I see Algiers, Tripoli, Derne, Mogadore, Timbuctoo, Mon-
    rovia,
I see the swarms of Pekin, Canton, Benares, Delhi, Calcutta,
    Tokio,
I see the Kruman in his hut, and the Dahoman and Ashantee-
    man in their huts,
I see the Turk smoking opium in Aleppo,
I see the picturesque crowds at the fairs of Khiva and those of
    Herat,
I see Teheran, I see Muscat and Medina and the intervening
    sands, I see the caravans toiling onward,
I see Egypt and the Egyptians, I see the pyramids and obelisks,
I look on chisell'd histories, records of conquering kings, dy-
    nasties, cut in slabs of sand-stone, or on gran-
    ite-blocks,
I see at Memphis mummy-pits containing mummies em-
    balm'd, swathed in linen cloth, lying there
    many centuries,
I look on the fall'n Theban, the large-ball'd eyes, the side-
    drooping neck, the hands folded across the
    breast.

I see all the menials of the earth, laboring,
I see all the prisoners in the prisons,
I see the defective human bodies of the earth,
The blind, the deaf and dumb, idiots, hunchbacks, lunatics,
The pirates, thieves, betrayers, murderers, slave-makers of the
    earth,
The helpless infants, and the helpless old men and women.

I see male and female everywhere,
I see the serene brotherhood of philosophs,
I see the constructiveness of my race,
I see the results of the perseverance and industry of my race,
I see ranks, colors, barbarisms, civilizations, I go among them,
    I mix indiscriminately,
And I salute all the inhabitants of the earth.

11

You whoever you are!
You daughter or son of England!
You of the mighty Slavic tribes and empires! you Russ in
    Russia!
You dim-descended, black, divine-soul'd African, large, fine-
    headed, nobly-form'd, superbly destin'd, on
    equal terms with me!
You Norwegian! Swede! Dane! Icelander! you Prussian!
You Spaniard of Spain! you Portuguese!

You Frenchwoman and Frenchman of France!
You Belge! you liberty-lover of the Netherlands! (you stock
      whence I myself have descended;)
You sturdy Austrian! you Lombard! Hun! Bohemian! farmer
      of Styria!
You neighbor of the Danube!
You working-man of the Rhine, the Elbe, or the Weser! you
      working-woman too!
You Sardinian! you Bavarian! Swabian! Saxon! Wallachian!
      Bulgarian!
You Roman! Neapolitan! you Greek!
You lithe matador in the arena at Seville!
You mountaineer living lawlessly on the Taurus or Cau-
      casus!
You Bokh horse-herd watching your mares and stallions feed-
      ing!
You beautiful-bodied Persian at full speed in the saddle shoot-
      ing arrows to the mark!
You Chinaman and Chinawoman of China! you Tartar of
      Tartary!
You women of the earth subordinated at your tasks!
You Jew journeying in your old age through every risk to
      stand once on Syrian ground!
You other Jews waiting in all lands for your Messiah!
You thoughtful Armenian pondering by some stream of the
      Euphrates! you peering amid the ruins of
      Nineveh! you ascending mount Ararat!
You foot-worn pilgrim welcoming the far-away sparkle of the
      minarets of Mecca!
You sheiks along the stretch from Suez to Bab-el-mandeb
      ruling your families and tribes!
You olive-grower tending your fruit on fields of Nazareth,
      Damascus, or lake Tiberias!
You Thibet trader on the wide inland or bargaining in the
      shops of Lassa!
You Japanese man or woman! you liver in Madagascar, Cey-
      lon, Sumatra, Borneo!
All you continentals of Asia, Africa, Europe, Australia, indif-
      ferent of place!
All you on the numberless islands of the archipelagoes of the
      sea!
And you of centuries hence when you listen to me!
And you each and everywhere whom I specify not, but include
      just the same!
Health to you! good will to you all, from me and America
      sent!

Each of us inevitable,

Each of us limitless—each of us with his or her right upon the
        earth,
Each of us allow'd the eternal purports of the earth,
Each of us here as divinely as any is here.

12

You Hottentot with clicking palate! you woolly-hair'd hordes!
You own'd persons dropping sweat-drops or blood-drops!
You human forms with the fathomless ever-impressive counte-
        nances of brutes!
You poor koboo whom the meanest of the rest look down
        upon for all your glimmering language and
        spirituality!
You dwarf'd Kamtschatkan, Greenlander, Lapp!
You Austral negro, naked, red, sooty, with protrusive lip,
        groveling, seeking your food!
You Caffre, Berber, Soudanese!
You haggard, uncouth, untutor'd Bedowee!
You plague-swarms in Madras, Nankin, Kaubul, Cairo!
You benighted roamer of Amazonia! you Patagonian! you
        Feejee-man!
I do not prefer others so very much before you either,
I do not say one word against you, away back there where you
        stand,
(You will come forward in due time to my side.)

13

My spirit has pass'd in compassion and determination around
        the whole earth,
I have look'd for equals and lovers and found them ready for
        me in all lands,
I think some divine rapport has equalized me with them.

You vapors, I think I have risen with you, moved away to
        distant continents, and fallen down there, for
        reasons,
I think I have blown with you you winds;
You waters I have finger'd every shore with you,
I have run through what any river or strait of the globe has
        run through.
I have taken my stand on the bases of peninsulas and on the
        high embedded rocks, to cry thence:

Salut au monde!
What cities the light or warmth penetrates I penetrate those
        cities myself,
All islands to which birds wing their way I wing my way
        myself.

Toward you all, in America's name,
I raise high the perpendicular hand, I make the signal,
To remain after me in sight forever,
For all the haunts and homes of men.

SONG OF THE OPEN ROAD

1

Afoot and light-hearted I take to the open road,
Healthy, free, the world before me,
The long brown path before me leading wherever I choose.

Henceforth I ask not good-fortune, I myself am good-fortune,
Henceforth I whimper no more, postpone no more, need
        nothing,
Done with indoor complaints, libraries, querulous criticisms,
Strong and content I travel the open road.

The earth, that is sufficient,
I do not want the constellations any nearer,
I know they are very well where they are,
I know they suffice for those who belong to them.

(Still here I carry my old delicious burdens,
I carry them, men and women, I carry them with me wherever
        I go,
I swear it is impossible for me to get rid of them,
I am fill'd with them; and I will fill them in return.)

2

You road I enter upon and look around, I believe you are not
                all that is here,
I believe that much unseen is also here.

Here the profound lesson of reception, nor preference nor
                denial,
The black with his woolly head, the felon, the diseas'd, the
                illiterate person, are not denied;
The birth, the hasting after the physician, the beggar's tramp,
                the drunkard's stagger, the laughing party of
                mechanics,
The escaped youth, the rich person's carriage, the fop, the
                eloping couple,
The early market-man, the hearse, the moving of furniture
                into the town, the return back from the town,
They pass, I also pass, any thing passes, none can be inter-
                dicted,
None but are accepted, none but shall be dear to me.

3

You air that serves me with breath to speak!
You objects that call from diffusion my meanings and give
    them shape!
You light that wraps me and all things in delicate equable
    showers!
You paths worn in the irregular hollows by the roadsides!
I believe you are latent with unseen existences, you are so
    dear to me.

You flagg'd walks of the cities! you strong curbs at the edges!
You ferries! you planks and posts of wharves! you timber-
    lined sides! you distant ships!
You rows of houses! you window-pierc'd façades! you roofs!
You porches and entrances! you copings and iron guards!
You windows whose transparent shells might expose so much!
You doors and ascending steps! you arches!
You gray stones of interminable pavements! you trodden
    crossings!
From all that has touch'd you I believe you have imparted to
    yourselves, and now would impart the same
    secretly to me,
From the living and the dead you have peopled your impassive
    surfaces, and the spirits thereof would be
    evident and amicable with me.

4

The earth expanding right hand and left hand,
The picture alive, every part in its best light,
The music falling in where it is wanted, and stopping where
    it is not wanted,
The cheerful voice of the public road, the gay fresh senti-
    ment of the road.

O highway I travel, do you say to me *Do not leave me?*
Do you say *Venture not—if you leave me you are lost?*
Do you say *I am already prepared, I am well-beaten and un-
denied, adhere to me?*

O public road, I say back I am not afraid to leave you, yet I
    love you,
You express me better than I can express myself,
You shall be more to me than my poem.

I think heroic deeds were all conceiv'd in the open air, and
    all free poems also,
I think I could stop here myself and do miracles,
I think whatever I shall meet on the road I shall like, and
    whoever beholds me shall like me,
I think whoever I see must be happy.

5

From this hour I ordain myself loos'd of limits and imagi-
        nary lines,
Going where I list, my own master total and absolute,
Listening to others, considering well what they say,
Pausing, searching, receiving, contemplating,
Gently, but with undeniable will, divesting myself of the holds
        that would hold me.

I inhale great draughts of space,
The east and the west are mine, and the north and the south
        are mine.

I am larger, better than I thought,
I did not know I held so much goodness.

All seems beautiful to me,
I can repeat over to men and women You have done such
        good to me I would do the same to you,
I will recruit for myself and you as I go,
I will scatter myself among men and women as I go,
I will toss a new gladness and roughness among them,
Whoever denies me it shall not trouble me,
Whoever accepts me he or she shall be blessed and shall bless
        me.

6

Now if a thousand perfect men were to appear it would not
        amaze me,
Now if a thousand beautiful forms of women appear'd it would
        not astonish me.

Now I see the secret of the making of the best persons,
It is to grow in the open air and to eat and sleep with the
        earth.

Here a great personal deed has room,
(Such a deed seizes upon the hearts of the whole race of men,
Its effusion of strength and will overwhelms law and mocks all
        authority and all argument against it.)

Here is the test of wisdom,
Wisdom is not finally tested in schools,
Wisdom cannot be pass'd from one having it to another not
        having it,
Wisdom is of the soul, is not susceptible of proof, is its own
        proof,
Applies to all stages and objects and qualities and is content,
Is the certainty of the reality and immortality of things, and
        the excellence of things;

Something there is in the float of the sight of things that pro-
        vokes it out of the soul.

Now I re-examine philosophies and religions,
They may prove well in lecture-rooms, yet not prove at all
        under the spacious clouds and along the
        landscape and flowing currents.

Here is realization,
Here is a man tallied—he realizes here what he has in him,
The past, the future, majesty, love—if they are vacant of you,
        you are vacant of them.

Only the kernel of every object nourishes;
Where is he who tears off the husks for you and me?
Where is he that undoes stratagems and envelopes for you
        and me?

Here is adhesiveness, it is not previously fashion'd, it is
        apropos;
Do you know what it is as you pass to be loved by strangers?
Do you know the talk of those turning eye-balls?

7

Here is the efflux of the soul,
The efflux of the soul comes from within through embower'd
        gates, ever provoking questions,
These yearnings why are they? these thoughts in the darkness
        why are they?
Why are there men and women that while they are nigh me
        the sunlight expands my blood?
Why when they leave me do my pennants of joy sink flat and
        lank?
Why are there trees I never walk under but large and melo-
        dious thoughts descend upon me?
(I think they hang there winter and summer on those trees
        and always drop fruit as I pass;)
What is it I interchange so suddenly with strangers?
What with some driver as I ride on the seat by his side?
What with some fisherman drawing his seine by the shore as
        I walk by and pause?
What gives me to be free to a woman's and man's good-will?
        what gives them to be free to mine?

8

The efflux of the soul is happiness, here is happiness,
I think it pervades the open air, waiting at all times,
Now it flows unto us, we are rightly charged.

Here rises the fluid and attaching character,

The fluid and attaching character is the freshness and sweet-
   ness of man and woman,
(The herbs of the morning sprout no fresher and sweeter
   every day out of the roots of themselves, than
   it sprouts fresh and sweet continually out
   of itself.)
Toward the fluid and attaching character exudes the sweat of
   the love of young and old,
From it falls distill'd the charm that mocks beauty and at-
   tainments,
Toward it heaves the shuddering longing ache of contact.

9

Allons! whoever you are come travel with me!
Traveling with me you find what never tires.

The earth never tires,
The earth is rude, silent, incomprehensible at first, Nature is
   rude and incomprehensible at first,
Be not discouraged, keep on, there are divine things well
   envelop'd,
I swear to you there are divine things more beautiful than
   words can tell.

Allons! we must not stop here,
However sweet these laid-up stores, however convenient this
   dwelling we cannot remain here,
However shelter'd this port and however calm these waters
   we must not anchor here,
However welcome the hospitality that surrounds us we are
   permitted to receive it but a little while.

10

Allons! the inducements shall be greater,
We will sail pathless and wild seas,
We will go where winds blow, waves dash, and the Yankee
   clipper speeds by under full sail.

Allons! with power, liberty, the earth, the elements,
Health, defiance, gayety, self-esteem, curiosity;
Allons! from all formules!
From your formules, O bat-eyed and materialistic priests.

The stale cadaver blocks up the passage—the burial waits no
   longer.

Allons! yet take warning!
He traveling with me needs the best blood, thews, endurance,
None may come to the trial till he or she bring courage and
   health,

Come not here if you have already spent the best of yourself,
Only those may come who come in sweet and determin'd
    bodies,
No diseas'd person, no rum-drinker or venereal taint is per-
    mitted here.

(I and mine do not convince by arguments, similes, rhymes,
We convince by our presence.)

11

Listen! I will be honest with you,
I do not offer the old smooth prizes, but offer rough new
    prizes,
These are the days that must happen to you:
You shall not heap up what is call'd riches,
You shall scatter with lavish hand all that you earn or achieve,
You but arrive at the city to which you were destin'd, you
    hardly settle yourself to satisfaction before
    you are call'd by an irresistible call to depart,
You shall be treated to the ironical smiles and mockings of
    those who remain behind you,
What beckonings of love you receive you shall only answer
    with passionate kisses of parting,
You shall not allow the hold of those who spread their
    reach'd hands toward you.

12

Allons! after the great Companions, and to belong to them!
They too are on the road—they are the swift and majestic
    men—they are the greatest women,
Enjoyers of calms of seas and storms of seas,
Sailors of many a ship, walkers of many a mile of land,
Habituès of many distant countries, habituès of far-distant
    dwellings,
Trusters of men and women, observers of cities, solitary
    toilers,
Pausers and contemplators of tufts, blossoms, shells of the
    shore,
Dancers at wedding-dances, kissers of brides, tender helpers
    of children, bearers of children,
Soldiers of revolts, standers by gaping graves, lowerers-down
    of coffins,
Journeyers over consecutive seasons, over the years, the curi-
    ous years each emerging from that which
    preceded it,
Journeyers as with companions, namely their own diverse
    phases,
Forth-steppers from the latent unrealized baby-days,
Journeyers gayly with their own youth, journeyers with their

bearded and well-grain'd manhood,
Journeyers with their womanhood, ample, unsurpass'd, content,
Journeyers with their own sublime old age of manhood or womanhood,
Old age, calm, expanded, broad with the haughty breadth of the universe,
Old age, flowing free with the delicious near-by freedom of death.

13

Allons! to that which is endless as it was beginningless,
To undergo much, tramps of days, rests of nights,
To merge all in the travel they tend to, and the days and nights they tend to,
Again to merge them in the start of superior journeys,
To see nothing anywhere but what you may reach it and pass it,
To conceive no time, however distant, but what you may reach it and pass it,
To look up or down no road but it stretches and waits for you, however long but it stretches and waits for you,
To see no being, not God's or any, but you also go thither,
To see no possession but you may possess it, enjoying all without labor or purchase, abstracting the feast yet not abstracting one particle of it,
To take the best of the farmer's farm and the rich man's elegant villa, and the chaste blessings of the well-married couple, and the fruits of orchards and flowers of gardens,
To take to your use out of the compact cities as you pass through,
To carry buildings and streets with you afterward wherever you go,
To gather the minds of men out of their brains as you encounter them, to gather the love out of their hearts,
To take your lovers on the road with you, for all that you leave them behind you,
To know the universe itself as a road, as many roads, as roads for traveling souls.

All parts away for the progress of souls,
All religion, all solid things, arts, governments—all that was or is apparent upon this globe or any globe, falls into niches and corners before the procession of souls along the grand roads of the universe.

Of the progress of the souls of men and women along the
        grand roads of the universe, all other prog-
        ress is the needed emblem and sustenance.

Forever alive, forever forward,
Stately, solemn, sad, withdrawn, baffled, mad, turbulent,
        feeble, dissatisfied,
Desperate, proud, fond, sick, accepted by men, rejected by
        men,
They go! they go! I know that they go, but I know not where
        they go,
But I know that they go toward the best—toward something
        great.

Whoever you are, come forth! or man or woman come forth!
You must not stay sleeping and dallying there in the house,
        though you built it, or though it has been
        built for you.

Out of the dark confinement! out from behind the screen!
It is useless to protest. I know all and expose it.

Behold through you as bad as the rest,
Through the laughter, dancing, dining, supping, of people,
Inside of dresses and ornaments, inside of those wash'd and
        trimm'd faces,
Behold a secret silent loathing and despair.

No husband, no wife, no friend, trusted to hear the con-
        fession,
Another self, a duplicate of every one, skulking and hiding it
        goes,
Formless and wordless through the streets of the cities, polite
        and bland in the parlors,
In the cars of railroads, in steamboats, in the public assembly,
Home to the houses of men and women, at the table, in the
        bedroom, everywhere,
Smartly attired, countenance smiling, form upright, death
        under the breast-bones, hell under the skull-
        bones,
Under the broadcloth and gloves, under the ribbons and arti-
        ficial flowers,
Keeping fair with the customs, speaking not a syllable of itself,
Speaking of any thing else but never of itself.

14

Allons! through struggles and wars!
The goal that was named cannot be countermanded.

Have the past struggles succeeded?
What has succeeded? yourself? your nation? Nature?

Now understand me well—it is provided in the essence of
        things that from any fruition of success, no
        matter what, shall come forth something to
        make a greater struggle necessary.

My call is the call of battle, I nourish active rebellion,
He going with me must go well arm'd,
He going with me goes often with spare diet, poverty, angry
        enemies, desertions.

15

Allons! the road is before us!
It is safe—I have tried it—my own feet have tried it well—
        be not detain'd!
Let the paper remain on the desk unwritten, and the book on
        the shelf unopen'd!
Let the tools remain in the workshop! let the money remain
        unearn'd!
Let the school stand! mind not the cry of the teacher!
Let the preacher preach in his pulpit! let the lawyer plead in
        the court, and the judge expound the law.

Camerado, I give you my hand!
I give you my love more precious than money,
I give you myself before preaching or law;
Will you give me yourself? will you come travel with me?
Shall we stick by each other as long as we live?

CROSSING BROOKLYN FERRY

1

Flood-tide below me! I see you face to face!
Clouds of the west—sun there half an hour high—I see you
        also face to face.

Crowds of men and women attired in the usual costumes, how
        curious you are to me!
On the ferry-boats the hundreds and hundreds that cross,
        returning home, are more curious to me than
        you suppose,
And you that shall cross from shore to shore years hence are
        more to me, and more in my meditations,
        than you might suppose.

2

The impalpable sustenance of me from all things at all hours
        of the day,
The simple, compact, well-join'd scheme, myself disintegrated,
        every one disintegrated yet part of the
        scheme,

The similitudes of the past and those of the future,
The glories strung like beads on my smallest sights and hear-
         ings, on the walk in the street and the
         passage over the river,
The current rushing so swiftly and swimming with me far
         away,
The others that are to follow me, the ties between me and
         them,
The certainty of others, the life, love, sight, hearing of others.

Others will enter the gates of the ferry and cross from shore
         to shore,
Others will watch the run of the flood-tide,
Others will see the shipping of Manhattan north and west, and
         the heights of Brooklyn to the south and
         east,
Others will see the islands large and small;
Fifty years hence, others will see them as they cross, the sun
         half an hour high,
A hundred years hence, or ever so many hundred years hence,
         others will see them,
Will enjoy the sunset, the pouring-in of the flood-tide, the
         falling-back to the sea of the ebb-tide.

3

It avails not, time nor place—distance avails not,
I am with you, you men and women of a generation, or ever
         so many generations hence,
Just as you feel when you look on the river and sky, so I felt,
Just as any of you is one of a living crowd, I was one of a
         crowd,
Just as you are refresh'd by the gladness of the river and the
         bright flow, I was refresh'd,
Just as you stand and lean on the rail, yet hurry with the
         swift current, I stood yet was hurried,
Just as you look on the numberless masts of ships and the
         thick-stemm'd pipes of steamboats, I look'd.

I too many and many a time cross'd the river of old,
Watched the Twelfth-month sea-gulls, saw them high in the
         air floating with motionless wings, oscillating
         their bodies,
Saw how the glistening yellow lit up parts of their bodies and
         left the rest in strong shadow,
Saw the slow-wheeling circles and the gradual edging toward
         the south,
Saw the reflection of the summer sky in the water,
Had my eyes dazzled by the shimmering track of beams,
Look'd at the fine centrifugal spokes of light round the shape
         of my head in the sunlit water,

Look'd on the haze on the hills southward and south-west-
 ward,
Look'd on the vapor as it flew in fleeces tinged with violet,
Look'd toward the lower bay to notice the vessels arriving,
Saw their approach, saw aboard those that were near me,
Saw the white sails of schooners and sloops, saw the ships at
 anchor,
The sailors at work in the rigging or out astride the spars,
The round masts, the swinging motion of the hulls, the slender
 serpentine pennants,
The large and small steamers in motion, the pilots in their
 pilot-houses,
The white wake left by the passage, the quick tremulous whirl
 of the wheels,
The flags of all nations, the falling of them at sunset,
The scallop-edged waves in the twilight, the ladled cups, the
 frolicsome crests and glistening,
The stretch afar growing dimmer and dimmer, the gray walls
 of the granite storehouses by the docks,
On the river the shadowy group, the big steam-tug closely
 flank'd on each side by the barges, the hay-
 boat, the belated lighter,
On the neighboring shore the fires from the foundry chimneys
 burning high and glaringly into the night,
Casting their flicker of black contrasted with wild red and
 yellow light over the tops of houses, and
 down into the clefts of streets.

4

These and all else were to me the same as they are to you,
I loved well those cities, loved well the stately and rapid river,
The men and women I saw were all near to me,
Others the same—others who look back on me because I
 look'd forward to them,
(The time will come, though I stop here to-day and to-night.)

5

What is it then between us?
What is the count of the scores or hundreds of years between
 us?

Whatever it is, it avails not—distance avails not, and place
 avails not,
I too lived, Brooklyn of ample hills was mine,
I too walk'd the streets of Manhattan island, and bathed in
 the waters around it,
I too felt the curious abrupt questionings stir within me.
In the day among crowds of people sometimes they came upon
 me,

In my walks home late at night or as I lay in my bed they
    came upon me,
I too had been struck from the float forever held in solution,
I too had receiv'd identity by my body,
That I was I knew was of my body, and what I should be I
    knew I should be of my body.

6

It is not upon you alone the dark patches fall,
The dark threw its patches down upon me also,
The best I had done seem'd to me blank and suspicious,
My great thoughts as I supposed them, were they not in reality
    meagre?
Nor is it you alone who know what it is to be evil,
I am he who knew what it was to be evil,
I too knitted the old knot of contrariety,
Blabb'd, blush'd, resented, lied, stole, grudg'd,
Had guile, anger, lust, hot wishes I dared not speak,
Was wayward, vain, greedy, shallow, sly, cowardly, malig-
    nant,
The wolf, the snake, the hog, not wanting in me,
The cheating look, the frivolous word, the adulterous wish,
    not wanting,
Refusals, hates, postponements, meanness, laziness, none of
    these wanting,
Was one with the rest, the days and haps of the rest,
Was call'd by my nighest name by clear loud voices of young
    men as they saw me approaching or passing,
Felt their arms on my neck as I stood, or the negligent lean-
    ing of their flesh against me as I sat,
Saw many I loved in the street or ferry-boat or public assem-
    bly, yet never told them a word,
Lived the same life with the rest, the same old laughing,
    gnawing, sleeping,
Play'd the part that still looks back on the actor or actress,
The same old role, the role that is what we make it, as great
    as we like,
Or as small as we like, or both great and small.

7

Closer yet I approach you,
What thought you have of me now, I had as much of you—I
    laid in my stores in advance,
I consider'd long and seriously of you before you were born.

Who was to know what should come home to me?
Who knows but I am enjoying this?
Who knows, for all the distance, but I am as good as looking
    at you now, for all you cannot see me?

8

Ah, what can ever be more stately and admirable to me than
mast-hemm'd Manhattan?
River and sunset and scallop-edg'd waves of flood-tide?
The sea-gulls oscillating their bodies, the hay-boat in the
twilight, and the belated lighter?
What gods can exceed these that clasp me by the hand, and
with voices I love call be promptly and loudly
by my nighest name as I approach?

What is more subtle than this which ties me to the woman or
man that looks in my face?
Which fuses me into you now, and pours my meaning into
you?

We understand then do we not?
What I promis'd without mentioning it, have you not ac-
cepted?
What the study could not teach—what the preaching could
not accomplish is accomplish'd, is it not?

9

Flow on, river! flow with the flood-tide, and ebb with the
ebb-tide!
Frolic on, crested and scallop-edg'd waves!
Gorgeous clouds of the sunset! drench with your splendor
me, or the men and women generations after
me!
Cross from shore to shore, countless crowds of passengers!
Stand up, tall masts of Mannahatta! stand up, beautiful hills of
Brooklyn!
Throb, baffled and curious brain! throw out questions and
answers!
Suspend here and everywhere, eternal float of solution!
Gaze, loving and thirsting eyes, in the house or street or public
assembly!
Sound out, voices of young men; loudly and musically call
me by my nighest name!
Live, old life! play the part that looks back on the actor or
actress!
Play the old role, the role that is great or small according as
one makes it!
Consider, you who peruse me, whether I may not in unknown
ways be looking upon you;
Be firm, rail over the river, to support those who lean idly,
yet haste with the hasting current;
Fly on, sea-birds! fly sideways, or wheel in large circles high
in the air;

Receive the summer sky, you water, and faithfully hold it till
        all downcast eyes have time to take it from
        you!
Diverge, fine spokes of light, from the shape of my head, or
        any one's head, in the sunlit water!
Come on, ships from the lower bay! pass up or down, white-
        sail'd schooners, sloops, lighters!
Flaunt away, flags of all nations! be duly lower'd at sunset!
Burn high you fires, foundry chimneys! cast black shadows at
        nightfall! cast red and yellow light over the
        tops of the houses!
Appearances, now or henceforth, indicate what you are,
You necessary film, continue to envelop the soul,
About my body for me, and your body for you, be hung our
        divinest aromas,
Thrive, cities—bring your freight, bring your shows, ample
        and sufficient rivers,
Expand, being than which none else is perhaps more spiritual,
Keep your places, objects than which none else is more lasting.

You have waited, you always wait, you dumb, beautiful min-
        isters,
We receive you with free sense at last, and are insatiate hence-
        forward,
Not you any more shall be able to foil us, or withhold your-
        selves from us,
We use you, and do not cast you aside—we plant you perma-
        nently within us,
We fathom you not—we love you—there is perfection in you
        also,
You furnish your parts toward eternity,
Great or small, you furnish your parts toward the soul.

SONG OF THE ANSWERER

1

Now list to my morning's romanza, I tell the signs of the
        Answerer,
To the cities and farms I sing as they spread in the sunshine
        before me.

A young man comes to me bearing a message from his brother,
How shall the young man know the whether and when of his
        brother?
Tell him to send me the signs.

And I stand before the young man face to face, and take his
        right hand in my left hand and his left hand
        in my right hand,

And I answer for his brother and for men, and I answer for
          him that answers for all, and send these
          signs.

Him all wait for, him all yield up to, his word is decisive and
          final,
Him they accept, in him lave, in him perceive themselves as
          amid light,
Him they immerse and he immerses them.

Beautiful women, the haughtiest nations, laws, the landscape,
          people, animals,
The profound earth and its attributes and the unquiet ocean,
          (so tell I my morning's romanza,)
All enjoyments and properties and money, and whatever
          money will buy,
The best farms, others toiling and planting and he unavoidably
          reaps,
The noblest and costliest cities, others grading and building
          and he domiciles there,
Nothing for any one but what is for him, near and far are
          for him, the ships in the offing,
The perpetual shows and marches on land are for him if they
          are for anybody.

He puts things in their attitudes,
He puts to-day out of himself with plasticity and love,
He places his own times, reminiscences, parents, brothers and
          sisters, associations, employment, politics, so
          that the rest never shame them afterward,
          nor assume to command them.

He is the Answerer,
What can be answer'd he answers, and what cannot be an-
          swer'd he shows how it cannot be answer'd.

A man is a summons and challenge,
(It is vain to skulk—do you hear that mocking and laughter?
          do you hear the ironical echoes?)

Books, friendships, philosophers, priests, action, pleasure,
          pride, beat up and down seeking to give satis-
          faction,
He indicates the satisfaction, and indicates them that beat up
          and down also.

Whichever the sex, whatever the season or place, he may go
          freshly and gently and safely by day or by
          night,
He has the pass-key of hearts, to him the response of the pry-
          ing of hands on the knobs.

His welcome is universal, the flow of beauty is not more wel-
come or universal than he is,
The person he favors by day or sleeps with at night is blessed.

Every existence has its idiom, every thing has an idiom and
tongue,
He resolves all tongues into his own and bestows it upon
men, and any man translates, and any man
translates himself also,
One part does not counteract another part, he is the joiner,
he sees how they join.

He says indifferently and alike *How are you friend?* to the
President at his levee,
He says *Good-day my brother,* to Cudge that hoes in the sugar-
field,
And both understand him and know that his speech is right.

He walks with perfect ease in the capitol,
He walks among the Congress, and one Representative says
to another, *Here is our equal appearing and
new.*

Then the mechanics take him for a mechanic,
And the soldiers suppose him to be a soldier, and the sailors
that he has follow'd the sea,
And the authors take him for an author, and the artists for an
artist,
And the laborers perceive he could labor with them and love
them,
No matter what the work is, that he is the one to follow it or
has follow'd it,
No matter what the nation, that he might find his brothers
and sisters there.

The English believe he comes of their English stock,
A Jew to the Jew he seems, a Russ to the Russ, usual and
near, removed from none.

Whoever he looks at in the traveler's coffee-house claims him,
The Italian or Frenchman is sure, the German is sure, the
Spaniard is sure, and the island Cuban is
sure,
The engineer, the deck-hand on the great lakes, or on the
Mississippi or St. Lawrence or Sacramento,
or Hudson or Paumanok sound, claims him.

The gentleman of perfect blood acknowledges his perfect
blood,
The insulter, the prostitute, the angry person, the beggar, see

themselves in the ways of him, he strangely
transmutes them,
They are not vile any more, they hardly know themselves
they are so grown.

2

The indications and tally of time,
Perfect sanity shows the master among philosophs,
Time, always without break, indicates itself in parts,
What always indicates the poet is the crowd of the pleasant
company of singers, and their words,
The words of the singers are the hours or minutes of the light
or dark, but the words of the maker of
poems are the general light and dark,
The makers of poems settles justice, reality, immortality,
His insight and power encircle things and the human race,
He is the glory and extract thus far of things and of the
human race.

The singers do not beget, only the Poet begets,
The singers are welcom'd, understood, appear often enough,
but rare has the day been, likewise the spot,
of the birth of the maker of poems, the An-
swerer,
(Not every century nor every five centuries has contain'd
such a day, for all its names.)

The singers of successive hours of centuries may have osten-
sible names, but the name of each of them
is one of the singers,
The name of each is, eye-singer, ear-singer, head-singer,
sweet - singer, night - singer, parlor - singer,
love-singer, weird-singer, or something else.

All this time and at all times wait the words of true poems,
The words of true poems do not merely please,
The true poets are not followers of beauty but the august mas-
ters of beauty;
The greatness of sons is the exuding of the greatness of
mothers and fathers,
The words of true poems are the tuft and final applause of
science.

Divine instinct, breadth of vision, the law of reason, health,
rudeness of body, withdrawness,
Gayety, sun-tan, air-sweetness, such are some of the words of
poems.

The sailor and traveler underlie the maker of poems, the
Answerer,

The builder, geometer, chemist, anatomist, phrenologist, artist,
   all these underlie the maker of poems, the
   Answerer.

The words of the true poems give you more than poems,
They give you to form for yourself poems, religions, politics,
   war, peace, behavior, histories, essays, daily
   life, and every thing else,
They balance ranks, colors, races, creeds, and the sexes,
They do not seek beauty, they are sought,
Forever touching them or close upon them follows beauty,
   longing, fain, love-sick.

They prepare for death, yet they are not the finish, but rather
   the outset,
They bring none to his or her terminus or to be content and
   full,
Whom they take they take into space to behold the birth of
   stars, to learn one of the meanings,
To launch off with absolute faith, to sweep through the cease-
   less rings and never be quiet again.

OUR OLD FEUILLAGE

Always our old feuillage!
Always Florida's green peninsula—always the priceless delta
   of Louisiana—always the cotton-fields of
   Alabama and Texas,
Always California's golden hills and hollows, and the silver
   mountains of New Mexico—always soft-
   breath'd Cuba,
Always the vast slope drain'd by the Southern sea, insepa-
   rable with the slopes drain'd by the Eastern
   and Western seas,
The area the eighty-third year of these States, the three and
   a half millions of square miles,
The eighteen thousand miles of sea-coast and bay-coast on
   the main, the thirty thousand miles of river
   navigation,
The seven millions of distinct families and the same number
   of dwellings—always these, and more,
   branching forth into numberless branches,
Always the free range and diversity—always the continent of
   Democracy;
Always the prairies, pastures, forests, vast cities, travelers,
   Kanada, the snows;
Always these compact lands tied at the hips with the belt
   stringing the huge oval lakes;
Always the West with strong native persons, the increasing

density there, the habitans, friendly, threat
ening, ironical, scorning invaders;
All sights, South, North, East—all deeds promiscuously done
at all times,
All characters, movements, growths, a few noticed, myriads
unnoticed,
Through Mannahatta's streets I walking, these things gath-
ering,
On interior rivers by night in the glare of pine knots, steam-
boats wooding up,
Sunlight by day on the valley of the Susquehanna, and on the
valleys of the Potomac and Rappahannock,
and the valleys of the Roanoke and Dela-
ware,
In their northerly wilds beasts of prey haunting the Adiron-
dacks the hills, or lapping the Saginaw waters
to drink,
In a lonesome inlet a sheldrake lost from the flock, sitting on
the water rocking silently,
In farmers' barns oxen in the stable, their harvest labor done,
they rest standing, they are too tired,
Afar on arctic ice the she-walrus lying drowsily while her
cubs play around,
The hawk sailing where men have not yet sail'd, the farthest
polar sea, ripply, crystalline, open, beyond
the floes,
White drift spooning ahead where the ship in the tempest
dashes,
On solid land what is done in cities as the bells strike mid-
night together,
In primitive woods the sounds there also sounding, the howl
of the wolf, the scream of the panther, and
the hoarse bellow of the elk,
In winter beneath the hard blue ice of Moosehead lake, in
summer visible through the clear waters, the
great trout swimming,
In lower latitudes in warmer air in the Carolinas the large
black buzzard floating slowly high beyond
the tree tops,
Below, the red cedar festoon'd with tylandria, the pines and
cypresses growing out of the white sand that
spreads far and flat,
Rude boats descending the big Pedee, climbing plants, para-
sites with color'd flowers and berries envel-
oping huge trees,
The waving drapery on the live-oak trailing long and low,
noiselessly waved by the wind,
The camp of Georgia wagoners just after dark, the supper-

fires and the cooking and eating by whites
and negroes,

Thirty or forty great wagons, the mules, cattle, horses, feeding
from troughs,

The shadows, gleams, up under the leaves of the old syca-
more-trees, the flames with the black smoke
from the pitch-pine curling and rising;

Southern fishermen fishing, the sounds and inlets of North
Carolina's coast, the shad-fishery and the
herring-fishery, the large sweep-seines, the
windlasses on shore work'd by horses, the
clearing, curing, and packing-houses;

Deep in the forest in piney woods turpentine dropping from
the incisions in the trees, there are the tur-
pentine works,

There are the negroes at work in good health, the ground in
all directions is cover'd with pine straw;

In Tennessee and Kentucky slaves busy in the coalings, at
the forge, by the furnace-blaze, or at the
corn-shucking,

In Virginia, the planter's son returning after a long absence,
joyfully welcom'd and kiss'd by the aged
mulatto nurse,

On rivers boatmen safely moor'd at nightfall in their boats
under shelter of high banks,

Some of the younger men dance to the sound of the banjo or
fiddle, others sit on the gunwale smoking and
talking;

Late in the afternoon the mocking-bird, the American mimic,
singing in the Great Dismal Swamp,

There are the greenish waters, the resinous odor, the plen-
teous moss, the cypress-tree, and the juniper-
tree;

Northward, young men of Mannahatta, the target company
from an excursion returning home at eve-
ning, the musket-muzzles all bear bunches of
flowers presented by women;

Children at play, or on his father's lap a young boy fallen
asleep, (how his lips move! how he smiles in
his sleep!)

The scout riding on horseback over the plains west of the
Mississippi, he ascends a knoll and sweeps his
eyes around;

California life, the miner, bearded, dress'd in his rude costume,
the stanch California friendship, the sweet
air, the graves one in passing meets solitary
just aside the horsepath;

Down in Texas the cotton-field, the negro-cabins, drivers driv-
ing mules or oxen before rude carts, cotton

bales piled on banks and wharves;

Encircling all, vast-darting up and wide, the American Soul, with equal hemispheres, one Love, one Dilation or Pride;

In arriere the peace-talk with the Iroquois the aborigines, the calumet, the pipe of good-will, arbitration, and indorsement,

The sachem blowing the smoke first toward the sun and then toward the earth,

The drama of the scalp-dance enacted with painted faces and guttural exclamations,

The setting out of the war-party, the long and stealthy march,

The single file, the swinging hatchets, the surprise and slaughter of enemies;

All the acts, scenes, ways, persons, attitudes of these States, reminiscences, institutions,

All these States compact, every square mile of these States without excepting a particle;

Me pleas'd, rambling in lanes and country fields, Paumanok's fields,

Observing the spiral flight of two little yellow butterflies shuffling between each other, ascending high in the air,

The darting swallow, the destroyer of insects, the fall traveler southward but returning northward early in the spring,

The country boy at the close of the day driving the herd of cows and shouting to them as they loiter to browse by the roadside,

The city wharf, Boston, Philadelphia, Baltimore, Charleston, New Orleans, San Francisco,

The departing ships when the sailors heave at the capstan;

Evening—me in my room—the setting sun,

The setting summer sun shining in my open window, showing the swarm of flies, suspended, balancing in the air in the centre of the room, darting athwart, up and down, casting swift shadows in specks on the opposite wall where the shine is;

The athletic American matron speaking in public to crowds of listeners,

Males, females, immigrants, combinations, the copiousness, the individuality of the States, each for itself —the money-makers,

Factories, machinery, the mechanical forces, the windlass, lever, pulley, all certainties,

The certainty of space, increase, freedom, futurity,

In space the sporades, the scatter'd islands, the stars—on the firm earth, the lands, my lands,

O lands! all so dear to me—what you are, (whatever it is,) I
  putting it at random in these songs, become
  a part of that, whatever it is,
Southward there, I screaming, with wings slow flapping, with
  the myriads of gulls wintering along the
  coasts of Florida, .
Otherways there atwixt the banks of the Arkansas, the Rio
  Grande, the Nueces, the Brazos, the Tom-
  bigbee, the Red River, the Saskatchawan or
  the Osage, I with the spring waters laughing
  and skipping and running,
Northward, on the sands, on some shallow bay of Paumanok,
  I with parties of snowy herons wading in the
  wet to seek worms and aquatic plants,
Retreating, triumphantly twittering, the king-bird, from pierc-
  ing the crow with its bill, for amusement—
  and I triumphantly twittering,
The migrating flock of wild geese alighting in autumn to re-
  fresh themselves, the body of the flock feed,
  the sentinels outside move around with erect
  heads watching, and are from time to time
  reliev'd by other sentinels—and I feeding
  and taking turns with the rest,
In Kanadian forests the moose, large as an ox, corner'd by
  hunters, rising desperately on his hind-feet,
  and plunging with his forefeet, the hoofs as
  sharp as knives—and I, plunging at the hunt-
  ers, corner'd and desperate,
In the Mannahatta, streets, piers, shipping, store-houses, and
  the countless workmen working in the shops,
And I too of the Mannahatta, singing thereof—and no less in
  myself than the whole of the Mannahatta in
  itself,
Singing the song of These, my ever-united lands—my body
  no more inevitably united, part to part, and
  made out of a thousand diverse contributions
  one identity, any more than my lands are
  inevitably united and made ONE IDENTITY.
Nativities, climates, the grass of the great pastoral Plains,
Cities, labors, death, animals, products, war, good and evil
  —these me,
These affording, in all their particulars, the old feuillage to
  me and to America, how can I do less than
  pass the clew of the union of them, to afford
  the like to you?
Whoever you are! how can I but offer you divine leaves, that
  you also be eligible as I am?

How can I but as here chanting, invite you for yourself to
        collect bouquets of the incomparable feuil-
        lage of these States?

A SONG OF JOYS

O to make the most jubilant song!
Full of music—full of manhood, womanhood, infancy!
Full of common employments—full of grain and trees.

O for the voices of animals—O for the swiftness and balance
        of fishes!
O for the dropping of raindrops in a song!
O for the sunshine and motion of waves in a song!

O the joy of my spirit—it is uncaged—it darts like light-
        ning!
It is not enough to have this globe or a certain time,
I will have thousands of globes and all time.

O the engineer's joys! to go with a locomotive!
To hear the hiss of steam, the merry shriek, the steam-whistle,
        the laughing locomotive!
To push with resistless way and speed off in the distance.

O the gleesome saunter over fields and hillsides!
The leaves and flowers of the commonest weeds, the moist
        fresh stillness of the woods,
The exquisite smell of the earth at daybreak, and all through
        the forenoon.

O the horseman's and horsewoman's joys!
The saddle, the gallop, the pressure upon the seat, the cool
        gurgling by the ears and hair.

O the fireman's joys!
I hear the alarm at dead of night,
I hear bells, shouts! I pass the crowd, I run!
The sight of the flames maddens me with pleasure.

O the joy of the strong-brawn'd fighter, towering in the arena
        in perfect condition, conscious of power,
        thirsting to meet his opponent.

O the joy of that vast elemental sympathy which only the
        human soul is capable of generating and
        emitting in steady and limitless floods.

O the mother's joys!
The watching, the endurance, the precious love, the anguish,
        the patiently yielded life.

O the joy of increase, growth, recuperation,
The joy of soothing and pacifying, the joy of concord and
harmony.

O to go back to the place where I was born,
To hear the birds sing once more,
To ramble about the house and barn and over the fields once
more,
And through the orchard and along the old lanes once more.

O to have been brought up on bays, lagoons, creeks, or along
the coast,
To continue and be employ'd there all my life,
The briny and damp smell, the shore, the salt weeds exposed
at low water,
The work of fishermen, the work of the eel-fisher and clam-
fisher;
I come with my clam-rake and spade, I come with my eel-
spear,
Is the tide out? I join the group of clam-diggers on the flats,
I laugh and work with them, I joke at my work like a mettle-
some young man;
In winter I take my eel-basket and eel-spear and travel out on
foot on the ice—I have a small axe to cut
holes in the ice,
Behold me well-clothed going gayly or returning in the after-
noon, my brood of tough boys accompanying
me,
My brood of grown and part-grown boys, who love to be with
no one else so well as they love to be with me,
By day to work with me, and by night to sleep with me.

Another time in warm weather out in a boat, to lift the lobster-
pots where they are sunk with heavy stones,
(I know the buoys,)
O the sweetness of the Fifth-month morning upon the water
as I row just before sunrise toward the buoys,
I pull the wicker pots up slantingly, the dark green lobsters are
desperate with their claws as I take them out,
I insert wooden pegs in the joints of their
pincers,
I go to all the places one after another, and then row back to
the shore,
There in a huge kettle of boiling water the lobsters shall be
boil'd till their color becomes scarlet.

Another time mackerel-taking,
Voracious, mad for the hook, near the surface, they seem to
fill the water for miles;

Another time fishing for rock-fish in Chesapeake Bay, I one
    of the brown-faced crew;
Another time trailing for blue-fish off Paumanok, I stand with
    braced body,
My left foot is on the gunwale, my right arm throws far out
    the coils of slender rope,
In sight around me the quick veering and darting of fifty skiffs,
    my companions.

O boating on the rivers,
The voyage down the St. Lawrence, the superb scenery, the
    steamers,
The ships sailing, the Thousand Islands, the occasional timber-
    raft and the raftsmen with long-reaching
    sweep-oars,
The little huts on the rafts, and the stream of smoke when they
    cook supper at evening.

(O something pernicious and dread!
Something far away from a puny and pious life!
Something unproved! something in a trance!
Something escaped from the anchorage and driving free.)

O to work in mines, or forging iron,
Foundry casting, the foundry itself, the rude high roof, the
    ample and shadow'd space,
The furnace, the hot liquid pour'd out and running.

O to resume the joys of the soldier!
To feel the presence of a brave commanding officer—to feel
    his sympathy!
To behold his calmness—to be warm'd in the rays of his smile!
To go to battle—to hear the bugles play and the drums beat!
To hear the crash of artillery—to see the glittering of the bayo-
    nets and musket-barrels in the sun!
To see men fall and die and not complain!
To taste the savage taste of blood—to be so devilish!
To gloat so over the wounds and deaths of the enemy.

O the whaleman's joys! O I cruise my old cruise again!
I feel the ship's motion under me, I feel the Atlantic breezes
    fanning me,
I hear the cry again sent down from the mast-head, *There—she
    blows!*
Again I spring up the rigging to look with the rest—we de-
    scend, wild with excitement,
I leap in the lower'd boat, we row toward our prey where he
    lies,
We approach stealthy and silent, I see the mountainous mass,
    lethargic, basking,

I see the harpooner standing up, I see the weapon dart from
      his vigorous arm;
O swift again far out in the ocean the wounded whale, set-
      tling, running to windward, tows me,
Again I see him rise to breathe, we row close again,
I see a lance driven through his side, press'd deep, turn'd in the
      wound,
Again we back off, I see him settle again, the life is leaving him
      fast,
As he rises he spouts blood, I see him swim in circles narrower
      and narrower, swiftly cutting the water—I
      see him die,
He gives one convulsive leap in the centre of the circle, and
      then falls flat and still in the bloody foam.

O the old manhood of me, my noblest joy of all!
My children and grand-children, my white hair and beard,
My largeness, calmness, majesty, out of the long stretch of
      my life.

O ripn'd joy of womanhood! O happiness at last!
I am more than eighty years of age, I am the most venerable
      mother,
How clear is my mind—how all people draw nigh to me!
What attractions are these beyond any before? what bloom
      more than the bloom of youth?
What beauty is this that descends upon me and rises out of me?

O the orator's joys!
To inflate the chest, to roll the thunder of the voice out from
      the ribs and throat,
To make the people rage, weep, hate, desire, with yourself,
To lead America—to quell America with a great tongue.

O the joy of my soul leaning pois'd on itself, receiving identity
      through materials and loving them, observing
      characters and absorbing them,
My soul vibrated back to me from them, from sight, hearing,
      touch, reason, articulation, comparison,
      memory, and the like,
The real life of my senses and flesh transcending my senses and
      flesh,
My body done with materials, my sight done with my material
      eyes,
Proved to me this day beyond cavil that it is not my material
      eyes which finally see,
Nor my material body which finally loves, walks, laughs,
      shouts, embraces, procreates.

O the farmer's joys!
Ohioan's, Illinoisian's, Wisconsinese', Kanadian's, Iowan's,
      Kansian's, Missourian's, Oregonese' joys!

To rise at peep of day and pass forth nimbly to work,
To plough land in the fall for winter-sown crops,
To plough land in the spring for maize,
To train orchards, to graft the trees, to gather apples in the fall.

O to bathe in the swimming-bath, or in a good place along
    shore,
To splash the water! to walk ankle-deep, or race naked along
    the shore.

O to realize space!
The plenteousness of all, that there are no bounds,
To emerge and be of the sky, of the sun and moon and flying
    clouds, as one with them.

O the joy of a manly self-hood!
To be servile to none, to defer to none, not to any tyrant known
    or unknown,
To walk with erect carriage, a step springy and elastic,
To look with calm gaze or with a flashing eye,
To speak with a full and sonorous voice out of a broad chest,
To confront with your personality all the other personalities
    of the earth.

Know'st thou the excellent joys of youth?
Joys of the dear companions and of the merry word and laugh-
    ing face?
Joy of the glad light-beaming day, joy of the wide-breath'd
    games?
Joy of sweet music, joy of the lighted ball-room and the
    dancers?
Joy of the plenteous dinner, strong carouse and drinking?

Yet O my soul supreme!
Know'st thou the joys of pensive thought?
Joys of the free and lonesome heart, the tender, gloomy heart?
Joys of the solitary walk, the spirit bow'd yet proud, the suf-
    fering and the struggle?
The agonistic throes, the ecstasies, joys of the solemn musings
    day or night?
Joys of the thought of Death, the great spheres Time and
    Space?
Prophetic joys of better, loftier love's ideals, the divine wife,
    the sweet, eternal, perfect comrade?
Joys all thine own undying one, joys worthy thee O soul.
O while I live to be the ruler of life, not a slave,
To meet life as a powerful conqueror,
No fumes, no ennui, no more complaints or scornful criti-
    cisms,
To these proud laws of the air, the water and the ground,
    proving my interior soul impregnable,

And nothing exterior shall ever take command of me.

For not life's joys alone I sing, repeating—the joy of death!
The beautiful touch of Death, soothing and benumbing a few
          moments, for reasons,
Myself discharging my excrementitious body to be burn'd, or
          render'd to powder, or buried,
My real body doubtless left to me for other spheres,
My voided body nothing more to me, returning to the purifica-
          tions, further offices, eternal uses of the
          earth.

O to attract by more than attraction!
How it is I know not—yet behold! the something which obeys
          none of the rest,
It is offensive, never defensive—yet how magnetic it draws.

O to struggle against great odds, to meet enemies undaunted!
To be entirely alone with them, to find how much one can
          stand!
To look strife, torture, prison, popular odium, face to face!
To mount the scaffold, to advance to the muzzles of guns with
          perfect nonchalance!
To be indeed a God!

O to sail to sea in a ship!
To leave this steady unendurable land,
To leave the tiresome sameness of the streets, the sidewalks
          and the houses,
To leave you O you solid motionless land, and entering a ship,
To sail and sail and sail!

O to have life henceforth a poem of new joys!
To dance, clap hands, exult, shout, skip, leap, roll on, float on!
To be a sailor of the world bound for all ports,
A ship itself, (see indeed these sails I spread to the sun and
          air,)
A swift and swelling ship full of rich words, full of joys.

SONG OF THE BROAD-AXE

1

Weapon shapely, naked, wan,
Head from the mother's bowels drawn,
Wooded flesh and metal bone, limb only one and lip only one,
Gray-blue leaf by red-heat grown, helve produced from a little
          seed sown,
Resting the grass amid and upon,
To be lean'd and to lean on.

Strong shapes and attributes of strong shapes, masculine trades,
       sights and sounds,
Long varied train of an emblem, dabs of music,
Fingers of the organist skipping staccato over the keys of the
       great organ.

2

Welcome are all earth's lands, each for its kind,
Welcome are lands of pine and oak,
Welcome are lands of the lemon and fig,
Welcome are lands of gold,
Welcome are lands of wheat and maize, welcome those of the
       grape,
Welcome are lands of sugar and rice,
Welcome the cotton-lands, welcome those of the white potato
       and sweet potato,
Welcome are mountains, flats, sands, forests, prairies,
Welcome the rich borders of rivers, table-lands, openings,
Welcome the measureless grazing-lands, welcome the teeming
       soil of orchards, flax, honey, hemp;
Welcome just as much the other more hard-faced lands,
Lands rich as lands of gold or wheat and fruit lands,
Lands of mines, lands of the manly and rugged ores,
Lands of coal, copper, lead, tin, zinc,
Lands of iron—lands of the make of the axe.

3

The log at the wood-pile, the axe supported by it,
The sylvan hut, the vine over the doorway, the space clear'd
       for a garden,
The irregular tapping of rain down on the leaves after the
       storm is lull'd,
The wailing and moaning at intervals, the thought of the sea,
The thought of ships struck in the storm and put on their
       beam ends, and the cutting away of masts,
The sentiment of the huge timbers of old-fashion'd houses and
       barns,
The remember'd print or narrative, the voyage at a venture
       of men, families, goods,
The disembarkation, the founding of a new city,
The voyage of those who sought a New England and found
       it, the outset anywhere,
The settlements of the Arkansas, Colorado, Ottawa, Willa-
       mette,
The slow progress, the scant fare, the axe, rifle, saddle-bags;
The beauty of all adventurous and daring persons,
The beauty of wood-boys and wood-men with their clear un-
       trimm'd faces,

The beauty of independence, departure, actions that rely on
    themselves,
The American contempt for statutes and ceremonies, the
    boundless impatience of restraint,
The loose drift of character, the inkling through random types,
    the solidification;
The butcher in the slaughter-house, the hands aboard schoon-
    ers and sloops, the raftsman, the pioneer,
Lumbermen in their winter camp, daybreak in the woods,
    stripes of snow on the limbs of trees, the
    occasional snapping,
The glad clear sound of one's own voice, the merry song, the
    natural life of the woods, the strong day's
    work,
The blazing fire at night, the sweet taste of supper, the talk,
    the bed of hemlock-boughs and the bear-skin;
The house-builder at work in cities or anywhere,
The preparatory jointing, squaring, sawing, mortising,
The hoist-up of beams, the push of them in their places, laying
    them regular,
Setting the studs by their tenons in the mortises according as
    they were prepared,
The blows of mallets and hammers, the attitudes of the men,
    their curv'd limbs,
Bending, standing, astride the beams, driving in pins, holding
    on by posts and braces,
The hook'd arm over the plate, the other arm wielding the axe,
The floor-men forcing the planks close to be nail'd,
Their postures bringing their weapons downward on the bear-
    ers,
The echoes resounding through the vacant building;
The huge storehouse carried up in the city well under way,
The six framing-men, two in the middle and two at each end,
    carefully bearing on their shoulders a heavy
    stick for a cross-beam,
The crowded line of masons with trowels in their right hands
    rapidly laying the long side-wall, two hun-
    dred feet from front to rear,
The flexible rise and fall of backs, the continual click of the
    trowels striking the bricks,
The bricks one after another each laid so workmanlike in its
    place, and set with a knock of the trowel-
    handle,
The piles of materials, the mortar on the mortar-boards, and
    the steady replenishing by the hod-men;
Spar-makers in the spar-yard, the swarming row of well-grown
    apprentices,
The swing of their axes on the square-hew'd log shaping it
    toward the shape of a mast,

The brisk short crackle of the steel driven slantingly into the
        pine,
The butter-color'd chips flying off in great flakes and slivers,
The limber motion of brawny young arms and hips in easy
        costumes,
The constructor of wharves, bridges, piers, bulk-heads, floats,
        stays against the sea;
The city fireman, the fire that suddenly bursts forth in the
        close-pack'd square,
The arriving engines, the hoarse shouts, the nimble stepping
        and daring,
The strong command through the fire-trumpets, the falling
        in line, the rise and fall of the arms forcing
        the water,
The slender, spasmic, blue-white jets, the bringing to bear of
        the hooks and ladders and their execution,
The crash and cut away of connecting wood-work, or through
        floors if the fire smoulders under them,
The crowd with their lit faces watching, the glare and dense
        shadows;
The forger at his forge-furnace and the user of iron after him,
The maker of the axe large and small, and the welder and
        temperer,
The chooser breathing his breath on the cold steel and trying
        the edge with his thumb,
The one who clean-shapes the handle and sets it firmly in the
        socket;
The shadowy processions of the portraits of the past users also,
The primal patient mechanics, the architects and engineers,
The far-off Assyrian edifice and Mizra edifice,
The Roman lictors preceding the consuls,
The antique European warrior with his axe in combat,
The uplifted arm, the clatter of blows on the helmeted head,
The death-howl, the limpsy tumbling body, the rush of friend
        and foe thither,
The siege of revolted lieges determin'd for liberty,
The summons to surrender, the battering at castle gates, the
        truce and parley,
The sack of an old city in its time,
The bursting in of mercenaries and bigots tumultuously and
        disorderly,
Roar, flames, blood, drunkenness, madness,
Goods freely rifled from houses and temples, screams of
        women in the grip of brigands,
Craft and thievery of camp-followers, men running, old per-
        sons despairing,
The hell of war, the cruelties of creeds,
The list of all executive deeds and words just or unjust,
The power of personality just or unjust.

4

Muscle and pluck forever!
What invigorates life invigorates death,
And the dead advance as much as the living advance,
And the future is no more uncertain than the present,
For the roughness of the earth and of man encloses as much as
        the delicatesse of the earth and of man,
And nothing endures but personal qualities.

What do you think endures?
Do you think a great city endures?
Or a teeming manufacturing state? or a prepared constitution?
        or the best-built steamships?
Or hotels of granite and iron? or any chef-d'œuvres of engi-
        neering, forts, armaments?
Away! these are not to be cherish'd for themselves,
They fill their hour, the dancers dance, the musicians play for
        them,
The show passes, all does well enough of course,
All does very well till one flash of defiance.

A great city is that which has the greatest men and women,
If it be a few ragged huts it is still the greatest city in the
        whole world.

5

The place where a great city stands is not the place of stretch'd
        wharves, docks, manufactures, deposits of
        produce merely,
Nor the place of ceaseless salutes of new-comers or the anchor-
        lifters of the departing,
Nor the place of the tallest and costliest buildings or shops sell-
        ing goods from the rest of the earth,
Nor the place of the best libraries and schools, nor the place
        where money is plentiest,
Nor the place of the most numerous population.

Where the city stands with the brawniest breed of orators and
        bards,
Where the city stands that is belov'd by these, and loves them
        in return and understands them,
Where no monuments exist to heroes but in the common words
        and deeds,
Where thrift is in its place, and prudence is in its place,
Where the men and women think lightly of the laws,
Where the slave ceases, and the master of slaves ceases,
Where the populace rise at once against the never-ending
        audacity of elected persons,
Where fierce men and women pour forth as the sea to the

whistle of death pours its sweeping and unript
waves,
Where outside authority enters always after the precedence of
inside authority,
Where the citizen is always the head and ideal, and President,
Mayor, Governor and what not, are agents
for pay,
Where children are taught to be laws to themselves, and to
depend on themselves,
Where equanimity is illustrated in affairs,
Where speculations on the soul are encouraged,
Where women walk in public processions in the streets the
same as the men,
Where they enter the public assembly and take places the same
as the men;
Where the city of the faithfulest friends stands,
Where the city of the cleanliness of the sexes stands,
Where the city of the healthiest fathers stands,
Where the city of the best-bodied mothers stands,
There the great city stands.

6

How beggarly appear arguments before a defiant deed!
How the floridness of the materials of cities shrivels before a
man's or woman's look!

All waits or goes by default till a strong being appears;
A strong being is the proof of the race and of the ability of
the universe,
When he or she appears materials are overaw'd,
The dispute on the soul stops,
The old customs and phrases are confronted, turn'd back, or
laid away.

What is your money-making now? what can it do now?
What is your respectability now?
What are your theology, tuition, society, traditions, statute-
books, now?
Where are your jibes of being now?
Where are your cavils about the soul now?

7

A sterile landscape covers the ore, there is as good as the best
for all the forbidding appearance,
There is the mine, there are the miners,
The forge-furnace is there, the melt is accomplish'd, the ham-
mers-men are at hand with their tongs and
hammers,
What always served and always serves is at hand.
Than this nothing has better served, it has served all,

Served the fluent-tongued and subtle-sensed Greek, and long
 ere the Greek,
Served in building the buildings that last longer than any,
Served the Hebrew, the Persian, the most ancient Hindu-
 stanee,
Served the mound-raiser on the Mississippi, served those whose
 relics remain in Central America,
Served Albic temples in woods or on plains, with unhewn
 pillars and the druids,
Served artificial clefts, vast, high, silent, on the snow-cover'd
 hills of Scandinavia,
Served those who time out of mind made on the granite walls
 rough sketches of the sun, moon, stars, ships,
 ocean waves,
Served the paths of the irruptions of the Goths, served the
 pastoral tribes and nomads,
Served the long distant Kelt, served the hardy pirates of the
 Baltic,
Served before any of those the venerable and harmless men of
 Ethiopia,
Served the making of helms for the galleys of pleasure and
 the making of those for war,
Served all great works on land and all great works on the sea,
For the mediæval ages and before the mediæval ages,
Served not the living only then as now, but served the dead.

8

I see the European headsman,
He stands mask'd, clothed in red, with huge legs and strong
 naked arms,
And leans on a ponderous axe.

(Whom have you slaughter'd lately European headsman?
Whose is that blood upon you so wet and sticky?)

I see the clear sunsets of the martyrs,
I see from the scaffolds the descending ghosts,
Ghosts of dead lords, uncrown'd ladies, impeach'd ministers,
 rejected kings,
Rivals, traitors, poisoners, disgraced chieftains and the rest.

I see those who in any land have died for the good cause,
The seed is spare, nevertheless the crop shall never run out,
(Mind you O foreign kings, O priests, the crop shall never run
 out.)

I see the blood wash'd entirely away from the axe,
Both blade and helve are clean,
They spirt no more the blood of European nobles, they clasp
 no more the necks of queens.

I see the headsman withdraw and become useless,
I see the scaffold untrodden and mouldy, I see no longer any
        axe upon it,
I see the mighty and friendly emblem of the power of my own
        race, the newest, largest race.

9

(America! I do not vaunt my love for you,
I have what I have.)

The axe leaps!
The solid forest gives fluid utterances,
They tumble forth, they rise and form,
Hut, tent, landing, survey,
Flail, plough, pick, crowbar, spade,
Shingle, rail, prop, wainscot, jamb, lath, panel, gable,
Citadel, ceiling, saloon, academy, organ, exhibition-house, li-
        brary,
Cornice, trellis, pilaster, balcony, window, turret, porch,
Hoe, rake, pitchfork, pencil, wagon, staff, saw, jack-plane,
        mallet, wedge, rounce,
Chair, tub, hoop, table, wicket, vane, sash, floor,
Work-box, chest, string'd instrument, boat, frame, and what
        not,
Capitols of States, and capitol of the nation of States,
Long stately rows in avenues, hospitals for orphans or for the
        poor or sick,
Manhattan steamboats and clippers taking the measure of all
        seas.

The shapes arise!
Shapes of the using of axes anyhow, and the users and all that
        neighbors them,
Cutters down of wood and haulers of it to the Penobscot or
        Kennebec,
Dwellers in cabins among the Californian mountains or by the
        little lakes, or on the Columbia,
Dwellers south on the banks of the Gila or Rio Grande,
        friendly gatherings, the characters and fun,
Dwellers along the St. Lawrence, or north in Kanada, or down
        by the Yellowstone, dwellers on coasts and
        off coasts,
Seal-fishers, whalers, arctic seamen breaking passages through
        the ice.

The shapes arise!
Shapes of factories, arsenals, foundries, markets,
Shapes of the two-threaded tracks of railroads,
Shapes of the sleepers of bridges, vast frameworks, girders,
        arches,

Shapes of the fleets of barges, tows, lake and canal craft, river craft,

Ship-yards and dry-docks along the Eastern and Western seas, and in many a bay and by-place,

The live-oak kelsons, the pine planks, the spars, the hackmatack-roots for knees,

The ships themselves on their ways, the tiers of scaffolds, the workmen busy outside and inside,

The tools lying around, the great auger and little auger, the adze, bolt, line, square, gouge, and bead-plane.

10

The shapes arise!

The shape measur'd, saw'd, jack'd, join'd, stain'd,

The coffin-shape for the dead to lie within in his shroud,

The shape got out in posts, in the bedstead posts, in the posts of the bride's bed,

The shape of the little trough, the shape of the rockers beneath, the shape of the babe's cradle,

The shape of the floor-planks, the floor-planks for dancer's feet,

The shape of the planks of the family home, the home of the friendly parents and children,

The shape of the roof of the home of the happy young man and woman, the roof over the well-married young man and woman,

The roof over the supper joyously cook'd by the chaste wife, and joyously eaten by the chaste husband, content after his day's work.

The shapes arise!

The shape of the prisoner's place in the court-room, and of him or her seated in the place,

The shape of the liquor-bar lean'd against by the young rum-drinker and the old rum-drinker,

The shape of the shamed and angry stairs trod by sneaking footsteps,

The shape of the sly settee, and the adulterous unwholesome couple,

The shape of the gambling-board with its devilish winnings and losings,

The shape of the step-ladder for the convicted and sentenced murderer, the murderer with haggard face and pinion'd arms,

The sheriff at hand with his deputies, the silent and white-lipp'd crowd, the dangling of the rope.

The shapes arise!
Shapes of doors giving many exits and entrances,
The door passing the dissever'd friend flush'd and in haste,
The door that admits good news and bad news,
The door whence the son left home confident and puff'd up,
The door he enter'd again from a long and scandalous ab-
           sence, diseas'd, broken down, without in-
           nocence, without means.

11

Her shape arises,
She less guarded than ever, yet more guarded than ever,
The gross and soil'd she moves among do not make her gross
           and soil'd,
She knows the thoughts as she passes, nothing is conceal'd
           from her,
She is none the less considerate or friendly therefor,
She is the best belov'd, it is without exception, she has no
           reason to fear and she does not fear,
Oaths, quarrels, hiccupp'd songs, smutty expressions are idle
           to her as she passes,
She is silent, she is possess'd of herself, they do not offend her,
She receives them as the laws of Nature receive them, she is
           strong,
She too is a law of Nature—there is no law stronger than she is.

12

The main shapes arise!
Shapes of Democracy total, result of centuries,
Shapes ever projecting other shapes,
Shapes of turbulent manly cities,
Shapes of the friends and home-givers of the whole earth,
Shapes bracing the earth and braced with the whole earth.

SONG OF THE EXPOSITION

1

(Ah little recks the laborer,
How near his work is holding him to God.
The loving Laborer through space and time.)

After all not to create only, or found only,
But to bring perhaps from afar what is already founded,
To give it our own identity, average, limitless, free,
To fill the gross the torpid bulk with vital religious fire,
Not to repel or destroy so much as accept, fuse, rehabilitate,
To obey as well as command, to follow more than to lead,
These also are the lessons of our New World;
While how little the New after all, how much the Old, Old
           World!

Long and long has the green been growing,
Long and long has the rain been falling,
Long has the globe been rolling round.

2

Come Muse migrate from Greece and Ionia,
Cross out please those immensely overpaid accounts,
That matter of Troy and Achilles wrath, and Æneas', Odys-
        seus' wanderings,
Placard "Removed" and "To Let" on the rocks of your snowy
        Parnassus,
Repeat at Jerusalem, place the notice high on Jaffa's gate and
        on Mount Moriah,
The same on the walls of your German, French and Spanish
        castles, and Italian collections,
For know a better, fresher, busier sphere, a wide, untried
        domain awaits, demands you.

3

Responsive to our summons,
Or rather to her long-nurs'd inclination,
Join'd with an irresistible, natural gravitation,
She comes! I hear the rustling of her gown,
I scent the odor of her breath's delicious fragrance,
I mark her step divine, her curious eyes a-turning, rolling,
Upon this very scene.

The dame of dames! can I believe then,
Thos ancient temples, sculptures classic, could none of them
        retain her?
Nor shades of Virgil and Dante, nor myriad memories, poems,
        old associations, magnetize and hold on to
        her?
But that she's left them all—and here?

Yes, if you will allow me to say so,
I, my friends, if you do not, can plainly see her,
The same undying soul of earth's, activity's, beauty's, heroism's
        expression,
Out from her evolutions hither come, ended the strata of her
        former themes,
Hidden and cover'd by to-day's, foundation of to-day's,
Ended, deceas'd through time, her voice by Castaly's foun-
        tain,
Silent the broken-lipp'd Sphynx in Egypt, silent all those cen-
        tury-baffling tombs,
Ended for aye the epics of Asia's, Europe's helmeted warriors,
        ended the primitive call of the muses,
Calliope's call forever closed, Clio, Melpomene, Thalia dead,

Ended the stately rhythmus of Una and Oriana, ended the
        quest of the Holy Graal,
Jerusalem a handful of ashes blown by the wind, extinct,
The Crusaders' streams of shadowy midnight troops sped with
        the sunrise,
Amadis, Tancred, utterly gone, Charlemagne, Roland, Oliver
        gone,
Palmerin, ogre, departed, vanish'd the turrets that Usk from
        its waters reflected,
Arthur vanish'd with all his knights, Merlin and Lancelot and
        Galahad, all gone, dissolv'd utterly like an
        exhalation;
Pass'd! pass'd! for us, forever pass'd, that once so mighty
        world, now void, inanimate, phantom world,
Embroider'd, dazzling, foreign world, with all its gorgeous
        legends, myths,
Its kings and castles proud, its priests and warlike lords and
        courtly dames,
Pass'd to its charnal vault, coffin'd with crown and armor on,
Blazon'd with Shakspere's purple page,
And dirged by Tennyson's sweet sad rhyme.

I say I see, my friends, if you do not, the illustrious emigré,
        (having it is true in her day, although the
        same, changed, journey'd considerable,)
Making directly for this rendezvous, vigorously clearing a path
        for herself, striding through the confusion,
By thud of machinery and shrill steam-whistle undismay'd,
Bluff'd not a bit by drain-pipe, gasometers, artificial fertilizers,
Smiling and pleas'd with palpable intent to stay,
She's here, install'd amid the kitchen ware!

4

But hold—don't I forget my manners?
To introduce the stranger, (what else indeed do I live to chant
        for?) to thee Columbia!
In liberty's name welcome immortal! clasp hands,
And ever henceforth sisters dear be both.

Fear not O Muse! truly new ways and days receive, surround
        you,
I candidly confess a queer, queer race, of novel fashion,
And yet the same old human race, the same within, without,
Faces and hearts the same, feelings the same, yearnings the
        same,
The same old love, beauty and use the same.

5

We do not blame thee elder World, nor really separate our-
        selves from thee,

(Would the son separate himself from the father?)
Looking back on thee, seeing thee to thy duties, grandeurs,
          through past ages bending, building,
We build to ours to-day.

Mightier than Egypt's tombs,
Fairer than Grecia's, Roma's temples,
Prouder than Milan's statued, spired cathedral,
More picturesque than Rhenish castle-keeps,
We plan even now to raise, beyond them all,
Thy great cathedral sacred industry, no tomb,
A keep for life for practical invention.

As in a waking vision,
E'en while I chant I see it rise, I scan and prophesy outside
          and in,
Its manifold ensemble.

Around a palace, loftier, fairer, ampler than any yet,
Earth's modern wonder, history's seven outstripping,
High rising tier on tier with glass and iron façades,
Gladdening the sun and sky, enhued in cheerfulest hues,
Bronze, lilac, robin's-egg, marine and crimson,
Over whose golden roof shall flaunt, beneath thy banner Free-
          dom,
The banners of the States and flags of every land,
A brood of lofty, fair, but lesser palaces shall cluster.

Somewhere within their walls shall all that forwards perfect
          human life be started,
Tried, taught, advanced, visibly exhibited.

Not only all the world of works, trade, products,
But all the workmen of the world here to be represented.

Here shall you trace in flowing operation,
In every state of practical, busy movement, the rills of civiliza-
          tion,
Materials here under your eye shall change their shape as if
          by magic,
The cotton shall be pick'd almost in the very field,
Shall be dried, clean'd, ginn'd, baled, spun into thread and
          cloth before you,
You shall see hands at work at all the old processes and all
          the new ones,
You shall see the various grains and how flour is made and
          then bread baked by the bakers,
You shall see the crude ores of California and Nevada passing
          on and on till they become bullion,
You shall watch how the printer sets type, and learn what a
          composing-stick is,

You shall mark in amazement the Hoe press whirling its cyl-
    inders, shedding the printed leaves steady
    and fast,
The photograph, model, watch, pin, nail, shall be created
    before you.

In large calm halls, a stately museum shall teach you the infi-
    nite lessons of minerals,
In another, woods, plants, vegetation shall be illustrated—in
    another animals, animal life and develop-
    ment.

One stately house shall be the music house,
Others for other arts—learning, the sciences, shall all be here,
None shall be slighted, none but shall here be honor'd, help'd,
    exampled.

6

(This, this and these, America, shall be *your* pyramids and
    obelisks,
Your Alexandrian Pharos, gardens of Babylon,
Your temple at Olympia.)

The male and female many laboring not,
Shall ever here confront the laboring many,
With precious benefits to both, glory to all,
To thee America, and thee eternal Muse.

And here shall ye inhabit powerful Matrons!
In your vast state vaster than all the old,
Echoed through long, long centuries to come,
To sound of different, prouder songs, with stronger themes,
Practical, peaceful life, the people's life, the People themselves,
Lifted, illumin'd, bathed in peace—elate, secure in peace.

7

Away with themes of war! away with war itself!
Hence from my shuddering sight to never more return that
    show of blacken'd, mutilated corpses!
That hell unpent and raid of blood, fit for wild tigers or for
    lop-tongued wolves, not reasoning men,
And in its stead speed industry's campaigns,
With thy undaunted armies, engineering,
Thy pennants labor, loosen'd to the breeze,
Thy bugles sounding loud and clear.

Away with old romance!
Away with novels, plots and plays of foreign courts,
Away with love-verses sugar'd in rhyme, the intrigues, amours
    of idlers,

Fitted for only banquets of the night where dancers to late
    music slide,
The unhealthy pleasures, extravagant dissipations of the few,
With perfumes, heat and wine, beneath the dazzling chande-
    liers.

To you ye reverent sane sisters,
I raise a voice for far superber themes for poets and for art,
To exalt the present and the real,
To teach the average man the glory of his daily walk and trade,
To sing in songs how exercise and chemical life are never to
    be baffled,
To manual work for each and all, to plough, hoe, dig,
To plant and tend the tree, the berry, vegetables, flowers,
For every man to see to it that he really do something, for
    every woman too;
To use the hammer and the saw, (rip, or cross-cut,)
To cultivate a turn for carpentering, plastering, painting,
To work as tailor, tailoress, nurse, hostler, porter,
To invent a little, something ingenious, to aid the washing,
    cooking, cleaning,
And hold it no disgrace to take a hand at them themselves.

I say I bring thee Muse to-day and here,
All occupations, duties broad and close,
Toil, healthy toil and sweat, endless, without cessation,
The old, old practical burdens, interests, joys,
The family, parentage, childhood, husband and wife,
The house-comforts, the house itself and all its belongings,
Food and its preservation, chemistry applied to it,
Whatever forms the average, strong, complete, sweet-blooded
    man or woman, the perfect longeve person-
    ality,
And helps its present life to health and happiness, and shapes
    its soul,
For the eternal real life to come.

With latest connections, works, the inter-transportation of the
    world,
Steam-power, the great express lines, gas, petroleum,
These triumphs of our time, the Atlantic's delicate cable,
The Pacific railroad, the Suez canal, the Mont Cenis and
    Gothard and Hoosac tunnels, the Brooklyn
    bridge,
This earth all spann'd with iron rails, with lines of steamships
    threading every sea,
Our own rondure, the current globe I bring.

8

And thou America,
Thy offspring towering e'er so high, yet higher Thee above all
          towering,
With Victory on thy left, and at thy right hand Law;
Thou Union holding all, fusing, absorbing, tolerating all,
Thee, ever thee, I sing.

Thou, also thou, a World,
With all thy wide geographies, manifold, different, distant,
Rounded by thee in one—one common orbic language,
One common indivisible destiny for All.

And by the spells which ye vouchsafe to those your ministers
          in earnest,
I here personify and call my themes, to make them pass before
          ye.

Behold, America! (and thou, ineffable guest and sister!)
For thee come trooping up thy waters and thy lands;
Behold! thy fields and farms, thy far-off woods and mountains,
As in procession coming.

Behold, the sea itself,
And on its limitless, heaving breast, the ships;
See, where their white sails, bellying in the wind, speckle the
          green and blue,
See, the steamers coming and going, steaming in or out of port,
See, dusky and undulating, the long pennants of smoke.

Behold, in Oregon, far in the north and west,
Or in Maine, far in the north and east, thy cheerful axemen,
Wielding all day their axes.

Behold, on the lakes, thy pilots at their wheels, thy oarsmen,
How the ash writhes under those muscular arms!
There by the furnace, and there by the anvil,
Behold thy sturdy blacksmiths swinging their sledges,
Overhand so steady, overhand they turn and fall with joyous
          clank,
Like a tumult of laughter.

Mark the spirit of invention everywhere, thy rapid patents,
Thy continual workshops, foundries, risen or rising,
See, from their chimneys how the tall flame-fires stream.

Mark, thy interminable farms, North, South,
Thy wealthy daughter-states, Eastern and Western,
The varied products of Ohio, Pennsylvania, Missouri, Geor-
          gia, Texas, and the rest,
Thy limitless crops, grass, wheat, sugar, oil, corn, rice, hemp,
          hops,

Thy barns all fill'd, the endless freight-train and the bulging
    storehouse,
The grapes that ripen on thy vines, the apples in thy orchards,
Thy incalculable lumber, beef, pork, potatoes, thy coal, thy
    gold and silver,
The inexhaustible iron in thy mines.

All thine, O sacred Union!
Ships, farms, shops, barns, factories, mines,
City and State, North, South, item and aggregate,
We dedicate, dread Mother, all to thee!

Protectress absolute, thou! bulwark of all!
For well we know that while thou givest each and all, (gen-
    erous as God,)
Without thee neither all nor each, nor land, home,
Nor ship, nor mine, nor any here this day secure,
Nor aught, nor any day secure.

9

And thou, the Emblem waving over all!
Delicate beauty, a word to thee, (it may be salutary,)
Remember thou hast not always been as here to-day so com-
    fortably ensovereign'd,
In other scenes than these have I observ'd thee flag,
Not quite so trim and whole and freshly blooming in folds of
    stainless silk,
But I have seen thee bunting, to tatters torn upon thy splin-
    ter'd staff,
Or clutch'd to some young color-bearer's breast with desper-
    ate hands,
Savagely struggled for, for life or death, fought over long,
'Mid cannons' thunder-crash and many a curse and groan and
    yell, and rifle-volleys cracking sharp,
And moving masses as wild demons surging, and lives as noth-
    ing risk'd,
For thy mere remnant grimed with dirt and smoke and sopp'd
    in blood,
For sake of that, my beauty, and that thou might'st dally as
    now secure up there,
Many a good man have I seen go under.

Now here and these and hence in peace, all thine, O flag!
And here and hence for thee, O universal Muse! and thou for
    them!
And here and hence O Union, all the work and workmen
    thine!
None separate from thee—henceforth One only, we and thou,
(For the blood of the children, what is it, only the blood
    maternal?

And lives and works, what are they all at last, except the roads
        to faith and death?)

While we rehearse our measureless wealth, it is for thee, dear
        Mother,
We own it all and several to-day indissoluble in thee;
Think not our chant, our show, merely for products gross or
        lucre—it is for thee, the soul in thee, electric,
        spiritual!
Our farms, inventions, crops, we own in thee! cities and States
        in thee!
Our freedom all in thee! our very lives in thee!

SONG OF THE REDWOOD-TREE

1

A California song,
A prophecy and indirection, a thought impalpable to breathe
        as air,
A chorus of dryads, fading, departing, or hamadryads depart-
        ing,
A murmuring, fateful, giant voice, out of the earth and sky,
Voice of a mighty dying tree in the redwood forest dense.

Farewell my brethren,
Farewell O earth and sky, farewell ye neighboring waters,
My time has ended, my term has come.

Along the northern coast,
Just back from the rock-bound shore and the caves,
In the saline air from the sea in the Mendocino country,
With the surge for base and accompaniment low and hoarse,
With crackling blows of axes sounding musically driven by
        strong arms,
Riven deep by the sharp tongues of the axes, there in the red-
        wood forest dense,
I heard the mighty tree its death-chant chanting.

The choppers heard not, the camp shanties echoed not,
The quick-ear'd teamsters and chain and jack-screw men
        heard not,
As the wood-spirits came from their haunts of a thousand
        years to join the refrain,
But in my soul I plainly heard.

Murmuring out of its myriad leaves,
Down from its lofty top rising two hundred feet high,
Out of its stalwart trunk and limbs, out of its foot-thick bark,
That chant of the seasons and time, chant not of the past only
        but the future.

You untold life of me,
And all you venerable and innocent joys,
Perennial hardy life of me with joys 'mid rain and many a
*   summer sun,*
And the white snows and night and the wild winds;
O the great patient rugged joys, my soul's strong joys unreck'd
*   by man,*
(For know I bear the soul befitting me, I too have conscious-
*   ness, identity,*
And all the rocks and mountains have, and all the earth,)
Joys of the life befitting me and brothers mine,
Our time, our term has come.

Nor yield we mournfully majestic brothers,
We who have grandly fill'd our time;
With Nature's calm content, with tacit huge delight,
We welcome what we wrought for through the past,
And leave the field for them.

For them predicted long,
For a superber race, they too to grandly fill their time,
For them we abdicate, in them ourselves ye forest kings!
In them these skies and airs, these mountain peaks, Shasta,
*   Nevadas,*
These huge precipitous cliffs, this amplitude, these valleys, far
*   Yosemite,*
To be in them absorb'd, assimilated.

Then to a loftier strain,
Still prouder, more ecstatic rose the chant,
As if the heirs, the deities of the West,
Joining with master-tongue bore part.

Not wan from Asia's fetiches,
Nor red from Europe's old dynastic slaughter-house,
(Area of murder-plots of thrones, with scent left yet of wars
*   and scaffolds everywhere,)*
But come from Nature's long and harmless throes, peacefully
*   builded thence,*
These virgin lands, lands of the Western shore,
To the new culminating man, to you, the empire new,
You promis'd long, we pledge, we dedicate.

You occult deep volitions,
You average spiritual manhood, purpose of all, pois'd on your-
*   self, giving not taking law,*
You womanhood divine, mistress and source of all, whence life
*   and love and aught that comes from life and*
*   love,*

You unseen moral essence of all the vast materials of America,
           (age upon age working in death the same as
           life,)
You that, sometimes known, oftener unknown, really shape
           and mould the New World, adjusting it to
           Time and Space,
You hidden national will lying in your abysms, conceal'd but
           ever alert,
You past and present purposes tenaciously pursued, may-be
           unconscious of yourselves,
Unswerv'd by all the passing errors, perturbations of the sur-
           face;
You vital, universal, deathless germs, beneath all creeds, arts,
           statutes, literatures,
Here build your homes for good, establish here, these areas
           entire, lands of the Western shore,
We pledge, we dedicate to you.

For man of you, your characteristic race,
Here may he hardy, sweet, gigantic grow, here tower propor-
           tionate to Nature,
Here climb the vast pure spaces unconfined, uncheck'd by wall
           or roof,
Here laugh with storm or sun, here joy, here patiently inure,
Here heed himself, unfold himself, (not others' formulas heed,)
           here fill his time,
To duty fall, to aid, unreck'd at last,
To disappear, to serve.

Thus on the northern coast,
In the echo of teamsters' calls and the clinking chains, and the
           music of choppers' axes,
The falling trunk and limbs, the crash, the muffled shriek, the
           groan,
Such words combined from the redwood-tree, as of voices
           ecstatic, ancient and rustling,
The century-lasting, unseen dryads, singing, withdrawing,
All their recesses of forests and mountains leaving,
From the Cascade range to the Wasatch, or Idaho far, or
           Utah,
To the deities of the modern henceforth yielding,
The chorus and indications, the vistas of coming humanity,
           the settlements, features all,
In the Mendocino woods I caught.

2

The flashing and golden pageant of California,
The sudden and gorgeous drama, the sunny and ample lands,
The long and varied stretch from Puget sound to Colorado
           south,

Lands bathed in sweeter, rarer, healthier air, valleys and
    mountain cliffs,
The fields of Nature long prepared and fallow, the silent, cyclic
    chemistry,
The slow and steady ages plodding, the unoccupied surface
    ripening, the rich ores forming beneath;
At last the New arriving, assuming, taking possession,
A swarming and busy race settling and organizing everywhere,
Ships coming in from the whole round world, and going out
    to the whole world,
To India and China and Australia and the thousand island
    paradises of the Pacific,
Populous cities, the latest inventions, the steamers on the
    rivers, the railroads, with many a thrifty
    farm, with machinery,
And wool and wheat and the grape, and diggings of yellow
    gold.

3

But more in you than these, lands of the Western shore,
(These but the means, the implements, the standing-ground,)
I see in you, certain to come, the promise of thousands of
    years, till now deferr'd,
Promis'd to be fulfill'd, our common kind, the race.

The new society at last, proportionate to Nature,
In man of you, more than your mountain peaks or stalwart
    trees imperial,
In woman more, far more, than all your gold or vines, or even
    vital air.

Fresh come, to a new world indeed, yet long prepared,
I see the genius of the modern, child of the real and ideal,
Clearing the ground for broad humanity, the true America,
    heir of the past so grand,
To build a grander future.

A SONG FOR OCCUPATIONS

1

A song for occupations!
In the labor of engines and trades and the labor of fields I find
    the developments,
And find the eternal meanings.

Workmen and Workwomen!
Were all educations practical and ornamental well display'd
    out of me, what would it amount to?

Were I as the head teacher, charitable proprietor, wise states-
        man, what would it amount to?
Were I to you as the boss employing and paying you, would
        that satisfy you?

The learn'd, virtuous, benevolent, and the usual terms,
A man like me and never the usual terms.

Neither a servant nor a master I,
I take no sooner a large price than a small price, I will have
        my own whoever enjoys me,
I will be even with you and you shall be even with me.

If you stand at work in a shop I stand as nigh as the nighest
        in the same shop,
If you bestow gifts on your brother or dearest friend I demand
        as good as your brother or dearest friend,
If your lover, husband, wife, is welcome by day or night, I
        must be personally as welcome,
If you become degraded, criminal, ill, then I become so for
        your sake,
If you remember your foolish and outlaw'd deeds, do you
        think I cannot remember my own foolish
        and outlaw'd deeds?
If you carouse at the table I carouse at the opposite side of
        the table,
If you meet some stranger in the streets and love him or her,
        why I often meet strangers in the street and
        love them.

Why what have you thought of yourself?
Is it you then that thought yourself less?
Is it you that thought the President greater than you?
Or the rich better off than you? or the educated wiser than
        you?

(Because you are greasy or pimpled, or were once drunk, or a
        thief,
Or that you are diseas'd, or rheumatic, or a prostitute,
Or from frivolity or impotence, or that you are no scholar and
        never saw your name in print,
Do you give in that you are any less immortal?)

2

Souls of men and women! it is not you I call unseen, unheard,
        untouchable and untouching,
It is not you I go argue pro and con about, and to settle
        whether you are alive or no,
I own publicly who you are, if nobody else owns.

Grown, half-grown and babe, of this country and every coun-
   try, doors and out-doors, one just as much as
   the other, I see,
And all else behind or through them.

The wife, and she is not one jot less than the husband,
The daughter, and she is just as good as the son,
The mother, and she is every bit as much as the father.

Offspring of ignorant and poor, boys apprenticed to trades,
Young fellows working on farms and old fellows working on
   farms,
Sailor-men, merchant-men, coasters, immigrants,
All these I see, but nigher and farther the same I see,
None shall escape me and none shall wish to escape me.

I bring what you much need yet always have,
Not money, amours, dress, eating, erudition, but as good,
I send no agent or medium, offer no representative of value,
   but offer the value itself.

There is something that comes to one now and perpetually,
It is not what is printed, preach'd, discussed, it eludes discus-
   sion and print,
It is not to be put in a book, it is not in this book,
It is for you whoever you are, it is no farther from you than
   your hearing and sight are from you,
It is hinted by nearest, commonest, readiest, it is ever pro-
   voked by them.

You may read in many languages, yet read nothing about it,
You may read the President's message and read nothing about
   it there,
Nothing in the reports from the State department or Treasury
   department, or in the daily papers or weekly
   papers,
Or in the census or revenue returns, prices current, or any
   accounts of stock.

3

The sun and stars that float in the open air,
The apple-shaped earth and we upon it, surely the drift of
   them is something grand,
I do not know what it is except that it is grand, and that it is
   happiness,
And that the enclosing purport of us here is not a speculation
   or bon-mot or reconnoissance,
And that it is not something which by luck may turn out well
   for us, and without luck must be a failure
   for us,

And not something which may yet be retracted in a certain
   contingency.

The light and shade, the curious sense of body and identity,
   the greed that with perfect complaisance de-
   vours all things,
The endless pride and outstretching of man, unspeakable joys
   and sorrows,
The wonder every one sees in every one else he sees, and the
   wonders that fill each minute of time for-
   ever,
What have you reckon'd them for, camerado?
Have you reckon'd them for your trade or farm-work? or for
   the profits of your store?
Or to achieve yourself a position? or to fill a gentleman's
   leisure, or a lady's leisure?

Have you reckon'd that the landscape took substance and
   form that it might be painted in a picture?
Or men and women that they might be written of, and songs
   sung?
Or the attraction of gravity, and the great laws and harmonious
   combinations and the fluids of the air, as sub-
   jects for the savans?
Or the brown land and the blue sea for maps and charts?
Or the stars to be put in constellations and named fancy
   names?
Or that the growth of seeds is for agricultural tables, or agri-
   culture itself?

Old institutions, these arts, libraries, legends, collections, and
   the practice handed along in manufactures,
   will we rate them so high?
Will we rate our cash and business high? I have no objection,
I rate them as high as the highest—then a child born of a
   woman and man I rate beyond all rate.

We thought our Union grand, and our Constitution grand,
I do not say they are not grand and good, for they are,
I am this day just as much in love with them as you,
Then I am in love with You, and with all my fellows upon
   the earth.

We consider bibles and religions divine—I do not say they
   are not divine,
I say they have all grown out of you, and may grow out of
   you still,
It is not they who give the life, it is you who give the life,
Leaves are not more shed from the trees, or trees from the
   earth, than they are shed out of you.

4

The sum of all known reverence I add up in you whoever you
    are,
The President is there in the White House for you, it is not
    you who are here for him,
The Secretaries act in their bureaus for you, not you here for
    them,
The Congress convenes every Twelfth-month for you,
Laws, courts, the forming of States, the charters of cities, the
    going and coming of commerce and mails,
    are all for you.

List close my scholars dear,
Doctrines, politics and civilization exurge from you,
Sculpture and monuments and any thing inscribed anywhere
    are tallied in you,
The gist of histories and statistics as far back as the records
    reach is in you this hour, and myths and
    tales the same,
If you were not breathing and walking here, where would
    they all be?
The most renown'd poems would be ashes, orations and plays
    would be vacuums.

All architecture is what you do to it when you look upon it,
(Did you think it was in the white or gray stone? or the lines
    of the arches and cornices?)
All music is what awakes from you when you are reminded
    by the instruments,
It is not the violins and the cornets, it is not the oboe nor the
    beating drums, nor the score of the baritone
    singer singing his sweet romanza, nor that of
    the men's chorus, nor that of the women's
    chorus,
It is nearer and farther than they.

5

Will the whole come back then?
Can each see signs of the best by a look in the looking-glass?
    is there nothing greater or more?
Does all sit there with you, with the mystic unseen soul?

Strange and hard that paradox true I give,
Objects gross and the unseen soul are one.

House-building, measuring, sawing the boards,
Blacksmithing, glass-blowing, nail-making, coopering, tin-
    roofing, shingle-dressing,
Ship-joining, dock-building, fish-curing, flagging of sidewalks
    by flaggers,

The pump, the pile-driver, the great derrick, the coal-kiln
      and brick-kiln,
Coal-mines and all that is down there, the lamps in the dark-
      ness, echoes, songs, what meditations, what
      vast native thoughts looking through
      smutch'd faces,
Iron-works, forge-fires in the mountains or by river-banks,
      men around feeling the melt with huge crow-
      bars, lumps of ore, the due combining of
      ore, limestone, coal,
The blast-furnace and the puddling-furnace, the loup-lump at
      the bottom of the melt at last, the rolling-mill,
      the stumpy bars of pig-iron, the strong, clean-
      shaped T-rail for railroads,
Oil-works, silk-works, white-lead-works, the sugar-house,
      steam-saws, the great mills and factories,
Stone-cutting, shapely trimmings for façades or window or
      door-lintels, the mallet, the tooth-chisel, the
      jib to protect the thumb,
The calking-iron, the kettle of boiling vault-cement, and the
      fire under the kettle,
The cotton-bale, the stevedore's hook, the saw and buck of the
      sawyer, the mould of the moulder, the work-
      ing knife of the butcher, the ice-saw, and all
      the work with ice,
The work and tools of the rigger, grappler, sail-maker, block-
      maker,
Goods of gutta-percha, papier-maché, colors, brushes, brush-
      making, glazier's implements,
The veneer and glue-pot, the confectioner's ornaments, the
      decanter and glasses, the shears and flat-iron,
The awl and knee-strap, the pint measure and quart measure,
      the counter and stool, the writing-pen of quill
      or metal, the making of all sorts of edged
      tools,
The brewery, brewing, the malt, the vats, everything that is
      done by brewers, wine-makers, vinegar-
      makers,
Leather-dressing, coach-making, boiler-making, rope-twisting,
      distilling, sign-painting, lime-burning, cotton-
      picking, electroplating, electrotyping, stereo-
      typing,
Stave-machines, planing-machines, reaping-machines, plough-
      ing-machines, thrashing - machines, steam
      wagons,
The cart of the carman, the omnibus, the ponderous dray,
Pyrotechny, letting off color'd fireworks at night, fancy figures
      and jets,

Beef on the butcher's stall, the slaughter-house of the butcher,
        the butcher in his killing-clothes,
The pens of live pork, the killing-hammer, the hog-hook, the
        scalder's tub, gutting, the cutter's cleaver, the
        packer's maul, and the pienteous winterwork
        of pork-packing,
Flour-works, grinding of wheat, rye, maize, rice, the barrels
        and the half and quarter barrels, the loaded
        barges, the high piles on wharves and levees,
The men and the work of the men on ferries, railroad, coast-
        ers, fish-boats, canals;
The hourly routine of your own or any man's life, the shop,
        yard, store, or factory,
These shows all near you by day and night—workman! who-
        ever you are, your daily life!
In that and them the heft of the heaviest—in that and them
        far more than you estimated, (and far less
        also,)
In them realities for you and me, in them poems for you and
        me,
In them, not yourself—you and your soul enclose all things,
        regardless of estimation,
In them the development good—in them all themes, hints,
        possibilities.

I do not affirm that what you see beyond is futile, I do not
        advise you to stop,
I do not say leadings you thought great are not great,
But I say that none lead to greater than these lead to.

6

Will you seek far off? you surely come back at last,
In things best known to you finding the best, or as good as
        the best,
In folks nearest to you finding the sweetest, strongest, lov-
        ingest,
Happiness, knowledge, not in another place but this place, not
        for another hour but this hour,
Man in the first you see or touch, always in friend, brother,
        nighest neighbor—woman in mother, sister,
        wife,
The popular tastes and employments taking precedence in
        poems or anywhere,
You workwomen and workmen of these States having your
        own divine and strong life,
And all else giving place to men and women like you.

When the psalm sings instead of the singer,
When the script preaches instead of the preacher,

When the pulpit descends and goes instead of the carver that
  carved the supporting desk,
When I can touch the body of books by night or by day, and
  when they touch my body back again,
When a university course convinces like a slumbering woman
  and child convince,
When the minted gold in the vault smiles like the night-watch-
  man's daughter,
When warrantee deeds loafe in chairs opposite and are my
  friendly companions,
I intend to reach them my hand, and make as much of them
  as I do of men and women like you.

A SONG OF THE ROLLING EARTH

1

A song of the rolling earth, and of words according,
Were you thinking that those were the words, those upright
  lines? those curves, angles, dots?
No, those are not the words, the substantial words are in the
  ground and sea,
They are in the air, they are in you.

Were you thinking that those were the words, those delicious
  sounds out of your friends' mouths?
No, the real words are more delicious than they.

Human bodies are words, myriads of words,
(In the best poems re-appears the body, man's or woman's,
  well-shaped, natural, gay,
Every part able, active, receptive, without shame or the need
  of shame.)

Air, soil, water, fire—those are words,
I myself am a word with them—my qualities interpenetrate
  with theirs—my name is nothing to them,
Though it were told in the three thousand languages, what
  would air, soil, water, fire, know of my
  name?

A healthy presence, a friendly or commanding gesture, are
  words, sayings, meanings,
The charms that go with the mere looks of some men and
  women, are sayings and meanings also.

The workmanship of souls is by those inaudible words of the
  earth,
The masters know the earth's words and use them more than
  audible words.

Amelioration is one of the earth's words,
The earth neither lags nor hastens,
It has all attributes, growths, effects, latent in itself from the
  jump,
It is not half beautiful only, defects and excrescences show
  just as much as perfections show.

The earth does not withhold, it is generous enough,
The truths of the earth continually wait, they are not so
  conceal'd either,
They are calm, subtle, untransmissible by print,
They are imbued through all things conveying themselves
  willingly,
Conveying a sentiment and invitation, I utter and utter,
I speak not, yet if you hear me not of what avail am I to you?
To bear, to better, lacking these of what avail am I?

(Accouche! accouchez!
Will you rot your own fruit in yourself there?
Will you squat and stifle there?)

The earth does not argue,
Is not pathetic, has no arrangements,
Does not scream, haste, persuade, threaten, promise,
Makes no discriminations, has no conceivable failures,
Closes nothing, refuses nothing, shuts none out,
Of all the powers, objects, states, it notifies, shuts none out.

The earth does not exhibit itself nor refuse to exhibit itself,
  possesses still underneath,
Underneath the ostensible sounds, the august chorus of heroes,
  the wail of slaves,
Persuasions of lovers, curses, gasps of the dying, laughter of
  young people, accents of bargainers,
Underneath these possessing words that never fail.

To her children the words of the eloquent dumb great mother
  never fail,
The true words do not fail, for motion does not fail and
  reflection does not fail,
Also the day and night do not fail, and the voyage we pursue
  does not fail.

Of the interminable sisters,
Of the ceaseless cotillions of sisters,
Of the centripetal and centrifugal sisters, the elder and younger
  sisters,
The beautiful sister we know dances on with the rest.

With her ample back towards every beholder,
With the fascinations of youth and the equal fascinations of
  age,

Sits she whom I too love like the rest, sits undisturb'd,
Holding up in her hand what has the character of a mirror,
        while her eyes glance back from it,
Glance as she sits, inviting none, denying none,
Holding a mirror day and night tirelessly before her own
        face.

Seen at hand or seen at a distance,
Duly the twenty-four appear in public every day,
Duly approach and pass with their companions or a com-
        panion,
Looking from no countenances of their own, but from the
        countenances of those who are with them,
From the countenances of children or women or the manly
        countenance,
From the open countenances of animals or from inanimate
        things,
From the landscape or waters or from the exquisite apparition
        of the sky,
From our countenances, mine and yours, faithfully returning
        them,
Every day in public appearing without fail, but never twice
        with the same companions.

Embracing man, embracing all, proceed the three hundred
        and sixty-five resistlessly round the sun;
Embracing all, soothing, supporting, follow close three hun-
        dred and sixty-five offsets of the first, sure
        and necessary as they.

Tumbling on steadily, nothing dreading,
Sunshine, storm, cold, heat, forever withstanding, passing,
        carrying,
The soul's realization and determination still inheriting,
The fluid vacuum around and ahead still entering and dividing,
No balk retarding, no anchor anchoring, on no rock striking,
Swift, glad, content, unbereav'd, nothing losing,
Of all able and ready at any time to give strict account,
The divine ship sails the divine sea.

2

Whoever you are! motion and reflection are especially for you,
The divine ship sails the divine sea for you.

Whoever you are! you are he or she for whom the earth is
        solid and liquid,
You are he or she for whom the sun and moon hang in the
        sky,
For none more than you are the present and the past,
For none more than you is immortality.

Each man to himself and each woman to herself, is the word
        of the past and present, and the true word of
        immortality;
No one can acquire for another—not one,
Not one can grow for another—not one.

The song is to the singer, and comes back most to him,
The teaching is to the teacher, and comes back most to him,
The murder is to the murderer, and comes back most to him,
The theft is to the thief, and comes back most to him,
The love is to the lover, and comes back most to him,
The gift is to the giver, and comes back most to him—it cannot
        fail,
The oration is to the orator, the acting is to the actor and
        actress not to the audience,
And no man understands any greatness or goodness but his
        own, or the indication of his own.

3

I swear the earth shall surely be complete to him or her who
        shall be complete,
The earth remains jagged and broken only to him or her who
        remains jagged and broken.

I swear there is no greatness or power that does not emulate
        those of the earth,
There can be no theory of any account unless it corroborate
        the theory of the earth,
No politics, song, religion, behavior, or what not, is of ac-
        count, unless it compare with the amplitude
        of the earth,
Unless it face the exactness, vitality, impartiality, rectitude of
        the earth.

I swear I begin to see love with sweeter spasms than that
        which responds love,
It is that which contains itself, which never invites and never
        refuses.

I swear I begin to see little or nothing in audible words,
All merges toward the presentation of the unspoken meanings
        of the earth,
Toward him who sings the songs of the body and of the truths
        of the earth,
Toward him who makes the dictionaries of words that print
        cannot touch.

I swear I see what is better than to tell the best,
It is always to leave the best untold.

When I undertake to tell the best I find I cannot,
My tongue is ineffectual on its pivots,
My breath will not be obedient to its organs,
I become a dumb man.

The best of the earth cannot be told anyhow, all or any is best,
It is not what you anticipated, it is cheaper, easier, nearer,
Things are not dismiss'd from the places they held before,
The earth is just as positive and direct as it was before,
Facts, religions, improvements, politics, trades, are as real as
    before,
But the soul is also real, it too is positive and direct,
No reasoning, no proof has establish'd it,
Undeniable growth has establish'd it.

4

These to echo the tones of souls and the phrases of souls,
(If they did not echo the phrases of souls what were they
    then?
If they had not reference to you in especial what were they
    then?)

I swear I will never henceforth have to do with the faith that
    tells the best,
I will have to do only with that faith that leaves the best untold.

Say on, sayers! sing on, singers!
Delve! mould! pile the words of the earth!
Work on, age after age, nothing is to be lost,
It may have to wait long, but it will certainly come in use,
When the materials are all prepared and ready, the architects
    shall appear.

I swear to you the architects shall appear without fail,
I swear to you they will understand you and justify you,
The greatest among them shall be he who best knows you,
    and encloses all and is faithful to all,
He and the rest shall not forget you, they shall perceive that
    you are not an iota less than they,
You shall be fully glorified in them.

YOUTH, DAY, OLD AGE AND NIGHT

Youth, large, lusty, loving—youth full of grace, force, fascina-
    tion,
Do you know that Old Age may come after you with equal
    grace, force, fascination?

Day full-blown and splendid—day of the immense sun, action,
    ambition, laughter,
The Night follows close with millions of suns, and sleep and
    restoring darkness.

BIRDS OF PASSAGE

SONG OF THE UNIVERSAL

1

Come said the Muse,
Sing me a song no poet yet has chanted,
Sing me the universal.

In this broad earth of ours,
Amid the measureless grossness and the slag,
Enclosed and safe within its central heart,
Nestles the seed perfection.

By every life a share or more or less,
None born but it is born, conceal'd or unconceal'd the seed is
                waiting.

2

Lo! keen-eyed towering science,
As from tall peaks the modern overlooking,
Successive absolute fiats issuing.

Yet again, lo! the soul, above all science,
For it has history gather'd like husks around the globe,
For it the entire star-myriads roll through the sky.

In spiral routes by long detours,
(As a much-tacking ship upon the sea,)
For it the partial to the permanent flowing,
For it the real to the ideal tends.

For it the mystic evolution,
Not the right only justified, what we call evil also justified.

Forth from their masks, no matter what,
From the huge festering trunk, from craft and guile and tears,
Health to emerge and joy, joy universal.

Out of the bulk, the morbid and the shallow,
Out of the bad majority, the varied countless frauds of men
              and states,
Electric, antiseptic yet, cleaving, suffusing all,
Only the good is universal.

3

Over the mountain-growths disease and sorrow,
An uncaught bird is ever hovering, hovering,
High in the purer, happier air.

From imperfection's murkiest cloud,
Darts always forth one ray of perfect light,
One flash of heaven's glory.

To fashion's, custom's discord,
To the mad Babel-din, the deafening orgies,
Soothing each lull a strain is heard, just heard,
From some far shore the final chorus sounding.

O the blest eyes, the happy hearts,
That see, that know the guiding thread so fine,
Along the mighty labyrinth.

4

And thou America,
For the scheme's culmination, its thought and its reality,
For these (not for thyself) thou hast arrived.

Thou too surroundest all,
Embracing carrying welcoming all, thou too by pathways
            broad and new,
To the ideal tendest.

The measur'd faiths of other lands, the grandeurs of the past,
Are not for thee, but grandeurs of thine own,
Deific faiths and amplitudes, absorbing, comprehending all,
All eligible to all.

All, all for immortality,
Love like the light silently wrapping all,
Nature's amelioration blessing all,
The blossoms, fruits of ages, orchards divine and certain,
Forms, objects, growths, humanities, to spiritual images ripen-
            ing.

Give me O God to sing that thought,
Give me, give him or her I love this quenchless faith
In Thy ensemble, whatever else withheld withhold not from
            us,
Belief in plan of Thee enclosed in Time and Space,
Health, peace, salvation universal.

Is it a dream?
Nay but the lack of it the dream,
And failing it life's lore and wealth a dream,
And all the world a dream.

PIONEERS! O PIONEERS!

        Come my tan-faced children,
Follow well in order, get your weapons ready,
Have you your pistols? have you your sharp-edged axes?
        Pioneers! O pioneers!

For we cannot tarry here,
We must march my darlings, we must bear the brunt of danger,
We the youthful sinewy races, all the rest on us depend,
      Pioneers! O pioneers!

O you youths, Western youths,
So impatient, full of action, full of manly pride and friend-
      ship,
Plain I see you Western youths, see you tramping with the
      foremost,
      Pioneers! O pioneers!

Have the elder races halted?
Do they droop and end their lesson, wearied over there be-
      yond the seas
We take up the task eternal, and the burden and the lesson,
      Pioneers! O pioneers!

All the past we leave behind,
We debouch upon a newer mightier world, varied world,
Fresh and strong the world we seize, world of labor and the
      march,
      Pioneers! O pioneers!

We detachments steady throwing,
Down the edges, through the passes, up the mountains steep,
Conquering, holding, daring, venturing as we go the unknown
      ways,
      Pioneers! O pioneers!

We primeval forests felling,
We the rivers stemming, vexing we and piercing deep the
      mines within,
We the surface broad surveying, we the virgin soil upheaving,
      Pioneers! O pioneers!

Colorado men are we,
From the peaks gigantic, from the great sierras and the high
      plateaus,
From the mine and from the gully, from the hunting trail we
      come,
      Pioneers! O pioneers!

From Nebraska, from Arkansas,
Central inland race are we, from Missouri, with the continental
      blood intervein'd,
All the hands of comrades clasping, all the Southern, all the
      Northern,
      Pioneers! O pioneers!

O resistless restless race!

O beloved race in all! O my breast aches with tender love for
      all!
O I mourn and yet exult, I am rapt with love for all,
      Pioneers! O pioneers!

      Raise the mighty mother mistress,
Waving high the delicate mistress, over all the starry mistress,
      (bend your heads all,)
Raise the fang'd and warlike mistress, stern, impassive,
      weapon'd mistress,
      Pioneers! O pioneers!

      See my children, resolute children,
By those swarms upon our rear we must never yield or falter,
Ages back in ghostly millions frowning there behind us
      urging,
      Pioneers! O pioneers!

      On and on the compact ranks,
With accessions ever waiting, with the places of the dead
      quickly fill'd,
Through the battle, through defeat, moving yet and never
      stopping,
      Pioneers! O pioneers!

      O to die advancing on!
Are there some of us to droop and die? has the hour come?
Then upon the march we fittest die, soon and sure the gap is
      fill'd,
      Pioneers! O pioneers!

      All the pulses of the world,
Falling in they beat for us, with the Western movement beat,
Holding single or together, steady moving to the front, all
      for us,
      Pioneers! O pioneers!

      Life's involv'd and varied pageants,
All the forms and shows, all the workmen at their work,
All the seamen and the landsmen, all the masters with their
      slaves,
      Pioneers! O pioneers!

      All the hapless silent lovers,
All the prisoners in the prisons, all the righteous and the
      wicked,
All the joyous, all the sorrowing, all the living, all the dying,
      Pioneers! O pioneers!

      I too with my soul and body,
We, a curious trio, picking, wandering on our way,

Through these shores amid the shadows, with the apparitions pressing,
    Pioneers! O pioneers!

Lo, the darting bowling orb!
Lo, the brother orbs around, all the clustering suns and planets,
All the dazzling days, all the mystic nights with dreams,
    Pioneers! O pioneers!

These are of us, they are with us,
All for primal needed work, while the followers there in embryo wait behind,
We to-day's procession heading, we the route for travel clearing,
    Pioneers! O pioneers!

O you daughters of the West!
O you young and elder daughters! O you mothers and you wives!
Never must you be divided, in our ranks you move united,
    Pioneers! O pioneers!

Minstrels latent on the prairies!
(Shrouded bards of other lands, you may rest, you have done your work,)
Soon I hear you coming warbling, soon you rise and tramp amid us,
    Pioneers! O pioneers!

Not for delectations sweet,
Not the cushion and the slipper, not the peaceful and the studious,
Not the riches safe and palling, not for us the tame enjoyment,
    Pioneers! O pioneers!

Do the feasters gluttonous feast?
Do the corpulent sleepers sleep? have they lock'd and bolted doors?
Still be ours the diet hard, and the blanket on the ground,
    Pioneers! O pioneers!

Has the night descended?
Was the road of late so toilsome? did we stop discouraged nodding on our way?
Yet a passing hour I yield you in your tracks to pause oblivious,
    Pioneers! O pioneers!

Till with sound of trumpet,
Far, far off the daybreak call—hark! how loud and clear I hear it wind,
Swift! to the head of the army!—swift! spring to your places,
    Pioneers! O pioneers!

TO YOU

Whoever you are, I fear you are walking the walk of dreams,
I fear these supposed realities are to melt from under your
        feet and hands,
Even now your features, joys, speech, house, trade, manners,
        troubles, follies, costume, crimes, dissipate
        away from you,
Your true soul and body appear before me,
They stand forth out of affairs, out of commerce, shops, work,
        farms, clothes, the house, buying, selling,
        eating, drinking, suffering, dying.

Whoever you are, now I place my hand upon you, that you
        be my poem,
I whisper with my lips close to your ear,
I have loved many women and men, but I love none better
        than you.

O I have been dilatory and dumb,
I should have made my way straight to you long ago,
I should have blabb'd nothing but you, I should have chanted
        nothing but you.

I will leave all and come and make the hymns of you,
None has understood you, but I understand you,
None has done justice to you, you have not done justice to
        yourself,
None but has found you imperfect, I only find no imperfec-
        tion in you,
None but would subordinate you, I only am he who will never
        consent to subordinate you,
I only am he who places over you no master, owner, better,
        God, beyond what waits intrinsically in your-
        self.

Painters have painted their swarming groups and the centre-
        figure of all,
From the head of the centre-figure spreading a nimbus of
        gold-color'd light,
But I paint myriads of heads, but paint no head without its
        nimbus of gold-color'd light,
From my hand from the brain of every man and woman it
        streams, effulgently flowing forever.

O I could sing such grandeurs and glories about you!
You have not known what you are, you have slumber'd upon
        yourself all your life,
Your eyelids have been the same as closed most of the time,
What you have done returns already in mockeries,

(Your thrift, knowledge, prayers, if they do not return in
        mockeries, what is their return?)

The mockeries are not you,
Underneath them and within them I see you lurk,
I pursue you where none else has pursued you,
Silence, the desk, the flippant expression, the night, the accus-
        tom'd routine, if these conceal you from
        others or from yourself, they do not conceal
        you from me,
The shaved face, the unsteady eye, the impure complexion,
        if these balk others they do not balk me,
The pert apparel, the deform'd attitude, drunkenness, greed,
        premature death, all these I part aside.

There is no endowment in man or woman that is not tallied
        in you,
There is no virtue, no beauty in man or woman, but as good
        is in you,
No pluck, no endurance in others, but as good is in you,
No pleasure waiting for others, but an equal pleasure waits
        for you.

As for me, I give nothing to any one except I give the like
        carefully to you,
I sing the songs of the glory of none, not God, sooner than I
        sing the songs of the glory of you.

Whoever you are! claim your own at any hazard!
These shows of the East and West are tame compared to you,
These immense meadows, these interminable rivers, you are
        immense and interminable as they,
These furies, elements, storms, motions of Nature, throes of
        apparent dissolution, you are he or she who
        is master or mistress over them,
Master or mistress in your own right over Nature, elements,
        pain, passion, dissolution.

The hopples fall from your ankles, you find an unfailing suf-
        ficiency,
Old or young, male or female, rude, low, rejected by the rest,
        whatever you are promulges itself,
Through birth, life, death, burial, the means are provided,
        nothing is scanted,
Through angers, losses, ambition, ignorance, ennui, what you
        are picks its way.

FRANCE

The 18th Year of these States.

A great year and place,
A harsh discordant natal scream out-sounding, to touch the
        mother's heart closer than any yet.

I walk'd the shores of my Eastern sea,
Heard over the waves the little voice,
Saw the divine infant where she woke mournfully wailing,
        amid the roar of cannon, curses, shouts,
        crash of falling buildings,
Was not so sick from the blood in the gutters running, nor
        from the single corpses, nor those in heaps,
        nor those borne away in the tumbrils,
Was not so desperate at the battues of death—was not so
        shock'd at the repeated fusillades of the guns.

Pale, silent, stern, what could I say to that long-accrued retri-
        bution?
Could I wish humanity different?
Could I wish the people made of wood and stone?
Or that there be no justice in destiny or time?

O Liberty! O mate for me!
Here too the blaze, the grape-shot and the axe, in reserve, to
        fetch them out in case of need,
Here too, though long represt, can never be destroy'd,
Here too could rise at last murdering and ecstatic,
Here too demanding full arrears of vengeance.

Hence I sign this salute over the sea,
And I do not deny that terrible red birth and baptism,
But remember the little voice that I heard wailing, and wait
        with perfect trust, no matter how long,
And from to-day sad and cogent I maintain the bequeath'd
        cause, as for all lands,
And I send these words to Paris with my love,
And I guess some chansonniers there will understand them,
For I guess there is latent music yet in France, floods of it,
O I hear already the bustle of instruments, they will soon be
        drowning all that would interrupt them,
O I think the east wind brings a triumphal and free march,
It reaches hither, it swells me to joyful madness,
I will run transpose it in words, to justify it,
I will yet sing a song for you ma femme.

MYSELF AND MINE

Myself and mine gymnastic ever,
To stand the cold or heat, to make good aim with a gun, to
        sail a boat, to manage horses, to beget superb
        children,
To speak readily and clearly, to feel at home among common
        people,
And to hold our own in terrible positions on land and sea.

Not for an embroiderer,
(There will always be plenty of embroiderers, I welcome them
        also,)
But for the fibre of things and for inherent men and women.

Not to chisel ornaments,
But to chisel with free stroke the heads and limbs of plen-
        teous supreme Gods, that the States may
        realize them walking and talking.

Let me have my own way,
Let others promulge the laws, I will make no account of the
        laws,
Let others praise eminent men and hold up peace, I hold up
        agitation and conflict,
I praise no eminent man, I rebuke to his face the one that
        was thought most worthy.

(Who are you? and what are you secretly guilty of all your
        life?
Will you turn aside all your life? will you grub and chatter all
        your life?
And who are you, blabbing by rote, years, pages, languages,
        reminiscences,
Unwitting to-day that you do not know how to speak properly
        a single word?)

Let others finish specimens, I never finish specimens,
I start them by exhaustless laws as Nature does, fresh and
        modern continually.

I give nothing as duties,
What others give as duties I give as living impulses,
(Shall I give the heart's action as a duty?)

Let others dispose of questions, I dispose of nothing, I arouse
        unanswerable questions,
Who are they I see and touch, and what about them?
What about these likes of myself that draw me so close by
        tender directions and indirections?

I call to the world to distrust the accounts of my friends, but
          listen to my enemies, as I myself do,
I charge you forever reject those who would expound me, for
          I cannot expound myself,
I charge that there be no theory or school founded out of me,
I charge you to leave all free, as I have left all free.

After me, vista!
O I see life is not short, but immeasurably long,
I henceforth tread the world chaste, temperate, an early riser,
          a steady grower,
Every hour the semen of centuries, and still of centuries.

I must follow up these continual lessons of the air, water,
          earth,
I perceive I have no time to lose.

YEAR OF METEORS

[1859–60]

Year of meteors! brooding year!
I would bind in words retrospective some of your deeds and
          signs,
I would sing your contest for the 19th Presidentiad,
I would sing how an old man, tall, with white hair, mounted
          the scaffold in Virginia,
(I was at hand, silent I stood with teeth shut close, I watch'd,
I stood very near you old man when cool and indifferent, but
          trembling with age and your unheal'd
          wounds, you mounted the scaffold;)
I would sing in my copious song your census returns of the
          States,
The tables of population and products, I would sing of your
          ships and their cargoes,
The proud black ships of Manhattan arriving, some fill'd with
          immigrants, some from the isthmus with car-
          goes of gold,
Songs thereof would I sing, to all that hitherward comes would
          I welcome give,
And you would I sing, fair stripling! welcome to you from me,
          young prince of England!
(Remember you surging Manhattan's crowds as you pass'd
          with your cortege of nobles?
There in the crowds stood I, and singled you out with at-
          tachment;)
Nor forget I to sing of the wonder, the ship as she swam up
          my bay,
Well-shaped and stately the Great Eastern swam up my bay,
          she was 600 feet long,

Her moving swiftly surrounded by myriads of small craft I
    forget not to sing;
Nor the comet that came unannounced out of the north flaring
    in heaven,
Nor the strange huge meteor-procession dazzling and clear
    shooting over our heads,
(A moment, a moment long it sail'd its balls of unearthly
    light over our heads,
Then departed, dropt in the night, and was gone;)
Of such, and fitful as they, I sing—with gleams from them
    would I gleam and patch these chants,
Your chants, O year all mottled with evil and good—year of
    forebodings!
Year of comets and meteors transient and strange—lo! even
    here one equally transient and strange!
As I flit through you hastily, soon to fall and be gone, what
    is this chant,
What am I myself but one of your meteors?

WITH ANTECEDENTS

1

With antecedents,
With my fathers and mothers and the accumulations of past
    ages,
With all which, had it not been, I would not now be here, as
    I am,
With Egypt, India, Phenicia, Greece and Rome,
With the Kelt, the Scandinavian, the Alb and the Saxon,
With antique maritime ventures, laws, artisanship, wars and
    journeys,
With the poet, the skald, the saga, the myth, and the oracle,
With the sale of slaves, with enthusiasts, with the trouba-
    dour, the crusader, and the monk,
With those old continents whence we have come to this new
    continent,
With the fading kingdoms and kings over there,
With the fading religions and priests,
With the small shores we look back to from our own large
    and present shores,
With countless years drawing themselves onward and arrived
    at these years,
You and me arrived—America arrived and making this year,
This year! sending itself ahead countless years to come.

2

O but it is not the years—it is I, it is You,
We touch all laws and tally all antecedents,

We are the skald, the oracle, the monk and the knight, we
    easily include them and more,
We stand amid time beginningless and endless, we stand amid
    evil and good,
All swings around us, there is as much darkness as light,
The very sun swings itself and its system of planets around us,
Its sun, and its again, all swing around us.

As for me, (torn, stormy, amid these vehement days,)
I have the idea of all, and am all and believe in all,
I believe materialism is true and spiritualism is true, I reject
    no part.

(Have I forgotten any part? any thing in the past?
Come to me whoever and whatever, till I give you recognition.)

I respect Assyria, China, Teutonia, and the Hebrews,
I adopt each theory, myth, god, and demi-god,
I see the old accounts, bibles, genealogies, are true, without
    exception,
I assert that all past days were what they must have been,
And that they could no-how have been better than they were,
And that to-day is what it must be, and that America is,
And that to-day and America could no-how be better than
    they are.

3

In the name of these States and in your and my name, the Past,
And in the name of these States and in your and my name, the
    Present time.

I know that the past was great and the future will be great,
And I know that both curiously conjoint in the present time,
(For the sake of him I typify, for the common average man's
    sake, your sake if you are he,)
And that where I am or you are this present day, there is the
    centre of all days, all races,
And there is the meaning to us of all that has ever come of
    races and days, or ever will come.

A BROADWAY PAGEANT

1

Over the Western sea hither from Niphon come,
Courteous, the swarth-cheek'd two-sworded envoys,
Leaning back in their open barouches, bare-headed, impassive,
Ride to-day through Manhattan.

Libertad! I do not know whether others behold what I behold,
In the procession along with the nobles of Niphon, the errand-
    bearers,

Bringing up the rear, hovering above, around, or in the ranks
      marching,
But I will sing you a song of what I behold Libertad.

When million-footed Manhattan unpent descends to her pave-
      ments,
When the thunder-cracking guns arouse me with the proud
      roar I love,
When the round-mouth'd guns out of the smoke and smell I
      love spit their salutes,
When the fire-flashing guns have fully alerted me, and heaven-
      clouds canopy my city with a delicate thin
      haze,
When gorgeous the countless straight stems, the forests at the
      wharves, thicken with colors,
When every ship richly drest carries her flag at the peak,
When pennants trail and street-festoons hang from the win-
      dows,
When Broadway is entirely given up to foot-passengers and
      foot-standers, when the mass is densest,
When the façades of the houses are alive with people, when
      eyes gaze riveted tens of thousands at a time,
When the guests from the islands advance, when the pageant
      moves forward visible,
When the summons is made, when the answer that waited
      thousands of years answers,
I too arising, answering, descend to the pavements, merge with
      the crowd, and gaze with them.

2

Superb-faced Manhattan!
Comrad Americanos! to us, then at last the Orient comes.

To us, my city,
Where our tall-topt marble and iron beauties range on oppo-
      site sides, to walk in the space between,
To-day our Antipodes comes.

The Originatress comes,
The nest of languages, the bequeather of poems, the race of
      eld,
Florid with blood, pensive, rapt with musings, hot with passion,
Sultry with perfume, with ample and flowing garments,
With sunburnt visage, with intense soul and glittering eyes,
The race of Brahma comes.

See my cantabile! these and more are flashing to us from the
      procession,
As it moves changing, a kaleidoscope divine it moves changing
      before us.

For not the envoys nor the tann'd Japanee from his island only,
Lithe and silent the Hindoo appears, the Asiatic continent it-
    self appears, the past, the dead,
The murky night-morning of wonder and fable inscrutable,
The envelop'd mysteries, the old and unknown hive-bees,
The north, the sweltering south, eastern Assyria, the Hebrews,
    the ancient of ancients,
Vast desolated cities, the gliding present, all of these and
    more are in the pageant-procession.

Geography, the world, is in it,
The Great Sea, the brood of islands, Polynesia, the coast be-
    yond,
The coast you henceforth are facing—you, Libertad! from
    your Western golden shores,
The countries there with their populations, the millions en-
    masse are curiously here,
The swarming market-places, the temples with idols ranged
    along the sides or at the end, bonze, brahmin,
    and llama,
Mandarin, farmer, merchant, mechanic, and fisherman,
The singing-girl and the dancing-girl, the ecstatic persons, the
    secluded emperors,
Confucius himself, the great poets and heroes, the warriors,
    the castes, all,
Trooping up, crowding from all directions, from the Altay
    mountains,
From Thibet, from the four winding and far-flowing rivers of
    China,
From the southern peninsulas and the demi-continental islands,
    from Malaysia,
These and whatever belongs to them palpable show forth to
    me, and are seiz'd by me,
And I am seiz'd by them, and friendlily held by them,
Till as here them all I chant, Libertad! for themselves and for
    you.

For I too raising my voice join the ranks of this pageant,
I am the chanter, I chant aloud over the pageant,
I chant the world on my Western sea,
I chant copious the islands beyond, thick as stars in the sky,
I chant the new empire grander than any before, as in a vision
    it comes to me,
I chant America the mistress, I chant a greater supremacy,
I chant projected a thousand blooming cities yet in time on
    those groups of sea-islands,
My sail-ships and steam-ships threading the archipelagoes,
My stars and stripes fluttering in the wind,

Commerce opening, the sleep of ages having done its work,
   races reborn, refresh'd,
Lives, works resumed—the object I know not—but the old,
   the Asiatic renew'd as it must be,
Commencing from this day surrounded by the world.

3

And you Libertad of the world!
You shall sit in the middle well-pois'd thousands and thou-
   sands of years,
As to-day from one side the nobles of Asia come to you,
As to-morrow from the other side the queen of England sends
   her eldest son to you.

The sign is reversing, the orb is enclosed,
The ring is circled, the journey is done,
The box-lid is but perceptibly open'd, nevertheless the per-
   fume pours copiously out of the whole box.

Young Libertad! with the venerable Asia, the all-mother,
Be considerate with her now and ever hot Libertad, for you
   are all,
Bend your proud neck to the long-off mother now sending
   messages over the archipelagoes to you,
Bend your proud neck low for once, young Libertad.

Were the children straying westward so long? so wide the
   tramping?
Were the precedent dim ages debouching westward from Par-
   adise so long?
Were the centuries steadily footing it that way, all the while
   unknown, for you, for reasons?

They are justified, they are accomplish'd, they shall now be
   turn'd the other way also, to travel toward
   you thence,
They shall now also march obediently eastward for your sake
   Libertad.

SEA-DRIFT

OUT OF THE CRADLE ENDLESSLY ROCKING

Out of the cradle endlessly rocking,
Out of the mocking-bird's throat, the musical shuttle,
Out of the Ninth-month midnight,

Over the sterile sands and the fields beyond, where the child
              leaving his bed wander'd alone, bareheaded,
              barefoot,
Down from the shower'd halo,
Up from the mystic play of shadows twining and twisting as
              if they were alive,
Out from the patches of briers and blackberries,
From the memories of the bird that chanted to me,
From your memories sad brother, from the fitful risings and
              fallings I heard,
From under that yellow half-moon late-risen and swollen as
              if with tears,
From those beginning notes of yearning and love there in the
              mist,
From the thousand responses of my heart never to cease,
From the myriad thence-arous'd words,
From the word stronger and more delicious than any,
From such as now they start the scene revisiting,
As a flock, twittering, rising, or overhead passing,
Borne hither, ere all eludes me, hurriedly,
A man, yet by these tears a little boy again,
Throwing myself on the sand, confronting the waves,
I, chanter of pains and joys, uniter of here and hereafter,
Taking all hints to use them, but swiftly leaping beyond them,
A reminiscence sing.

Once Paumanok,
When the lilac-scent was in the air and Fifth-month grass was
              growing,
Up this seashore in some briers,
Two feather'd guests from Alabama, two together,
And their nest, and four light-green eggs spotted with brown,
And every day the he-bird to and fro near at hand,
And every day the she-bird crouch'd on her nest, silent, with
              bright eyes,
And every day I, a curious boy, never too close, never disturb-
              ing them,
Cautiously peering, absorbing, translating.

Shine! shine! shine!
Pour down your warmth, great sun!
While we bask, we two together.

Two together!
Winds blow south, or winds blow north,
Day come white, or night come black,
Home, or rivers and mountains from home,
Singing all time, minding no time,
While we two keep together.

Till of a sudden,
May-be kill'd, unknown to her mate,
One forenoon the she-bird crouch'd not on the nest,
Nor return'd that afternoon, nor the next,
Nor ever appear'd again.

And thenceforward all summer in the sound of the sea,
And at night under the full of the moon in calmer weather,
Over the hoarse surging of the sea,
Or flitting from brier to brier by day,
I saw, I heard at intervals the remaining one, the he-bird,
The solitary guest from Alabama.

Blow! blow! blow!
Blow up sea-winds along Paumanok's shore;
I wait and I wait till you blow my mate to me.

Yes, when the stars glisten'd,
All night long on the prong of a moss-scallop'd stake,
Down almost amid the slapping waves,
Sat the lone singer wonderful causing tears.

He call'd on his mate,
He pour'd forth the meanings which I of all men know.

Yes my brother I know,
The rest might not, but I have treasur'd every note,
For more than once dimly down to the beach gliding,
Silent, avoiding the moonbeams, blending myself with the
                    shadows,
Recalling now the obscure shapes, the echoes, the sounds and
                    sights after their sorts,
The white arms out in the breakers tirelessly tossing,
I, with bare feet, a child, the wind wafting my hair,
Listen'd long and long.

Listen'd to keep, to sing, now translating the notes,
Following you my brother.

Soothe! soothe! soothe!
Close on its wave soothes the wave behind,
And again another behind embracing and lapping, every one
                    close,
But my love soothes not me, not me.

Low hangs the moon, it rose late,
It is lagging—O I think it is heavy with love, with love.

O madly the sea pushes upon the land,
With love, with love.

*O night! do I not see my love fluttering out among the
        breakers?*
What is that little black thing I see there in the white?

Loud! loud! loud!
Loud I call to you, my love!
High and clear I shoot my voice over the waves,
Surely you must know who is here, is here,
You must know who I am, my love.

Low-hanging moon!
What is that dusky spot in your brown yellow?
O it is the shape, the shape of my mate!
O moon do not keep her from me any longer.

Land! land! O land!
*Whichever way I turn, O I think you could give me my mate
        back again if you only would,*
For I am almost sure I see her dimly whichever way I look.

O rising stars!
*Perhaps the one I want so much will rise, will rise with some
        of you.*

O throat! O trembling throat!
Sound clearer through the atmosphere!
Pierce the woods, the earth,
Somewhere listening to catch you must be the one I want.

Shake out carols!
Solitary here, the night's carols!
Carols of lonesome love! death's carols!
Carols under that lagging, yellow, waning moon!
O under the moon where she droops almost down into the sea!
O reckless despairing carols.

But soft! sink low!
Soft! let me just murmur,
And do you wait a moment you husky-nois'd sea,
For somewhere I believe I heard my mate responding to me,
So faint, I must be still, be still to listen,
*But not altogether still, for then she might not come imme-
        diately to me.*

Hither my love!
Here I am! here!
With this just-sustain'd note I announce myself to you,
This gentle call is for you my love, for you.

Do not be decoy'd elsewhere,
That is the whistle of the wind, it is not my voice,
That is the fluttering, the fluttering of the spray,
Those are the shadows of leaves.

O darkness! O in vain!
O I am very sick and sorrowful.

O brown halo in the sky near the moon, drooping upon the sea!
O troubled reflection in the sea!

O throat! O throbbing heart!
And I singing uselessly, uselessly all the night.

O past! O happy life! O songs of joy!
In the air, in the woods, over fields,
Loved! loved! loved! loved! loved!
But my mate no more, no more with me!
We two together no more.

The aria sinking,
All else continuing, the stars shining,
The winds blowing, the notes of the bird continuous echoing,
With angry moans the fierce old mother incessantly moaning,
On the sands of Paumanok's shore gray and rustling,
The yellow half-moon enlarged, sagging down, drooping, the
    face of the sea almost touching,
The boy ecstatic, with his bare feet the waves, with his hair
    the atmosphere dallying,
The love in the heart long pent, now loose, now at last tumul-
    tuously bursting,
The aria's meaning, the ears, the soul, swiftly depositing,
The strange tears down the cheeks coursing,
The colloquy there, the trio, each uttering,
The undertone, the savage old mother incessantly crying,
To the boy's soul's questions sullenly timing, some drown'd
    secret hissing,
To the outsetting bard.

Demon or bird! (said the boy's soul,)
Is it indeed toward your mate you sing? or is it really to me?
For I, that was a child, my tongue's use sleeping, now I have
    heard you,
Now in a moment I know what I am for, I awake,
And already a thousand singers, a thousand songs, clearer,
    louder and more sorrowful than yours,
A thousand warbling echoes have started to life within me,
    never to die.

O you singer solitary, singing by yourself, projecting me,
O solitary me listening, never more shall I cease perpetuating
    you,
Never more shall I escape, never more the reverberations,
Never more the cries of unsatisfied love be absent from me,
Never again leave me to be the peaceful child I was before
    what there in the night,

By the sea under the yellow and sagging moon,
The messenger there arous'd, the fire, the sweet hell within,
The unknown want, the destiny of me.

O give me the clew! (it lurks in the night here somewhere,)
O if I am to have so much, let me have more!

A word then, (for I will conquer it,)
The word final, superior to all,
Subtle, sent up—what is it?—I listen;
Are you whispering it, and have been all the time, you sea
                    waves?
Is that it from your liquid rims and wet sands?

Whereto answering, the sea,
Delaying not, hurrying not,
Whisper'd me through the night, and very plainly before day-
                    break,
Lisp'd to me the low and delicious word death,
And again death, death, death, death,
Hissing melodious, neither like the bird nor like my arous'd
                    child's heart,
But edging near as privately for me rustling at my feet,
Creeping thence steadily up to my ears and laving me softly
                    all over,
Death, death, death, death, death.

Which I do not forget,
But fuse the song of my dusky demon and brother,
That he sang to me in the moonlight on Paumanok's gray
                    beach,
With the thousand responsive songs at random,
My own songs awaked from that hour,
And with them the key, the word up from the waves,
The word of the sweetest song and all songs,
That strong and delicious word which, creeping to my feet,
(Or like some old crone rocking the cradle, swathed in sweet
                    garments, bending aside,)
The sea whisper'd me.

AS I EBB'D WITH THE OCEAN OF LIFE

1

As I ebb'd with the ocean of life,
As I wended the shores I know,
As I walk'd where the ripples continually wash you Paumanok,
Where they rustle up hoarse and sibilant,
Where the fierce old mother endlessly cries for her castaways,
I musing late in the autumn day, gazing off southward,

Held by this electric self out of the pride of which I utter
poems,
Was seiz'd by the spirit that trails in the lines underfoot,
The rim, the sediment that stands for all the water and all the
land of the globe.
Fascinated, my eyes reverting from the south, dropt, to follow
those slender windrows,
Chaff, straw, splinters of wood, weeds, and the sea-gluten,
Scum, scales from shining rocks, leaves of salt-lettuce, left by
the tide,
Miles walking, the sound of breaking waves the other side of
me,
Paumanok there and then as I thought the old thought of like-
nesses,
These you presented to me you fish-shaped island,
As I wended the shores I know,
As I walk'd with that electric self-seeking types.

2

As I wend to the shores I know not,
As I list to the dirge, the voices of men and women wreck'd,
As I inhale the impalpable breezes that set in upon me,
As the ocean so mysterious rolls toward me closer and closer,
I too but signify at the utmost a little wash'd-up drift,
A few sands and dead leaves to gather,
Gather, and merge myself as part of the sands and drift.

O baffled, balk'd, bent to the very earth,
Oppress'd with myself that I have dared to open my mouth,
Aware now that amid all that blab whose echoes recoil upon
me I have not once had the least idea who
or what I am,
But that before all my arrogant poems the real Me stands yet
untouch'd, untold, altogether unreach'd,
Withdrawn far, mocking me with mock-congratulatory signs
and bows,
With peals of distant ironical laughter at every word I have
written,
Pointing in silence to these songs, and then to the sand beneath.
I perceive I have not really understood any thing, not a single
object, and that no man ever can,
Nature here in sight of the sea taking advantage of me to dart
upon me and sting me,
Because I have dared to open my mouth to sing at all.

3

You oceans both, I close with you,
We murmur alike reproachfully rolling sands and drift, know-
        ing not why,
These little shreds indeed standing for you and me and all.

You friable shore with trails of debris,
You fish-shaped island, I take what is underfoot,
What is yours is mine my father.

I too Paumanok,
I too have bubbled up, floated the measureless float, and been
        wash'd on your shores,
I too am but a trail of drift and debris,
I too leave little wrecks upon you, you fish-shaped island.

I throw myself upon your breast my father,
I cling to you so that you cannot unloose me,
I hold you so firm till you answer me something.

Kiss me my father,
Touch me with your lips as I touch those I love,
Breathe to me while I hold you close the secret of the mur-
        muring I envy.

4

Ebb, ocean of life (the flow will return,)
Cease not your moaning you fierce old mother,
Endlessly cry for your castaways, but fear not, deny not me,
Rustle not up so hoarse and angry against my feet as I touch
        you or gather from you.

I mean tenderly by you and all,
I gather for myself and for this phantom looking down where
        we lead, and following me and mine.

Me and mine, loose windrows, little corpses,
Froth, snowy white, and bubbles,
(See, from my dead lips the ooze exuding at last,
See, the prismatic colors glistening and rolling,)
Tufts of straw, sands, fragments,
Buoy'd hither from many moods, one contradicting another,
From the storm, the long calm, the darkness, the swell,
Musing, pondering, a breath, a briny tear, a dab of liquid or
        soil,
Up just as much out of fathomless workings fermented and
        thrown,
A limp blossom or two, torn, just as much over waves floating,
        drifted at random,
Just as much for us that sobbing dirge of Nature,

Just as much whence we come that blare of the cloud-trum-
  pets,
We, capricious, brought hither we know not whence, spread
  out before you,
You up there walking or sitting,
Whoever you are, we too lie in drifts at your feet.

TEARS

Tears! tears! tears!
In the night, in solitude, tears,
On the white shore dripping, dripping, suck'd in by the sand,
Tears, not a star shining, all dark and desolate,
Moist tears from the eyes of a muffled head;
O who is that ghost? that form in the dark, with tears?
What shapeless lump is that, bent, crouch'd there on the sand?
Streaming tears, sobbing tears, throes, choked with wild cries;
O storm, embodied, rising, careering with swift steps along
  the beach!
O wild and dismal night storm, with wind—O belching and
  desperate!
O shade so sedate and decorous by day, with calm countenance
  and regulated pace,
But away at night as you fly, none looking—O then the un-
  loosen'd ocean,
Of tears! tears! tears!

TO THE MAN-OF-WAR-BIRD

Thou who has slept all night upon the storm,
Waking renew'd on thy prodigious pinions,
(Burst the wild storm? above it thou ascended'st,
And rested on the sky, thy slave that cradled thee,)
Now a blue point, far, far in heaven floating,
As to the light emerging here on deck I watch thee,
(Myself a speck, a point on the world's floating vast.)
Far, far at sea,
After the night's fierce drifts have strewn the shore with
  wrecks,
With re-appearing day as now so happy and serene,
The rosy and elastic dawn, the flashing sun,
The limpid spread of air cerulean,
Thou also re-appearest.

Thou born to match the gale, (thou art all wings,)
To cope with heaven and earth and sea and hurricane,
Thou ship of air that never furl'st thy sails,
Days, even weeks untired and onward, through spaces, realms
  gyrating,
At dusk that look'st on Senegal, at morn America,

That sport'st amid the lightning-flash and thunder-cloud,
In them, in thy experiences, had'st thou my soul,
What joys! what joys were thine!

ABOARD AT A SHIP'S HELM

Aboard at a ship's helm,
A young steersman steering with care.

Through fog on a sea-coast dolefully ringing,
An ocean-bell—O a warning bell, rock'd by the waves.

O you give good notice indeed, you bell by the sea-reefs ring-
ing,
Ringing, ringing, to warn the ship from its wreck-place.

For as on the alert O steersman, you mind the loud admoni-
tion,
The bows turn, the freighted ship tacking speeds away under
her gray sails,
The beautiful and noble ship with all her precious wealth
speeds away gayly and safe.

But O the ship, the immortal ship! O ship aboard the ship!
Ship of the body, ship of the soul, voyaging, voyaging, voyag-
ing.

ON THE BEACH AT NIGHT

On the beach at night,
Stands a child with her father,
Watching the east, the autumn sky.

Up through the darkness,
While ravening clouds, the burial clouds, in black masses
spreading,
Lower sullen and fast athwart and down the sky,
Amid a transparent clear belt of ether yet left in the east,
Ascends large and calm the lord-star Jupiter,
And nigh at hand, only a very little above,
Swim the delicate sisters the Pleiades.

From the beach the child holding the hand of her father,
Those burial clouds that lower victorious soon to devour all,
Watching, silently weeps.

Weep not, child,
Weep not, my darling,
With these kisses let me remove your tears,
The ravening clouds shall not long be victorious,
They shall not long possess the sky, they devour the stars only
in apparition,

Jupiter shall emerge, be patient, watch again another night,
    the Pleiades shall emerge,
They are immortal, all those stars both silvery and golden shall
    shine out again,
The great stars and the little ones shall shine out again, they
    endure,
The vast immortal suns and the long-enduring pensive moons
    shall again shine.

Then dearest child mournest thou only for Jupiter?
Considerest thou alone the burial of the stars?

Something there is,
(With my lips soothing thee, adding I whisper,
I give thee the first suggestion, the problem and indirection,)
Something there is more immortal even than the stars,
(Many the burials, many the days and nights, passing away,)
Something that shall endure longer even than lustrous Jupiter,
Longer than sun or any revolving satellite,
Or the radiant sisters the Pleiades.

THE WORLD BELOW THE BRINE

The world below the brine,
Forests at the bottom of the sea, the branches and leaves,
Sea-lettuce, vast lichens, strange flowers and seeds, the thick
    tangle, openings, and pink turf,
Different colors, pale gray and green, purple, white, and gold,
    the play of light through the water,
Dumb swimmers there among the rocks, coral, gluten, grass,
    rushes, and the aliment of the swimmers,
Sluggish existences grazing there suspended, or slowly crawl-
    ing close to the bottom,
The sperm-whale at the surface blowing air and spray, or
    disporting with his flukes,
The leaden-eyed shark, the walrus, the turtle, the hairy sea-
    leopard, and the sting-ray,
Passions there, wars, pursuits, tribes, sight in those ocean-
    depths, breathing that thick-breathing air, as
    so many do,
The change thence to the sight here, and to the subtle air
    breathed by beings like us who walk this
    sphere,
The change onward from ours to that of beings who walk other
    spheres.

ON THE BEACH AT NIGHT ALONE

On the beach at night alone,
As the old mother sways her to and fro singing her husky song,

As I watch the bright stars shining, I think a thought of the
        clef of the universes and of the future.

A vast similitude interlocks all,
All spheres, grown, ungrown, small, large, suns, moons,
        planets,
All distances of place however wide,
All distances of time, all inanimate forms,
All souls, all living bodies though they be ever so different,
        or in different worlds,
All gaseous, watery, vegetable, mineral processes, the fishes,
        the brutes,
All nations, colors, barbarisms, civilizations, languages,
All identities that have existed or may exist on this globe, or
        any globe
All lives and deaths, all of the past, present, future,
This vast similitude spans them, and always has spann'd,
And shall forever span them and compactly hold and enclose
        them.

SONG FOR ALL SEAS, ALL SHIPS

1

To-day a rude brief recitative,
Of ships sailing the seas, each with its special flag or ship-
        signal,
Of unnamed heroes in the ships—of waves spreading and
        spreading far as the eye can reach,
Of dashing spray, and the winds piping and blowing,
And out of these a chant for the sailors of all nations,
Fitful, like a surge.

Of sea-captains young or old, and the mates, and of all in-
        trepid sailors,
Of the few, very choice, taciturn, whom fate can never surprise
        nor death dismay,
Pick'd sparingly without noise by thee old ocean, chosen by
        thee,
Thou sea that pickest and cullest the race in time, and unitest
        nations,
Suckled by thee, old husky nurse, embodying thee,
Indomitable, untamed as thee.

(Ever the heroes on water or on land, by ones or twos appear-
        ing,
Ever the stock preserv'd and never lost, though rare, enough
        for seed preserv'd.)

2

Flaunt out O sea your separate flags of nations!
Flaunt out visible as ever the various ship-signals!
But do you reserve especially for yourself and for the soul of
        man one flag above all the rest,
A spiritual woven signal for all nations, emblem of man elate
        above death,
Token of all brave captains and all intrepid sailors and mates,
And all that went down doing their duty,
Reminiscent of them, twined from all intrepid captains young
        or old,
A pennant universal, subtly waving all time, o'er all brave
        sailors,
All seas, all ships.

PATROLING BARNEGAT

Wild, wild the storm, and the sea high running,
Steady the roar of the gale, with incessant undertone mutter-
        ing,
Shouts of demoniac laughter fitfully piercing and pealing,
Waves, air, midnight, their savagest trinity lashing,
Out in the shadows there milk-white combs careering,
On beachy slush and sand spirts of snow fierce slanting,
Where through the murk the easterly death-wind breasting,
Through cutting swirl and spray watchful and firm advancing,
(That in the distance! is that a wreck? is the red signal flaring?)
Slush and sand of the beach tireless till daylight wending,
Steadily, slowly, through hoarse roar never remitting,
Along the midnight edge by those milk-white combs careering,
A group of dim, weird forms, struggling, the night confronting,
That savage trinity warily watching.

AFTER THE SEA-SHIP

After the sea-ship, after the whistling winds,
After the white-gray sails taut to their spars and ropes,
Below, a myriad myriad waves hastening, lifting up their necks,
Tending in ceaseless flow toward the track of the ship,
Waves of the ocean bubbling and gurgling, blithely prying,
Waves, undulating waves, liquid, uneven, emulous waves,
Toward that whirling current, laughing and buoyant, with
        curves,
Where the great vessel sailing and tacking displaced the sur-
        face,
Larger and smaller waves in the spread of the ocean yearnfully
        flowing,

The wake of the sea-ship after she passes, flashing and frolic-
    some under the sun,
A motley procession with many a fleck of foam and many
    fragments,
Following the stately and rapid ship, in the wake following.

BY THE ROADSIDE

A BOSTON BALLAD

[1854]

To get betimes in Boston town I rose this morning early,
Here's a good place at the corner, I must stand and see the
    show.

Clear the way there Jonathan!
Way for the President's marshal—way for the government
    cannon!
Way for the Federal foot and dragoons, (and the apparitions
    copiously tumbling.)

I love to look on the Stars and Stripes, I hope the fifes will play
    Yankee Doodle.

How bright shine the cutlasses of the foremost troops!
Every man holds his revolver, marching stiff through Boston
    town.

A fog follows, antiques of the same come limping,
Some appear wooden-legged, and some appear bandaged and
    bloodless.

Why this is indeed a show—it has called the dead out of the
    earth!
The old graveyards of the hills have hurried to see!
Phantoms! phantoms countless by flank and rear!
Cock'd hats of mothy mould—crutches made of mist!
Arms in slings—old men leaning on young men's shoulders.

What troubles you Yankee phantoms? what is all this chatter-
    ing of bare gums?
Does the ague convulse your limbs? do you mistake your
    crutches for firelocks and level them?

If you blind your eyes with tears you will not see the Presi-
    dent's marshal,
If you groan such groans you might balk the government can-
    non.

For shame old maniacs—bring down those toss'd arms, and let
      your white hair be,
Here gape your great-grandsons, their wives gaze at them from
      the windows,
See how well dress'd, see how orderly they conduct themselves.

Worse and worse—can't you stand it? are you retreating?
Is this hour with the living too dead for you?

Retreat then—pell-mell!
To your graves—back—back to the hills old limpers!
I do not think you belong here anyhow.

But there is one thing that belongs here—shall I tell you what
      it is, gentlemen of Boston?

I will whisper it to the Mayor, he shall send a committee to
      England,
They shall get a grant from the Parliament, go with a cart to
      the royal vault,
Dig out King George's coffin, unwrap him quick from the
      grave-clothes, box up his bones for a journey,
Find a swift Yankee clipper—here is freight for you, black-
      bellied clipper,
Up with your anchor—shake out your sails—steer straight
      toward Boston bay.

Now call for the President's marshal again, bring out the
      government cannon,
Fetch home the roarers from Congress, make another proces-
      sion, guard it with foot and dragoons.

This centre-piece for them;
Look, all orderly citizens—look from the windows, women!

The committee open the box, set up the regal ribs, glue those
      that will not stay,
Clap the skull on top of the ribs, and clap a crown on top of
      the skull.

You have got your revenge, old buster—the crown is come to
      its own, and more than its own.
Stick your hands in your pockets, Jonathan—you are a made
      man from this day,
You are mighty cute—and here is one of your bargains.

EUROPE

The 72d and 73d Years of These States

Suddenly out of its stale and drowsy lair, the lair of slaves,
Like lightning it le'pt half startled at itself,
Its feet upon the ashes and the rags, its hand tight to the throats
      of kings.

O hope and faith!
O aching close of exiled patriots' lives!
O many a sicken'd heart!
Turn back unto this day and make yourselves afresh.

And you, paid to defile the People—you liars, mark!
Not for numberless agonies, murders, lusts,
For court thieving in its manifold mean forms, worming from
    his simplicity the poor man's wages,
For many a promise sworn by royal lips and broken and
    laugh'd at in the breaking,
Then in their power not for all these did the blows strike
    revenge, or the heads of the nobles fall;
The People scorn'd the ferocity of kings.

But the sweetness of mercy brew'd bitter destruction, and the
    frighten'd monarchs come back,
Each comes in state with his train, hangman, priest, tax-gath-
    erer,
Soldier, lawyer, lord, jailer, and sycophant.

Yet behind all lowering stealing, lo, a shape,
Vague as the night, draped interminably, head, front and form,
    in scarlet folds,
Whose face and eyes none may see,
Out of its robes only this, the red robes lifted by the arm,
One finger crook'd pointed high over the top, like the head of
    a snake appears.

Meanwhile corpses lie in new-made graves, bloody corpses of
    young men,
The rope of the gibbet hangs heavily, the bullets of princes are
    flying, the creatures of power laugh aloud,
And all these things bear fruits, and they are good.

Those corpses of young men,
Those martyrs that hang from the gibbets, those hearts pierc'd
    by the gray lead,
Cold and motionless as they seem live elsewhere with un-
    slaughter'd vitality.

They live in other young men O kings!
They live in brothers again ready to defy you,
They were purified by death, they were taught and exalted.

Not a grave of the murder'd for freedom but grows seed for
    freedom, in its turn to bear seed,
Which the winds carry afar and re-sow, and the rains and the
    snows nourish.

Not a disembodied spirit can the weapons of tyrants let loose,
But it stalks invisibly over the earth, whispering, counseling,
          cautioning.

Liberty, let others despair of you—I never despair of you.

Is the house shut? is the master away?
Nevertheless, be ready, be not weary of watching,
He will soon return, his messengers come anon.

A HAND-MIRROR

Hold it up sternly—see this it sends back, (who is it? is it you?)
Outside fair costume, within ashes and filth,
No more a flashing eye, no more a sonorous voice or springy
          step,
Now some slave's eye, voice, hands, step,
A drunkard's breath, unwholesome eater's face, venerealee's
          flesh,
Lungs rotting away piecemeal, stomach sour and cankerous,
Joints rheumatic, bowels clogged with abomination,
Blood circulating dark and poisonous streams,
Words babble, hearing and touch callous,
No brain, no heart left, no magnetism of sex;
Such from one look in this looking-glass ere you go hence,
Such a result so soon—and from such a beginning!

GODS

Lover divine and perfect Comrade,
Waiting content, invisible yet, but certain,
Be thou my God.

Thou, thou, the Ideal Man,
Fair, able, beautiful, content, and loving,
Complete in body and dilate in spirit,
Be thou my God.

O Death, (for Life has served its turn,)
Opener and usher to the heavenly mansion,
Be thou my God.

Aught, aught of mightiest, best I see, conceive, or know,
(To break the stagnant tie—thee, thee to free, O soul,)
Be thou my God.

All great ideas, the races' aspirations,
All heroisms, deeds of rapt enthusiasts,
Be ye my Gods.

Or Time and Space,
Or shape of Earth divine and wondrous,
Or some fair shape I viewing, worship,
Or lustrous orb of sun or star by night,
Be ye my Gods.

GERMS

Forms, qualities, lives, humanity, language, thoughts,
The ones known, and the ones unknown, the ones on the stars,
The stars themselves, some shaped, others unshaped,
Wonders as of those countries, the soil, trees, cities, inhabi-
        tants, whatever they may be,
Splendid suns, the moons and rings, the countless combina-
        tions and effects,
Such-like, and as good as such-like, visible here or anywhere,
        stand provided for in a handful of space,
        which I extend my arm and half enclose with
        my hand,
That containing the start of each and all, the virtue, the germs
        of all.

THOUGHTS

Of ownership—as if one fit to own things could not at pleasure
        enter upon all, and incorporate them into
        himself or herself;
Of vista—suppose some sight in arriere through the formative
        chaos, presuming the growth, fulness, life,
        now attain'd on the journey,
(But I see the road continued, and the journey ever con-
        tinued;)
Of what was once lacking on earth, and in due time has
        become supplied—and of what will yet be
        supplied,
Because all I see and know I believe to have its main purport
        in what will yet be supplied.

WHEN I HEARD THE LEARN'D ASTRONOMER

When I heard the learn'd astronomer,
When the proofs, the figures, were ranged in columns before
        me,
When I was shown the charts and diagrams, to add, divide, and
        measure them,
When I sitting heard the astronomer where he lectured with
        much applause in the lecture-room,
How soon unaccountable I became tired and sick,
Till rising and gliding out I wander'd off by myself,
In the mystical moist night-air, and from time to time,
Look'd up in perfect silence at the stars.

PERFECTIONS

Only themselves understand themselves and the like of them-
     selves,
As souls only understand souls.

O ME! O LIFE!

O me! O life! of the questions of these recurring,
Of the endless trains of the faithless, of cities fill'd with the
     foolish,
Of myself forever reproaching myself, (for who more foolish
     than I, and who more faithless?)
Of eyes that vainly crave the light, of the objects mean, of the
     struggle ever renew'd,
Of the poor results of all, of the plodding and sordid crowds
     I see around me,
Of the empty and useless years of the rest, with the rest me
     intertwined,
The question, O me! so sad, recurring—What good amid these,
     O me, O life?

Answer

That you are here—that life exists and identity,
That the powerful play goes on, and you may contribute a
     verse.

TO A PRESIDENT

All you are doing and saying is to America dangled mirages,
You have not learn'd of Nature—of the politics of Nature you
     have not learn'd the great amplitude, recti-
     tude, impartiality,
You have not seen that only such as they are for these States,
And that what is less than they must sooner or later lift off
     from these States.

I SIT AND LOOK OUT

I sit and look out upon all the sorrows of the world, and upon
     all oppression and shame,
I hear secret convulsive sobs from young men at anguish with
     themselves, remorseful after deeds done,
I see in low life the mother misused by her children, dying,
     neglected, gaunt, desperate,
I see the wife misused by her husband, I see the treacherous
     seducer of young women,
I mark the ranklings of jealousy and unrequited love attempted
     to be hid, I see these sights on the earth,

I see the workings of battle, pestilence, tyranny, I see mar-
       tyrs and prisoners,
I observe a famine at sea, I observe the sailors casting lots who
       shall be kill'd to preserve the lives of the rest,
I observe the slights and degradations cast by arrogant persons
       upon laborers, the poor, and upon negroes,
       and the like;
All these—all the meanness and agony without end I sitting
       look out upon,
See, hear, and am silent.

TO RICH GIVERS

What you give me I cheerfully accept,
A little sustenance, a hut and garden, a little money, as I ren-
       dezvous with my poems,
A traveler's lodging and breakfast as I journey through the
       States,—why should I be ashamed to own
       such gifts? why to advertise for them?
For I myself am not one who bestows nothing upon man and
       woman,
For I bestow upon any man or woman the entrance to all the
       gifts of the universe.

THE DALLIANCE OF THE EAGLES

Skirting the river road, (my forenoon walk, my rest,)
Skyward in air a sudden muffled sound, the dalliance of the
       eagles,
The rushing amorous contact high in space together,
The clinching interlocking claws, a living, fierce, gyrating
       wheel,
Four beating wings, two beaks, a swirling mass tight grappling,
In tumbling turning clustering loops, straight downward falling,
Till o'er the river pois'd, the twain yet one, a moment's lull,
A motionless still balance in the air, then parting, talons loos-
       ing,
Upward again on slow-firm pinions slanting, their separate
       diverse flight,
She hers, he his, pursuing.

ROAMING IN THOUGHT
[After reading *Hegel*]

Roaming in thought over the Universe, I saw the little that is
       Good steadily hastening towards immortal-
       ity,
And the vast all that is call'd Evil I saw hastening to merge
       itself and become lost and dead.

A FARM PICTURE

Through the ample open door of the peaceful country barn,
A sunlit pasture field with cattle and horses feeding,
And haze and vista, and the far horizon fading away.

A CHILD'S AMAZE

Silent and amazed even when a little boy,
I remember I heard the preacher every Sunday put God in his
statements,
As contending against some being or influence.

THE RUNNER

On a flat road runs the well-train'd runner,
He is lean and sinewy with muscular legs,
He is thinly clothed, he leans forward as he runs,
With lightly closed fists and arms partially rais'd.

BEAUTIFUL WOMEN

Women sit or move to and fro, some old, some young,
The young are beautiful—but the old are more beautiful than
the young.

MOTHER AND BABE

I see the sleeping babe nestling the breast of its mother,
The sleeping mother and babe—hush'd, I study them long
and long.

THOUGHT

Of obedience, faith, adhesiveness;
As I stand aloof and look there is to me something profoundly
affecting in large masses of men following the
lead of those who do not believe in men.

VISOR'D

A mask, a perpetual natural disguiser of herself,
Concealing her face, concealing her form,
Changes and transformations every hour, every moment,
Falling upon her even when she sleeps.

THOUGHT

Of Justice—as if Justice could be any thing but the same ample
law, expounded by natural judges and saviors,
As if it might be this thing or that thing, according to decisions.

GLIDING O'ER ALL

Gliding o'er all, through all,
Through Nature, Time, and Space,
As a ship on the waters advancing,
The voyage of the soul—not life alone,
Death, many deaths I'll sing.

HAST NEVER COME TO THEE AN HOUR

Hast never come to thee an hour,
A sudden gleam divine, precipitating, bursting all these bub-
    bles, fashions, wealth?
These eager business aims—books, politics, art, amours,
To utter nothingness?

THOUGHT

Of Equality—as if it harm'd me, giving others the same chances
            and rights as myself—as if it were not indis-
            pensable to my own rights that others possess
            the same.

TO OLD AGE

I see in you the estuary that enlarges and spreads itself grandly
            as it pours in the great sea.

LOCATIONS AND TIMES

Locations and times—what is it in me that meets them all,
            whenever and wherever, and makes me at
            home?
Forms, colors, densities, odors—what is it in me that corre-
            sponds with them?

OFFERINGS

A thousand perfect men and women appear,
Around each gathers a cluster of friends, and gay children
            and youths, with offerings.

TO THE STATES

To Identify the 16th, 17th, or 18th Presidentiad.

Why reclining, interrogating? why myself and all drowsing?
What deepening twilight—scum floating atop of the waters,
Who are they as bats and night-dogs askant in the capitol?
What a filthy Presidentiad! (O South, your torrid suns! O
            North, your arctic freezings!)
Are those really Congressmen? are those the great Judges? is
            that the President?
Then I will sleep awhile yet, for I see that these States sleep,
            for reasons;

(With gathering murk, with muttering thunder and lambent
shoots we all duly awake,
South, North, East, West, inland and seaboard, we will surely
awake.)

DRUM-TAPS

FIRST O SONGS FOR A PRELUDE

First O songs for a prelude,
Lightly strike on the stretch'd tympanum pride and joy in my
city,
How she led the rest to arms, how she gave the cue,
How at once with lithe limbs unwaiting a moment she sprang,
(O superb! O Manhattan, my own, my peerless!
O strongest you in the hour of danger, in crisis! O truer than
steel!)
How you sprang—how you threw off the costumes of peace
with indifferent hand,
How your soft opera-music changed, and the drum and fife
were heard in their stead,
How you led to the war, (that shall serve for our prelude, songs
of soldiers,)
How Manhattan drum-taps led.

Forty years had I in my city seen soldiers parading,
Forty years as a pageant, till unawares the lady of this teeming
and turbulent city,
Sleepless amid her ships, her houses, her incalculable wealth,
With her million children around her, suddenly,
At dead of night, at news from the south,
Incens'd struck with clinch'd hand the pavement.

A shock electric, the night sustain'd it,
Till with ominous hum our hive at daybreak pour'd out its
myriads.

From the houses then and the workshops, and through all the
doorways,
Leapt they tumultuous, and lo! Manhattan arming.

To the drum-taps prompt,
The young men falling in and arming,
The mechanics arming, (the trowel, the jack-plane, the black-
smith's hammer, tost aside with precipita-
tion,)

The lawyer leaving his office and arming, the judge leaving the
        court,
The driver deserting his wagon in the street, jumping down,
        throwing the reins abruptly down on the
        horses' backs,
The salesman leaving the store, the boss, book-keeper, porter,
        all leaving,
Squads gather everywhere by common consent and arm,
The new recruits, even boys, the old men show them how to
        wear their accoutrements, they buckle the
        straps carefully,
Outdoors arming, indoors arming, the flash of the musket-
        barrels,
The white tents cluster in camps, the arm'd sentries around,
        the sunrise cannon and again at sunset,
Arm'd regiments arrive every day, pass through the city, and
        embark from the wharves,
(How good they look as they tramp down to the river, sweaty,
        with their guns on their shoulders!
How I love them! how I could hug them, with their brown
        faces and their clothes and knapsacks cover'd
        with dust!)
The blood of the city up—arm'd! arm'd! the cry everywhere,
The flags flung out from the steeples of churches and from
        all the public buildings and stores,
The tearful parting, the mother kisses her son, the son kisses
        his mother,
(Loth is the mother to part, yet not a word does she speak
        to detain him,)
The tumultuous escort, the ranks of policemen preceding,
        clearing the way,
The unpent enthusiasm, the wild cheers of the crowd for their
        favorites,
The artillery, the silent cannons bright as gold, drawn along,
        rumble lightly over the stones,
(Silent cannons, soon to cease your silence,
Soon unlimber'd to begin the red business;)
All the mutter of preparation, all the determin'd arming,
The hospital service, the lint, bandages and medicines,
The women volunteering for nurses, the work begun for in
        earnest, no mere parade now;
War! an arm'd race is advancing! the welcome for battle, no
        turning away;
War! be it weeks, months, or years, an arm'd race is advancing
        to welcome it.
Mannahatta a-march—and it's O to sing it well!
It's O for a manly life in the camp.

And the sturdy artillery,
The guns bright as gold, the work for giants, to serve well the
   guns,
Unlimber them! (no more as the past forty years for salute
   or courtesies merely,
Put in something now besides powder and wadding.)

And you lady of ships, you Mannahatta,
Old matron of this proud, friendly, turbulent city,
Often in peace and wealth you were pensive or covertly
   frown'd amid all your children,
But now you smile with joy exulting old Mannahatta.

EIGHTEEN SIXTY-ONE

Arm'd year—year of the struggle,
No dainty rhymes or sentimental love verses for you terrible
   year,
Not you as some pale poetling seated at a desk lisping cadenzas
   piano,
But as a strong man erect, clothed in blue clothes, advancing,
   carrying a rifle on your shoulder,
With well-gristled body and sunburnt face and hands, with a
   knife in the belt at your side,
As I heard you shouting loud, your sonorous voice ringing
   across the continent,
Your masculine voice O year, as rising amid the great cities,
Amid the men of Manhattan I saw you as one of the workmen,
   the dwellers in Manhattan,
Or with large steps crossing the prairies out of Illinois and
   Indiana,
Rapidly crossing the West with springy gait and descending
   the Alleghanies,
Or down from the great lakes or in Pennsylvania, or on deck
   along the Ohio river,
Or southward along the Tennessee or Cumberland rivers, or at
   Chattanooga on the mountain top,
Saw I your gait and saw I your sinewy limbs clothed in blue,
   bearing weapons, robust year,
Heard your determin'd voice launch'd forth again and again,
Year that suddenly sang by the mouths of the round-lipp'd
   cannon,
I repeat you, hurrying, crashing, sad, distracted year.

BEAT! BEAT! DRUMS!

Beat! beat! drums—blow! bugles, blow!
Through the windows—through doors—burst like a ruthless
   force,
Into the solemn church, and scatter the congregation,
Into the school where the scholar is studying;

Leave not the bridegroom quiet—no happiness must he have
  now with his bride,
Nor the peaceful farmer any peace, ploughing his field or
  gathering his grain,
So fierce you whirr and pound you drums—so shrill you bugles
  blow.

Beat! beat! drums—blow! bugles! blow!
Over the traffic of cities—over the rumble of wheels in the
  streets;
Are beds prepared for sleepers at night in the houses? no
  sleepers must sleep in those beds,
No bargainers' bargains by day—no brokers or speculators—
  would they continue?
Would the talkers be talking? would the singer attempt to sing?
Would the lawyers rise in the court to state his case before the
  judge?
Then rattle quicker, heavier drums—you bugles wilder blow.

Beat! beat! drums!—blow! bugles! blow!
Make no parley—stop for no expostulation,
Mind not the timid—mind not the weeper or prayer,
Mind not the old man beseeching the young man,
Let not the child's voice be heard, nor the mother's entreaties,
Make even the trestles to shake the dead where they lie await-
  ing the hearses,
So strong you thump O terrible drums—so loud you bugles
  blow.

FROM PAUMANOK STARTING I FLY LIKE A BIRD

From Paumanok starting I fly like a bird,
Around and around to soar to sing the idea of all,
To the north betaking myself to sing there arctic songs,
To Kanada till I absorb Kanada in myself, to Michigan then,
To Wisconsin, Iowa, Minnesota, to sing their songs, (they are
  inimitable;)
Then to Ohio and Indiana to sing theirs, to Missouri and Kan-
  sas and Arkansas to sing theirs,
To Tennessee and Kentucky, to the Carolinas and Georgia to
  sing theirs,
To Texas and so along up toward California, to roam accepted
  everywhere;
To sing first, (to the tap of the war-drum if need be,)
The idea of all, of the Western world one and inseparable,
And then the song of each member of these States.

SONG OF THE BANNER AT DAYBREAK

Poet

O a new song, a free song,
Flapping, flapping, flapping, flapping, by sounds, by voices
    clearer,
By the wind's voice and that of the drum,
By the banner's voice and child's voice and sea's voice and
    father's voice,
Low on the ground and high in the air,
On the ground where father and child stand,
In the upward air where their eyes turn,
Where the banner at daybreak is flapping.

Words! book-words! what are you?
Words no more, for hearken and see,
My song is there in the open air, and I must sing,
With the banner and pennant a-flapping.

I'll weave the chord and twine in,
Man's desire and babe's desire, I'll twine them in, I'll put in life,
I'll put the bayonet's flashing point, I'll let bullets and slugs
    whizz,
(As one carrying a symbol and menace far into the future,
Crying with trumpet voice, *Arouse and beware! Beware and
    arouse!*)
I'll pour the verse with streams of blood, full of volition, full
    of joy,
Then loosen, launch forth, to go and compete,
With the banner and pennant a-flapping.

Pennant

Come up here, bard, bard,
Come up here, soul, soul,
Come up here, dear little child,
To fly in the clouds and winds with me, and play with the
    measureless light.

Child

Father what is that in the sky beckoning to me with long finger?
And what does it say to me all the while?

Father

Nothing my babe you see in the sky,
And nothing at all to you it says—but look you my babe,
Look at these dazzling things in the houses, and see you the
    money-shops opening,
And see you the vehicles preparing to crawl along the streets
    with goods;

These, ah these, how valued and toil'd for these!
How envied by all the earth!

Poet

Fresh and rosy red the sun is mounting high,
On floats the sea in distant blue careering through its channels,
On floats the wind over the breast of the sea setting in toward
    land,
The great steady wind from west or west-by-south,
Floating so buoyant with milk-white foam on the waters.

But I am not the sea nor the red sun,
I am not the wind with girlish laughter,
Not the immense wind which strengthens, not the wind which
    lashes,
Not the spirit that ever lashes its own body to terror and death,
But I am that which unseen comes and sings, sings, sings,
Which babbles in brooks and scoots in showers on the land,
Which the birds know in the woods mornings and evenings,
And the shore-sands know and the hissing wave, and that
    banner and pennant,
Aloft there flapping and flapping.

Child

O father it is alive—it is full of people—it has children,
O now it seems to me it is talking to its children,
I hear it—it talks to me—O it is wonderful!
O it stretches—it spreads and runs so fast—O my father,
It is so broad it covers the whole sky.

Father

Cease, cease, my foolish babe,
What you are saying is sorrowful to me, much it displeases me;
Behold with the rest again I say, behold not banners and pen-
    nants aloft,
But the well-prepared pavements behold, and mark the solid-
    wall'd houses.

Banner and Pennant

Speak to the child O bard out of Manhattan,
To our children all, or north or south of Manhattan,
Point this day, leaving all the rest, to us over all—and yet we
    know not why,
For what are we, mere strips of cloth profiting nothing,
Only flapping in the wind?

Poet

I hear and see not strips of cloth alone,
I hear the tramp of armies, I hear the challenging sentry,

I hear the jubilant shouts of millions of men, I hear Liberty!
I hear the drums beat and the trumpets blowing,
I myself move abroad swift-rising flying then,
I use the wings of the land-bird and use the wings of the sea-
    bird, and look down as from a height,
I do not deny the precious results of peace, I see populous cities
    with wealth incalculable,
I see numberless farms, I see the farmers working in their fields
    or barns,
I see mechanics working, I see buildings everywhere founded,
    going up, or finish'd,
I see trains of cars swiftly speeding along railroad tracks drawn
    by the locomotives,
I see the stores, depots, of Boston, Baltimore, Charleston, New
    Orleans,
I see far in the West the immense area of grain, I dwell awhile
    hovering,
I pass to the lumber forests of the North, and again to the
    Southern plantation, and again to California;
Sweeping the whole I see the countless profit, the busy gath-
    erings, earn'd wages,
See the Identity formed out of thirty-eight spacious and
    haughty States, (and many more to come,)
See forts on the shores of harbors, see ships sailing in and out;
Then over all, (aye! aye!) my little and lengthen'd pennant
    shaped like a sword,
Runs swiftly up indicating war and defiance—and now the
    halyards have rais'd it,
Side of my banner broad and blue, side of my starry banner,
Discarding peace over all the sea and land.

Banner and Pennant

Yet louder, higher, stronger, bard! yet farther, wider cleave!
No longer let our children deem us riches and peace alone,
We may be terror and carnage, and are so now,
Not now are we any one of these spacious and haughty States,
    (nor any five, nor ten,)
Nor market nor depot we, nor money-bank in the city,
But these and all, and the brown and spreading land, and the
    mines below, are ours,
And the shores of the sea are ours, and the rivers great and
    small,
And the fields they moisten, and the crops and the fruits are
    ours,
Bays and channels and ships sailing in and out are ours—while
    we over all,
Over the area spread below, the three or four millions of square
    miles, the capitals,

The forty millions of people,—O bard! in life and death
    supreme,
We, even we, henceforth flaunt out masterful, high up above,
Not for the present alone, for a thousand years chanting
    through you,
This song to the soul of one poor little child.

Child

O my father I like not the houses,
They will never to me be anything, nor do I like money,
But to mount up there I would like, O father dear, that banner
    I like,
That pennant I would be and must be.

Father

Child of mine you fill me with anguish,
To be that pennant would be too fearful,
Little you know what it is this day, and after this day, forever,
It is to gain nothing, but risk and defy everything,
Forward to stand in front of wars—and O, such wars!—what
    have you to do with them?
With passions of demons, slaughter, premature death?

Banner

Demons and death then I sing,
Put in all, aye will I, sword-shaped pennant for war,
And a pleasure new and ecstatic, and the prattled yearning of
    children,
Blent with the sounds of the peaceful land and the liquid wash
    of the sea,
And the black ships fighting on the sea envelop'd in smoke,
And the icy cool of the far, far north, with rustling cedars
    and pines,
And the whirr of drums and the sound of soldiers marching,
    and the hot sun shining south,
And the beach-waves combing over the beach on my Eastern
    shore, and my Western shore the same,
And all between those shores, and my ever running Mississippi
    with bends and chutes,
And my Illinois fields, and my Kansas fields, and my fields of
    Missouri,
The Continent, devoting the whole identity without reserving
    an atom,
Pour in! whelm that which asks, which sings, with all and the
    yield of all,
Fusing and holding, claiming, devouring the whole,
No more with tender lip, nor musical labial sound,

But out of the night emerging for good, our voice persuasive
    no more,
Croaking like crows here in the wind.

Poet

My limbs, my veins dilate, my theme is clear at last,
Banner so broad advancing out of the night, I sing you haughty
    and resolute,
I burst through where I waited long, too long, deafen'd and
    blinded,
My hearing and tongue are come to me, (a little child taught
    me,)
I hear from above O pennant of war your ironical call and
    demand,
Insensate! insensate! (yet I at any rate chant you,) O banner!
Not houses of peace indeed are you, nor any nor all their
    prosperity, (if need be, you shall again have
    every one of those houses to destroy them,
You thought not to destroy those valuable houses, standing
    fast, full of comfort, built with money,
May they stand fast, then? not an hour except you above
    them and all stand fast;)
O banner, not money so precious are you, not farm produce
    you, nor the material good nutriment,
Nor excellent stores, nor landed on wharves from the ships,
Not the superb ships with sail-power or steam-power, fetching
    and carrying cargoes,
Nor machinery, vehicles, trade, nor revenues—but you as
    henceforth I see you,
Running up out of the night, bringing your cluster of stars,
    (ever-enlarging stars,)
Divider of daybreak you, cutting the air, touch'd by the sun,
    measuring the sky,
(Passionately seen and yearn'd for by one poor little child,
While others remain busy or smartly talking, forever teaching
    thrift, thrift;)
O you up there! O pennant! where you undulate like a snake
    hissing so curious,
Out of reach, an idea only, yet furiously fought for, risking
    bloody death, loved by me,
So loved—O you banner leading the day with stars brought
    from the night!
Valueless, object of eyes, over all and demanding all—(abso-
    lute owner of all)—O banner and pennant!
I too leave the rest—great as it is, it is nothing—houses, ma-
    chines are nothing—I see them not,
I see but you, O warlike pennant! O banner so broad, with
    stripes, I sing you only,
Flapping up there in the wind.

RISE O DAYS FROM YOUR FATHOMLESS DEEPS

1

Rise O days from your fathomless deeps, till you loftier, fiercer
        sweep,
Long for my soul hungering gymnastic I devour'd what the
        earth gave me,
Long I roam'd the woods of the north, long I watch'd Niagara
        pouring,
I travel'd the prairies over and slept on their breast, I cross'd
        the Nevadas, I cross'd the Plateaus,
I ascended the towering rocks along the Pacific, I sail'd out to
        sea,
I sail'd through the storm, I was refresh'd by the storm,
I watch'd with joy the threatening maws of the waves,
I mark'd the white combs where they career'd so high, curling
        over,
I heard the wind piping, I saw the black clouds,
Saw from below what arose and mounted, (O superb! O wild
        as my heart, and powerful!)
Heard the continuous thunder as it bellow'd after the light-
        ning,
Noted the slender and jagged threads of lightning as sudden
        and fast amid the din they chased each other
        across the sky;
These, and such as these, I, elate, saw—saw with wonder, yet
        pensive and masterful,
All the menacing might of the globe uprisen around me,
Yet there with my soul I fed, I fed content, supercilious.

2

'Twas well, O soul—'twas a good preparation you gave me,
Now we advance our latent and ampler hunger to fill,
Now we go forth to receive what the earth and the sea never
        gave us,
Not through the mighty woods we go, but through the mightier
        cities,
Something for us is pouring now more than Niagara pouring,
Torrents of men, (sources and rills of the Northwest are you
        indeed inexhaustible?)
What, to pavements and homesteads here, what were those
        storms of the mountains and sea?
What, to passions I witness around me to-day? was the sea
        risen?
Was the wind piping the pipe of death under the black clouds?
Lo! from deeps more unfathomable, something more deadly
        and savage,

Manhattan rising, advancing with menacing front—Cincin-
    nati, Chicago, unchain'd;
What was that swell I saw on the ocean? behold what comes
    here,
How it climbs with daring feet and hands—how it dashes!
How the true thunder bellows after the lightning—how bright
    the flashes of lightning!
How Democracy with desperate vengeful port strides on,
    shown through the dark by those flashes of
    lightning!
(Yet a mournful wail and low sob I fancied I heard through
    the dark,
In a lull of the deafening confusion.)

3

Thunder on! stride on, Democracy! strike with vengeful
    stroke!
And do you rise higher than ever yet O days, O cities!
Crash heavier, heavier yet O storms! you have done me good,
My soul prepared in the mountains absorbs your immortal
    strong nutriment,
Long had I walk'd my cities, my country roads through farms,
    only half satisfied,
One doubt nauseous undulating like a snake, crawl'd on the
    ground before me
Continually preceding my steps, turning upon me oft, ironi-
    cally hissing low;
The cities I loved so well I abandon'd and left, I sped to the
    certainties suitable to me,
Hungering, hungering, hungering, for primal energies and
    Nature's dauntlessness,
I refresh'd myself with it only, I could relish it only,
I waited the bursting forth of the pent fire—on the water and
    air I waited long;
But now I no longer wait, I am fully satisfied, I am glutted,
I have witness'd the true lightning, I have witness'd my cities
    electric,
I have lived to behold man burst forth and warlike America
    rise,
Hence I will seek no more the food of the northern solitary
    wilds,
No more the mountains roam or sail the stormy sea.

VIRGINIA—THE WEST

The noble sire fallen on evil days,
I saw with hand uplifted, menacing, brandishing,
(Memories of old in abeyance, love and faith in abeyance,)
The insane knife toward the Mother of All.

The noble son on sinewy feet advancing,
I saw, out of the land of prairies, land of Ohio's waters and
of Indiana,
To the rescue the stalwart giant hurry his plenteous offspring,
Drest in blue, bearing their trusty rifles on their shoulders.

Then the Mother of All with calm voice speaking,
As to you Rebellious, (I seemed to hear her say,) why strive
against me, and why seek my life?
When you yourself forever provide to defend me?
For you provided me Washington—and now these also.

CITY OF SHIPS

City of Ships!
(O the black ships! O the fierce ships!
O the beautiful sharp-bow'd steam-ships and sail-ships!)
City of the world! (for all races are here,
All the lands of the earth make contributions here;)
City of the sea! city of hurried and glittering tides!
City whose gleeful tides continually rush or recede, whirling
in and out with eddies and foam!
City of wharves and stores—city of tall façades of marble and
iron!
Proud and passionate city—mettlesome, mad, extravagant
city!
Spring up O city—not for peace alone, but be indeed your-
self, warlike!
Fear not—submit not to no models but your own O city!
Behold me—incarnate me as I have incarnated you!
I have rejected nothing you offer'd me—whom you adopted I
have adopted,
Good or bad I never question you—I love all—I do not
condemn anything,
I chant and celebrate all that is yours—yet peace no more,
In peace I chanted peace, but now the drum of war is mine,
War, red war is my song through your streets, O city!

THE CENTENARIAN'S STORY

Volunteer of 1861-2 [at Washington Park, Brooklyn, assisting the
Centenarian]

Give me your hand old Revolutionary,
The hill-top is nigh, but a few steps, (make room gentlemen,)
Up the path you have follow'd me well, spite of your hundred
and extra years,
You can walk old man, though your eyes are almost done,
Your faculties serve you, and presently I must have them
serve me.

Rest, while I tell what the crowd around us means,
On the plain below recruits are drilling and exercising,
There is the camp, one regiment departs to-morrow,
Do you hear the officers giving their orders?
Do you hear the clank of the muskets?

Why what comes over you now old man?
Why do you tremble and clutch my hand so convulsively?
The troops are but drilling, they are yet surrounded with
    smiles,
Around them at hand the well-drest friends and the women,
While splendid and warm the afternoon sun shines down,
Green the midsummer verdure and fresh blows the dallying
    breeze,
O'er proud and peaceful cities and arm of the sea between.

But drill and parade are over, they march back to quarters,
Only hear that approval of hands! hear what a clapping!

As wending the crowd now part and disperse—but we old
    man,
Not for nothing have I brought you hither—we must remain,
You to speak in your turn, and I to listen and tell.

The Centenarian

When I clutch'd your hand it was not with terror,
But suddenly pouring about me here on every side,
And below there where the boys were drilling, and up the
    slopes they ran,
And where tents are pitch'd, and wherever you see south
    and south-east and south-west,
Over hills, across lowlands and in the skirts of woods,
And along the shores in mire (now fill'd over) came again
    and suddenly raged,
As eighty-five years a-gone no mere parade receiv'd with
    applause of friends,
But a battle which I took part in myself—aye, long ago as it
    is, I took part in it,
Walking then this hilltop, this same ground.

Aye, this is the ground,
My blind eyes even as I speak behold it re-peopled from
    graves,
The years recede, pavements and stately houses disappear,
Rude forts appear again, the old hoop'd guns are mounted,
I see the lines of rais'd earth stretching from river to bay,
I mark the vista of waters, I mark the uplands and slopes;
Here we lay encamp'd, it was this time in summer also.

As I talk I remember all, I remember the Declaration,

It was read here, the whole army paraded, it was read to us
    here,
By his staff surrounded the General stood in the middle, he
    held up his unsheath'd sword,
It glitter'd in the sun in full sight of the army.

'Twas a bold act then—the English war-ships had just arrived,
We could watch down the lower bay where they lay at anchor,
And the transports swarming with soldiers.

A few days more and they landed, and then the battle.

Twenty thousand were brought against us,
A veteran force furnish'd with good artillery.

I tell not now the whole of the battle,
But one brigade early in the forenoon order'd forward to
    engage the red-coats,
Of that brigade I tell, and how steadily it march'd,
And how long and well it stood confronting death.

Who do you think that was marching steadily sternly con-
    fronting death?
It was the brigade of the youngest men, two thousand strong,
Rais'd in Virginia and Maryland, and most of them known
    personally to the General.

Jauntily forward they went with quick step toward Gowanus'
    waters,
Till of a sudden unlook'd for by defiles through the woods,
    gain'd at night,
The British advancing, rounding in from the east, fiercely
    playing their guns,
That brigade of the youngest was cut off and at the enemy's
    mercy.

The General watch'd them from this hill,
They made repeated desperate attempts to burst their environ-
    ment,
Then drew close together, very compact, their flag flying in
    the middle,
But O from the hills how the cannon were thinning and thin-
    ning them!

It sickens me yet, that slaughter!
I saw the moisture gather in drops on the face of the General.
I saw how he wrung his hands in anguish.

Meanwhile the British manœuvr'd to draw us out for a pitch'd
    battle,
But we dared not trust the chances of a pitch'd battle.

We fought the fight in detachments,
Sallying forth we fought at several points, but in each the luck
        was against us,
Our foe advancing, steadily getting the best of it, push'd us
        back to the works on this hill,
Till we turn'd menacing here, and then he left us.

That was the going out of the brigade of the youngest men,
        two thousand strong,
Few return'd, nearly all remain in Brooklyn.

That and here my General's first battle,
No women looking on nor sunshine to bask in, it did not
        conclude with applause,
Nobody clapp'd hands here then.

But in darkness in mist on the ground under a chill rain,
Wearied that night we lay foil'd and sullen,
While scornfully laugh'd many an arrogant lord off against
        us encamp'd,
Quite within hearing, feasting, clinking wineglasses together
        over their victory.

So dull and damp and another day,
But the night of that, mist lifting, rain ceasing,
Silent as a ghost while they thought they were sure of him,
        my General retreated.

I saw him at the river-side,
Down by the ferry lit by torches, hastening the embarcation;
My General waited till the soldiers and wounded were all
        pass'd over,
And then, (it was just ere sunrise,) these eyes rested on him
        for the last time.

Every one else seem'd fill'd with gloom,
Many no doubt thought of capitulation.

But when my General pass'd me,
As he stood in his boat and look'd toward the coming sun,
I saw something different from capitulation.

Terminus

Enough, the Centenarian's story ends,
The two, the past and present, have interchanged,
I myself as connecter, a chansonnier of a great future, am now
        speaking.

And is this the ground Washington trod?
And these waters I listlessly daily cross, are these the waters
        he cross'd,

As resolute in defeat as other generals in their proudest tri-
umphs?

I must copy the story, and send it eastward and westward,
I must preserve that look as it beam'd on you rivers of
Brooklyn.

See—as the annual round returns the phantoms return,
It is the 27th of August and the British have landed,
The batttle begins and goes against us, behold through the
smoke Washington's face,
The brigade of Virginia and Maryland have march'd forth to
intercept the enemy,
They are cut off, murderous artillery from the hills plays upon
them,
Rank after rank falls, while over them silently droops the
flag,
Baptized that day in many a young man's bloody wounds,
In death, defeat, and sisters', mothers' tears.

Ah, hills and slopes of Brooklyn! I perceive you are more
valuable than your owners supposed;
In the midst of you stands an encampment very old,
Stands forever the camp of that dead brigade.

CAVALRY CROSSING A FORD

A line in long array where they wind betwixt green islands,
They take a serpentine course, their arms flash in the sun—
hark to the musical clank,
Behold the silvery river, in it the splashing horses loitering
stop to drink,
Behold the brown-faced men, each group, each person a pic-
ture, the negligent rest on the saddles,
Some emerge on the opposite bank, others are just entering
the ford—while,
Scarlet and blue and snowy white,
The guidon flags flutter gayly in the wind.

BIVOUAC ON A MOUNTAIN SIDE

I see before me now a traveling army halting,
Below a fertile valley spread, with barns and the orchards of
summer,
Behind, the terraced sides of a mountain, abrupt, in places
rising high,
Broken, with rocks, with clinging cedars, with tall shapes
dingily seen,
The numerous camp-fires scatter'd near and far, some away
up on the mountain,

The shadowy forms of men and horses, looming, large-sized,
    flickering,
And over all the sky—the sky! far, far out of reach, studded,
    breaking out, the eternal stars.

AN ARMY CORPS ON THE MARCH

With its cloud of skirmishers in advance,
With now the sound of a single shot snapping like a whip, and
    now an irregular volley,
The swarming ranks press on and on, the dense brigades press
    on,
Glittering dimly, toiling under the sun—the dust-cover'd men,
In columns rise and fall to the undulations of the ground,
With artillery interspers'd—the wheels rumble, the horses
    sweat,
As the army corps advances.

BY THE BIVOUAC'S FITFUL FLAME

By the bivouac's fitful flame,
A procession winding around me, solemn and sweet and slow
    —but first I note,
The tents of the sleeping army, the fields' and woods' dim
    outline,
The darkness lit by spots of kindled fire, the silence,
Like a phantom far or near an occasional figure moving,
The shrubs and trees, (as I lift my eyes they seem to be
    stealthily watching me,)
While wind in procession thoughts, O tender and wondrous
    thoughts,
Of life and death, of home and the past and loved, and of
    those that are far away;
A solemn and slow procession there as I sit on the ground,
By the bivouac's fitful flame.

COME UP FROM THE FIELDS FATHER

Come up from the fields father, here's a letter from our Pete,
And come to the front door mother, here's a letter from thy
    dear son.

Lo, 'tis autumn,
Lo, where the trees, deeper green, yellower and redder,
Cool and sweeten Ohio's villages with leaves fluttering in the
    moderate wind,
Where apples ripe in the orchards hang and grapes on the
    trellis'd vines,
(Smell you the smell of the grapes on the vines?
Smell you the buckwheat where the bees were lately buzzing?)

Above all, lo, the sky so calm, so transparent after the rain,
      and with wondrous clouds,
Below too, all calm, all vital and beautiful, and the farm
      prospers well.

Down in the fields all prospers well,
But now from the fields come father, come at the daughter's
      call,
And come to the entry mother, to the front door come right
      away.

Fast as she can she hurries, something ominous, her steps
      trembling,
She does not tarry to smooth her hair nor adjust her cap.

Open the envelope quickly,
O this is not our son's writing, yet his name is sign'd,
O a strange hand writes for our dear son, O stricken mother's
      soul!
All swims before her eyes, flashes with black, she catches the
      main words only,
Sentences broken, *gunshot wound in the breast, cavalry skir-
      mish, taken to hospital,*
At present low, but will soon be better.

Ah now the single figure to me,
Amid all teeming and wealthy Ohio with all its cities and
      farms,
Sickly white in the face and dull in the head, very faint,
By the jamb of a door leans.

Grieve not so, dear mother, (the just-grown daughter speaks
      through her sobs,
The little sisters huddle around speechless and dismay'd,)
See, dearest mother, the letter says Pete will soon be better.

Alas poor boy, he will never be better, (nor may-be needs to
      be better, that brave and simple soul,)
While they stand at home at the door he is dead already,
The only son is dead.

But the mother needs to be better,
She with thin form presently drest in black,
By day her meals untouch'd, then at night fitfully sleeping,
      often waking,
In the midnight waking, weeping, longing with one deep
      longing,
O that she might withdraw unnoticed, silent from life escape
      and withdraw,
To follow, to seek, to be with her dear dead son.

VIGIL STRANGE I KEPT ON THE FIELD
ONE NIGHT

Vigil strange I kept on the field one night;
When you my son and my comrade dropt at my side that day,
One look I but gave which your dear eyes return'd with a look
        I shall never forget,
One touch of your hand to mine O boy, reach'd up as you
        lay on the ground,
Then onward I sped in the battle, the even-contested battle,
Till late in the night reliev'd to the place at last again I made
        my way,
Found you in death so cold dear comrade, found your body
        son of responding kisses, (never again on
        earth responding,)
Bared your face in the starlight, curious the scene, cool blew
        the moderate night-wind,
Long there and then in vigil I stood, dimly around me the
        battlefield spreading,
Vigil wondrous and vigil sweet there in the fragrant silent
        night,
But not a tear fell, not even a long-drawn sigh, long, long I
        gazed,
Then on the earth partially reclining sat by your side leaning
        my chin in my hands,
Passing sweet hours, immortal and mystic hours with you
        dearest comrade—not a tear, not a word,
Vigil of silence, love and death, vigil for you my son and my
        soldier,
As onward silently stars aloft, eastward new ones upward stole,
Vigil final for you brave boy, (I could not save you, swift was
        your death,
I faithfully loved you and cared for you living, I think we
        shall surely meet again,)
Till at latest lingering of the night, indeed just as the dawn
        appear'd,
My comrade I wrapt in his blanket, envelop'd well his form,
Folded the blanket well, tucking it carefully over head and
        carefully under feet,
And there and then and bathed by the rising sun, my son in
        his grave, in his rude-dug grave I deposited,
Ending my vigil strange with that, vigil of night and battle-
        field dim,
Vigil for boy of responding kisses, (never again on earth re-
        sponding,)
Vigil for comrade swiftly slain, vigil I never forget, how as
        day brighten'd,
I rose from the chill ground and folded my soldier well in his
        blanket,
And buried him where he fell.

A MARCH IN THE RANKS HARD-PREST

A march in the ranks hard-prest, and the road unknown,
A route through a heavy wood with muffled steps in the dark-
ness,
Our army foil'd with loss severe, and the sullen remnant re-
treating,
Till after midnight glimmer upon us the lights of a dim-lighted
building,
We come to an open space in the woods, and halt by the dim-
lighted building,
'Tis a large old church at the crossing roads, now an im-
promptu hospital,
Entering but for a minute I see a sight beyond all the pictures
and poems ever made,
Shadows of deepest, deepest black, just lit by moving candles
and lamps,
And by one great pitchy torch stationary with wild red flame
and clouds of smoke,
By these, crowds, groups of forms vaguely I see on the floor,
some in the pews laid down,
At my feet more distinctly a soldier, a mere lad, in danger of
bleeding to death, (he is shot in the abdo-
men,)
I stanch the blood temporarily, (the youngster's face is white
as a lily,)
Then before I depart I sweep my eyes o'er the scene fain to
absorb it all,
Faces, varieties, postures beyond description, most in ob-
scurity, some of them dead,
Surgeons operating, attendants holding lights, the smell of
ether, the odor of blood,
The crowd, O the crowd of the bloody forms, the yard outside
also fill'd,
Some on the bare ground, some on planks or stretchers, some
in the death-spasm sweating,
An occasional scream or cry, the doctor's shouted orders or
calls,
The glisten of the little steel instruments catching the glint of
the torches,
These I resume as I chant, I see again the forms, I smell the
odor,
Then hear outside the orders given, *Fall in, my men, fall in;*
But first I bend to the dying lad, his eyes open, a half-smile
gives he me,
Then the eyes close, calmly close, and I speed forth to the
darkness,
Resuming, marching, ever in darkness marching, on in the
ranks,
The unknown road still marching.

A SIGHT IN CAMP IN THE DAYBREAK GRAY AND DIM

A sight in camp in the daybreak gray and dim,
As from my tent I emerge so early sleepless,
As slow I walk in the cool fresh air the path near by the hos-
        pital tent,
Three forms I see on stretchers lying, brought out there un-
        tended lying,
Over each the blanket spread, ample brownish woolen blanket,
Gray and heavy blanket, folding, covering all.

Curious I halt and silent stand,
Then with light fingers I from the face of the nearest the first
        just lift the blanket;
Who are you elderly man so gaunt and grim, with well-gray'd
        hair, and flesh all sunken about the eyes?
Who are you my dear comrade?

Then to the second I step—and who are you my child and
        darling?
Who are you sweet boy with cheeks yet blooming?

Then to the third—a face nor child nor old, very calm, as of
        beautiful yellow-white ivory;
Young man I think I know you—I think this face is the face
        of the Christ himself,
Dead and divine and brother of all, and here again he lies.

AS TOILSOME I WANDER'D VIRGINIA'S WOODS

As toilsome I wander'd Virginia's woods,
To the music of rustling leaves kick'd by my feet, (for 'twas
        autumn,)
I mark'd at the foot of a tree the grave of a soldier;
Mortally wounded he and buried on the retreat, (easily all
        could I understand,)
The halt of a mid-day hour, when up! no time to lose—yet
        this sign left,
On a tablet scrawl'd and nail'd on the tree by the grave,
Bold, cautious, true, and my loving comrade.

Long, long I muse, then on my way go wandering,
Many a changeful season to follow, and many a scene of life,
Yet at times through changeful season and scene, abrupt,
        alone, or in the crowded street,
Comes before me the unknown soldier's grave, comes the
        inscription rude in Virginia's woods,
Bold, cautious, true, and my loving comrade.

NOT THE PILOT

Not the pilot has charged himself to bring his ship into port,
        though beaten back and many times baffled;
Not the pathfinder penetrating inland weary and long,
By deserts parch'd, snows chill'd, rivers wet, perseveres till he
        reaches his destination,
More than I have charged myself, heeded or unheeded, to
        compose a march for these States,
For a battle-call, rousing to arms if need be, years, centuries
        hence.

YEAR THAT TREMBLED AND REEL'D
BENEATH ME

Year that trembled and reel'd beneath me!
Your summer wind was warm enough, yet the air I breathed
        froze me,
A thick gloom fell through the sunshine and darken'd me,
Must I change my triumphant songs? said I to myself,
Must I indeed learn to chant the cold dirges of the baffled?
And sullen hymns of defeat?

THE WOUND-DRESSER

1

An old man bending I come among new faces,
Years looking backward resuming in answer to children,
Come tell us old man, as from young men and maidens that
        love me,
(Arous'd and angry, I'd thought to beat the alarum, and urge
        relentless war,
But soon my fingers fail'd me, my face droop'd and I resign'd
        myself,
To sit by the wounded and soothe them, or silently watch the
        dead;)
Years hence of these scenes, of these furious passions, these
        chances,
Of unsurpass'd heroes, (was one side so brave? the other was
        equally brave;)
Now be witness again, paint the mightiest armies of earth,
Of those armies so rapid so wondrous what saw you to tell us?
What stays with you latest and deepest? of curious panics,
Of hard-fought engagements or sieges tremendous what deep-
        est remains?

2

O maidens and young men I love and that love me,
What you ask of my days those the strangest and sudden your
        talking recalls,

Soldier alert I arrive after a long march cover'd with sweat
    and dust,
In the nick of time I come, plunge in the fight, loudly shout
    in the rush of successful charge,
Enter the captur'd works—yet lo, like a swift-running river
    they fade,
Pass and are gone they fade—I dwell not on soldiers' perils or
    soldiers' joys,
(Both I remember well—many of the hardships, few the joys,
    yet I was content.)

But in silence, in dreams' projections,
While the world of gain and appearance and mirth goes on,
So soon what is over forgotten, and waves wash the imprints
    off the sand,
With hinged knees returning I enter the doors, (while for you
    up there,
Whoever you are, follow without noise and be of strong heart.)

Bearing the bandages, water and sponge,
Straight and swift to my wounded I go,
Where they lie on the ground after the battle brought in,
Where their priceless blood reddens the grass the ground,
Or to the rows of the hospital tent, or under the roof'd hos-
    pital,
To the long rows of cots up and down each side I return,
To each and all one after another I draw near, not one do I
    miss,
An attendant follows holding a tray, he carries a refuse pail,
Soon to be fill'd with clotted rags and blood, emptied, and fill'd
    again.

I onward go, I stop,
With hinged knees and steady hand to dress wounds,
I am firm with each, the pangs are sharp yet unavoidable,
One turns to me his appealing eyes—poor boy! I never knew
    you,
Yet I think I could not refuse this moment to die for you, if
    that would save you.

3

On, on I go, (open doors of time! open hospital doors!)
The crush'd head I dress, (poor crazed hand tear not the
    bandage away,)
The neck of the cavalry-man with the bullet through and
    through I examine,
Hard the breathing rattles, quite glazed already the eye, yet
    life struggles hard,
(Come sweet death! be persuaded O beautiful death!
In mercy come quickly.)

From the stump of the arm, the amputated hand,
I undo the clotted lint, remove the slough, wash off the matter
  and blood,
Back on his pillow the soldier bends with curv'd neck and
  side falling head,
His eyes are closed, his face is pale, he dares not look on the
  bloody stump,
And has not yet look'd on it.

I dress a wound in the side, deep, deep,
But a day or two more, for see the frame all wasted and
  sinking,
And the yellow-blue countenance see.

I dress the perforated shoulder, the foot with the bullet-wound,
Cleanse the one with a gnawing and putrid gangrene, so sick-
  ening, so offensive,
While the attendant stands behind aside me holding the tray
  and pail.

I am faithful, I do not give out,
The fractur'd thigh, the knee, the wound in the abdomen,
These and more I dress with impassive hand, (yet deep in my
  breast a fire, a burning flame.)

4

Thus in silence in dreams' projections,
Returning, resuming, I thread my way through the hospitals,
The hurt and wounded I pacify with soothing hand,
I sit by the restless all the dark night, some are so young,
Some suffer so much, I recall the experience sweet and sad,
(Many a soldier's loving arms about this neck have cross'd and
  rested,
Many a soldier's kiss dwells on these bearded lips.)

LONG, TOO LONG AMERICA

Long, too long America,
Traveling roads all even and peaceful you learn'd from joys
  and prosperity only,
But now, ah now, to learn from crises of anguish, advancing,
  grappling with direst fate and recoiling not,
And now to conceive and show to the world what your children
  en-masse really are,
(For who except myself has yet conceiv'd what your children
  en-masse really are?)

GIVE ME THE SPLENDID SILENT SUN

1

Give me the splendid silent sun with all his beams full-
dazzling,
Give me juicy autumnal fruit ripe and red from the orchard,
Give me a field where the unmow'd grass grows,
Give me an arbor, give me the trellis'd grape,
Give me fresh corn and wheat, give me serene-moving animals
teaching content,
Give me nights perfectly quiet as on high plateaus west of the
Mississippi, and I looking up at the stars,
Give me odorous at sunrise a garden of beautiful flowers
where I can walk undisturb'd,
Give me for marriage a sweet-breath'd woman of whom I
should never tire,
Give me a perfect child, give me away aside from the noise of
the world a rural domestic life,
Give me to warble spontaneous songs recluse by myself, for
my own ears only,
Give me solitude, give me Nature, give me again O Nature
your primal sanities!

These demanding to have them, (tired with ceaseless excite-
ment, and rack'd by the war-strife,)
These to procure incessantly asking, rising in cries from my
heart,
While yet incessantly asking still I adhere to my city,
Day upon day and year upon year O city, walking your streets,
Where you hold me enchain'd a certain time refusing to give
me up,
Yet giving to make me glutted, enrich'd of soul, you give me
forever faces;
(O I see what I sought to escape, confronting, reversing my
cries,
I see my own soul trampling down what is ask'd for.)

2

Keep your splendid silent sun,
Keep your woods O Nature, and the quiet places by the woods,
Keep your fields of clover and timothy, and your corn-fields
and orchards,
Keep the blossoming buckwheat fields where the Ninth-month
bees hum;
Give me faces and streets, give me these phantoms incessant
and endless along the trottoirs!
Give me interminable eyes—give me women—give me com-
rades and lovers by the thousand!

Let me see new ones every day—let me hold new ones by
    the hand every day!
Give me such shows—give me the streets of Manhattan!
Give me Broadway, with the soldiers marching—give me the
    sound of the trumpets and drums!
(The soldiers in companies or regiments—some starting away,
    flush'd and reckless,
Some, their time up, returning with thinn'd ranks, young,
    yet very old, worn, marching, noticing noth-
    ing;)
Give me the shores and wharves heavy-fringed with black
    ships!
O such for me! O an intense life, full to repletion and varied!
The life of the theatre, bar-room, huge hotel, for me!
The saloon of the steamer! the crowded excursion for me! the
    torchlight procession!
The dense brigade bound for the war, with high piled military
    wagons following;
People, endless, streaming, with strong voices, passions,
    pageants,
Manhattan streets with their powerful throbs, with beating
    drums as now,
The endless and noisy chorus, the rustle and clank of muskets,
    (even the sight of the wounded,)
Manhattan crowds, with their turbulent musical chorus!
Manhattan faces and eyes forever for me.

DIRGE FOR TWO VETERANS

    The last sunbeam
Lightly falls from the finish'd Sabbath,
On the pavement here, and there beyond it is looking,
    Down a new-made double grave.

    Lo, the moon ascending,
Up from the east the silvery round moon,
Beautiful over the house-tops, ghastly, phantom moon,
    Immense and silent moon.

    I see a sad procession,
And I hear the sound of coming full-key'd bugles,
All the channels of the city streets they're flooding,
    As with voices and with tears.

    I hear the great drums pounding,
And the small drums steady whirring,
And every blow of the great convulsive drums,
    Strikes me through and through.

    For the son is brought with the father,
(In the foremost ranks of the fierce assault they fell,

Two veterans son and father dropt together,
  And the double grave awaits them.)

Now nearer blow the bugles,
And the drums strike more convulsive,
And the daylight o'er the pavement quite has faded,
  And the strong dead-march enwraps me.

In the eastern sky up-buoying,
The sorrowful vast phantom moves illumin'd,
('Tis some mother's large transparent face,
  In heaven brighter growing.)

O strong dead-march you please me!
O moon immense with your silvery face you soothe me!
O my soldiers twain! O my veterans passing to burial!
  What I have I also give you.

The moon gives you light,
And the bugles and the drums give you music,
And my heart, O my soldiers, my veterans,
  My heart gives you love.

OVER THE CARNAGE ROSE PROPHETIC A VOICE

Over the carnage rose prophetic a voice,
Be not dishearten'd, affection shall solve the problems of free-
  dom yet,
Those who love each other shall become invincible,
They shall yet make Columbia victorious.

Sons of the Mother of All, you shall yet be victorious,
You shall yet laugh to scorn the attacks of all the remainder
  of the earth.

No danger shall balk Columbia's lovers,
If need be a thousand shall sternly immolate themselves for
  one.

One from Massachusetts shall be a Missourian's comrade,
From Maine and from hot Carolina, and another an Ore-
  gonese, shall be friends triune,
More precious to each other than all the riches of the earth.

To Michigan, Florida perfumes shall tenderly come,
Not the perfumes of flowers, but sweeter, and wafted beyond
  death.

It shall be customary in the houses and streets to see manly
  affection,
The most dauntless and rude shall touch face to face lightly,
The dependence of Liberty shall be lovers,
The continuance of Equality shall be comrades.

These shall tie you and band you stronger than hoops of iron,
I, ecstatic, O partners! O lands! with the love of lovers tie you.

(Were you looking to be held together by lawyers?
Or by an agreement on a paper? or by arms?
Nay, nor the world, nor any living thing, will so cohere.)

I SAW OLD GENERAL AT BAY

I saw old General at bay,
(Old as he was, his gray eyes yet shone out in battle like stars,)
His small force was now completely hemm'd in, in his works,
He call'd for volunteers to run the enemy's lines, a desperate
emergency,
I saw a hundred and more step forth from the ranks, but two
or three were selected,
I saw them receive their orders aside, they listen'd with care,
the adjutant was very grave,
I saw them depart with cheerfulness, freely risking their lives.

THE ARTILLERYMAN'S VISION

While my wife at my side lies slumbering, and the wars are
over long,
And my head on the pillow rests at home, and the vacant mid-
night passes,
And through the stillness, through the dark, I hear, just hear,
the breath of my infant,
There in the room as I wake from sleep this vision presses
upon me;
The engagement opens there and then in fantasy unreal,
The skirmishers begin, they crawl cautiously ahead, I hear the
irregular snap! snap!
I hear the sounds of the different missiles, the short *t-h-t! t-h-t!*
of the rifle-balls,
I see the shells exploding leaving small white clouds, I hear
the great shells shrieking as they pass,
The grape like the hum and whirr of wind through the trees,
(tumultuous now the contest rages,)
All the scenes at the batteries rise in detail before me again,
The crashing and smoking, the pride of the men in their pieces,
The chief-gunner ranges and sights his piece and selects a
fuse of the right time,
After firing I see him lean aside and look eagerly off to note
the effect;
Elsewhere I hear the cry of a regiment charging, (the young
colonel leads himself this time with bran-
dish'd sword,)
I see the gaps cut by the enemy's volleys, (quickly fill'd up, no
delay,)

I breathe the suffocating smoke, then the flat clouds hover low concealing all;
Now a strange lull for a few seconds, not a shot fired on either side,
Then resumed the chaos louder than ever, with eager calls and orders of officers,
While from some distant part of the field the wind wafts to my ears a shout of applause, (some special success,)
And ever the sound of the cannon far or near, (rousing even in dreams a devilish exultation and all the old mad joy in the depths of my soul,)
And ever the hastening of infantry shifting positions, batteries, cavalry, moving hither and thither,
(The falling, dying, I heed not, the wounded dripping and red I heed not, some to the rear are hobbling,)
Grime, heat, rush, aides-de-camp galloping by or on a full run,
With the patter of small arms, the warning *s-s-t* of the rifles, (these in my vision I hear or see,)
And bombs bursting in air, and at night the vari-color'd rockets.

ETHIOPIA SALUTING THE COLORS

Who are you dusky woman, so ancient hardly human,
With your woolly-white and turban'd head, and bare bony feet?
Why rising by the roadside here, do you the colors greet?

('Tis while our army lines Carolina's sands and pines,
Forth from thy hovel door thou Ethiopa com'st to me,
As under doughty Sherman I march toward the sea.)

Me master years a hundred since from my parents sunder'd,
A little child, they caught me as the savage beast is caught,
Then hither me across the sea the cruel slaver brought.

No further does she say, but lingering all the day,
Her high-borne turban'd head she wags, and rolls her darkling eye,
And courtesies to the regiments, the guidons moving by.

What is it fateful woman, so blear, hardly human?
Why wag your head with turban bound, yellow, red and green?
Are the things so strange and marvelous you see or have seen?

NOT YOUTH PERTAINS TO ME

Not youth pertains to me,
Nor delicatesse, I cannot beguile the time with talk,
Awkward in the parlor, neither a dancer nor elegant,

In the learn'd coterie sitting constrain'd and still, for learning
    inures not to me,
Beauty, knowledge, inure not to me—yet there are two or
    three things inure to me,
I have nourish'd the wounded and sooth'd many a dying sol-
    dier,
And at intervals waiting or in the midst of camp,
Composed these songs.

RACE OF VETERANS

Race of veterans—race of victors!
Race of the soil, ready for conflict—race of the conquering
    march!
(No more credulity's race, abiding-temper'd race,)
Race henceforth owning no law but the law of itself,
Race of passion and the storm.

WORLD TAKE GOOD NOTICE

World take good notice, silver stars fading,
Milky hue ript, weft of white detaching,
Coals thirty-eight, baleful and burning,
Scarlet, significant, hands off warning,
Now and henceforth flaunt from these shores.

O TAN-FACED PRAIRIE-BOY

O tan-faced prairie-boy,
Before you came to camp came many a welcome gift,
Praises and presents came and nourishing food, till at last
    among the recruits,
You came, taciturn, with nothing to give—we but look'd on
    each other,
When lo! more than all the gifts of the world you gave me.

LOOK DOWN FAIR MOON

Look down fair moon and bathe this scene,
Pour softly down night's nimbus floods on faces ghastly,
    swollen, purple,
On the dead on their backs with arms toss'd wide,
Pour down your unstinted nimbus sacred moon.

RECONCILIATION

Word over all, beautiful as the sky,
Beautiful that war and all its deeds of carnage must in time be
    utterly lost,
That the hands of the sisters Death and Night incessantly
    softly wash again, and ever again, this soil'd
    world;

For my enemy is dead, a man divine as myself is dead,
I look where he lies white-faced and still in the coffin—I draw near,
Bend down and touch lightly with my lips the white face in the coffin.

HOW SOLEMN AS ONE BY ONE

[Washington City, 1865]

How solemn as one by one,
As the ranks returning worn and sweaty, as the men file by where I stand,
As the faces the masks appear, as I glance at the faces studying the masks,
(As I glance upward out of this page studying you, dear friend, whoever you are,)
How solemn the thought of my whispering soul to each in the ranks, and to you!
I see behind each mask that wonder a kindred soul,
O the bullet could never kill what you really are, dear friend,
Nor the bayonet stab what you really are;
The soul! yourself I see, great as any, good as the best,
Waiting secure and content, which the bullet could never kill,
Nor the bayonet stab O friend.

AS I LAY WITH MY HEAD IN YOUR LAP CAMERADO

As I lay with my head in your lap camerado,
The confession I made I resume, what I said to you and the open air I resume,
I know I am restless and make others so,
I know my words are weapons full of danger, full of death,
For I confront peace, security, and all the settled laws, to unsettle them,
I am more resolute because all have denied me than I could ever have been had all accepted me,
I heed not and have never heeded either experience, cautions, majorities, nor ridicule,
And the threat of what is call'd hell is little or nothing to me,
And the lure of what is call'd heaven is little or nothing to me;
Dear camerado! I confess I have urged you onward with me, and still urge you, without the least idea what is our destination,
Or whether we shall be victorious, or utterly quell'd and defeated.

DELICATE CLUSTER

Delicate cluster! flag of teeming life!
Covering all my lands—all my seashores lining!
Flag of death! (how I watch'd you through the smoke of battle
    pressing!
How I heard you flap and rustle, cloth defiant!)
Flag cerulean—sunny flag, with the orbs of night dappled!
Ah my silvery beauty—ah my woolly white and crimson!
Ah to sing the song of you, my matron mighty!
My sacred one, my mother!

TO A CERTAIN CIVILIAN

Did you ask dulcet rhymes from me?
Did you seek the civilian's peaceful and languishing rhymes?
Did you find what I sang erewhile so hard to follow?
Why I was not singing erewhile for you to follow, to under-
    stand—nor am I now;
(I have been born of the same as the war was born,
The drum-corps' rattle is ever to me sweet music, I love well
    the martial dirge,
With slow wail and convulsive throb leading the officer's
    funeral;)
What to such as you anyhow such a poet as I? therefore leave
    my works,
And go lull yourself with what you can understand, and with
    piano-tunes,
For I lull nobody, and you will never understand me.

LO, VICTRESS ON THE PEAKS

Lo, Victress on the peaks,
Where thou with mighty brow regarding the world,
(The world O Libertad, that vainly conspired against thee,)
Out of its countless beleaguering toils, after thwarting them
    all,
Dominant, with the dazzling sun around thee,
Flauntest now unharm'd in immortal soundness and bloom—
    lo, in these hours supreme,
No poem proud, I chanting bring to thee, nor mastery's rap-
    turous verse,
But a cluster containing night's darkness and blood-dripping
    wounds,
And psalms of the dead.

SPIRIT WHOSE WORK IS DONE

[Washington City, 1865]

Spirit whose work is done—spirit of dreadful hours!
Ere departing fade from my eyes your forests of bayonets;

Spirit of gloomiest fears and doubts, (yet onward ever un-
 faltering pressing,)
Spirit of many a solemn day and many a savage scene—
 electric spirit,
That with muttering voice through the war now closed, like
 a tireless phantom flitted,
Rousing the land with breath of flame, while you beat and
 beat the drum,
Now as the sound of the drum, hollow and harsh to the last,
 reverberates round me,
As your ranks, your immortal ranks, return, return from the
 battles,
As the muskets of the young men yet lean over their shoulders,
As I look on the bayonets bristling over their shoulders,
As those slanted bayonets, whole forests of them appearing
 in the distance, approach and pass on, re-
 turning homeward,
Moving with steady motion, swaying to and fro to the right
 and left,
Evenly, lightly rising and falling while the steps keep time;
Spirit of hours I knew, all hectic red one day, but pale as death
 next day,
Touch my mouth ere you depart, press my lips close,
Leave me your pulses of rage—bequeath them to me—fill me
 with currents convulsive,
Let them scorch and blister out of my chants when you are
 gone,
Let them identify you to the future in these songs.

ADIEU TO A SOLDIER

Adieu O soldier,
You of the rude campaigning, (which we shared,)
The rapid march, the life of the camp,
The hot contention of opposing fronts, the long manœuvre,
Red battles with their slaughter, the stimulus, the strong ter-
 rific game,
Spell of all brave and manly hearts, the trains of time through
 you and like of you all fill'd,
With war and war's expression.

Adieu dear comrade,
Your mission is fulfill'd—but I, more warlike,
Myself and this contentious soul of mine,
Still on our own campaigning bound,
Through untried roads with ambushes opponents lined,
Through many a sharp defeat and many a crisis, often baffled,
Here marching, ever marching on, a war fight out—aye here,
To fiercer, weightier battles give expression.

TURN O LIBERTAD

Turn O Libertad, for the war is over,
From it and all henceforth expanding, doubting no more,
   resolute, sweeping the world,
Turn from lands retrospective recording proofs of the past,
From the singers that sing the trailing glories of the past,
From the chants of the feudal world, the triumphs of kings,
   slavery, caste,
Turn to the world, the triumphs reserv'd and to come—give
   up that backward world,
Leave to the singers of hitherto, give them the trailing past,
But what remains remains for singers for you—wars to come
   are for you,
(Lo, how the wars of the past have duly inured to you, and the
   wars of the present also inure;)
Then turn, and be not alarm'd O Libertad—turn your un-
   dying face,
To where the future, greater than all the past,
Is swiftly, surely preparing for you.

TO THE LEAVEN'D SOIL THEY TROD

To the leaven'd soil they trod calling I sing for the last,
(Forth from my tent emerging for good, loosing, untying the
   tent-ropes,)
In the freshness the forenoon air, in the far-stretching circuits
   and vistas again to peace restored,
To the fiery fields emanative and the endless vistas beyond, to
   the South and the North,
To the leaven'd soil of the general Western world to attest my
   songs,
To the Alleghanian hills and the tireless Mississippi,
To the rocks I calling sing, and all the trees in the woods,
To the plains of the poems of heroes, to the prairies spreading
   wide,
To the far-off sea and the unseen winds, and the sane impal-
   pable air;
And responding they answer all, (but not in words,)
The average earth, the witness of war and peace, acknowl-
   edges mutely,
The prairie draws me close, as the father to bosom broad the
   son,
The Northern ice and rain that began me nourish me to the
   end,
But the hot sun of the South is to fully ripen my songs.

MEMORIES OF PRESIDENT LINCOLN

WHEN LILACS LAST IN THE DOORYARD BLOOM'D

1

When lilacs last in the dooryard bloom'd,
And the great star early droop'd in the western sky in the
    night,
I mourn'd, and yet shall mourn with ever-returning spring.

Ever-returning spring, trinity sure to me you bring,
Lilac blooming perennial and drooping star in the west,
And thought of him I love.

2

O powerful western fallen star!
O shades of night—O moody, tearful night!
O great star disappear'd—O the black murk that hides the
    star!
O cruel hands that hold me powerless—O helpless soul of me!
O harsh surrounding cloud that will not free my soul.

3

In the dooryard fronting an old farm-house near the white-
    wash'd palings,
Stands the lilac-bush tall-growing with heart-shaped leaves of
    rich green,
With many a pointed blossom rising delicate, with the perfume
    strong I love,
With every leaf a miracle—and from this bush in the dooryard,
With delicate-color'd blossoms and heart-shaped leaves of
    rich green,
A sprig with its flower I break.

4

In the swamp in secluded recesses,
A shy and hidden bird is warbling a song.

Solitary the thrush,
The hermit withdrawn to himself, avoiding the settlements,
Sings by himself a song.

Song of the bleeding throat,
Death's outlet song of life, (for well dear brother I know,
If thou wast not granted to sing thou would'st surely die.)

5

Over the breast of the spring, the land, amid cities,
Amid lanes and through old woods, where lately the violets
      peep'd from the ground, spotting the gray
      debris,
Amid the grass in the fields each side of the lanes, passing the
      endless grass,
Passing the yellow-spear'd wheat, every grain from its shroud
      in the dark-brown fields uprisen,
Passing the apple-tree blows of white and pink in the orchards,
Carrying a corpse to where it shall rest in the grave,
Night and day journeys a coffin.

6

Coffin that passes through lanes and streets,
Through day and night with the great cloud darkening the
      land,
With the pomp of the inloop'd flags with the cities draped in
      black,
With the show of the States themselves as of crape-veil'd
      women standing,
With processions long and winding and the flambeaus of the
      night,
With the countless torches lit, with the silent sea of faces and
      the unbared heads,
With the waiting depot, the arriving coffin, and the sombre
      faces,
With dirges through the night, with the thousand voices rising
      strong and solemn,
With all the mournful voices of the dirges pour'd around the
      coffin,
The dim-lit churches and the shuddering organs—where amid
      these you journey,
With the tolling tolling bells' perpetual clang,
Here, coffin that slowly passes,
I give you my sprig of lilac.

7

(Nor for you, for one alone,
Blossoms and branches green to coffins all I bring,
For fresh as the morning, thus would I chant a song for you
      O sane and sacred death.

All over bouquets of roses,
O death, I cover you over with roses and early lilies,
But mostly and now the lilac that blooms the first,
Copious I break, I break the sprigs from the bushes,
With loaded arms I come, pouring for you,
For you and the coffins all of you O death.)

8

O western orb sailing the heaven,
Now I know what you must have meant as a month since I
    walk'd,
As I walk'd in silence the transparent shadowy night,
As I saw you had something to tell as you bent to me night
    after night,
As you droop'd from the sky low down as if to my side, (while
    the other stars all look'd on,)
As we wander'd together the solemn night, (for something I
    know not what kept me from sleep,)
As the night advanced, and I saw on the rim of the west how
    full you were of woe,
As I stood on the rising ground in the breeze in the cool trans-
    parent night,
As I watch'd where you pass'd and was lost in the netherward
    black of the night,
As my soul in its trouble dissatisfied sank, as where you sad
    orb,
Concluded, dropt in the night, and was gone.

9

Sing on there in the swamp,
O singer bashful and tender, I hear your notes, I hear your call,
I hear, I come presently, I understand you,
But a moment I linger, for the lustrous star has detain'd me,
The star my departing comrade holds and detains me.

10

O how shall I warble myself for the dead one there I loved?
And how shall I deck my song for the large sweet soul that
    has gone?
And what shall my perfume be for the grave of him I love?

Sea-winds blown from east and west,
Blown from the Eastern sea and blown from the Western sea,
    till there on the prairies meeting,
These and with these and the breath of my chant,
I'll perfume the grave of him I love.

11

O what shall I hang on the chamber walls?
And what shall the pictures be that I hang on the walls,
To adorn the burial-house of him I love?

Pictures of growing spring and farms and homes,
With the Fourth-month eve at sundown, and the gray smoke
    lucid and bright,

With floods of the yellow gold of the gorgeous, indolent, sink-
      ing sun, burning, expanding the air,
With the fresh sweet herbage under foot, and the pale green
      leaves of the trees prolific,
In the distance the flowing glaze, the breast of the river, with
      a wind-dapple here and there,
With ranging hills on the banks, with many a line against the
      sky, and shadows,
And the city at hand with dwellings so dense, and stacks of
      chimneys,
And all the scenes of life and the workshops, and the workmen
      homeward returning.

12

Lo, body and soul—this land,
My own Manhattan with spires, and the sparkling and hurry-
      ing tides, and the ships,
The varied and ample land, the South and the North in the
      light, Ohio's shores and flashing Missouri,
And ever the far-spreading prairies cover'd with grass and
      corn.

Lo, the most excellent sun so calm and haughty,
The violet and purple morn with just-felt breezes,
The gentle soft-born measureless light,
The miracle spreading bathing all, the fulfill'd noon,
The coming eve delicious, the welcome night and the stars,
Over my cities shining all, enveloping man and land.

13

Sing on, sing on you gray-brown bird,
Sing from the swamps, the recesses, pour your chant from the
      bushes,
Limitless out of the dusk, out of the cedars and pines.

Sing on dearest brother, warble your reedy song,
Loud human song, with voice of uttermost woe.

O liquid and free and tender!
O wild and loose to my soul—O wondrous singer!
You only I hear—yet the star holds me, (but will soon depart,)
Yet the lilac with mastering odor holds me.

14

Now while I sat in the day and look'd forth,
In the close of the day with its light and the fields of spring,
      and the farmers preparing their crops,
In the large unconscious scenery of my land with its lakes and
      forests,

In the heavenly aerial beauty, (after the perturb'd winds and
  the storms,)
Under the arching heavens of the afternoon swift passing, and
  the voices of children and women,
The many-moving sea-tides, and I saw the ships how they
  sail'd,
And the summer approaching with richness, and the fields all
  busy with labor,
And the infinite separate houses, how they all went on, each
  with its meals and minutia of daily usages,
And the streets how their throbbings throbb'd, and the cities
  pent—lo, then and there,
Falling upon them all and among them all, enveloping me
  with the rest,
Appear'd the cloud, appear'd the long black trail,
And I knew death, its thought, and the sacred knowledge of
  death.

Then with the knowledge of death as walking one side of me,
And the thought of death close-walking the other side of me,
And I in the middle as with companions, and as holding the
  hands of companions,
I fled forth to the hiding receiving night that talks not,
Down to the shores of the water, the path by the swamp in
  the dimness,
To the solemn shadowy cedars and ghostly pines so still.

And the singer so shy to the rest receiv'd me,
The gray-brown bird I know receiv'd us comrades three,
And he sang the carol of death, and a verse for him I love.

From deep secluded recesses,
From the fragrant cedars and the ghostly pines so still,
Came the carol of the bird.

And the charm of the carol rapt me,
As I held as if by their hands my comrades in the night,
And the voice of my spirit tallied the song of the bird.

Come lovely and soothing death,
Undulate round the world, serenely arriving, arriving,
In the day, in the night, to all, to each,
Sooner or later delicate death.

Prais'd be the fathomless universe,
For life and joy, and for objects and knowledge curious,
And for love, sweet love—but praise! praise! praise!
For the sure-enwinding arms of cool-enfolding death.

Dark mother always gliding near with soft feet,
Have none chanted for thee a chant of fullest welcome?

Then I chant it for thee, I glorify thee above all,
I bring thee a song that when thou must indeed come, come
    unfalteringly.

Approach strong deliveress,
When it is so, when thou hast taken them I joyously sing the
    dead,
Lost in the loving floating ocean of thee,
Laved in the flood of thy bliss O death.

From me to thee glad serenades,
Dances for thee I propose saluting thee, adornments and
    feastings for thee,
And the sights of the open landscape and the high-spread sky
    are fitting,
And life and the fields, and the huge and thoughtful night.

The night in silence under many a star,
The ocean shore and the husky whispering wave whose voice
    I know,
And the soul turning to thee O vast and well-veil'd death,
And the body gratefully nestling close to thee.

Over the tree-tops I float thee a song,
Over the rising and sinking waves, over the myriad fields and
    the prairies wide,
Over the dense-pack'd cities all and the teeming wharves and
    ways,
I float this carol with joy, with joy to thee O death.

15

To the tally of my soul,
Loud and strong kept up the gray-brown bird,
With pure deliberate notes spreading filling the night.

Loud in the pines and cedars dim,
Clear in the freshness moist and the swamp-perfume,
And I with my comrades there in the night.

While my sight that was bound in my eyes unclosed,
As to long panoramas of visions.

And I saw askant the armies,
I saw as in noiseless dreams hundreds of battle-flags,
Borne through the smoke of the battles and pierc'd with
    missiles I saw them,
And carried hither and yon through the smoke, and torn and
    bloody,
And at last but a few shreds left on the staffs, (and all in
    silence,)
And the staffs all splinter'd and broken.

I saw battle-corpses, myriads of them,
And the white skeletons of young men, I saw them,
I saw the debris and debris of all the slain soldiers of the war,
But I saw they were not as was thought,
They themselves were fully at rest, they suffer'd not,
The living remain'd and suffer'd, the mother suffer'd,
And the wife and the child and the musing comrade suffer'd,
And the armies that remain'd suffer'd.

16

Passing the visions, passing the night,
Passing, unloosing the hold of my comrades' hands,
Passing the song of the hermit bird and the tallying song of
    my soul,
Victorious song, death's outlet song, yet varying ever-altering
    song,
As low and wailing, yet clear the notes, rising and falling,
    flooding the night,
Sadly sinking and fainting, as warning and warning, and yet
    again bursting with joy,
Covering the earth and filling the spread of the heaven,
As that powerful psalm in the night I heard from recesses,
Passing, I leave thee lilac with heart-shaped leaves,
I leave thee there in the dooryard, blooming, returning with
    spring.

I cease from my song for thee,
From my gaze on thee in the west, fronting the west, com-
    muning with thee,
O comrade lustrous with silver face in the night.

Yet each to keep and all, retrievements out of the night,
The song, the wondrous chant of the gray-brown bird,
And the tallying chant, the echo arous'd in my soul,
With the lustrous and drooping star with the countenance full
    of woe,
With the holders holding my hand nearing the call of the bird,
Comrades mine and I in the midst, and their memory ever
    to keep, for the dead I loved so well,
For the sweetest, wisest soul of all my days and lands—and
    this for his dear sake,
Lilac and star and bird twined with the chant of my soul,
There in the fragrant pines and the cedars dusk and dim.

O CAPTAIN! MY CAPTAIN!

O Captain! my Captain! our fearful trip is done,
The ship has weather'd every rack, the prize we sought is won,
The port is near, the bells I hear, the people all exulting,

While follow eyes the steady keel, the vessel grim and daring;
But O heart! heart! heart!
O the bleeding drops of red,
Where on the deck my Captain lies,
Fallen cold and dead.

O Captain! my Captain! rise up and hear the bells;
Rise up—for you the flag is flung—for you the bugle trills,
For you bouquets and ribbon'd wreaths—for you the shores a-
crowding,
For you they call, the swaying mass, their eager faces turning;
Here Captain! dear father!
The arm beneath your head!
It is some dream that on the deck,
You've fallen cold and dead.

My Captain does not answer, his lips are pale and still,
My father does not feel my arm, he has no pulse nor will,
The ship is anchor'd safe and sound, its voyage closed and
done,
From fearful trip the victor ship comes in with object won:
Exult O shores, and ring O bells!
But I with mournful tread,
Walk the deck my Captain lies,
Fallen cold and dead.

HUSH'D BE THE CAMPS TO-DAY

[May 4, 1865]

Hush'd be the camps to-day,
And soldiers let us drape our war-worn weapons,
And each with musing soul retire to celebrate,
Our dear commander's death.

No more for him life's stormy conflicts,
Nor victory, nor defeat—no more time's dark events,
Charging like ceaseless clouds across the sky.

But sing poet in our name,
Sing of the love we bore him—because you—dweller in camps,
know it truly.

As they invault the coffin there,
Sing—as they close the doors of earth upon him—one verse,
For the heavy hearts of soldiers.

THIS DUST WAS ONCE THE MAN

This dust was once the man,
Gentle, plain, just and resolute, under whose cautious hand,
Against the foulest crime in history known in any land or age,
Was saved the Union of these States.

BY BLUE ONTARIO'S SHORE

1

By blue Ontario's shore,
As I mused of these warlike days and of peace return'd, and
the dead that return no more,
A Phantom gigantic superb, with stern visage accosted me,
Chant me the poem, it said, *that comes from the soul of
America, chant me the carol of victory,*
*And strike up the marches of Libertad, marches more pow-
erful yet,*
*And sing me before you go the song of the throes of De-
mocracy.*

(Democracy, the destin'd conquerer, yet treacherous lip-smiles
everywhere,
And death and infidelity at every step.)

2

A Nation announcing itself,
I myself make the only growth by which I can be appreciated,
I reject none, accept all, then reproduce all in my own forms.

A breed whose proof is in time and deeds,
What we are we are, nativity is answer enough to objections,
We wield ourselves as a weapon is wielded,
We are powerful and tremendous in ourselves,
We are executive in ourselves, we are sufficient in the variety
of ourselves,
We are the most beautiful to ourselves and in ourselves,
We stand self-pois'd in the middle, branching thence over the
world,
From Missouri, Nebraska, or Kansas, laughing attacks to scorn.

Nothing is sinful to us outside of ourselves,
Whatever appears, whatever does not appear, we are beautiful
or sinful in ourselves only.

(O Mother—O Sisters dear!
If we are lost, no victor else has destroy'd us,
It is by ourselves we go down to eternal night.)

3

Have you thought there could be but a single supreme?
There can be any number of supremes—one does not counter-
vail another any more than one eyesight
countervails another, or one life countervails
another.

All is eligible to all,
All is for individuals, all is for you,
No condition is prohibited, not God's or any.

All comes by the body, only health puts you rapport with the
    universe.

Produce great Persons, the rest follows.

4

Piety and conformity to them that like,
Peace, obesity, allegiance, to them that like,
I am he who tauntingly compels men, women, nations,
Crying, Leap from your seats and contend for your lives!

I am he who walks the States with a barb'd tongue, questioning
    every one I meet,
Who are you that wanted only to be told what you knew
    before?
Who are you that wanted only a book to join you in your non-
    sense?

(With pangs and cries as thine own O bearer of many children,
These clamors wild to a race of pride I give.)
O lands, would you be freer than all that has even been before?
If you would be freer than all that has been before, come listen
    to me.

Fear grace, elegance, civilization, delicatesse,
Fear the mellow sweet, the sucking of honey-juice,
Beware the advancing mortal ripening of Nature,
Beware what precedes the decay of the ruggedness of states and
    men.

5

Ages, precedents, have long been accumulating undirected ma-
    terials,
America brings builders, and brings its own styles.

The immortal poets of Asia and Europe have done their work
    and pass'd to other spheres,
A work remains, the work of surpassing all they have done.

America, curious toward foreign characters, stands by its own
    at all hazards,
Stands removed, spacious, composite, sound, initiates the true
    use of precedents,
Does not repel them or the past or what they have produced
    under their forms,
Takes the lesson with calmness, perceives the corpse slowly
    borne from the house,

Perceives that it waits a little while in the door, that it was
    fittest for its days,
That its life has descended to the stalwart and well-shaped heir
    who approaches,
And that he shall be fittest for his days.

Any period one nation must lead,
One land must be the promise and reliance of the future.

These States are the amplest poem,
Here is not merely a nation but a teeming Nation of nations,
Here the doings of men correspond with the broadcast doings
    of the day and night,
Here is what moves in magnificent masses careless of particu-
    lars,
Here are the roughs, beards, friendliness, combativeness, the
    soul loves,
Here the flowing trains, here the crowds, equality, diversity, the
    soul loves.

6

Land of lands and bards to corroborate!
Of them standing among them, one lifts to the light a west-
    bred face,
To him the hereditary countenance bequeath'd both mother's
    and father's,
His first parts substances, earth, water, animals, trees,
Built of the common stock, having room for far and near,
Used to dispense with other lands, incarnating this land,
Attracting it body and soul to himself, hanging on its neck with
    incomparable love,
Plunging his seminal muscle into its merits and demerits,
Making its cities, beginnings, events, diversities, wars, vocal
    in him,
Making its rivers, lakes, bays, embouchure in him,
Mississippi with yearly freshets and changing chutes, Colum-
    bia, Niagara, Hudson, spending themselves
    lovingly in him,
If the Atlantic coast stretch or the Pacific coast stretch, he
    stretching with them North or South,
Spanning between them East and West, and touching whatever
    is between them,
Growths growing from him to offset the growths of pine, cedar,
    hemlock, live-oak, locust, chestnut, hickory,
    cottonwood, orange, magnolia,
Tangles as tangled in him as any canebrake or swamp,
He likening sides and peaks of mountains, forests coated with
    northern transparent ice,
Off him pasturage sweet and natural as savanna, upland,
    prairie,

Through him flights, whirls, screams, answering those of the
        fish-hawk, mocking-bird, night-heron, and
        eagle,
His spirit surrounding his country's spirit, unclosed to good
        and evil,
Surrounding the essences of real things, old times and present
        times,
Surrounding just found shores, islands, tribes of red aborigines,
Weather-beaten vessels, landings, settlements, embryo stature
        and muscle,
The haughty defiance of the Year One, war, peace, the forma-
        tion of the Constitution,
The separate States, the simple elastic scheme, the immigrants,
The Union always swarming with blatherers and always sure
        and impregnable,
The unsurvey'd interior, log-houses, clearings, wild animals,
        hunters, trappers,
Surrounding the multiform agriculture, mines, temperature,
        the gestation of new States,
Congress convening every Twelfth-month, the members duly
        coming up from the uttermost parts,
Surrounding the noble character of mechanics and farmers,
        especially the young men,
Responding their manners, speech, dress, friendships, the gait
        they have of persons who never knew how it
        felt to stand in the presence of superiors,
The freshness and candor of their physiognomy, the copious-
        ness and decision of their phrenology,
The picturesque looseness of their carriage, their fierceness
        when wrong'd,
The fluency of their speech, their delight in music, their curi-
        osity, good temper and open-handedness, the
        whole composite make,
The prevailing ardor and enterprise, the large amativeness,
The perfect equality of the female with the male, the fluid
        movement of the population,
The superior marine, free commerce, fisheries, whaling, gold-
        digging,
Wharf-hemm'd cities, railroad and steamboat lines intersecting
        all points,
Factories, mercantile life, labor-saving machinery, the North-
        east, Northwest, Southwest,
Manhattan firemen, the Yankee swap, southern plantation life,
Slavery—the murderous, treacherous conspiracy to raise it
        upon the ruins of all the rest,
On and on to the grapple with it—Assassin! then your life
        or ours be the stake, and respite no more.

7

(Lo, high toward heaven, this day,
Libertad, from the conqueress' field return'd,
I mark the new aureola around your head,
No more of soft astral, but dazzling and fierce,
With war's flames and the lambent lightnings playing,
And your port immovable where you stand,
With still the inextinguishable glance and the clinch'd and
        lifted fist,
And your foot on the neck of the menacing one, the scorner
        utterly crush'd beneath you,
The menacing arrogant one that strode and advanced with his
        senseless scorn, bearing the murderous knife,
The wide-swelling one, the braggart that would yesterday do
        so much,
To-day a carrion dead and damn'd, the despised of all the
        earth,
An offal rank, to the dunghill maggots spurn'd.)

8

Others take finish, but the Republic is ever constructive and
        ever keeps vista,
Others adorn the past, but you O days of the present, I adorn
        you,
O days of the future I believe in you—I isolate myself for your
        sake,
O America because you build for mankind I build for you,
O well-beloved stone-cutters, I lead them who plan with deci-
        sion and science,
Lead the present with friendly hand toward the future.

(Bravas to all impulses sending sane children to the next age!
But damn that which spends itself with no thought of the
        stain, pains, dismay, feebleness, it is be-
        queathing.)

9

I listened to the Phantom by Ontario's shore,
I heard the voice arising demanding bards,
By them all native and grand, by them alone can these States
        be fused into the compact organism of a Na-
        tion.

To hold men together by paper and seal or by compulsion is
        no account,
That only holds men together which aggregates all in a living
        principle, as the hold of the limbs of the body
        or the fibres of plants.
Of all races and eras these States with veins full of poetical

stuff most need poets, and are to have the
greatest, and use them the greatest,
Their Presidents shall not be their common referee so much as
their poets shall.

(Soul of love and tongue of fire!
Eye to pierce the deepest deeps and sweep the world!
Ah Mother, prolific and full in all besides, yet how long barren,
barren?)

10

Of these States the poet is the equable man,
Not in him but off from him things are grotesque, eccentric,
fail of their full returns,
Nothing out of its place is good, nothing in its place is bad,
He bestows on every object or quality its fit proportion, neither
more nor less,
He is the arbiter of the diverse, he is the key,
He is the equalizer of his age and land,
He supplies what wants supplying, he checks what wants check-
ing,
In peace out of him speaks the spirit of peace, large, rich,
thrifty, building populous towns, encouraging
agriculture, arts, commerce, lighting the study
of man, the soul, health, immortality, govern-
ment,
In war he is the best backer of the war, he fetches artillery as
good as the engineer's, he can make every
word he speaks draw blood,
The years straying toward infidelity he withholds by his steady
faith,
He is no arguer, he is judgment, (Nature accepts him abso-
lutely,)
He judges not as the judge judges but as the sun falling round
a helpless thing,
As he sees the farthest he has the most faith,
His thoughts are the hymns of the praise of things,
In the dispute on God and eternity he is silent,
He sees eternity less like a play with a prologue and denoue-
ment,
He sees eternity in men and women, he does not see men and
women as dreams or dots.

For the great Idea, the idea of perfect and free individuals,
For that, the bard walks in advance, leader of leaders,
The attitude of him cheers up slaves and horrifies foreign
despots.

Without extinction is Liberty, without retrograde is Equality,
They live in the feelings of young men and the best women.

(Not for nothing have the indomitable heads of the earth been
always ready to fall for Liberty.)

11

For the great Idea,
That, O my brethren, that is the mission of poets.

Songs of stern defiance ever ready,
Songs of the rapid arming and the march,
The flag of peace quick-folded, and instead the flag we know.
Warlike flag of the great Idea.

(Angry cloth I saw there leaping!
I stand again in leaden rain your flapping folds saluting,
I sing you over all, flying beckoning through the fight—O the
hard contested fight!
The cannons ope their rosy-flashing muzzles—the hurtled balls
scream,
The battle-front forms amid the smoke—the volleys pour in-
cessant from the line,
Hark, the ringing word *Charge!*—now the tussle and the furi-
ous maddening yells,
Now the corpses tumble curl'd upon the ground,
Cold, cold in death, for precious life of you,
Angry cloth I saw there leaping.)

12

Are you he who would assume a place to teach or be a poet
here in the States?
The place is august, the terms obdurate.

Who would assume to teach here may well prepare himself
body and mind,
He may well survey, ponder, arm, fortify, harden, make lithe
himself,
He shall surely be question'd beforehand by me with many and
stern questions.

Who are you indeed who would talk or sing to America?
Have you studied out the land, its idioms and men?
Have you learn'd the physiology, phrenology, politics, geog-
raphy, pride, freedom, friendship of the land?
its substratums and objects?
Have you consider'd the organic compact of the first day of the
first year of Independence, sign'd by the Com-
missioners, ratified by the States, and read by
Washington at the head of the army?
Have you possess'd yourself of the Federal Constitution?
Do you see who have left all feudal processes and poems be-
hind them, and assumed the poems and proc-
esses of Democracy?

Are you faithful to things? do you teach what the land and
    sea, the bodies of men, womanhood, amative-
    ness, heroic angers, teach?
Have you sped through fleeting customs, popularities?
Can you hold your hand against all seductions, follies, whirls,
    fierce contentions? are you very strong? are
    you really of the whole People?
Are you not of some coterie? some school or mere religion?
Are you done with reviews and criticisms of life? animating
    now to life itself?
Have you vivified yourself from the maternity of these States?
Have you too the old ever-fresh forbearance and impartiality?
Do you hold the like love for those hardening to maturity? for
    the last-born? little and big? and for the er-
    rant?

What is this you bring my America?
Is it uniform with my country?
Is it not something that has been better told or done before?
Have you not imported this or the spirit of it in some ship?
Is it not a mere tale? a rhyme? a prettiness?—is the good old
    cause in it?
Has it not dangled long at the heels of the poets, politicians,
    literats, of enemies' lands?
Does it not assume that what is notoriously gone is still here?
Does it answer universal needs? will it improve manners?
Does it sound with trumpet-voice the proud victory of the
    Union in that secession war?
Can your performance face the open fields and the seaside?
Will it absorb into me as I absorb food, air, to appear again in
    my strength, gait, face?
Have real employments contributed to it? original makers, not
    mere amanuenses?
Does it meet modern discoveries, calibres, facts, face to face?
What does it mean to American persons, progresses, cities?
    Chicago, Kanada, Arkansas?
Does it see behind the apparent custodians the real custodians
    standing, menacing, silent, the mechanics,
    Manhattanese, Western men, Southerners,
    significant alike in their apathy, and in the
    promptness of their love?
Does it see what finally befalls, and has always finally befallen,
    each temporizer, patcher, outsider, partialist,
    alarmist, infidel, who has ever ask'd anything
    of America?
What mocking and scornful negligence?
The track strew'd with the dust of skeletons,
By the roadside others disdainfully toss'd.

13

Rhymes and rhymers pass away, poems distill'd from poems
pass away,
The swarms of reflectors and the polite pass, and leave ashes,
Admirers, importers, obedient persons, make but the soil of
literature,
America justifies itself, give it time, no disguise can deceive it
or conceal from it, it is impassive enough,
Only toward the likes of itself will it advance to meet them,
If its poets appear it will in due time advance to meet them,
there is no fear of mistake,
(The proof of a poet shall be sternly deferr'd till his country
absorbs him as affectionately as he has ab-
sorb'd it.)

He masters whose spirit masters, he tastes sweetest who results
sweetest in the long run,
The blood of the brawn beloved of time is unconstraint;
In the need of songs, philosophy, an appropriate native grand-
opera. shipcraft, any craft,
He or she is greatest who contributes the greatest original
practical example.

Already a nonchalant breed, silently emerging, appears on the
streets,
People's lips salute only doers, lovers, satisfiers, positive know-
ers,
There will shortly be no more priests, I say their work is done,
Death is without emergencies here, but life is perpetual emer-
gencies here,
Are your body, days, manners, superb? after death you shall
be superb,
Justice, health, self-esteem, clear the way with irresistible
power;
How dare you place any thing before a man?

14

Fall behind me States!
A man before all—myself, typical, before all.

Give me the pay I have served for,
Give to sing the songs of the great Idea, take all the rest,
I have loved the earth, sun, animals, I have despised riches,
I have given alms to every one that ask'd, stood up for the
stupid and crazy, devoted my income and
labor to others,
Hated tyrants, argued not concerning God, had patience and
indulgence toward the people, taken off my
hat to nothing known or unknown,

Gone freely with powerful uneducated persons and with the
      young, and with the mothers of families,
Read these leaves to myself in the open air, tried them by trees,
      stars, rivers,
Dismiss'd whatever insulted my own soul or defiled my body,
Claim'd nothing to myself which I have not carefully claim'd
      for others on the same terms,
Sped to the camps, and comrades found and accepted from
      every State,
(Upon this breast has many a dying soldier lean'd to breathe
      his last,
This arm, this hand, this voice, have nourish'd, rais'd, restored,
To life recalling many a prostrate form;)
I am willing to wait to be understood by the growth of the
      taste of myself,
Rejecting none, permitting all.
(Say O Mother, have I not to your thought been faithful?
Have I not through life kept you and yours before me?)

15

I swear I begin to see the meaning of these things,
It is not the earth, it is not America who is so great,
It is I who am great or to be great, it is You up there, or any
      one,
It is to walk rapidly through civilization, governments, theories,
Through poems, pageants, shows, to form individuals.

Underneath all, individuals,
I swear nothing is good to me now that ignores individuals,
The American compact is altogether with individuals,
The only government is that which makes minute of individ-
      uals,
The whole theory of the universe is directed unerringly to one
      single individual—namely to You.

(Mother! with subtle sense severe, with the naked sword in
      your hand,
I saw you at last refuse to treat but directly with individuals.)

16

Underneath all, Nativity,
I swear I will stand by my own nativity, pious or impious so
      be it;
I swear I am charm'd with nothing except nativity,
Men, women, cities, nations, are only beautiful from nativity.

Underneath all is the Expression of love for men and women,
(I swear I have seen enough of mean and impotent modes of
      expressing love for men and women.

After this day I take my own modes of expressing love for men
        and women.)

I swear I will have each quality of my race in myself,
(Talk as you like, he only suits these States whose manners
        favor the audacity and sublime turbulence of
        the States.)

Underneath the lessons of things, spirits, Nature, govern-
        ments, ownerships, I swear I perceive other
        lessons,
Underneath all to me is myself, to you yourself, (the same
        monotonous old song.)

17

O I see flashing that this America is only you and me,
Its power, weapons, testimony, are you and me,
Its crimes, lies, thefts, defections, are you and me,
Its Congress is you and me, the officers, capitols, armies, ships,
        are you and me,
Its endless gestations of new States are you and me,
The war, (that war so bloody and grim, the war I will hence-
        forth forget,) was you and me,
Natural and artificial are you and me,
Freedom, language, poems, employments, are you and me,
Past, present, future, are you and me.

I dare not shirk any part of myself,
Not any part of America good or bad,
Not to build for that which builds for mankind,
Not to balance ranks, complexions, creeds, and the sexes,
Not to justify science nor the march of equality,
Nor to feed the arrogant blood of the brawn belov'd of time.

I am for those that have never been master'd,
For men and women whose tempers have never been master'd,
For those whom laws, theories, conventions, can never master.

I am for those who walk abreast with the whole earth,
Who inaugurate one to inaugurate all.

I will not be outfaced by irrational things,
I will penetrate what it is in them that is sarcastic upon me,
I will make cities and civilizations defer to me,
This is what I have learnt from America—it is the amount, and
        it I teach again.

(Democracy, while weapons were everywhere aim'd at your
        breast,
I saw you serenely give birth to immortal children, saw in
        dreams your dilating form,
Saw you with spreading mantel covering the world.)

18

I will confront these shows of the day and night,
I will know if I am to be less than they,
I will see if I am not as majestic as they,
I will see if I am not as subtle and real as they,
I will see if I am to be less generous than they,
I will see if I have no meaning, while the houses and ships
                have meaning,
I will see if the fishes and birds are to be enough for them-
                selves, and I am not to be enough for myself.

I match my spirit against yours you orbs, growths, mountains,
                brutes,
Copious as you are I absorb you all in myself, and become the
                master myself,
America isolated yet embodying all, what is it finally except
                myself?
These States, what are they except myself?

I know now why the earth is gross, tantalizing, wicked, it is
                for my sake,
I take you specially to be mine, you terrible, rude forms.

(Mother, bend down, bend close to me your face,
I know not what these plots and wars and deferments are for,
I know not fruition's success, but I know that through war and
                crime your work goes on, and must yet go
                on.)

19

Thus by blue Ontario's shore,
While the winds fann'd me and the waves came trooping
                toward me,
I thrill'd with the power's pulsations, and the charm of my
                theme was upon me,
Till the tissues that held me parted their ties upon me.

And I saw the free souls of poets,
The loftiest bards of past ages strode before me,
Strange large men, long unwaked, undisclosed, were disclosed
                to me.

20

O my rapt verse, my call, mock me not!
Not for the bards of the past, not to invoke them have I
                launch'd you forth,
Not to call even those lofty bards here by Ontario's shores,
Have I sung so capricious and loud my savage song.

Bards for my own land only I invoke,
(For the war, the war is over, the field is clear'd,)

Till they strike up marches henceforth triumphant and on-
    ward,
To cheer O Mother your boundless expectant soul.

Bards of the great Idea! bards of the peaceful inventions! (for
    the war, the war is over!)
Yet bards of latent armies, a million soldiers waiting ever-
    ready,
Bards with songs as from burning coals or the lightning's fork'd
    stripes!
Ample Ohio's, Kanada's bards—bards of California! inland
    bards—bards of the war!
You by my charm I invoke.

REVERSALS

Let that which stood in front go behind,
Let that which was behind advance to the front,
Let bigots, fools, unclean persons, offer new propositions,
Let the old propositions be postponed,
Let a man seek pleasure everywhere except in himself,
Let a woman seek happiness everywhere except in herself.

AUTUMN RIVULETS

AS CONSEQUENT, Etc.

As consequent from store of summer rains,
Or wayward rivulets in autumn flowing,
Or many a herb-lined brook's reticulations,
Or subterranean sea-rills making for the sea,
Songs of continued years I sing.

Life's ever-modern rapids first, (soon, soon to blend,
With the old streams of death.)

Some threading Ohio's farm-fields or the woods,
Some down Colorado's cañons from sources of perpetual snow,
Some half-hid in Oregon, or away southward in Texas,
Some in the north finding their way to Erie, Niagara, Ottawa,
Some to Atlantica's bays, and so to the great salt brine.

In you whoe'er you are my book perusing,
In I myself, in all the world, these currents flowing,
All, all toward the mystic ocean tending.

Currents for starting a continent new,
Overtures sent to the solid out of the liquid,

Fusion of ocean and land, tender and pensive waves,
(Not safe and peaceful only, waves rous'd and ominous too,
Out of the depths the storm's abysmic waves, who knows
      whence?
Raging over the vast, with many a broken spar and tatter'd
      sail.)

Or from the sea of Time, collecting vasting all, I bring,
A windrow-drift of weeds and shells.

O little shells, so curious-convolute, so limpid-cold and voice-
      less,
Will you not little shells to the tympans of temples held,
Murmurs and echoes still call up, eternity's music faint and
      far,
Wafted inland, sent from Atlantica's rim, strains for the soul
      of the prairies,
Whisper'd reverberations, chords for the ear of the West
      joyously sounding,
Your tidings old, yet ever new and untranslatable,
Infinitesimals out of my life, and many a life,
(For not my life and years alone I give—all, all I give,)
These waifs from the deep, cast high and dry,
Wash'd on America's shores?

THE RETURN OF THE HEROES

1

For the lands and for these passionate days and for myself,
Now I awhile retire to thee O soil of autumn fields,
Reclining on thy breast, giving myself to thee,
Answering the pulses of thy sane and equable heart,
Tuning a verse for thee.

O earth that hast no voice, confide to me a voice,
O harvest of my lands—O boundless summer growths,
O lavish brown parturient earth—O infinite teeming womb,
A song to narrate thee.

2

Ever upon this stage,
Is acted God's calm annual drama,
Gorgeous processions, songs of birds,
Sunrise that fullest feeds and freshens most the soul,
The heaving sea, the waves upon the shore, the musical, strong
      waves,
The woods, the stalwart trees, the slender, tapering trees,
The liliput countless armies of the grass,
The heat, the showers, the measureless pasturages,
The scenery of the snows, the winds' free orchestra,

The stretching light-hung roof of clouds, the clear cerulean
        and the silvery fringes,
The high dilating stars, the placid beckoning stars,
The moving flocks and herds, the plains and emerald mead-
        ows,
The shows of all the varied lands and all the growths and
        products.

3

Fecund America—to-day,
Thou art all over set in births and joys!
Thou groan'st with riches, thy wealth clothes thee as a swath-
        ing-garment,
Thou laughest loud with ache of great possessions,
A myriad-twining life like interlacing vines binds all thy vast
        demesne,
As some huge ship freighted to water's edge thou ridest into
        port,
As rain falls from the heaven and vapors rise from earth, so
        have the precious values fallen upon thee and
        risen out of thee;
Thou envy of the globe! thou miracle!
Thou, bathed, choked, swimming in plenty,
Thou lucky Mistress of the tranquil barns,
Thou Prairie Dame that sittest in the middle and lookest out
        upon thy world, and lookest East and look-
        est West,
Dispensatress, that by a word givest a thousand miles, a million
        farms, and missest nothing,
Thou all-acceptress—thou hospitable, (thou only art hospi-
        table as God is hospitable.)

4

When late I sang sad was my voice,
Sad were the shows around me with deafening noises of hatred
        and smoke of war;
In the midst of the conflict, the heroes, I stood,
Or pass'd with slow step through the wounded and dying.

But now I sing not war,
Nor the measur'd march of soldiers, nor the tents of camps,
Nor the regiments hastily coming up deploying in line of battle;
No more the sad, unnatural shows of war.

Ask'd room those flush'd immortal ranks, the first forth-step-
        ping armies?
Ask room alas the ghastly ranks, the armies dread that follow'd.

(Pass, pass, ye proud brigades, with your tramping sinewy
        legs,

With your shoulders young and strong, with your knapsacks
    and your muskets;
How elate I stood and watch'd you, where starting off you
    march'd.

Pass—then rattle drums again,
For an army heaves in sight, O another gathering army,
Swarming, trailing on the rear, O you dread accruing army,
O you regiments so piteous, with your mortal diarrhœa, with
    your fever,
O my land's maim'd darlings, with the plenteous bloody band-
    age and the crutch,
Lo, your pallid army follows.)

5

But on these days of brightness,
On the far-stretching beauteous landscape, the roads and lanes,
    the high-piled farm-wagons, and the fruits
    and barns,
Should the dead intrude?

Ah the dead to me mar not, they fit well in Nature,
They fit very well in the landscape, under the trees and grass,
And along the edge of the sky in the horizon's far margin.

Nor do I forget you Departed,
Nor in your winter or summer my lost ones,
But most in the open air as now when my soul is rapt and at
    peace, like pleasing phantoms,
Your memories rising glide silently by me.

6

I saw the day the return of the heroes,
(Yet the heroes never surpass'd shall never return,
Them that day I saw not.)

I saw the interminable corps, I saw the processions of armies,
I saw them approaching, defiling by with divisions,
Streaming northward, their work done, camping awhile in
    clusters of mighty camps.

No holiday soldiers—youthful, yet veterans,
Worn, swart, handsome, strong, of the stock of homestead and
    workshop,
Harden'd of many a long campaign and sweaty march,
Inured on many a hard-fought bloody field.

A pause—the armies wait,
A million flush'd embattled conquerors wait,
The world too waits, then soft as breaking night and sure as
    dawn,
They melt, they disappear.

Exult O lands! victorious lands!
Not there your victory on those red shuddering fields,
But here and hence your victory.

Melt, melt away ye armies—disperse ye blue-clad soldiers,
Resolve ye back again, give up for good your deadly arms,
Other the arms the fields henceforth for you, or South or North,
With saner wars, sweet wars, life-giving wars.

7

Loud O my throat, and clear O soul!
The season of thanks and the voice of full-yielding,
The chant of joy and power for boundless fertility.

All till'd and untill'd fields expand before me,
I see the true arenas of my race, or first or last,
Man's innocent and strong arenas.

I see the heroes at other toils,
I see well-wielded in their hands the better weapons.

I see where the Mother of All,
With full-spanning eye gazes forth, dwells long,
And counts the varied gathering of the products.

Busy the far, the sunlit panorama,
Prairie, orchard, and yellow grain of the North,
Cotton and rice of the South and Louisianian cane,
Open unseeded fallows, rich fields of clover and timothy,
Kine and horses feeding, and droves of sheep and swine,
And many a stately river flowing and many a jocund brook,
And healthy uplands with herby-perfumed breezes,
And the good green grass, that delicate miracle the ever-recur-
        ring grass.

8

Toil on heroes! harvest the products!
Not alone on those warlike fields the Mother of All,
With dilated form and lambent eyes watch'd you.

Toil on heroes! toil well! handle the weapons well!
The Mother of All, yet here as ever she watches you.

Well-pleased America thou beholdest,
Over the fields of the West those crawling monsters,
The human-divine inventions, the labor-saving implements;
Beholdest moving in every direction imbued as with life the
        revolving hay-rakes,
The steam-power reaping-machines and the horse-power ma-
        chines,

The engines, thrashers of grain and cleaners of grain, well sep-
   arating the straw, the nimble work of the
   patent pitch-fork,
Beholdest the newer saw-mill, the southern cotton-gin, and
   the rice-cleanser.

Beneath thy look O Maternal,
With these and else and with their own strong hands the heroes
   harvest.

All gather and all harvest,
Yet but for thee O Powerful, not a scythe might swing as now
   in security,
Not a maize-stalk dangle as now its silken tassels in peace.

Under thee only thy harvest, even but a wisp of hay under thy
   great face only,
Harvest the wheat of Ohio, Illinois, Wisconsin, every barbed
   spear under thee,
Harvest the maize of Missouri, Kentucky, Tennessee, each ear
   in its light-green sheath,
Gather the hay to its myriad mows in the odorous tranquil
   barns,
Oats to their bins, the white potato, the buckwheat of Michi-
   gan, to theirs;
Gather the cotton in Mississippi or Alabama, dig and hoard
   the golden the sweet potato of Georgia and
   the Carolinas,
Clip the wool of California or Pennsylvania,
Cut the flax in the Middle States, or hemp or tobacco in the
   Borders,
Pick the pea and the bean, or pull apples from the trees or
   bunches of grapes from the vines,
Or aught that ripens in all these States or North or South.
Under the beaming sun and under thee.

THERE WAS A CHILD WENT FORTH

There was a child went forth every day,
And the first object he look'd upon, that object he became,
And that object became part of him for the day or a certain
   part of the day,
Or for many years or stretching cycles of years.

The early lilacs became part of this child,
And grass and white and red morning-glories, and white and
   red clover, and the song of the phœbe-bird,
And the Third-month lambs and the sow's pink-faint litter,
   and the mare's foal and the cow's calf,
And the noisy brood of the barnyard or by the mire of the
   pond-side,

And the fish suspending themselves so curiously below there,
and the beautiful curious liquid,
And the water-plants with their graceful flat heads, all became
part of him.

The field-sprouts of Fourth-month and Fifth-month became
part of him,
Winter-grain sprouts and those of the light-yellow corn, and
the esculent roots of the garden,
And the apple-trees cover'd with blossoms and the fruit after-
ward, and wood-berries, and the commonest
weeds by the road,
And the old drunkard staggering home from the outhouse of
the tavern whence he had lately risen,
And the schoolmistress that pass'd on her way to the school,
And the friendly boys that pass'd, and the quarrelsome boys,
And the tidy and fresh-cheek'd girls, and the barefoot negro
boy and girl,
And all the changes of city and country wherever he went.

His own parents, he that had father'd him and she that had
conceiv'd him in her womb and birth'd him,
They gave this child more of themselves than that,
They gave him afterward every day, they became part of him.

The mother at home quietly placing the dishes on the supper-
table,
The mother with mild words, clean her cap and gown, a whole-
some odor falling off her person and clothes
as she walks by,
The father, strong, self-sufficient, manly, mean, anger'd, unjust,
The blow, the quick loud word, the tight bargain, the crafty
lure,
The family usages, the language, the company, the furniture,
the yearning and swelling heart,
Affection that will not be gainsay'd, the sense of what is real,
the thought if after all it should prove unreal,
The doubts of day-time and the doubts of night-time, the curi-
ous whether and how,
Whether that which appears so is so, or is it all flashes and
specks?
Men and women crowding fast in the streets, if they are not
flashes and specks what are they?
The streets themselves and the façades of houses, and goods in
the windows,
Vehicles, teams, the heavy-plank'd wharves, the huge crossing
at the ferries,
The village on the highland seen from afar at sunset, the river
between,

Shadows, aureola and mist, the light falling on roofs and gables
    of white or brown two miles off,
The schooner near by sleepily dropping down the tide, the little
    boat slack-tow'd astern,
The hurrying tumbling waves, quick-broken crests, slapping,
The strata of color'd clouds, the long bar of maroon-tint away
    solitary by itself, the spread of purity it lies
    motionless in,
The horizon's edge, the flying sea-crow, the fragrance of salt
    marsh and shore mud,
These became part of that child who went forth every day,
    and who now goes, and will always go forth
    every day.

OLD IRELAND

Far hence amid an isle of wondrous beauty,
Crouching over a grave an ancient sorrowful mother,
Once a queen, now lean and tatter'd seated on the ground,
Her old white hair drooping dishevel'd round her shoulders,
At her feet fallen an unused royal harp,
Long silent, she too long silent, mourning her shrouded hope
    and heir,
Of all the earth her heart most full of sorrow because most
    full of love.

Yet a word ancient mother,
You need crouch there no longer on the cold ground with fore-
    head between your knees,
O you need not sit there veil'd in your old white hair so
    dishevel'd,
For know you the one you mourn is not in that grave,
It was an illusion, the son you love was not really dead,
The Lord is not dead, he is risen again young and strong in
    another country,
Even while you wept there by your fallen harp by the grave,
What you wept for was translated, pass'd from the grave,
The winds favor'd and the sea sail'd it,
And now with rosy and new blood,
Moves to-day in a new country.

THE CITY DEAD-HOUSE

By the city dead-house by the gate,
As idly sauntering wending my way from the clangor,
I curious pause, for lo, an outcast form, a poor dead prostitute
    brought,
Her corpse they deposit unclaim'd, it lies on the damp brick
    pavement,
The divine woman, her body, I see the body, I look on it alone,

That house once full of passion and beauty, all else I notice not,
Nor stillness so cold, nor running water from faucet, nor odors
        morbific impress me,
But the house alone—that wondrous house—that delicate fair
        house—that ruin!
That immortal house more than all the rows of dwellings ever
        built!
Or white-domed capitol with majestic figure surmounted, or all
        the old high-spired cathedrals.

That little house alone more than them all—poor, desperate
        house!
Fair, fearful wreck—tenement of a soul—itself a soul,
Unclaim'd, avoided house—take one breath from my tremu-
        lous lips,
Take one tear dropt aside as I go for thought of you,
Dead house of love—house of madness and sin, crumbled,
        crush'd,
House of life, erewhile talking and laughing—but ah, poor
        house, dead even then,
Months, years, an echoing, garnish'd house—but dead, dead,
        dead.

THIS COMPOST

1

Something startles me where I thought I was safest,
I withdraw from the still woods I loved,
I will not go now on the pastures to walk,
I will not strip the clothes from my body to meet my lover the
       sea,
I will not touch my flesh to the earth as to other flesh to renew
       me.

O how can it be that the ground itself does not sicken?
How can you be alive you growths of spring?
How can you furnish health you blood of herbs, roots, or-
       chards, grain?
Are they not continually putting distemper'd corpses within
       you?
Is not every continent work'd over and over with sour dead?

Where have you disposed of their carcasses?
Those drunkards and gluttons of so many generations?
Where have you drawn off all the foul liquid and meat?
I do not see any of it upon you to-day, or perhaps I am deceiv'd,
I will run a furrow with my plough, I will press my spade
       through the sod and turn it up underneath,
I am sure I shall expose some of the foul meat.

2

Behold this compost! behold it well!
Perhaps every mite has once form'd part of a sick person—
        yet behold!
The grass of spring covers the prairies,
The bean bursts noiselessly through the mould in the garden,
The delicate spear of the onion pierces upward,
The apple-buds cluster together on the apple-branches,
The resurrection of the wheat appears with pale visage out of
        its graves,
The tinge awakes over the willow-tree and the mulberry-tree,
The he-birds carol mornings and evenings while the she-birds
        sit on their nests,
The young of poultry break through the hatch'd eggs,
The new-born of animals appear, the calf is dropt from the
        cow, the colt from the mare,
Out of its little hill faithfully rise the potato's dark green leaves,
Out of its hill rises the yellow maize-stalk, the lilacs bloom in
        the dooryards,
The summer growth is innocent and disdainful above all those
        strata of sour dead.

What chemistry!
That the winds are really not infectious,
That this is no cheat, this transparent green-wash of the sea
        which is so amorous after me,
That it is safe to allow it to lick my naked body all over with
        its tongues,
That it will not endanger me with the fevers that have depos-
        ited themselves in it,
That all is clean forever and forever,
That the cool drink from the well tastes so good,
That blackberries are so flavorous and juicy,
That the fruits of the apple-orchard and the orange-orchard,
        that melons, grapes, peaches, plums, will
        none of them poison me,
That when I recline on the grass I do not catch any disease,
Though probably every spear of grass rises out of what was
        once a catching disease.

Now I am terrified at the Earth, it is that calm and patient,
It grows such sweet things out of such corruptions,
It turns harmless and stainless on its axis, with such endless
        successions of diseas'd corpses,
It distills such exquisite winds out of such infused fetor,
It renews with such unwitting looks its prodigal, annual, sump-
        tuous crops,
It gives such divine materials to men, and accepts such leavings
        from them at last.

TO A FOIL'D EUROPEAN REVOLUTIONAIRE

Courage yet, my brother or my sister!
Keep on—Liberty is to be subserv'd whatever occurs;
That is nothing that is quell'd by one or two failures, or any
      number of failures,
Or by the indifference or ingratitude of the people, or by any
      unfaithfulness,
Or the show of the tushes of power, soldiers, cannon, penal
      statutes.

What we believe in waits latent forever through all the conti-
      nents,
Invites no one, promises nothing, sits in calmness and light, is
      positive and composed, knows no discour-
      agement,
Waiting patiently, waiting its time.

(Not songs of loyalty alone are these,
But songs of insurrection also,
For I am the sworn poet of every dauntless rebel the world
      over,
And he going with me leaves peace and routine behind him,
And stakes his life to be lost at any moment.)

The battle rages with many a loud alarm and frequent ad-
      vance and retreat,
The infidel triumphs, or supposes he triumphs,
The prison, scaffold, garrote, handcuffs, iron necklace and
      lead-balls do their work,
The named and unnamed heroes pass to other spheres,
The great speakers and writers are exiled, they lie sick in dis-
      tant lands,
The cause is asleep, the strongest throats are choked with their
      own blood,
The young men droop their eyelashes toward the ground when
      they meet;
But for all this Liberty has not gone out of the place, nor the
      infidel enter'd into full possession.

When Liberty goes out of a place it is not the first to go, nor
      the second or third to go,
It waits for all the rest to go, it is the last.

When there are no more memories of heroes and martyrs,
And when all life and all the souls of men and women are
      discharged from any part of the earth,
Then only shall liberty or the idea of liberty be discharged
      from that part of the earth,
And the infidel come into full possession.

Then courage European revolter, revoltress!
For till all ceases neither must you cease.

I do not know what you are for, (I do not know what I am for
        myself, nor what any thing is for,)
But I will search carefully for it even in being foil'd,
In defeat, poverty, misconception, imprisonment—for they
        too are great.

Did we think victory great?
So it is—but now it seems to me, when it cannot be help'd, that
        defeat is great,
And that death and dismay are great.

UNNAMED LANDS

Nations ten thousand years before these States, and many times
        ten thousand years before these States,
Garner'd clusters of ages that men and women like us grew up
        and travel'd their course and pass'd on,
What vast-built cities, what orderly republics, what pastoral
        tribes and nomads,
What histories, rulers, heroes, perhaps transcending all others,
What laws, customs, wealth, arts, traditions,
What sort of marriage, what costumes, what physiology and
        phrenology,
What of liberty and slavery among them, what they thought
        of death and the soul,
Who were witty and wise, who beautiful and poetic, who brut-
        ish and undevelop'd,
Not a mark, not a record remains—and yet all remains.

O I know that those men and women were not for nothing, any
        more than we are for nothing,
I know that they belong to the scheme of the world every bit
        as much as we now belong to it.

Afar they stand, yet near to me they stand,
Some with oval countenances learn'd and calm,
Some naked and savage, some like huge collections of insects,
Some in tents, herdsmen, patriarchs, tribes, horsemen,
Some prowling through woods, some living peaceably on farms,
        laboring, reaping, filling barns,
Some traversing paved avenues, amid temples, palaces, facto-
        ries, libraries, shows, courts, theatres, won-
        derful monuments.

Are those billions of men really gone?
Are those women of the old experience of the earth gone?
Do their lives, cities, arts, rest only with us?
Did they achieve nothing for good for themselves?

I believe of all those men and women that fill'd the unnamed
      lands, every one exists this hour here or else-
      where, invisible to us,
In exact proportion to what he or she grew from in life, and
      out of what he or she did, felt, became, loved,
      sinn'd, in life.

I believe that was not the end of those nations or any person
      of them, any more than this shall be the end
      of my nation, or of me;
Of their languages, governments, marriage, literature, prod-
      ucts, games, wars, manners, crimes, prisons,
      slaves, heroes, poets,
I suspect their results curiously await in the yet unseen world,
      counterparts of what accrued to them in the
      seen world,
I suspect I shall meet them there,
I suspect I shall there find each old particular of those un-
      named lands.

SONG OF PRUDENCE

Manhattan's streets I saunter'd, pondering
On Time, Space, Reality—on such as these, and abreast with
      them Prudence.

The last explanation always remains to be made about pru-
      dence,
Little and large alike drop quietly aside from the prudence that
      suits immortality.

The soul is of itself,
All verges to it, all has reference to what ensues,
All that a person does, says, thinks, is of consequence,
Not a move can a man or woman make, that affects him or
      her in a day, month, any part of the direct
      lifetime, or the hour of death,
But the same affects him or her onward afterward through the
      indirect lifetime.

The indirect is just as much as the direct,
The spirit receives from the body just as much as it gives to the
      body, if not more.

Not one word or deed, not venereal sore, discoloration, privacy
      of the onanist,
Putridity of gluttons or rum-drinkers, peculation, cunning, be-
      trayal, murder, seduction, prostitution,
But has results beyond death as really as before death.

Charity and personal force are the only investments worth any
      thing.

No specification is necessary, all that a male or female does,
    that is vigorous, benevolent, clean, is so much
    profit to him or her,
In the unshakable order of the universe and through the whole
    scope of it forever.

Who has been wise receives interest,
Savage, felon, President, judge, farmer, sailor, mechanic, lit-
    terat, young, old, it is the same,
The interest will come round—all will come round.

Singly, wholly, to affect now, affected their time, will forever
    affect, all of the past, and all of the present
    and all of the future,
All the brave actions of war and peace,
All help given to relatives, strangers, the poor, old, sorrowful,
    young children, widows, the sick, and to
    shunn'd persons,
All self-denial that stood steady and aloof on wrecks, and saw
    others fill the seats of the boats,
All offering of substance or life for the good old cause, or for
    a friend's sake, or opinion's sake,
All pains of enthusiasts scoff'd at by their neighbors,
All the limitless sweet love and precious suffering of mothers,
All honest men baffled in strifes recorded or unrecorded,
All the grandeur and good of ancient nations whose fragments
    we inherit,
All the good of the dozens of ancient nations unknown to us
    by name, date, location,
All that was ever manfully begun, whether it succeeded or no,
All suggestions of the divine mind of man or the divinity of his
    mouth, or the shaping of his great hands,
All that is well thought or said this day on any part of the globe,
    or on any of the wandering stars, or on any of
    the fix'd stars, by those there as we are here,
All that is henceforth to be thought or done by you whoever
    you are, or by any one,
These inure, have inured, shall inure, to the identities from
    which they sprang, or shall spring.

Did you guess any thing lived only its moment?
The world does not so exist, no parts palpable or impalpable
    so exist,
No consummation exists without being from some long pre-
    vious consummation, and that from some
    other,
Without the farthest conceivable one coming a bit nearer the
    beginning than any.

Whatever satisfies souls is true;
Prudence entirely satisfies the craving and glut of souls,

Itself only finally satisfies the soul,
The soul has that measureless pride which revolts from every
      lesson but its own.

Now I breathe the word of the prudence that walks abreast
      with time, space, reality,
That answers the pride which refuses every lesson but its own.

What is prudence is indivisible,
Declines to separate one part of life from every part,
Divides not the righteous from the unrighteous or the living
      from the dead,
Matches every thought or act by its correlative,
Knows no possible forgiveness or deputed atonement,
Knows that the young man who composedly peril'd his life and
      lost it has done exceedingly well for himself
      without doubt,
That he who never peril'd his life, but retains it to old age in
      riches and ease, has probably achiev'd noth-
      ing for himself worth mentioning,
Knows that only that person has really learn'd who has learn'd
      to prefer results,
Who favors body and soul the same,
Who perceives the indirect assuredly following the direct,
Who in his spirit in any emergency whatever neither hurries
      nor avoids death.

THE SINGER IN THE PRISON

1

O sight of pity, shame and dole!
O fearful thought—a convict soul.

Rang the refrain along the hall, the prison,
Rose to the roof, the vaults of heaven above,
Pouring in floods of melody in tones so pensive sweet and
      strong the like whereof was never heard,
Reaching the far-off sentry and the armed guards, who ceas'd
      their pacing,
Making the hearer's pulses stop for ecstasy and awe.

2

The sun was low in the west one winter day,
When down a narrow aisle amid the thieves and outlaws of
      the land,
(There by the hundreds seated, sear-faced murderers, wily
      counterfeiters,
Gather'd to Sunday church in prison walls, the keepers round,
Plenteous, well-armed, watching with vigilant eyes,)

Calmly a lady walk'd holding a little innocent child by either
  hand,
Whom seating on their stools beside her on the platform,
She, first preluding with the instrument a low and musical prel-
  ude,
In voice surpassing all, sang forth a quaint old hymn.

A soul confined by bars and bands,
Cries, help! O help! and wrings her hands,
Blinded her eyes, bleeding her breast,
Nor pardon finds, nor balm of rest.

Ceaseless she paces to and fro,
O heart-sick days! O nights of woe!
Nor hand of friend, nor loving face,
Nor favor comes, nor word of grace.

It was not I that sinn'd the sin,
The ruthless body dragg'd me in;
Though long I strove courageously,
The body was too much for me.

Dear prison'd soul bear up a space,
For soon or late the certain grace;
To see thee free and bear thee home,
The heavenly pardoner death shall come.

Convict no more, nor shame, nor dole!
Depart—a God-enfranchis'd soul!

3

The singer ceas'd,
One glance swept from her clear calm eyes o'er all those
  upturn'd faces,
Strange sea of prison faces, a thousand varied, crafty, brutal,
  seam'd and beauteous faces,
Then rising, passing back along the narrow aisle between
  them,
While her gown touch'd them rustling in the silence,
She vanish'd with her children in the dusk.

While upon all, convicts and armed keepers ere they stirr'd,
(Convict forgetting prison, keeper his loaded pistol,)
A hush and pause fell down a wondrous minute,
With deep half-stifled sobs and sound of bad men bow'd and
  moved to weeping,
And youth's convulsive breathings, memories of home,
The mother's voice in lullaby, the sister's care, the happy
  childhood,
The long-pent spirit rous'd to reminiscence;
A wondrous minute then—but after in the solitary night, to
  many, many there,

Years after, even in the hour of death, the sad refrain, the
    tune, the voice, the words,
Resumed, the large calm lady walks the narrow aisle,
The wailing melody again, the singer in the prison sings,

> *O sight of pity, shame and dole!*
> *O fearful thought—a convict soul.*

WARBLE FOR LILAC-TIME

Warble me now for joy of lilac-time, (returning in remi-
    niscence,)
Sort me O tongue and lips for Nature's sake, souvenirs of
    earliest summer,
Gather the welcome signs, (as children with pebbles or string-
    ing shells,)
Put in April and May, the hylas croaking in the ponds, the
    elastic air,
Bees, butterflies, the sparrow with its simple notes,
Blue-bird and darting swallow, nor forget the high-hole flash-
    ing his golden wings,
The tranquil sunny haze, the clinging smoke, the vapor,
Shimmer of waters with fish in them, the cerulean above,
All that is jocund and sparkling, the brooks running,
The maple woods, the crisp February days and the sugar-
    making,
The robin where he hops, bright-eyed, brown-breasted,
With musical clear call at sunrise, and again at sunset,
Or flitting among the trees of the apple-orchard, building the
    nest of his mate,
The melted snow of March, the willow sending forth its yellow-
    green sprouts,
For spring-time is here! the summer is here! and what is this
    in it and from it?
Thou, soul, unloosen'd—the restlessness after I know not what;
Come, let us lag here no longer, let us be up and away!
O if one could but fly like a bird!
O to escape, to sail forth as in a ship!
To glide with thee O soul, o'er all, in all, as a ship o'er the
    waters;
Gathering these hints, the preludes, the blue sky, the grass,
    the morning drops of dew,
The lilac-scent, the bushes with dark green heart-shaped leaves,
Wood-violets, the little delicate pale blossoms called inno-
    cence,
Samples and sorts not for themselves alone, but for their
    atmosphere,
To grace the bush I love—to sing with the birds,
A warble for joy of lilac-time, returning in reminiscence.

OUTLINES FOR A TOMB
[G. P., Buried 1870]

1

What may we chant, O thou within this tomb?
What tablets, outlines, hang for thee, O millionaire?
The life thou lived'st we know not,
But that thou walk'dst thy years in barter, 'mid the haunts of
         brokers,
Nor heroism thine, nor war, nor glory.

2

Silent, my soul,
With drooping lids, as waiting, ponder'd,
Turning from all the samples, monuments of heroes.

While through the interior vistas,
Noiseless uprose, phantasmic, (as by night Auroras of the
         north,)
Lambent tableaus, prophetic, bodiless scenes,
Spiritual projections.

In one, among the city streets a laborer's home appear'd,
After his day's work done, cleanly, sweet-air'd, the gaslight
         burning,
The carpet swept and a fire in the cheerful stove.

In one, the sacred parturition scene,
A happy painless mother birth'd a perfect child.

In one, at a bounteous morning meal,
Sat peaceful parents with contented sons.

In one, by twos and threes, young people,
Hundreds concentring, walk'd the paths and streets and roads,
Toward a tall-domed school.

In one a trio beautiful,
Grandmother, loving daughter, loving daughter's daughter, sat,
Chatting and sewing.

In one, along a suite of noble rooms,
'Mid plenteous books and journals, paintings on the walls, fine
         statuettes,
Were groups of friendly journeymen, mechanics young and
         old,
Reading, conversing.

All, all the shows of laboring life,
City and country, women's, men's and children's,

Their wants provided for, hued in the sun and tinged for once
        with joy
Marriage, the street, the factory, farm, the house-room, lodg-
        ing-room,
Labor and toil, the bath, gymnasium, playground, library,
        college,
The student, boy or girl, led forward to be taught,
The sick cared for, the shoeless shod, the orphan father'd and
        mother'd,
The hungry fed, the houseless housed;
(The intentions perfect and divine,
The workings, details, haply human.)

3

O thou within this tomb,
From thee such scenes, thou stintless, lavish giver,
Tallying the gifts of earth, large as the earth,
Thy name an earth, with mountains, fields and tides.

Nor by your streams alone, you rivers,
By you, your banks Connecticut,
By you and all your teeming life old Thames,
By you Potomac laving the ground Washington trod, by you
        Patapsco,
You Hudson, you endless Mississippi—nor you alone,
But to the high seas launch, my thought, his memory.

OUT FROM BEHIND THIS MASK

[To Confront a Portrait]

1

Out from behind this bending rough-cut mask,
These lights and shades, this drama of the whole,
This common curtain of the face contain'd in me for me, in
        you for you, in each for each,
(Tragedies, sorrows, laughter, tears—O heaven!
The passionate teeming plays this curtain hid!)
This glaze of God's serenest purest sky,
This film of Satan's seething pit,
This heart's geography's map, this limitless small continent,
        this soundless sea;
Out from the convolutions of this globe,
This subtler astronomic orb than sun or moon, than Jupiter,
        Venus, Mars,
This condensation of the universe, (nay here the only universe,
Here the idea, all in this mystic handful wrapt;)
These burin'd eyes, flashing to you to pass to future time,
To launch and spin through space revolving sideling, from
        these to emanate,
To you whoe'er you are—a look.

2

A traveler of thoughts and years, of peace and war,
Of youth long sped and middle age declining,
(As the first volume of a tale perused and laid away, and this the
    second,
Songs, ventures, speculations, presently to close,)
Lingering a moment here and now, to you I opposite turn,
As on the road or at some crevice door by chance, or open'd
    window,
Pausing, inclining, baring my head, you specially I greet,
To draw and clinch your soul for once inseparably with mine,
Then travel travel on.

VOCALISM

1

Vocalism, measure, concentration, determination, and the di-
    vine power to speak words;
Are you full-lung'd and limber-lipp'd from long trial? from vig-
    orous practice? from physique?
Do you move in these broad lands as broad as they?
Come duly to the divine power to speak words?
For only at last after many years, after chastity, friendship,
    procreation, prudence, and nakedness,
After treading ground and breasting river and lake,
After a loosn'd throat, after absorbing eras, temperaments,
    races, after knowledge, freedom, crimes,
After complete faith, after clarifyings, elevations, and remov-
    ing obstructions,
After these and more, it is just possible there comes to a man,
    a woman, the divine power to speak words;
Then toward that man or that woman swiftly hasten all—none
    refuse, all attend,
Armies, ships, antiquities, libraries, paintings, machines, cit-
    ies, hate, despair, amity, pain, theft, murder,
    aspiration, form in close ranks,
They debouch as they are wanted to march obediently through
    the mouth of that man or that woman.

2

O what is it in me that makes me tremble so at voices?
Surely whoever speaks to me in the right voice, him or her I
    shall follow,
As the water follows the moon, silently, with fluid steps, any-
    where around the globe.

All waits for the right voices;
Where is the practis'd and perfect organ? where is the de-
    velop'd soul?

For I see every word utter'd thence has deeper, sweeter, new
        sounds, impossible on less terms.

I see brains and lips closed, tympans and temples unstruck,
Until that comes which has the quality to strike and to unclose,
Until that comes which has the quality to bring forth what lies
        slumbering forever ready in all words.

TO HIM THAT WAS CRUCIFIED

My spirit to yours dear brother,
Do not mind because many sounding your name do not under-
        stand you,
I do not sound your name, but I understand you,
I specify you with joy O my comrade to salute you, and to
        salute those who are with you, before and
        since, and those to come also,
That we all labor together transmitting the same charge and
        succession,
We few equals indifferent of lands, indifferent of times,
We, enclosers of all continents, all castes, allowers of all
        theologies,
Compassionaters, perceivers, rapport of men,
We walk silent among disputes and assertions, but reject not
        the disputers nor any thing that is asserted,
We hear the bawling and din, we are reach'd at by divisions,
        jealousies, recriminations on every side,
They close peremptorily upon us to surround us, my com-
        rade,
Yet we walk unheld, free, the whole earth over, journeying
        up and down till we make our ineffaceable
        mark upon time and the diverse eras,
Till we saturate time and eras, that the men and women of
        races, ages to come, may prove brethren and
        lovers as we are.

YOU FELONS ON TRIAL IN COURTS

You felons on trial in courts,
You convicts in prison-cells, you sentenced assassins chain'd
        and handcuff'd with iron,
Whom am I too that I am not on trial or in prison?
Me ruthless and devilish as any, that my wrists are not chain'd
        with iron, or my ankles with iron?
You prostitutes flaunting over the trottoirs or obscene in your
        rooms,
Who am I that I should call you more obscene than myself?

O culpable! I acknowledge—I exposé!
(O admirers, praise not me—compliment not me—you make
        me wince,
I see what you do not—I know what you do not.)

Inside these breast-bones I lie smutch'd and choked,
Beneath this face that appears so impassive hell's tides con-
    tinually run.
Lusts and wickedness are acceptable to me,
I walk with delinquents with passionate love,
I feel I am of them—I belong to those convicts and prosti-
    tutes myself,
And henceforth I will not deny them—for how can I deny
    myself?

LAWS FOR CREATIONS

Laws for creations,
For strong artists and leaders, for fresh broods of teachers and
    perfect literats for America,
For noble savans and coming musicians.

All must have reference to the ensemble of the world, and the
    compact truth of the world,
There shall be no subject too pronounced—all works shall
    illustrate the divine law of indirections.

What do you suppose creation is?
What do you suppose will satisfy the soul, except to walk free
    and own no superior?
What do you suppose I would intimate to you in a hundred
    ways, but that man or woman is as good as
    God?
And that there is no God any more divine than Yourself?
And that that is what the oldest and newest myths finally
    mean?
And that you or any one must approach creations through
    such laws?

TO A COMMON PROSTITUTE

Be composed—be at ease with me—I am Walt Whitman, lib-
    eral and lusty as Nature,
Not till the sun excludes you do I exclude you,
Not till the waters refuse to glisten for you and the leaves to
    rustle for you, do my words refuse to glisten
    and rustle for you.

My girl I appoint with you an appointment, and I charge you
    that you make preparations to be worthy to
    meet me,
And I charge you that you be patient and perfect till I come.

Till then I salute you with a significant look that you do not
    forget me.

I WAS LOOKING A LONG WHILE

I was looking a long while for Intentions,
For a clew to the history of the past for myself, and for these
        chants—and now I have found it,
It is not in those paged fables in the libraries, (them I neither
        accept nor reject,)
It is not more in the legends than in all else,
It is in the present—it is this earth to-day,
It is in Democracy—(the purport and aim of all the past,)
It is the life of one man or one woman to-day—the average
        man of to-day,
It is in languages, social customs, literatures, arts,
It is in the broad show of artificial things, ships, machinery,
        politics, creeds, modern improvements, and
        the interchange of nations,
All for the modern—all for the average man of to-day.

THOUGHT

Of persons arrived at high positions, ceremonies, wealth, schol-
        arships, and the like;
(To me all that those persons have arrived at sinks away from
        them, except as it results to their bodies and
        souls,
So that often to me they appear gaunt and naked,
And often to me each one mocks the others, and mocks
        himself or herself,
And of each one the core of life, namely happiness, is full of
        the rotten excrement of maggots,
And often to me those men and women pass unwittingly the
        true realities of life, and go toward false
        realities,
And often to me they are alive after what custom has served
        them, but nothing more,
And often to me they are sad, hasty, unwaked sonnambules
        walking the dusk.)

MIRACLES

Why, who makes much of a miracle?
As to me I know of nothing else but miracles,
Whether I walk the streets of Manhattan,
Or dart my sight over the roofs of houses toward the sky,
Or wade with naked feet along the beach just in the edge of
        the water,
Or stand under trees in the woods,
Or talk by day with any one I love, or sleep in the bed at night
        with any one I love,
Or sit at table at dinner with the rest,

Or look at strangers opposite me riding in the car,
Or watch honey-bees busy around the hive of a summer fore-
    noon,
Or animals feeding in the fields,
Or birds, or the wonderfulness of insects in the air,
Or the wonderfulness of the sundown, or of stars shining so
    quiet and bright,
Or the exquisite delicate thin curve of the new moon in spring;
These with the rest, one and all, are to me miracles,
The whole referring, yet each distinct and in its place.

To me every hour of the light and dark is a miracle,
Every cubic inch of space is a miracle,
Every square yard of the surface of the earth is spread with
    the same,
Every foot of the interior swarms with the same.

To me the sea is a continual miracle,
The fishes that swim—the rocks—the motion of the waves—
    the ships with men in them,
What stranger miracles are there?

SPARKLES FROM THE WHEEL

Where the city's ceaseless crowd moves on the livelong day,
Withdrawn I join a group of children watching, I pause aside
    with them.

By the curb toward the edge of the flagging,
A knife-grinder works at his wheel sharpening a great knife,
Bending over he carefully holds it to the stone, by foot and
    knee,
With measur'd tread he turns rapidly, as he presses with light
    but firm hand,
Forth issue then in copious golden jets,
Sparkles from the wheel.

The scene and all its belongings, how they seize and affect me,
The sad sharp-chinn'd old man with worn clothes and broad
    shoulder-band of leather,
Myself effusing and fluid, a phantom curiously floating, now
    here absorb'd and arrested,
The group, (an unminded point set in a vast surrounding,)
The attentive, quiet children, the loud, proud, restive base of
    the streets,
The low hoarse purr of the whirling stone, the light-press'd
    blade,
Diffusing, dropping, sideways-darting, in tiny showers of gold,
Sparkles from the wheel.

TO A PUPIL

Is reform needed? is it through you?
The greater the reform needed, the greater the Personality you
        need to accomplish it.

You! do you not see how it would serve to have eyes, blood,
        complexion, clean and sweet?
Do you not see how it would serve to have such a body and
        soul that when you enter the crowd an at-
        mosphere of desire and command enters with
        you, and every one is impress'd with your
        Personality?

O the magnet! the flesh over and over!
Go, dear friend, if need be give up all else, and commence
        to-day to inure yourself to pluck, reality, self-
        esteem, definiteness, elevatedness,
Rest not till you rivet and publish yourself of your own Per-
        sonality.

UNFOLDED OUT OF THE FOLDS

Unfolded out of the folds of the woman man comes unfolded,
        and is always to come unfolded,
Unfolded only out of the superbest woman of the earth is to
        come the superbest man of the earth,
Unfolded out of the friendliest woman is to come the friendli-
        est man,
Unfolded only out of the perfect body of a woman can a man
        be form'd of perfect body,
Unfolded only out of the inimitable poems of woman can
        come the poems of man, (only thence have
        my poems come;)
Unfolded out of the strong and arrogant woman I love, only
        thence can appear the strong and arrogant
        man I love,
Unfolded by brawny embraces from the well-muscled woman
        I love, only thence come the brawny em-
        braces of the man.
Unfolded out of the folds of the woman's brain come all the
        folds of the man's brain, duly obedient,
Unfolded out of the justice of the woman all justice is un-
        folded,
Unfolded out of the sympathy of the woman is all sympathy;
A man is a great thing upon the earth and through eternity,
        but every jot of the greatness of man is un-
        folded out of woman;
First the man is shaped in the woman, he can then be shaped
        in himself.

WHAT AM I AFTER ALL

What am I after all but a child, pleas'd with the sound of my
own name? repeating it over and over;
I stand apart to hear—it never tires me.

To you your name also;
Did you think there was nothing but two or three pronuncia-
tions in the sound of your name?

KOSMOS

Who includes diversity and is Nature,
Who is the amplitude of the earth, and the coarseness and
sexuality of the earth, and the great charity
of the earth, and the equilibrium also,
Who has not look'd forth from the windows the eyes for noth-
ing, or whose brain held audience with mes-
sengers for nothing,
Who contains believers and disbelievers, who is the most
majestic lover,
Who holds duly his or her triune proportion of realism, spirit-
ualism, and of the æsthetic or intellectual,
Who having consider'd the body finds all its organs and parts
good,
Who, out of the theory of the earth and of his or her body
understands by subtle analogies all other
theories,
The theory of a city, a poem, and of the large politics of these
States;
Who believes not only in our globe with its sun and moon,
but in other globes with their suns and
moons,
Who, constructing the house of himself or herself, not for a
day but for all time, sees races, eras, dates,
generations,
The past, the future, dwelling there, like space, inseparable
together.

OTHERS MAY PRAISE WHAT THEY LIKE

Others may praise what they like;
But I, from the banks of the running Missouri, praise nothing
in art or aught else,
Till it has well inhaled the atmosphere of this river, also the
western prairie-scent,
And exudes it all again.

WHO LEARNS MY LESSON COMPLETE?

Who learns my lesson complete?
Boss, journeyman, apprentice, churchman and atheist,
The stupid and the wise thinker, parents and offspring, mer-
         chant, clerk, porter and customer,
Editor, author, artist, and schoolboy—draw nigh and com-
         mence;
It is no lesson—it lets down the bars to a good lesson,
And that to another, and every one to another still.

The great laws take and effuse without argument,
I am of the same style, for I am their friend,
I love them quits and quits, I do not halt and make salaams.

I lie abstracted and hear beautiful tales of things and the
         reasons of things,
They are so beautiful I nudge myself to listen.

I cannot say to any person what I hear—I cannot say it to
         myself—it is very wonderful.

It is no small matter, this round and delicious globe moving
         so exactly in its orbit for ever and ever, with-
         out one jolt or the untruth of a single second,
I do not think it was made in six days, nor in ten thousand
         years, nor ten billions of years,
Nor plann'd and built one thing after another as an architect
         plans and builds a house.

I do not think seventy years is the time of a man or woman,
Nor that seventy millions of years is the time of a man or
         woman,
Nor that years will ever stop the existence of me, or any one
         else.

Is it wonderful that I should be immortal? as every one is
         immortal;
I know it is wonderful, but my eyesight is equally wonderful,
         and how I was conceived in my mother's
         womb is equally wonderful,
And pass'd from a babe in the creeping trance of a couple of
         summers and winters to articulate and walk
         —all this is equally wonderful.

And that my soul embraces you this hour, and we affect each
         other without ever seeing each other, and
         never perhaps to see each other, is every bit
         as wonderful.

And that I can think such thoughts as these is just as won-
　　derful,
And that I can remind you, and you think them and know
　　them to be true, is just as wonderful.

And that the moon spins round the earth and on with the
　　earth, is equally wonderful,
And that they balance themselves with the sun and stars is
　　equally wonderful.

TESTS

All submit to them where they sit, inner, secure, unapproach-
　　able to analysis in the soul,
Not traditions, not the outer authorities are the judges,
They are the judges of outer authorities and of all traditions,
They corroborate as they go only whatever corroborates them-
　　selves, and touches themselves;
For all that, they have it forever in themselves to corroborate
　　far and near without one exception.

THE TORCH

On my Northwest coast in the midst of the night a fishermen's
　　group stands watching,
Out on the lake that expands before them, others are spearing
　　salmon,
The canoe, a dim shadowy thing, moves across the black
　　water,
Bearing a torch ablaze at the prow.

O STAR OF FRANCE
[1870-71]

O star of France,
The brightness of thy hope and strength and fame,
Like some proud ship that led the fleet so long,
Beseems to-day a wreck driven by the gale, a mastless hulk,
And 'mid its teeming madden'd half-drown'd crowds,
Nor helm nor helmsman.

Dim smitten star,
Orb not of France alone, pale symbol of my soul, its dearest
　　hopes,
The struggle and the daring, rage divine for liberty,
Of aspirations toward the far ideal, enthusiast's dreams of
　　brotherhood,
Of terror to the tyrant and the priest.

Star crucified—by traitors sold,
Star panting o'er a land of death, heroic land,
Strange, passionate, mocking, frivolous land.

Miserable! yet for thy errors, vanities, sins, I will not now
              rebuke thee,
Thy unexampled woes and pangs have quell'd them all,
And left thee sacred.

In that amid thy many faults thou ever aimedst highly,
In that thou wouldst not really sell thyself however great the
              price,
In that thou surely wakedst weeping from thy drugg'd sleep,
In that alone among thy sisters thou, giantess, didst rend the
              ones that shamed thee,
In that thou couldst not, wouldst not, wear the usual chains,
This cross, thy livid face, thy pierced hands and feet,
The spear thrust in thy side.

O star! O ship of France, beat back and baffled long!
Bear up O smitten orb! O ship continue on!

Sure as the ship of all, the Earth itself,
Product of deathly fire and turbulent chaos,
Forth from its spasms of fury and its poisons,
Issuing at last in perfect power and beauty,
Onward beneath the sun following its course,
So thee O ship of France!

Finish'd the days, the clouds dispel'd,
The travail o'er, the long-sought extrication,
When lo! reborn, high o'er the European world,
(In gladness answering thence, as face afar to face, reflecting
              ours Columbia,)
Again thy star O France, fair lustrous star,
In heavenly peace, clearer, more bright than ever,
Shall beam immortal.

THE OX-TAMER

In a far-away northern country in the placid pastoral region,
Lives my farmer friend, the theme of my recitative, a famous
              tamer of oxen,
There they bring him the three-year-olds and the four-year-
              olds to break them,
He will take the wildest steer in the world and break him and
              tame him,
He will go fearless without any whip where the young bullock
              chafes up and down the yard,
The bullock's head tosses restless high in the air with raging
              eyes,
Yet see you! how soon his rage subsides—how soon this tamer
              tames him;
See you! on the farms hereabouts a hundred oxen young and
              old, and he is the man who has tamed them,

They all know him, all are affectionate to him;
See you! some are such beautiful animals, so lofty looking;
Some are buff-color'd, some mottled, one has a white line
              running along his back, some are brindled,
Some have wide flaring horns (a good sign)—see you! the
              bright hides,
See, the two with stars on their foreheads—see, the round
              bodies and broad backs,
How straight and square they stand on their legs—what fine
              sagacious eyes!
How they watch their tamer—they wish him near them—how
              they turn to look after him!
What yearning expression! how uneasy they are when he
              moves away from them;
Now I marvel what it can be he appears to them, (books, poli-
              tics, poems, depart—all else departs,)
I confess I envy only his fascination—my silent, illiterate
              friend,
Whom a hundred oxen love there in his life on farms,
In the northern country far, in the placid pastoral region.

AN OLD MAN'S THOUGHT OF SCHOOL

[For the Inauguration of a Public School, Camden, New Jersey, 1874]

An old man's thought of school,
An old man gathering youthful memories and blooms that
              youth itself cannot.

Now only do I know you,
O fair auroral skies—O morning dew upon the grass!
And these I see, these sparkling eyes,
These stores of mystic meaning, these young lives,
Building, equipping like a fleet of ships, immortal ships,
Soon to sail out over the measureless seas,
On the soul's voyage.

Only a lot of boys and girls?
Only the tiresome spelling, writing, ciphering classes?
Only a public school?

Ah more, infinitely more;
(As George Fox rais'd his warning cry, "Is it this pile of brick
              and mortar, these dead floors, windows, rails,
              you call the church?
Why this is not the church at all—the church is living, ever
              living souls.")

And you America,
Cast you the real reckoning for your present?
The lights and shadows of your future, good or evil?
To girlhood, boyhood look, the teacher and the school.

WANDERING AT MORN

Wandering at morn,
Emerging from the night from gloomy thoughts, thee in my
        thoughts,
Yearning for thee harmonious Union! thee, singing bird divine!
Thee coil'd in evil times my country, with craft and black
        dismay, with every meanness, treason thrust
        upon thee,
This common marvel I beheld—the parent thrush I watch'd
        feeding its young,
The singing thrush whose tones of joy and faith ecstatic,
Fail not to certify and cheer my soul.
There ponder'd, felt I,
If worms, snakes, loathsome grubs, may to sweet spiritual
        songs be turn'd,
If vermin so transposed, so used and bless'd may be,
Then may I trust in you, your fortunes, days, my country;
Who knows but these may be the lessons fit for you?
From these your future song may rise with joyous trills,
Destin'd to fill the world.

ITALIAN MUSIC IN DAKOTA

["The Seventeenth—the finest Regimental Band I ever heard."]

Through the soft evening air enwinding all,
Rocks, woods, fort, cannon, pacing sentries, endless wilds,
In dulcet streams, in flutes' and cornets' notes,
Electric, pensive, turbulent, artificial,
(Yet strangely fitting even here, meanings unknown before,
Subtler than ever, more harmony, as if born here, related here,
Not to the city's fresco'd rooms, not to the audience of the
        opera house,
Sounds, echoes, wandering strains, as really here at home,
Sonnambula's innocent love, trios with *Norma's* anguish,
And thy ecstatic chorus *Poliuto;*)
Ray'd in the limpid yellow slanting sundown,
Music, Italian music in Dakota.

While Nature, sovereign of this gnarl'd realm,
Lurking in hidden barbaric grim recesses,
Acknowledging rapport however far remov'd,
(As some old root or soil of earth its last-born flower or fruit,)
Listens well pleas'd.

WITH ALL THY GIFTS

With all thy gifts America,
Standing secure, rapidly tending, overlooking the world,
Power, wealth, extent, vouchsafed to thee—with these and
        like of these vouchsafed to thee,

What if one gift thou lackest? (the ultimate human problem
      never solving,)
The gift of perfect women fit for thee—what if that gift of
      gifts thou lackest?
The towering feminine of thee? the beauty, health, completion,
      fit for thee?
The mothers fit for thee?

MY PICTURE-GALLERY

In a little house keep I pictures suspended, it is not a fix'd
      house,
It is round, it is only a few inches from one side to the other;
Yet behold, it has room for all the shows of the world, all
      memories!
Here the tableaus of life, and here the groupings of death;
Here, do you know this? this is cicerone himself,
With finger rais'd he points to the prodigal pictures.

THE PRAIRIE STATES

A newer garden of creation, no primal solitude,
Dense, joyous, modern, populous millions, cities and farms,
With iron interlaced, composite, tied, many in one,
By all the world contributed—freedom's and law's and thrift's
      society,
The crown and teeming paradise, so far, of time's accumu-
      lations,
To justify the past.

PROUD MUSIC OF THE STORM

1

Proud music of the storm,
Blast that careers so free, whistling across the prairies,
Strong hum of forest tree-tops—wind of the mountains,
Personified dim shapes—you hidden orchestras,
You serenades of phantoms with instruments alert,
Bending with Nature's rhythmus all the tongues of nations;
You chords left as by vast composers—you choruses,
You formless, free, religious dances—you from the Orient,
You undertone of rivers, roar of pouring cataracts,
You sounds from distant guns with galloping cavalry,
Echoes of camps with all the different bugle-calls,
Trooping tumultuous, filling the midnight late, bending me
      powerless,
Entering my lonesome slumber-chamber, why have you seiz'd
      me?

2

Come forward O my soul, and let the rest retire,
Listen, lose not, it is toward thee they tend,
Parting the midnight, entering my slumber-chamber,
For thee they sing and dance O soul.

A festival song,
The duet of the bridegroom and the bride, a marriage-march,
With lips of love, and hearts of lovers fill'd to the brim with
love,
The red-flush'd cheeks and perfumes, the cortege swarming
full of friendly faces young and old,
To flutes' clear notes and sounding harps' cantabile.

Now loud approaching drums,
Victoria! see'st thou in powder-smoke the banners torn but
flying? the rout of the baffled?
Hearest those shouts of a conquering army?

(Ah soul, the sobs of women, the wounded groaning in agony,
The hiss and crackle of flames, the blacken'd ruins, the embers
of cities,
The dirge and desolation of mankind.)

Now airs antique and mediæval fill me,
I see and hear old harpers with their harps at Welsh festivals,
I hear the minnesingers singing their lays of love,
I hear the minstrels, gleemen, troubadours, of the middle ages.

Now the great organ sounds,
Tremulous, while underneath, (as the hid footholds of the
earth,
On which arising rest, and leaping forth depend,
All shapes of beauty, grace and strength, all hues we know,
Green blades of grass and warbling birds, children that gam-
bol and play, the clouds of heaven above,)
The strong base stands, and its pulsations intermits not,
Bathing, supporting, merging all the rest, maternity of all the
rest,
And with it every instrument in multitudes,
The players playing, all the world's musicians,
The solemn hymns and masses rousing adoration,
All passionate heart-chants, sorrowful appeals,
The measureless sweet vocalists of ages,
And for their solvent setting earth's own diapason,
Of winds and woods and mighty ocean waves,
A new composite orchestra, binder of years and climes, ten-
fold renewer,
As of the far-back days the poets tell, the Paradiso,

The straying thence, the separation long, but now the wander-
        ing done,
The journey done, the journeyman come home,
And man and art with Nature fused again.

Tutti! for earth and heaven;
(The Almighty leader now for once has signal'd with his
        wand.)

The manly strophe of the husbands of the world,
And all the wives responding.

The tongues of violins,
(I think O tongues ye tell this heart, that cannot tell itself,
This brooding yearning heart, that cannot tell itself.)

3

Ah from a little child,
Thou knowest soul how to me all sounds became music,
My mother's voice in lullaby or hymn,
(The voice, O tender voices, memory's loving voices,
Last miracle of all, O dearest mother's, sister's, voices;)
The rain, the growing corn, the breeze among the long-leav'd
        corn,
The measur'd sea-surf beating on the sand,
The twittering bird, the hawk's sharp scream,
The wild-fowl's notes at night as flying low migrating north
        or south,
The psalm in the country church or mid the clustering trees,
        the open air camp-meeting,
The fiddler in the tavern, the glee, the long-strung sailor-song,
The lowing cattle, bleating sheep, the crowing cock at dawn.

All songs of current lands come sounding round me,
The German airs of friendship, wine and love,
Irish ballads, merry jigs and dances, English warbles,
Chansons of France, Scotch tunes, and o'er the rest,
Italia's peerless compositions.

Across the stage with pallor on her face, yet lurid passion,
Stalks Norma brandishing the dagger in her hand.

I see poor crazed Lucia's eyes' unnatural gleam,
Her hair down her back falls loose and dishevel'd.

I see where Ernani walking the bridal garden,
Amid the scent of night-roses, radiant, holding his bride by
        the hand,
Hears the infernal call, the death-pledge of the horn.

To crossing swords and gray hairs bared to heaven,
The clear electric base and baritone of the world,
The trombone duo, Libertad forever!

From Spanish chestnut trees' dense shade,
By old and heavy convent walls a wailing song,
Song of lost love, the torch of youth and life quench'd in
     despair,
Song of the dying swan, Fernando's heart is breaking.

Awaking from her woes at last retriev'd Amina sings,
Copious as stars and glad as morning light the torrents of her
     joy.

(The teeming lady comes,
The lustrous orb, Venus contralto, the blooming mother,
Sister of loftiest gods, Alboni's self I hear.)

4

I hear those odes, symphonies, operas,
I hear in the *William Tell* the music of an arous'd and angry
     people,
I hear Meyerbeer's *Huguenots*, the *Prophet*, or *Robert*,
Gounod's *Faust*, or Mozart's *Don Juan*.

I hear the dance-music of all nations,
The waltz, some delicious measure, lapsing, bathing me in
     bliss,
The bolero to tinkling guitars and clattering castanets.

I see religious dances old and new,
I hear the sound of the Hebrew lyre,
I see the crusaders marching bearing the cross on high, to
     the martial clang of cymbals,
I hear dervishes monotonously chanting, interspers'd with
         frantic shouts, as they spin around turning
         always towards Mecca,
I see the rapt religious dances of the Persians and the Arabs,
Again, at Eleusis, home of Ceres, I see the modern Greeks
     dancing,
I hear them clapping their hands as they bend their bodies,
I hear the metrical shuffling of their feet.

I see again the wild old Corybantian dance, the performers
     wounding each other,
I see the Roman youth to the shrill sound of flageolets throw-
     ing and catching their weapons,
As they fall on their knees and rise again.

I hear from the Mussulman mosque the muezzin calling,
I see the worshippers within, nor form nor sermon, argument
     nor word,
But silent, strange, devout, rais'd, glowing heads, ecstatic
     faces.

I hear the Egyptian harp or many strings,
The primitive chants of the Nile boatmen,
The sacred imperial hymns of China,
To the delicate sounds of the king, (the stricken wood and
       stone,)
Or to Hindu flutes and the fretting twang of the vina,
A band of bayaderes.

5

Now Asia, Africa leave me, Europe seizing inflates me,
To organs huge and bands I hear as from vast concourses of
       voices,
Luther's strong hymn *Eine feste Burg ist unser Gott*,
Rossini's *Stabat Mater dolorosa*,
Or floating in some high cathedral dim with gorgeous color'd
       windows,
The passionate *Agnus Dei* or *Gloria in Excelsis*.

Composers! mighty maestros!
And you, sweet singers of old lands, soprani, tenori, bassi!
To you a new bard caroling in the West,
Obeisant sends his love.

(Such led to thee O soul,
All senses, shows and objects, lead to thee,
But now it seems to me sound leads o'er all the rest.)

I hear the annual singing of the children in St. Paul's cathe-
       dral,
Or, under the high roof of some colossal hall, the symphonies,
       oratorios of Beethoven, Handel, or Haydn,
The *Creation* in billows of godhood laves me.

Give me to hold all sounds, (I madly struggling cry,)
Fill me with all the voices of the universe,
Endow me with their throbbings, Nature's also,
The tempests, waters, winds, operas and chants, marches and
       dances,
Utter, pour in, for I would take them all!

6

Then I woke softly,
And pausing, questioning awhile the music of my dream,
And questioning all those reminiscences, the tempest in its
       fury,
And all the songs of sopranos and tenors,
And those rapt oriental dances of religious fervor,
And the sweet varied instruments, and the diapason of organs,
And all the artless plaints of love and grief and death,
I said to my silent curious soul out of the bed of the slumber-
       chamber,

Come, for I have found the clew I sought so long,
Let us go forth refresh'd amid the day,
Cheerfully tallying life, walking the world, the real,
Nourish'd henceforth by our celestial dream.

And I said, moreover,
Haply what thou hast heard O soul was not the sound of winds,
Nor dream of raging storm, nor sea-hawk's flapping wings nor
        harsh scream,
Nor vocalism of sun-bright Italy,
Nor German organ majestic, nor vast concourse of voices,
        nor layers of harmonies,
Nor strophes of husbands and wives, nor sound of marching
        soldiers,
Nor flutes, nor harps, nor the bugle-calls of camps,
But to a new rhythmus fitted for thee,
Poems bridging the way from Life to Death, vaguely wafted
        in night air, uncaught, unwritten,
Which let us go forth in the bold day and write.

PASSAGE TO INDIA

1

Singing my days,
Singing the great achievements of the present,
Singing the strong light works of engineers,
Our modern wonders, (the antique ponderous Seven outvied,)
In the Old World the east the Suez canal,
The New by its mighty railroad spann'd,
The seas inlaid with eloquent gentle wires;
Yet first to sound, and ever sound, the cry with thee O soul,
The Past! the Past! the Past!

The Past—the dark unfathom'd retrospect!
The teeming gulf—the sleepers and the shadows!
The past—the infinite greatness of the past!
For what is the present after all but a growth out of the past?
(As a projectile form'd, impell'd, passing a certain line, still
        keeps on,
So the present, utterly form'd, impell'd by the past.)

2

Passage O soul to India!
Eclaircise the myths Asiatic, the primitive fables.

Not you alone proud truths of the world,
Nor you alone ye facts of modern science,
But myths and fables of eld, Asia's, Africa's fables,
The far-darting beams of the spirit, the unloos'd dreams,
The deep diving bibles and legends,
The daring plots of the poets, the elder religions;

O you temples fairer than lilies pour'd over by the rising sun!
O you fables spurning the known, eluding the hold of the
        known, mounting to heaven!
You lofty and dazzling towers, pinnacled, red as roses, bur-
        nish'd with gold!
Towers of fables immortal fashion'd from mortal dreams!
You too I welcome and fully the same as the rest!
You too with joy I sing.

Passage to India!
Lo, soul, seest thou not God's purpose from the first?
The earth to be spann'd, connected by network,
The races, neighbors, to marry and be given in marriage,
The oceans to be cross'd, the distant brought near,
The lands to be welded together.

A worship new I sing,
You captains, voyagers, explorers, yours,
You engineers, you architects, machinists, yours,
You, not for trade or transportation only,
But in God's name, and for thy sake O soul.

3

Passage to India!
Lo soul for thee of tableaus twain.
I see in one the Suez canal initiated, open'd,
I see the procession of steamships, the Empress Eugenie's lead-
        ing the van,
I mark from on deck the strange landscape, the pure sky, the
        level sand in the distance,
I pass swiftly the picturesque groups, the workmen gather'd,
The gigantic dredging machines.

In one again, different, (yet thine, all thine, O soul, the same,)
I see over my own continent the Pacific railroad surmounting
        every barrier,
I see continual trains of cars winding along the Platte carrying
        freight and passengers,
I hear the locomotives rushing and roaring, and the shrill
        steam-whistle,
I hear the echoes reverberate through the grandest scenery in
        the world,
I cross the Laramie plains, I note the rocks in grotesque shapes,
        the buttes,
I see the plentiful larkspur and wild onions, the barren, color-
        less, sage-deserts,
I see in glimpses afar or towering immediately above me the
        great mountains, I see the Wind river and the
        Wahsatch mountains,

I see the Monument mountain and the Eagle's Nest, I pass the
        Promontory, I ascend the Nevadas,
I scan the Noble Elk mountain and wind around its base,
I see the Humboldt range, I thread the valley and cross the
        river,
I see the clear waters of lake Tahoe, I see forests of majestic
        pines,
Or crossing the great desert, the alkaline plains, I behold
        enchanting mirages of waters and meadows,
Marking through these and after all, in duplicate slender lines,
Bridging the three or four thousand miles of land travel,
Tying the Eastern to the Western sea,
The road between Europe and Asia.

(Ah Genoese thy dream! thy dream!
Centuries after thou art laid in thy grave,
The shore thou foundest verifies thy dream.)

4

Passage to India!
Struggles of many a captain, tales of many a sailor dead,
Over my mood stealing and spreading they come,
Like clouds and cloudlets in the unreach'd sky.

Along all history, down the slopes,
As a rivulet running, sinking now, and now again to the sur-
        face rising,
A ceaseless thought, a varied train—lo, soul, to thee, thy
        sight, they rise,
The plans, the voyages again, the expeditions;
Again Vasco de Gama sails forth,
Again the knowledge gain'd, the mariner's compass,
Lands found and nations born, thou born America,
For purpose vast, man's long probation fill'd,
Thou rondure of the world at last accomplish'd.

5

O vast Rondure, swimming in space,
Cover'd all over with visible power and beauty,
Alternate light and day and the teeming spiritual darkness,
Unspeakable high processions of sun and moon and countless
        stars above,
Below, the manifold grass and waters, animals, mountains,
        trees,
With inscrutable purpose, some hidden prophetic intention,
Now first it seems my thought begins to span thee.

Down from the gardens of Asia descending radiating,
Adam and Eve appear, then their myriad progeny after them,

Wandering, yearning, curious, with restless explorations,
With questionings, baffled, formless, feverish, with never-
    happy hearts,
With that sad incessant refrain, *Wherefore unsatisfied soul?*
    and *Whither O mocking life?*

Ah who shall soothe these feverish children?
Who justify these restless explorations?
Who speak the secret of impassive earth?
Who bind it to us? what is this separate Nature so unnatural?
What is this earth to our affections? (unloving earth, without
    a throb to answer ours,
Cold earth, the place of graves.)

Yet soul be sure the first intent remains, and shall be carried
    out,
Perhaps even now the time has arrived.

After the seas are all cross'd, (as they seem already cross'd,)
After the great captains and engineers have accomplish'd
    their work,
After the noble inventors, after the scientists, the chemist,
    the geologist, ethnologist,
Finally shall come the poet worthy of that name,
The true son of God shall come singing his songs.

Then not your deeds only O voyagers, O scientists and in-
    ventors, shall be justified,
All these hearts as of fretted children shall be sooth'd,
All affection shall be fully responded to, the secret shall be told,
All these separations and gaps shall be taken up and hook'd
    and link'd together,
The whole earth, this cold, impassive, voiceless earth, shall
    be completely justified,
Trinitas divine shall be gloriously accomplish'd and compacted
    by the true son of God, the poet,
(He shall indeed pass the straits and conquer the mountains,
He shall double the cape of Good Hope to some purpose,)
Nature and Man shall be disjoin'd and diffused no more,
The true son of God shall absolutely fuse them.

6

Year at whose wide-flung door I sing!
Year of the purpose accomplish'd!
Year of the marriage of continents, climates and oceans!
(No mere doge of Venice now wedding the Adriatic,)
I see O year in you the vast terraqueous globe given and giving
    all,
Europe to Asia, Africa join'd, and they to the New World,

The lands, geographies, dancing before you, holding a festival
garland,
As brides and bridegrooms hand in hand.

Passage to India!
Cooling airs from Caucasus, far, soothing cradle of man,
The river Euphrates flowing, the past lit up again.

Lo soul, the retrospect brought forward,
The old, most populous, wealthiest of earth's lands,
The streams of the Indus and the Ganges and their many
affluents,
(I my shores of America walking to-day behold, resuming all,)
The tale of Alexander on his warlike marches suddenly dying,
On one side China and on the other Persia and Arabia,
To the south the great seas and the bay of Bengal,
The flowing literatures, tremendous epics, religions, castes,
Old occult Brahma interminably far back, the tender and
junior Buddha,
Central and southern empires and all their belongings, pos-
sessors,
The wars of Tamerlane, the reign of Aurungzebe,
The traders, rulers, explorers, Moslems, Venetians, Byzan-
tium, the Arabs, Portuguese,
The first traveler famous yet, Marco Polo, Patouta, the Moor,
Doubts to be solv'd, the map incognita, blanks to be fill'd,
The foot of man unstay'd, the hands never at rest,
Thyself O soul that will not brook a challenge.

The mediæval navigators rise before me,
The world of 1492, with its awaken'd enterprise,
Something swelling in humanity now like the sap of the earth
in spring,
The sunset splendor of chivalry declining.

And who art thou sad shade?
Gigantic, visionary, thyself a visionary,
With majestic limbs and pious beaming eyes,
Spreading around with every look of thine a golden world,
Enhuing it with gorgeous hues.

As the chief histrion,
Down to the footlights walks in some great scena,
Dominating the rest I see the Admiral himself,
(History's type of courage, action, faith,)
Behold him sail from Palos leading his little fleet,
His voyage behold, his return, his great fame,
His misfortunes, calumniators, behold him a prisoner, chain'd,
Behold his dejection, poverty, death.

(Curious in time I stand, noting the efforts of heroes,
Is the deferment long? bitter the slander, poverty, death?
Lies the seed unreck'd for centuries in the ground? lo, to God's
          due occasion,
Uprising in the night, it sprouts, blooms,
And fills the earth with use and beauty.)

7

Passage indeed O soul to primal thought,
Not lands and seas alone, thy own clear freshness,
The young maturity of brood and bloom,
To realms of budding bibles.

O soul, repressless, I with thee and thou with me,
Thy circumnavigation of the world begin,
Of man, the voyage of his mind's return,
To reason's early paradise,
Back, back to wisdom's birth, to innocent intuitions,
Again with fair creation.

8

O we can wait no longer,
We too take ship O soul,
Joyous we too launch out on trackless seas,
Fearless for unknown shores on waves of ecstasy to sail,
Amid the wafting winds, (thou pressing me to thee, I thee to
          me, O soul,)
Caroling free, singing our song of God,
Chanting our chant of pleasant exploration.

With laugh and many a kiss,
(Let others deprecate, let others weep for sin, remorse, hu-
          miliation,)
O soul thou pleasest me, I thee.

Ah more than any priest O soul we too believe in God,
But with the mystery of God we dare not dally.

O soul thou pleasest me, I thee,
Sailing these seas or on the hills, or waking in the night,
Thoughts, silent thoughts, of Time and Space and Death, like
          waters flowing,
Bear me indeed as through the regions infinite,
Whose air I breathe, whose ripples hear, lave me all over,
Bathe me O God in thee, mounting to thee,
I and my soul to range in range of thee.

O Thou transcendent,
Nameless, the fibre and the breath,
Light of the light, shedding forth universes, thou centre of
          them,

Thou mightier centre of the true, the good, the loving,
Thou moral, spiritual fountain—affection's source—thou
        reservoir,
(O pensive soul of me—O thirst unsatisfied—waitest not
        there?
Waitest not haply for us somewhere there the Comrade per-
        fect?)
Thou pulse—thou motive of the stars, sun, systems,
That, circling, move in order, safe, harmonious,
Athwart the shapeless vastness of space,
How should I think, how breathe a single breath, how speak,
        if out of myself,
I could not launch, to those, superior universes?

Swiftly I shrivel at the thought of God,
At Nature and its wonders, Time and Space and Death,
But that I, turning, call to thee O soul, thou actual Me,
And lo, thou gently masterest the orbs,
Thou matest Time, smilest content at Death,
And fillest, swellest full the vastnesses of Space.

Greater than stars or suns,
Bounding O soul thou journeyest forth;
What love than thine and ours could wider amplify?
What aspirations, wishes, outvie thine and ours O soul?
What dreams of the ideal? what plans of purity, perfection,
        strength,
What cheerful willingness for others' sake to give up all?
For others' sake to suffer all?

Reckoning ahead O soul, when thou, the time achiev'd,
The seas all cross'd, weather'd the capes, the voyage done,
Surrounded, copest, frontest God, yieldest, the aim attain'd,
As fill'd with friendship, love complete, the Elder Brother
        found,
The Younger melts in fondness in his arms.

9

Passage to more than India!
Are thy wings plumed indeed for such far flights?
O soul, voyagest thou indeed on voyages like those?
Disportest thou on waters such as those?
Soundest below the Sanscrit and the Vedas?
Then have thy bent unleash'd.

Passage to you, your shores, ye aged fierce enigmas!
Passage to you, to mastership of you, ye strangling problems!
You, strew'd with the wrecks of skeletons, that, living, never
        reach'd you.

Passage to more than India!
O secret of the earth and sky!
Of you O waters of the sea! O winding creeks and rivers!
Of you O woods and fields! of you strong mountains of my
          land!
Of you O prairies! of you gray rocks!

O morning red! O clouds! O rain and snows!
O day and night, passage to you!

O sun and moon and all you stars! Sirius and Jupiter!
Passage to you!

Passage, immediate passage! the blood burns in my veins!
Away O soul! hoist instantly the anchor!
Cut the hawsers—haul out—shake out every sail!
Have we not stood here like trees in the ground long enough?
Have we not grovel'd here long enough, eating and drinking
          like mere brutes?
Have we not darken'd and dazed ourselves with books long
          enough?

Sail forth—steer for the deep waters only,
Reckless O soul, exploring, I with thee, and thou with me,
For we are bound where mariner has not yet dared to go,
And we will risk the ship, ourselves and all.

O brave soul!
O farther farther sail!
O daring joy, but safe! are they not all the seas of God?
O farther, farther, farther sail!

PRAYER OF COLUMBUS

A batter'd, wreck'd old man,
Thrown on this savage shore, far, far from home,
Pent by the sea and dark rebellious brows, twelve dreary
          months,
Sore, stiff with many toils, sicken'd and nigh to death,
I take my way along the island's edge,
Venting a heavy heart.

I am too full of woe!
Haply I may not live another day;
I cannot rest O God, I cannot eat or drink or sleep,
Till I put forth myself, my prayer, once more to Thee.
Breathe, bathe myself once more in Thee, commune with
          Thee,
Report myself once more to Thee.

Thou knowest my years entire, my life,

My long and crowded life of active work, not adoration
 merely;
Thou knowest the prayers and vigils of my youth,
Thou knowest my manhood's solemn and visionary medita-
 tions,
Thou knowest how before I commenced I devoted all to come
 to Thee,
Thou knowest I have in age ratified all those vows and strictly
 kept them,
Thou knowest I have not once lost nor faith nor ecstasy in
 Thee,
In shackles, prison'd, in disgrace, repining not,
Accepting all from Thee, as duly come from Thee.

All my emprises have been fill'd with Thee,
My speculations, plans, begun and carried on in thought of
 Thee,
Sailing the deep or journeying the land for Thee;
Intentions, purports, aspirations mine, leaving results to Thee.

O I am sure they really came from Thee,
The urge, the ardor, the unconquerable will,
The potent, felt, interior command, stronger than words,
A message from the Heavens whispering to me even in sleep,
These sped me on.

By me and these the work so far accomplished,
By me earth's elder cloy'd and stifled lands uncloy'd, unloos'd,
By me the hemispheres rounded and tied, the unknown to the
 known.

The end I know not, it is all in Thee,
O small or great I know not—haply what broad fields, what
 lands,
Haply the brutish measureless human undergrowth I know,
Transplanted there may rise to stature, knowledge worthy
 Thee,
Haply the swords I know may there indeed be turn'd to reap-
 ing-tools,
Haply the lifeless cross I know, Europe's dead cross, may bud
 and blossom there.

One effort more, my altar this bleak sand;
That Thou O God my life hast lighted,
With ray of light, steady, ineffable, vouchsafed of Thee,
Light rare untellable, lighting the very light,
Beyond all signs, descriptions, languages;
For that O God, be it my latest word, here on my knees,
Old, poor, and paralyzed, I thank Thee.

My terminus near,
The clouds already closing in upon me,
The voyage balk'd, the course disputed, lost,
I yield my ships to Thee.

My hands, my limbs grow nerveless,
My brain feels rack'd, bewilder'd,
Let the old timbers part, I will not part,
I will cling fast to Thee, O God, though the waves buffet me,
Thee, Thee at least I know.

Is it the prophet's thought I speak, or am I raving?
What do I know of life? what of myself?
I know not even my own work past or present,
Dim ever-shifting guesses of it spread before me,
Of newer better worlds, their mighty parturition,
Mocking, perplexing me.

And these things I see suddenly, what mean they?
As if some miracle, some hand divine unseal'd my eyes,
Shadowy vast shapes smile through the air and sky,
And on the distant waves sail countless ships,
And anthems in new tongues I hear saluting me.

THE SLEEPERS

1

I wander all night in my vision,
Stepping with light feet, swiftly and noiselessly stepping and
            stopping,
Bending with open eyes over the shut eyes of sleepers,
Wandering and confused, lost to myself, ill-assorted, con-
            tradictory,
Pausing, gazing, bending, and stopping.

How solemn they look there, stretch'd and still,
How quiet they breathe, the little children in their cradles.

The wretched features of ennuyés, the white features of
            corpses, the livid faces of drunkards, the
            sick-gray faces of onanists,
The gash'd bodies on battle-fields, the insane in their strong-
            door'd rooms, the sacred idiots, the new-
            born emerging from gates, and the dying
            emerging from gates,
The night pervades them and infolds them.

The married couple sleep calmly in their bed, he with his
            palm on the hip of the wife, and she with
            her palm on the hip of the husband,
The sisters sleep lovingly side by side in their bed,

The men sleep lovingly side by side in theirs,
And the mother sleeps with her little child carefully wrapt.

The blind sleep, and the deaf and dumb sleep,
The prisoner sleeps well in the prison, the runaway son sleeps,
The murderer that is to be hung next day, how does he sleep?
And the murder'd person, how does he sleep?

The female that loves unrequited sleeps,
And the male that loves unrequited sleeps,
The head of the money-maker that plotted all day sleeps,
And the enraged and treacherous dispositions, all, all sleep.

I stand in the dark with drooping eyes by the worst-suffer-
ing and the most restless,
I pass my hands soothingly to and fro a few inches from them,
The restless sink in their beds, they fitfully sleep.

Now I pierce the darkness, new beings appear,
The earth recedes from me into the night,
I saw that it was beautiful, and I see that what is not the earth
is beautiful.

I go from bedside to bedside, I sleep close with the other
sleepers each in turn,
I dream in my dream all the dreams of the other dreamers,
And I become the other dreamers.

I am a dance—play up there! the fit is whirling me fast!

I am the ever-laughing—it is new moon and twilight,
I see the hiding of douceurs, I see nimble ghosts whichever
way I look,
Cache and cache again deep in the ground and sea, and
where it is neither ground nor sea.

Well do they do their jobs those journeymen divine,
Only from me can they hide nothing, and would not if they
could,
I reckon I am their boss and they make me a pet besides,
And surround me and lead me and run ahead when I walk,
To lift their cunning covers to signify me with stretch'd arms,
and resume the way;
Onward we move, a gay gang of blackguards! with mirth-
shouting music and wild-flapping pennants of
joy!

I am the actor, the actress, the voter, the politician,
The emigrant and the exile, the criminal that stood in the box,
He who has been famous and he who shall be famous after
to-day,

The stammerer, the well-formed person, the wasted or feeble
    person.

I am she who adorn'd herself and folded her hair expectantly,
My truant lover has come, and it is dark.

Double yourself and receive me darkness,
Receive me and my lover too, he will not let me go without
    him.

I roll myself upon you as upon a bed, I resign myself to the
    dusk.

He whom I call answers me and takes the place of my lover,
He rises with me silently from the bed.

Darkness, you are gentler than my lover, his flesh was sweaty
    and panting,
I feel the hot moisture yet that he left me.

My hands are spread forth, I pass them in all directions,
I would sound up the shadowy shore to which you are jour-
    neying.

Be careful darkness! already what was it touch'd me?
I thought my lover had gone, else darkness and he are one,
I hear the heart-beat, I follow, I fade away.

2

I descend my western course, my sinews are flaccid,
Perfume and youth course through me and I am their wake.

It is my face yellow and wrinkled instead of the old woman's,
I sit low in a straw-bottom chair and carefully darn my grand-
    son's stockings.

It is I too, the sleepless widow looking out on the winter mid-
    night,
I see the sparkles of starshine on the icy and pallid earth.

A shroud I see and I am the shroud, I wrap a body and lie
    in the coffin,
It is dark here under ground, it is not evil or pain here, it is
    blank here, for reasons.

(It seems to me that everything in the light and air ought to
    be happy,
Whoever is not in his coffin and the dark grave let him know
    he has enough.)

3

I see a beautiful gigantic swimmer swimming naked through
    the eddies of the sea,

His brown hair lies close and even to his head, he strikes out
        with courageous arms, he urges himself with
        his legs,
I see his white body, I see his undaunted eyes,
I hate the swift-running eddies that would dash him head-
        foremost on the rocks.

What are you doing unruffianly red-trickled waves?
Will you kill the courageous giant? will you kill him in the
        prime of his middle age?

Steady and long he struggles,
He is baffled, bang'd, bruis'd, he holds out while his strength
        holds out,
The slapping eddies are spotted with his blood, they bear him
        away, they roll him, swing him, turn him,
His beautiful body is borne in the circling eddies, it is con-
        tinually bruis'd on rocks,
Swiftly and out of sight is borne the brave corpse.

4

I turn but do not extricate myself,
Confused, a past-reading, another, but with darkness yet.

The beach is cut by the razory ice-wind, the wreck-guns sound,
The tempest lulls, the moon comes floundering through the
        drifts.

I look where the ship helplessly heads end on, I hear the
        burst as she strikes, I hear the howls of dis-
        may, they grow fainter and fainter.

I cannot aid with my wringing fingers,
I can but rush to the surf and let it drench me and freeze upon
        me.

I search with the crowd, not one of the company is wash'd
        to us alive,
In the morning I help pick up the dead and lay them in rows
        in a barn.

5

Now of the older war-days, the defeat at Brooklyn,
Washington stands inside the lines, he stands on the intrench'd
        hills amid a crowd of officers,
His face is cold and damp, he cannot repress the weeping
        drops,
He lifts the glass perpetually to his eyes, the color is blanch'd
        from his cheeks,
He sees the slaughter of the southern braves confided to him
        by their parents.

The same at last and at last when peace is declared,
He stands in the room of the old tavern, the well-belov'd
    soldiers all pass through,
The officers speechless and slow draw near in their turns,
The chief encircles their necks with his arm and kisses them
    on the cheek,
He kisses lightly the wet cheeks one after another, he shakes
    hands and bids good-by to the army.

6

Now what my mother told me one day as we sat at dinner
    together,
Of when she was a nearly grown girl living home with her
    parents on the old homestead.

A red squaw came one breakfast-time to the old homestead,
On her back she carried a bundle of rushes for rush-bottom-
    ing chairs,
Her hair, straight, shiny, coarse, black, profuse, half-envelop'd
    her face,
Her step was free and elastic, and her voice sounded ex-
    quisitely as she spoke.

My mother look'd in delight and amazement at the stranger,
She look'd at the freshness of her tall-borne face and full
    and pliant limbs,
The more she look'd upon her she loved her,
Never before had she seen such wonderful beauty and purity,
She made her sit on a bench by the jamb of the fireplace, she
    cook'd food for her,
She had no work to give her, but she gave her remembrance
    and fondness,

The red squaw staid all the forenoon, and toward the middle
    of the afternoon she went away,
O my mother was loth to have her go away,
All the week she thought of her, she watch'd for her many a
    month,
She remember'd her many a winter and many a summer,
But the red squaw never came nor was heard of there again.

7

A show of the summer softness—a contact of something un-
    seen—an amour of the light and air,
I am jealous and overwhelm'd with friendliness,
And will go gallivant with the light and air myself.

O love and summer, you are in the dreams and in me,
Autumn and winter are in the dreams, the farmer goes with
    his thrift,

The droves and crops increase, the barns are well-fill'd.

Elements merge in the night, ships make tacks in the dreams,
The sailor sails, the exile returns home,
The fugitive returns unharm'd, the immigrant is back beyond
    months and years,
The poor Irishman lives in the simple house of his childhood
    with the well-known neighbors and faces,
They warmly welcome him, he is barefoot again, he forgets he
    is well off,
The Dutchman voyages home, and the Scotchman and Welsh-
    man voyage home, and the native of the
    Mediterranean voyages home,
To every port of England, France, Spain, enter well-fill'd ships,
The Swiss foots it toward his hills, the Prussian goes his way,
    the Hungarian his way, and the Pole his way,
The Swede returns, and the Dane and Norwegian return.

The homeward bound and the outward bound,
The beautiful lost swimmer, the ennuyé, the onanist, the female
    that loves unrequited, the money-maker,
The actor and actress, those through with their parts and those
    waiting to commence,
The affectionate boy, the husband and wife, the voter, the nom-
    inee that is chosen and the nominee that has
    fail'd,
The great already known and the great any time after to-day,
The stammerer, the sick, the perfect-form'd, the homely,
The criminal that stood in the box, the judge that sat and sen-
    tenced him, the fluent lawyers, the jury, the
    audience,
The laughter and weeper, the dancer, the midnight widow, the
    red squaw,
The consumptive, the erysipalite, the idiot, he that is wrong'd,
The antipodes, and every one between this and them in the
    dark,
I swear they are averaged now—one is no better than the
    other,
The night and sleep have liken'd them and restored them.

I swear they are all beautiful,
Every one that sleeps is beautiful, every thing in the dim light
    is beautiful,
The wildest and bloodiest is over, and all is peace.

Peace is always beautiful,
The myth of heaven indicates peace and night.
The myth of heaven indicates the soul,
The soul is always beautiful, it appears more or it appears less,
    it comes or it lags behind,

It comes from its embower'd garden and looks pleasantly on
      itself and encloses the world,
Perfect and clean the genitals previously jetting, and perfect
      and clean the womb cohering,
The head well-grown proportion'd and plumb, and the bowels
      and joints proportion'd and plumb.

The soul is always beautiful,
The universe is duly in order, every thing is in its place,
What has arrived is in its place and what waits shall be in its
      place,
The twisted skull waits, the watery or rotten blood waits,
The child of the glutton or venerealee waits long, and the
      child of the drunkard waits long, and the
      drunkard himself waits long,
The sleepers that lived and died wait, the far advanced are to
      go on in their turns, and the far behind are to
      come on in their turns,
The diverse shall be no less diverse, but they shall flow and
      unite—they unite now.

8

The sleepers are very beautiful as they lie unclothed,
They flow hand in hand over the whole earth from east to west
      as they lie unclothed,
The Asiatic and African are hand in hand, the European and
      American are hand in hand,
Learn'd and unlearn'd are hand in hand, and male and female
      are hand in hand,
The bare arm of the girl crosses the bare breast of her lover,
      they press close without lust, his lips press her
      neck,
The father holds his grown or ungrown son in his arms with
      measureless love, and the son holds the father
      in his arms with measureless love,
The white hair of the mother shines on the white wrist of the
      daughter,
The breath of the boy goes with the breath of the man, friend
      is inarm'd by friend,

The scholar kisses the teacher and the teacher kisses the
      scholar, the wrong'd is made right,
The call of the slave is one with the master's call, and the mas-
      ter salutes the slave,
The felon steps forth from the prison, the insane becomes sane,
      the suffering of sick persons is reliev'd,
The sweatings and fevers stop, the throat that was unsound is
      sound, the lungs of the consumptive are re-
      sumed, the poor distress'd head is free,

The joints of the rheumatic move as smoothly as ever, and
      smoother than ever,
Stiflings and passages open, the paralyzed become supple,
The swell'd and convuls'd and congested awake to themselves
      in condition,
They pass the invigoration of the night and the chemistry of
      the night, and awake.

I too pass from the night,
I stay a while away O night, but I return to you again and love
      you.

Why should I be afraid to trust myself to you?
I am not afraid, I have been well brought forward by you,
I love the rich running day, but I do not desert her in whom
      I lay so long,
I know not how I came of you and I know not where I go
      with you, but I know I came well and shall
      go well.

I will stop only a time with the night, and rise betimes,
I will duly pass the day O my mother, and duly return to you.

TRANSPOSITIONS

Let the reformers descend from the stands where they are
      forever bawling—let an idiot or insane per-
      son appear on each of the stands;
Let judges and criminals be transposed—let the prison-keepers
      be put in prison—let those that were prison-
      ers take the keys;
Let them that distrust birth and death lead the rest.

TO THINK OF TIME

1

To think of time—of all that restrospection,
To think of to-day, and the ages continued henceforward.

Have you guess'd you yourself would not continue?
Have you dreaded these earth-beetles?
Have you fear'd the future would be nothing to you?

Is to-day nothing? is the beginningless past nothing?
If the future is nothing they are just as surely nothing.

To think that the sun rose in the east—that men and women
      were flexible, real, alive—that every thing
      was alive,
To think that you and I did not see, feel, think, nor bear our
      part,
To think that we are now here and bear our part.

2

Not a day passes, not a minute or second without an accouche-
          ment,
Not a day passes, not a minute or second without a corpse.

The dull nights go over and the dull days also,
The soreness of lying so much in bed goes over,
The physician after long putting off gives the silent and terrible
          look for an answer,
The children come hurried and weeping, and the brothers and
          sisters are sent for,
Medicines stand unused on the shelf, (the camphor-smell has
          long pervaded the rooms,)
The faithful hand of the living does not desert the hand of the
          dying,
The twitching lips press lightly on the forehead of the dying,
The breath ceases and the pulse of the heart ceases,
The corpse stretches on the bed and the living look upon it,
It is palpable as the living are palpable.

The living look upon the corpse with their eyesight,
But without eyesight lingers a different living and looks curi-
          ously on the corpse.

3

To think the thought of death merged in the thought of mate-
          rials,
To think of all these wonders of city and country, and others
          taking great interest in them, and we taking
          no interest in them.

To think how eager we are in building our houses,
To think others shall be just as eager, and we quite indifferent.

(I see one building the house that serves him a few years, or
          seventy or eighty years at most,
I see one building the house that serves him longer than that.)

Slow-moving and black lines creep over the whole earth—they
          never cease—they are the burial lines,
He that was President was buried, and he that is now President
          shall surely be buried.

4

A reminiscence of the vulgar fate,
A frequent sample of the life and death of workmen,
Each after his kind.

Cold dash of waves at the ferry-wharf, posh and ice in the
          river, half-frozen mud in the streets,

A gray discouraged sky overhead, the short last daylight of
December,
A hearse and stages, the funeral of an old Broadway stage-
driver, the cortege mostly drivers.

Steady the trot to the cemetery, duly rattles the death-bell,
The gate is pass'd, the new-dug grave is halted at, the living
alight, the hearse uncloses,
The coffin is pass'd out, lower'd and settled, the whip it laid on
the coffin, the earth is swiftly shovel'd in,
The mound above is flatted with the spades—silence,
A minute—no one moves or speaks—it is done,
He is decently put away—is there any thing more?

He was a good fellow, free-mouth'd, quick-temper'd, not bad-
looking,
Ready with life or death for a friend, fond of women, gambled,
ate hearty, drank hearty,
Had known what it was to be flush, grew low-spirited toward
the last, sicken'd, was help'd by a contribu-
tion,
Died, aged forty-one years—and that was his funeral.

Thumb extended, finger uplifted, apron, cape, gloves, strap,
wet-weather clothes, whip carefully chosen,
Boss, spotter, starter, hostler, somebody loafing on you, you
loafing on somebody, headway, man before
and man behind,
Good day's work, bad day's work, pet stock, mean stock, first
out, last out, turning-in at night,
To think that these are so much and so nigh to other drivers,
and he there takes no interest in them.

5

The markets, the government, the working-man's wages, to
think what account they are through our
nights and days,
To think that other working-men will make just as great ac-
count of them, yet we make little or no ac-
count.

The vulgar and the refined, what you call sin and what you
call goodness, to think how wide a differ-
ence,
To think the difference will still continue to others, yet we lie
beyond the difference.

To think how much pleasure there is,
Do you enjoy yourself in the city? or engaged in business? or

planning a nomination and election? or with
your wife and family?
Or with your mother and sisters? or in womanly housework?
or the beautiful maternal cares?
These also flow onward to others, you and I flow onward,
But in due time you and I shall take less interest in them.

Your farm, profits, crops—to think how engross'd you are,
To think there will still be farms, profits, crops, yet for you of
what avail?

6

What will be will be well, for what is is well,
To take interest is well, and not to take interest shall be well.

The domestic joys, the daily housework or business, the build-
ing of houses, are not phantasms, they have
weight, form, location,
Farms, profits, crops, markets, wages, government, are none
of them phantasms,
The difference between sin and goodness is no delusion,
The earth is not an echo, man and his life and all the things
of his life are well-consider'd.

You are not thrown to the winds, you gather certainly and
safely around yourself,
Yourself, yourself! yourself, for ever and ever!

7

It is not to diffuse you that you were born of your mother and
father, it is to identify you,
It is not that you should be undecided, but that you should be
decided,
Something long preparing and formless is arrived and form'd
in you,
You are henceforth secure, whatever comes or goes,

The threads that were spun are gather'd, the weft crosses the
warp, the pattern is systematic.

The preparations have every one been justified,
The orchestra have sufficiently tuned their instruments, the
baton has given the signal.

The guest that was coming, he waited long, he is now housed,
He is one of those who are beautiful and happy, he is one of
those that to look upon and be with is enough.

The law of the past cannot be eluded,
The law of the present and future cannot be eluded,
The law of the living cannot be eluded, it is eternal,

The law of promotion and transformation cannot be eluded,
The law of heroes and good-doers cannot be eluded,
The law of drunkards, informers, mean persons, not one iota
thereof can be eluded.

8

Slow moving and black lines go ceaselessly over the earth,
Northerner goes carried and Southerner goes carried, and they
on the Atlantic side and they on the Pacific,
And they between, and all through the Mississippi country, and
all over the earth.

The great masters and kosmos are well as they go, the heroes
and good-doers are well,
The known leaders and inventors and the rich owners and
pious and distinguish'd may be well,
But there is more account than that, there is strict account
of all.

The interminable hordes of the ignorant and wicked are not
nothing,
The barbarians of Africa and Asia are not nothing,
The perpetual successions of shallow people are not nothing as
they go.

Of and in all these things,
I have dream'd that we are not to be changed so much, nor the
law of us changed,
I have dream'd that heroes and good-doers shall be under the
present and past law,
And that murderers, drunkards, liars, shall be under the pres-
ent and past law,
For I have dream'd that the law they are under now is enough.

And I have dream'd that the purpose and essence of the known
life, the transient,
Is to form and decide identity for the unknown life, the per-
manent.

If all came but to ashes of dung,
If maggots and rats ended us, then Alarum! for we are be-
tray'd,
Then indeed suspicion of death.

Do you suspect death? if I were to suspect death I should die
now,
Do you think I could walk pleasantly and well-suited toward
annihilation?

Pleasantly and well-suited I walk,
Whither I walk I cannot define, but I know it is good,
The whole universe indicates that it is good,
The past and the present indicate that it is good.

How beautiful and perfect are the animals!
How perfect the earth, and the minutest thing upon it!
What is called good is perfect, and what is called bad is just
as perfect,
The vegetables and minerals are all perfect, and the impon-
derable fluids perfect;
Slowly and surely they have pass'd on to this, and slowly and
surely they yet pass on.

9

I swear I think now that every thing without exception has an
eternal soul!
The trees have, rooted in the ground! the weeds of the sea
have! the animals!

I swear I think there is nothing but immortality!
That the exquisite scheme is for it, and the nebulous float is for
it, and the cohering is for it!
And all preparation is for it—and identity is for it—and life
and materials are altogether for it!

WHISPERS OF HEAVENLY DEATH

DAREST THOU NOW O SOUL

Darest thou now O soul,
Walk out with me toward the unknown region,
Where neither ground is for the feet nor any path to follow?

No map there, nor guide,
Nor voice sounding, nor touch of human hand,
Nor face with blooming flesh, nor lips, nor eyes, are in that
land.

I know it not O soul,
Nor dost thou, all is a blank before us,
All waits undream'd of in that region, that inaccessible land.

Till when the ties loosen,
All but the ties eternal, Time and Space,
Nor darkness, gravitation, sense, nor any bounds bounding us.

Then we burst forth, we float,
In Time and Space O soul, prepared for them,
Equal, equipt at last, (O joy! O fruit of all!) them to fulfil
O soul.

WHISPERS OF HEAVENLY DEATH

Whispers of heavenly death murmur'd I hear,
Labial gossip of night, sibilant chorals,
Footsteps gently ascending, mystical breezes wafted soft and
    low,
Ripples of unseen rivers, tides of a current flowing, forever
    flowing,
(Or is it the plashing of tears? the measureless waters of human
    tears?)

I see, just see skyward, great cloud-masses,
Mournfully slowly they roll, silently swelling and mixing,
With at times a half-dimm'd, sadden'd far-off star,
Appearing and disappearing.

(Some parturition rather, some solemn immortal birth;
On the frontiers to eyes impenetrable,
Some soul is passing over.)

CHANTING THE SQUARE DEIFIC

1

Chanting the square deific, out of the One advancing, out of
    the sides,
Out of the old and new, out of the square entirely divine,
Solid, four-sided, (all the sides needed,) from this side Jehovah
    am I,
Old Brahm I, and I Saturnius am;
Not Time affects me—I am Thine, old, modern as any,
Unpersuadable, relentless, executing righteous judgments,
As the Earth, the Father, the brown old Kronos, with laws,
Aged beyond computation, yet ever new, ever with those
    mighty laws rolling,
Relentless I forgive no man—whoever sins dies—I will have
    that man's life;
Therefore let none expect mercy—have the seasons, gravita-
    tion, the appointed days, mercy? no more
    have I,
But as the seasons and gravitation, and as all the appointed
    days that forgive not,
I dispense from this side judgments inexorable without the
    least remorse.

2

Consolator most mild, the promis'd one advancing,
With gentle hand extended, the mightier God am I,
Foretold by prophets and poets in their most rapt prophecies
    and poems,

From this side, lo! the Lord Christ gazes—lo! Hermes—I—lo!
    mine is Hercules' face,
All sorrow, labor, suffering, I, tallying it, absorb in myself,
Many times have I been rejected, taunted, put in prison, and
    crucified, and many times shall be again,
All the world have I given up for my dear brothers' and sisters'
    sake, for the soul's sake,
Wending my way through the homes of men, rich or poor, with
    the kiss of affection,
For I am affection, I am the cheer-bringing God, with hope
    and all enclosing charity,
With indulgent words as to children, with fresh and sane
    words, mine only,
Young and strong I pass knowing well I am destin'd myself to
    an early death;
But my charity has no death—my wisdom dies not, neither
    early nor late,
And my sweet love bequeath'd here and elsewhere never dies.

3

Aloof, dissatisfied, plotting revolt,
Comrade of criminals, brother of slaves,
Crafty, despised, a drudge, ignorant,
With sudra face and worn brow, black, but in the depths of
    my heart, proud as any,
Lifted now and always against whoever scorning assumes to
    rule me,
Morose, full of guile, full of reminiscences, brooding, with
    many wiles,
(Though it was thought I was baffled and dispel'd, and my
    wiles done, but that will never be,)
Defiant, I, Satan, still live, still utter words, in new lands duly
    appearing, (and old ones also,)
Permanent here from my side, warlike, equal with any, real
    as any,
Nor time nor change shall ever change me or my words.

4

Santa Spirita, breather, life,
Beyond the light, lighter than light,
Beyond the flames of hell, joyous, leaping easily above hell,
Beyond Paradise, perfumed solely with mine own perfume,
Including all life on earth, touching, including God, including
    Saviour and Satan,
Ethereal, pervading all, (for without me what were all? what
    were God?)
Essence of forms, life of the real identities, permanent, posi-
    tive, (namely the unseen,)

Life of the great round world, the sun and stars, and of man,
    I, the general soul,
Here the square finishing, the solid, I the most solid,
Breathe my breath also through these songs.

OF HIM I LOVE DAY AND NIGHT

Of him I love day and night I dream'd I heard he was dead,
And I dream'd I went where they had buried him I love, but
    he was not in that place,
And I dream'd I wander'd searching among burial-places to
    find him,
And I found that every place was a burial-place;
The houses full of life were equally full of death, (this house
    is now,)
The streets, the shipping, the places of amusement, the Chi-
    cago, Boston, Philadelphia, the Mannahatta,
    were as full of the dead as of the living,
And fuller, O vastly fuller of the dead than of the living;
And what I dream'd I will henceforth tell to every person and
    age,
And I stand henceforth bound to what I dream'd,
And now I am willing to disregard burial-places and dispense
    with them,
And if the memorials of the dead were put up indifferently
    everywhere, even in the room where I eat or
    sleep, I should be satisfied,
And if the corpse of any one I love, or if my own corpse, be
    duly render'd to powder and pour'd in the
    sea, I shall be satisfied,
Or if it be distributed to the winds I shall be satisfied.

YET, YET, YE DOWNCAST HOURS

Yet, yet, ye downcast hours, I know ye also,
Weights of lead, how ye clog and cling at my ankles,
Earth to a chamber of mourning turns—I hear the o'erween-
    ing, mocking voice,
*Matter is conqueror—matter, triumphant only, continues on-
    ward.*

Despairing cries float ceaselessly toward me,
The call of my nearest lover, putting forth, alarm'd, uncertain,
The sea I am quickly to sail, come tell me,
Come tell me where I am speeding, tell me my destination.

I understand your anguish, but I cannot help you,
I approach, hear, behold, the sad mouth, the look out of the
    eyes, your mute inquiry,
Whither I go from the bed I recline on, come tell me;

Old age, alarm'd, uncertain—a young woman's voice, appeal-
        ing to me for comfort;
A young man's voice, *Shall I not escape?*

AS IF A PHANTOM CARESS'D ME

As if a phantom caress'd me,
I thought I was not alone walking here by the shore;
But the one I thought was with me as now I walk by the shore,
        the one I loved that caress'd me,
As I lean and look through the glimmering light, that one has
        utterly disappear'd,
And those appear that are hateful to me and mock me.

ASSURANCES

I need no assurances, I am a man who is pre-occupied of his
        own soul;
I do not doubt that from under the feet and beside the hands
        and face I am cognizant of, are now looking
        faces I am not cognizant of, calm and actual
        faces,
I do not doubt but the majesty and beauty of the world are
        latent in any iota of the world,
I do not doubt I am limitless, and that the universes are limit-
        less, in vain I try to think how limitless,
I do not doubt that the orbs and the systems of orbs play their
        swift sports through the air on purpose, and
        that I shall one day be eligible to do as much
        as they, and more than they,
I do not doubt that temporary affairs keep on and on millions
        of years,
I do not doubt interiors have their interiors, and exteriors have
        their exteriors, and that the eyesight has
        another eyesight, and the hearing another
        hearing, and the voice another voice,
I do not doubt that the passionately-wept deaths of young men
        are provided for, and that the deaths of
        young women and the deaths of little children
        are provided for,
(Did you think Life was so well provided for, and Death, the
        purport of all Life, is not well provided for?)
I do not doubt that wrecks at sea, no matter what the horrors
        of them, no matter whose wife, child, hus-
        band, father, lover, has gone down, are pro-
        vided for, to the minutest points,
I do not doubt that whatever can possibly happen anywhere at
        any time, is provided for in the inherences of
        things,
I do not think Life provides for all and for Time and Space,
        but I believe Heavenly Death provides for all.

QUICKSAND YEARS

Quicksand years that whirl me I know not whither,
Your schemes, politics, fail, lines give way, substances mock
        and elude me,
Only the theme I sing, the great and strong-possess'd soul,
        eludes not,
One's-self must never give way—that is the final substance—
        that out of all is sure,
Out of politics, triumphs, battles, life, what at last finally
        remains?
When shows break up what but One's-Self is sure?

THAT MUSIC ALWAYS ROUND ME

That music always round me, unceasing, unbeginning, yet long
        untaught I did not hear,
But now the chorus I hear and am elated,
A tenor, strong, ascending with power and health, with glad
        notes of daybreak I hear,
A soprano at intervals sailing buoyantly over the tops of im-
        mense waves,
A transparent base shuddering lusciously under and through
        the universe,
The triumphant tutti, the funeral wailings with sweet flutes
        and violins, all these I fill myself with,
I hear not the volumes of sound merely, I am moved by the
        exquisite meanings,
I listen to the different voices winding in and out, striving,
        contending with fiery vehemence to excel
        each other in emotion;
I do not think the performers know themselves—but now I
        think I begin to know them.

WHAT SHIP PUZZLED AT SEA

What ship puzzled at sea, cons for the true reckoning?
Or coming in, to avoid the bars and follow the channel a
        perfect pilot needs?
Here, sailor! here, ship! take aboard the most perfect pilot,
Whom, in a little boat, putting off and rowing, I hailing you
        offer.

A NOISELESS PATIENT SPIDER

A noiseless patient spider,
I mark'd where on a little promontory it stood isolated,
Mark'd how to explore the vacant vast surrounding,
It launch'd forth filament, filament, filament, out of itself,
Ever unreeling them, ever tirelessly speeding them.

And you O my soul where you stand,
Surrounded, detached, in measureless oceans of space,
Ceaselessly musing, venturing, throwing, seeking the spheres
    to connect them,
Till the bridge you will need be form'd, till the ductile anchor
    hold,
Till the gossamer thread you fling catch somewhere, O my soul.

O LIVING ALWAYS, ALWAYS DYING

O living always, always dying!
O the burials of me past and present,
O me while I stride ahead, material, visible, imperious as ever;
O me, what I was for years, now dead, (I lament not, I am
    content;)
O to disengage myself from those corpses of me, which I turn
    and look at where I cast them,
To pass on, (O living! always living!) and leave the corpses
    behind.

TO ONE SHORTLY TO DIE

From all the rest I single out you, having a message for you,
You are to die—let others tell you what they please, I cannot
    prevaricate,
I am exact and merciless, but I love you—there is no escape
    for you.

Softly I lay my right hand upon you, you just feel it,
I do not argue, I bend my head close and half envelop it,
I sit quietly by, I remain faithful,
I am more than nurse, more than parent or neighbor,
I absolve you from all except yourself spiritual bodily, that is
    eternal, you yourself will surely escape,
The corpse you will leave will be but excrementitious.

The sun bursts through in unlooked-for directions,
Strong thoughts fill you and confidence, you smile,
You forget you are sick, as I forget you are sick,
You do not see the medicines, you do not mind the weeping
    friends, I am with you,
I exclude others from you, there is nothing to be commiserated,
I do not commiserate, I congratulate you.

NIGHT ON THE PRAIRIES

Night on the prairies,
The supper is over, the fire on the ground burns low,
The wearied emigrants sleep, wrapt in their blankets;
I walk by myself—I stand and look at the stars, which I think
    now I never realized before.

Now I absorb immortality and peace,
I admire death and test propositions.
How plenteous! how spiritual! how resumé!
The same old man and soul—the same old aspirations, and the
    same content.

I was thinking the day most splendid till I saw what the not-
    day exhibited,
I was thinking this globe enough till there sprang out so noise-
    less around me myriads of other globes.

Now while the great thoughts of space and eternity fill me I will
    measure myself by them,
And now touch'd with the lives of other globes arrived as far
    along as those of the earth,
Or waiting to arrive, or pass'd on farther than those of the
    earth,
I henceforth no more ignore them than I ignore my own life,
Or the lives of the earth arrived as far as mine, or waiting to
    arrive.

O I see now that life cannot exhibit all to me, as the day can-
    not,
I see that I am to wait for what will be exhibited by death.

THOUGHT

As I sit with others at a great feast, suddenly while the music
    is playing,
To my mind, (whence it comes I know not,) spectral in mist
    of a wreck at sea,
Of certain ships, how they sail from port with flying streamers
    and wafted kisses, and that is the last of them,
Of the solemn and murky mystery about the fate of the Presi-
    dent,
Of the flower of the marine science of fifty generations foun-
    der'd off the Northeast coast and going down
        —of the steamship Arctic going down,
Of the veil'd tableau—women gather'd together on deck, pale,
    heroic, waiting the moment that draws so
    close—O the moment!
A huge sob—a few bubbles—the white foam spirting up—and
    then the women gone,
Sinking there while the passionless wet flows on—and I now
    pondering, Are those women indeed gone?
Are souls drown'd and destroy'd so?
Is only matter triumphant?

THE LAST INVOCATION

At the last, tenderly,
From the walls of the powerful fortress'd house,
From the clasp of the knitted locks, from the keep of the well-
closed doors,
Let me be wafted.

Let me glide noiselessly forth;
With the key of softness unlock the locks—with a whisper,
Set ope the doors O soul.

Tenderly—be not impatient,
(Strong is your hold O mortal flesh,
Strong is your hold O love.)

AS I WATCH'D THE PLOUGHMAN PLOUGHING

As I watch'd the ploughman ploughing,
Or the sower sowing in the fields, or the harvester harvesting,
I saw there too, O life and death, your analogies;
(Life, life is the tillage, and Death is the harvest according.)

PENSIVE AND FALTERING

Pensive and faltering,
The words *the Dead* I write,
For living are the Dead,
(Haply the only living, only real,
And I the apparition, I the spectre.)

THOU MOTHER WITH THY EQUAL BROOD

1

Thou Mother with thy equal brood,
Thou varied chain of different States, yet one identity only,
A special song before I go I'd sing o'er all the rest,
For thee, the future.

I'd sow a seed for thee of endless Nationality,
I'd fashion thy ensemble including body and soul,
I'd show away ahead thy real Union, and how it may be ac-
complish'd.

The paths to the house I seek to make,
But leave to those to come the house itself.

Belief I sing, and preparation;
As Life and Nature are not great with reference to the
present only,
But greater still from what is yet to come,
Out of that formula for thee I sing.

2

As a strong bird on pinions free,
Joyous, the amplest spaces heavenward cleaving,
Such be the thought I'd think of thee America,
Such be the recitative I'd bring for thee.

The conceits of the poets of other lands I'd bring thee not,
Nor the compliments that have served their turn so long,
Nor rhyme, nor the classics, nor perfume of foreign court or
        indoor library;
But an odor I'd bring as from forests of pine in Maine, or
        breath of an Illinois prairie,
With open airs of Virginia or Georgia or Tennessee, or from
        Texas uplands, or Florida's glades,
Or the Saguenay's black stream, or the wide blue spread of
        Huron,
With presentment of Yellowstone's scenes, or Yosemite,
And murmuring under, pervading all, I'd bring the rustling
        sea-sound,
That endlessly sounds from the two Great Seas of the world.

And for thy subtler sense subtler refrains dread Mother,
Preludes of intellect tallying these and thee, mind-formulas
             fitted for thee, real and sane and large as
             these and thee,
Thou! mounting higher, diving deeper than we knew, thou
        transcendental Union!
By the fact to be justified, blended with thought,
Thought of man justified, blended with God,
Through thy idea, lo, the immortal reality!
Through thy reality, lo, the immortal idea!

3

Brain of the New World, what a task is thine,
To formulate the Modern—out of the peerless grandeur of the
        modern,
Out of thyself, comprising science, to recast poems, churches,
        art,
(Recast, maybe discard them, end them—maybe their work
        is done, who knows?)
By vision, hand, conception, on the background of the mighty
        past, the dead,
To limn with absolute faith the mighty living present.
And yet thou living present brain, heir of the dead, the Old
        World brain,
Thou that lay folded like an unborn babe within its folds so
        long,
Thou carefully prepared by it so long—haply thou but unfold-
        est it, only maturest it,

It to eventuate in thee—the essence of the by-gone time con-
tain'd in thee,
Its poems, churches, arts, unwitting to themselves, destined
with reference to thee;
Thou but the apples, long, long, long a-growing,
The fruit of all the Old ripening to-day in thee.

4

Sail, sail thy best, ship of Democracy,
Of value is thy freight, 'tis not the Present only,
The Past is also stored in thee,
Thou holdest not the venture of thyself alone, not of the West-
ern continent alone,
Earth's *résumé* entire floats on thy keel O ship, is steadied by
thy spars,
With thee Time voyages in trust, the antecedent nations sink
or swim with thee,
With all their ancient struggles, martyrs, heroes, epics, wars,
thou bear'st the other continents,
Theirs, theirs as much as thine, the destination-port triumph-
ant;
Steer then with good strong hand and wary eye O helmsman,
thou carriest great companions,
Venerable priestly Asia sails this day with thee,
And royal feudal Europe sails with thee.

5

Beautiful world of new superber birth that rises to my eyes,
Like a limitless golden cloud filling the western sky,
Emblem of general maternity lifted above all,
Sacred shape of the bearer of daughters and sons,
Out of thy teeming womb thy giant babes in ceaseless proces-
sion issuing,
Acceding from such gestation, taking and giving continual
strength and life,
World of the real—world of the twain in one,
World of the soul, born by the world of the real alone, led to
identity, body, by it alone,
Yet in beginning only, incalculable masses of composite pre-
cious materials,
By history's cycles forwarded, by every nation, language,
hither sent,
Ready, collected here, a freer, vast, electric world, to be con-
structed here,
(The true New World, the world of orbic science, morals, lit-
eratures to come,)
Thou wonder world yet undefined, unform'd, neither do I
define thee,
How can I pierce the impenetrable blank of the future?

I feel thy ominous greatness evil as well as good,
I watch thee advancing, absorbing the present, transcending
      the past,
I see thy light lighting, and thy shadow shadowing, as if the
      entire globe,
But I do not undertake to define thee, hardly to comprehend
      thee,
I but thee name, thee prophesy, as now,
I merely thee ejaculate!

Thee in thy future,
Thee in thy only permanent life, career, thy own unloosen'd
      mind, thy soaring spirit,
Thee as another equally needed son, radiant, ablaze, swift-
      moving fructifying all,
Thee risen in potent cheerfulness and joy, in endless great hi-
      larity,
Scattering for good the cloud that hung so long, that weigh'd
      so long upon the mind of man,
The doubt, suspicion, dread, of gradual, certain decadence of
      man;
Thee in thy larger, saner brood of female, male—thee in thy
      athletes, moral, spiritual, South, North, West,
      East,
(To thy immortal breasts, Mother of All, thy every daughter,
      son, endear'd alike, forever equal,)
Thee in thy own musicians, singers, artists, unborn yet, but
      certain,
Thee in thy moral wealth and civilization, (until which thy
      proudest material civilization must remain in
      vain,)
Thee in thy all-supplying, all-enclosing worship—thee in no
      single bible saviour, merely,
Thy saviours countless, latent within thyself, thy bibles in-
      cessant within thyself, equal to any, divine as
      any,
(Thy soaring course thee formulating, not in thy two great
      wars, nor in thy century's visible growth,
But far more in these leaves and chants, thy chants, great
      Mother!)
Thee in an education grown of thee, in teachers, studies,
      students, born of thee,
Thee in thy democratic fêtes en-masse, thy high original
      festivals, operas, lecturers, preachers,
Thee in thy ultimata, (the preparations only now completed,
      the edifice on sure foundations tied,)
Thee in thy pinnacles, intellect, thought, thy topmost rational
      joys, thy love and godlike aspiration,

In thy resplendent coming literati, thy full-lung'd orators, thy
      sacerdotal bards, kosmic savans,
These! these in thee, (certain to come,) to-day I prophesy.

6

Land tolerating all, accepting all, not for the good alone, all
      good for thee,
Land in the realms of God to be a realm unto thyself,
Under the rule of God to be a rule unto thyself.

(Lo, where arise three peerless stars,
To be thy natal stars my country, Ensemble, Evolution, Free-
      dom,
Set in the sky of Law.)

Land of unprecedented faith, God's faith,
Thy soil, thy very subsoil, all upheav'd,
The general inner earth so long so sedulously draped over,
      now hence for what it is boldly laid bare,
Open'd by thee to heaven's light for benefit or bale.

Not for success alone,
Not to fair-sail unintermitted always,
The storm shall dash thy face, the murk of war and worse
      than war shall cover thee all over,
(Wert capable of war, its tug and trials? be capable of peace,
      its trials,
For the tug and mortal strain of nations come at last in
      prosperous peace, not war;)
In many a smiling mask death shall approach beguiling thee,
      thou in disease shalt swelter,
The livid cancer spread its hideous claws, clinging upon thy
      breasts, seeking to strike thee deep within,
Consumption of the worst, moral consumption, shall rouge
      thy face with hectic,
But thou shalt face thy fortunes, thy diseases, and surmount
      them all,
Whatever they are to-day and whatever through time they
      may be,
They each and all shall lift and pass away and cease from
      thee,
While thou, Time's spirals rounding, out of thyself, thyself
      still extricating, fusing,
Equable, natural, mystical Union thou, (the mortal with im-
      mortal blent,)
Shalt soar toward the fulfilment of the future, the spirit of the
      body and the mind,
The soul, its destinies.

The soul, its destinies, the real real,
(Purport of all these apparitions of the real;)
In thee America, the soul, its destinies,
Thou globe of globes! thou wonder nebulous!
By many a throe of heat and cold convuls'd, (by these thy-
        self solidifying,)
Thou mental, moral orb—thou New, indeed new, Spiritual
        World!
The Present holds thee not—for such vast growth as thine,
For such unparallel'd flight as thine, such brood as thine,
The Future only holds thee and can hold thee.

A PAUMANOK PICTURE

Two boats with nets lying off the sea-beach, quite still,
Ten fishermen waiting—they discover a thick school of moss-
        bonkers—they drop the join'd seine-ends in
        the water,
The boats separate and row off, each on its rounding course
        to the beach, enclosing the mossbonkers,
The net is drawn in by a windlass by those who stop ashore,
Some of the fishermen lounge in their boats, others stand
        ankle-deep in the water, pois'd on strong
        legs,
The boats partly drawn up, the water slapping against them,
Strew'd on the sand in heaps and windrows, well out from
        the water, the green-back'd spotted moss-
        bonkers.

FROM NOON TO STARRY NIGHT

THOU ORB ALOFT FULL-DAZZLING

Thou orb aloft full-dazzling! thou hot October noon!
Flooding with sheeny light the gray beach sand,
The sibilant near sea with vistas far and foam,
And tawny streaks and shades and spreading blue;
O sun of noon refulgent! my special word to thee.

Hear me illustrious!
Thy lover me, for always I have loved thee,
Even as basking babe, then happy boy alone by some wood
        edge, thy touching-distant beams enough,
Or man matured, or young or old, as now to thee I launch my
        invocation.

(Thou canst not with thy dumbness me deceive,
I know before the fitting man all Nature yields,
Thought answering not in words, the skies, trees, hear his
      voice—and thou O sun,
As for thy throes, thy perturbations, sudden breaks and shafts
      of flame gigantic,
I understand them, I know those flames, those perturbations
      well.)

Thou that with fructifying heat and light,
O'er myriad farms, o'er lands and waters North and South,
O'er Mississippi's endless course, o'er Texas' grassy plains,
      Kanada's woods,
O'er all the globe that turns its face to thee shining in space,
Thou that impartially infoldest all, not only continents, seas,
Thou that to grapes and weeds and little wild flowers givest so
      liberally,
Shed, shed thyself on mine and me, with but a fleeting ray out
      of thy million millions,
Strike though these chants.

Nor only launch thy subtle dazzle and thy strength for these,
Prepare the later afternoon of me myself—prepare my length-
      ening shadows,
Prepare my starry nights.

FACES

1

Sauntering the pavement or riding the country by-road, lo,
      such faces!
Faces of friendship, precision, caution, suavity, ideality,
The spiritual-prescient face, the always welcome common
      benevolent face,
The face of the singing of music, the grand faces of natural
      lawyers and judges broad at the back-top,
The faces of hunters and fishers bulged at the brows, the
      shaved blanch'd faces of orthodox citizens,
The pure, extravagant, yearning, questioning artist's face,
The ugly face of some beautiful soul, the handsome detested
      or despised face,
The sacred faces of infants, the illuminated face of the mother
      of many children,
The face of an amour, the face of veneration,
The face as of a dream, the face of an immobile rock,
The face withdrawn of its good and bad, a castrated face,
A wild hawk, his wings clipp'd by the clipper,
A stallion that yielded at last to the thongs and knife of the
      gelder.

Sauntering the pavement thus, or crossing the ceaseless ferry,
    faces and faces and faces,
I see them and complain not, and am content with all.

2

Do you suppose I could be content with all if I thought them
    their own finalè?

This now is too lamentable a face for a man,
Some abject louse asking leave to be, cringing for it,
Some milk-nosed maggot blessing what lets it wrig to its hole.

This face is a dog's snout sniffing for garbage,
Snakes nest in that mouth, I hear the sibilant threat.

This face is a haze more chill than the arctic sea,
Its sleepy and wabbling icebergs crunch as they go.

This is a face of bitter herbs, this an emetic, they need no
    label,
And more of the drug-shelf, laudanum, caoutchouc, or hog's-
    lard.

This face is an epilepsy, its wordless tongue gives out the un-
    earthly cry,
Its veins down the neck distend, its eyes roll till they show
    nothing but their whites,
Its teeth grit, the palms of the hands are cut by the turn'd-in
    nails,
The man falls struggling and foaming to the ground, while he
    speculates well.

This face is bitten by vermin and worms,
And this is some murderer's knife with a half-pull'd scab-
    bard.

This face owes to the sexton his dismalest fee,
An unceasing death-bell tolls there.

3

Features of my equals would you trick me with your creas'd
    and cadaverous march?
Well, you cannot trick me.

I see your rounded never-erased flow,
I see 'neath the rims of your haggard and mean disguises.

Splay and twist as you like, poke with the tangling fores of
    fishes or rats,
You'll be unmuzzled, you certainly will.

I saw the face of the most smear'd and slobbering idiot they
        had at the asylum,
And I knew for my consolation what they knew not,
I knew of the agents that emptied and broke my brother,
The same wait to clear the rubbish from the fallen tenement,
And I shall look again in a score or two of ages,
And I shall meet the real landlord perfect and unharm'd, every
        inch as good as myself.

4

The Lord advances, and yet advances,
Always the shadow in front, always the reach'd hand bringing
        up the laggards.

Out of this face emerge banners and horses—O superb! I see
        what is coming,
I see the high pioneer-caps, see staves of runners clearing
        the way,
I hear victorious drums.

This face is a life-boat,
This is the face commanding and bearded, it asks no odds
        of the rest,
This face is flavor'd fruit ready for eating,
This face of a healthy honest boy is the programme of all
        good.

These faces bear testimony slumbering or awake,
They show their descent from the Master himself.

Of the word I have spoken I except not one—red, white, black,
        are all deific,
In each house is the ovum, it comes forth after a thousand
        years.

Spots or cracks at the windows do not disturb me,
Tall and sufficient stand behind and make signs to me,
I read the promise and patiently wait.

This is a full-grown lily's face,
She speaks to the limber-hipp'd man near the garden pickets,
Come here she blushingly cries, *Come nigh to me limber-*
        hipp'd man,
Stand at my side till I lean as high as I can upon you,
Fill me with albescent honey, bend down to me,
Rub to me with your chafing beard, rub to my breast and
        shoulders.

5

The old face of the mother of many children,
Whist! I am fully content.

Lull'd and late is the smoke of the First-day morning,
It hangs low over the rows of trees by the fences,
It hangs thin by the sassafras and wild-cherry and cat-brier
    under them.

I saw the rich ladies in full dress at the soiree,
I heard what the singers were singing so long,
Heard who sprang in crimson youth from the white froth
    and the water-blue.

Behold a woman!
She looks out from her quaker cap, her face is clearer and
    more beautiful than the sky.

She sits in an armchair under the shaded porch of the farm-
    house,
The sun just shines on her old white head.

Her ample gown is of cream-hued linen,
Her grandsons raised the flax, and her grand-daughters spin
    it with the distaff and the wheel.

The melodious character of the earth,
The finish beyond which philosophy cannot go and does not
    wish to go,
The justified mother of men.

THE MYSTIC TRUMPETER

1

Hark, some wild trumpeter, some strange musician,
Hovering unseen in air, vibrates capricious tunes to-night.

I hear thee trumpeter, listening alert I catch thy notes,
Now pouring, whirling like a tempest round me,
Now low, subdued, now in the distance lost.

2

Come nearer bodiless one, haply in thee resounds
Some dead composer, haply thy pensive life
Was fill'd with aspirations high, unform'd ideals,
Waves, oceans musical, chaotically surging,
That now ecstatic ghost, close to me bending, thy cornet
    echoing, pealing,
Gives out to no one's ears but mine, but freely gives to mine,
That I may thee translate.

3

Blow trumpeter free and clear, I follow thee,
While at thy liquid prelude, glad, serene,

The fretting world, the streets, the noisy hours of day with-
    draw,
A holy calm descends like dew upon me,
I walk in cool refreshing night the walks of Paradise,
I scent the grass, the moist air and the roses;
Thy song expands my numb'd imbonded spirit, thou freest,
    launchest me,
Floating and basking upon heaven's lake.

4

Blow again trumpeter! and for my sensuous eyes,
Bring the old pageants, show the feudal world.

What charm thy music works! thou makest pass before me,
Ladies and cavaliers long dead, barons are in their castle halls,
    the troubadors are singing,
Arm'd knights go forth to redress wrongs, some in quest of
    the holy Graal;
I see the tournament, I see the contestants incased in heavy
    armor seated on stately champing horses,
I hear the shouts, the sounds of blows and smiting steel;
I see the Crusaders' tumultuous armies—hark, how the cym-
    bals clang,
Lo, where the monks walk in advance, bearing the cross on
    high.

5

Blow again trumpeter! and for thy theme,
Take now the enclosing theme of all, the solvent and the
    setting,
Love, that is pulse of all, the sustenance and the pang,
The heart of man and woman all for love,
No other theme but love—knitting, enclosing, all-diffusing
    love.

O how the immortal phantoms crowd around me!
I see the vast alembic ever working, I see and know the flames
    that heat the world,
The glow, the blush, the beating hearts of lovers,
So blissful happy some, and some so silent, dark, and nigh to
    death;
Love, that is all the earth to lovers—love, that mocks time and
    space,
Love, that is day and night—love, that is sun and moon and
    stars,
Love, that is crimson, sumptuous, sick with perfume,
No other words but words of love, no other thought but love.

6

Blow again trumpeter—conjure war's alarums.

Swift to thy spell a shuddering hum like distant thunder rolls,
Lo, where the arm'd men hasten—lo, mid the clouds of dust
    the glint of bayonets,
I see the grime-faced cannoneers, I mark the rosy flash amid
    the smoke, I hear the cracking of the guns;
Nor war alone—thy fearful music-song, wild prayer, brings
    every sight of fear,
The deeds of ruthless brigands, rapine, murder—I hear the
    cries for help!
I see ships foundering at sea, I behold on deck and below
    deck the terrible tableaus.

7

O trumpeter, methinks I am myself the instrument thou
    playest,
Thou melt'st my heart, my brain—thou movest, drawest,
    changest them at will;
And now thy sullen notes send darkness through me,
Thou takest away all cheering light, all hope,
I see the enslaved, the overthrown, the hurt, the opprest of the
    whole earth,
I feel the measureless shame and humiliation of my race, it
    becomes all mine,
Mine too the revenges of humanity, the wrongs of ages, baffled
    feuds and hatreds,
Utter defeat upon me weighs—all lost—the foe victorious,
(Yet 'mid the ruins Pride colossal stands unshaken to the last,
Endurance, resolution to the last.)

8

Now trumpeter for thy close,
Vouchsafe a higher strain than any yet,
Sing to my soul, renew its languishing faith and hope,
Rouse up my slow belief, give me some vision of the future,
Give me for once its prophecy and joy.

O glad, exulting, culminating song!
A vigor more than earth's is in thy notes,
Marches of victory—man disenthral'd—the conqueror at last,
Hymns to the universal God from universal man—all joy!
A reborn race appears—a perfect world, all joy!
Women and men in wisdom innocence and health—all joy!
Riotous laughing bacchanals fill'd with joy!
War, sorrow, suffering gone—the rank earth purged—nothing
    but joy left!
The ocean fill'd with joy—the atmosphere all joy!

Joy! joy! in freedom, worship, love! joy in the ecstasy of life!
Enough to merely be! enough to breathe!
Joy! joy! all over joy!

TO A LOCOMOTIVE IN WINTER

Thee for my recitative,
Thee in the driving storm even as now, the snow, the winter-
    day declining,
Thee in thy panoply, thy measur'd dual throbbing and thy
    beat convulsive,
The black cylindric body, golden brass and silvery steel,
Thy ponderous side-bars, parallel and connecting rods, gyrat-
    ing, shuttling at thy sides,
Thy metrical, now swelling pant and roar, now tapering in
    the distance,
Thy great protruding head-light fix'd in front,
Thy long, pale, floating vapor-pennants, tinged with delicate
    purple,
The dense and murky clouds out-belching from thy smoke-
    stack,
Thy knitted frame, thy springs and valves, the tremulous
    twinkle of thy wheels,
Thy train of cars, behind, obedient, merrily following,
Through gale or calm, now swift, now slack, yet steadily
    careering;
Type of the modern—emblem of motion and power—pulse of
    the continent,
For once come serve the Muse and merge in verse, even as
    here I see thee,
With storm and buffeting gusts of wind and falling snow,
By day thy warning ringing bell to sound its notes,
By night thy silent signal lamps to swing.

Fierce-throated beauty!
Roll through my chant with all thy lawless music, thy swing-
    ing lamps at night,
Thy madly-whistled laughter, echoing, rumbling like an earth-
    quake, rousing all,
Law of thyself complete, thine own track firmly holding,
(No sweetness debonair of tearful harp or glib piano thine,)
Thy trills of shrieks by rock and hills return'd,
Launch'd o'er the prairies wide, across the lakes,
To the free skies unpent and glad and strong.

O MAGNET-SOUTH

O magnet-South! O glistening perfumed South! my South!
O quick mettle, rich blood, impulse and love! good and evil!
    O all dear to me!

O dear to me my birth-things—all moving things and the trees
         where I was born—the grains, plants, rivers,
Dear to me my own slow sluggish rivers where they flow,
         distant, over flats of silvery sands or through
         swamps,
Dear to me the Roanoke, the Savannah, the Altamahaw, the
         Pedee, the Tombigbee, the Santee, the Coosa,
         and the Sabine,
O pensive, faraway wandering, I return with my soul to haunt
         their banks again,
Again in Florida I float on transparent lakes, I float on the
         Okeechobee, I cross the hummock-land or
         through pleasant openings or dense forests,
I see the parrots in the woods, I see the pawpaw-tree and the
         blossoming titi;
Again, sailing in my coaster on deck, I coast off Georgia, I
         coast up the Carolinas,
I see where the live-oak is growing, I see where the yellow-pine,
         the scented bay-tree, the lemon and orange,
         the cypress, the graceful palmetto,
I pass rude sea-headlands and enter Pamlico sound through
         an inlet, and dart my vision inland;
O the cotton plant! the growing fields of rice, sugar, hemp!
The cactus guarded with thorns, the laurel-tree with large white
         flowers,
The range afar, the richness and barrenness, the old woods
         charged with mistletoe and trailing moss,
The piney odor and the gloom, the awful natural stillness,
         (here in these dense swamps the freebooter
         carries his gun, and the fugitive has his
         conceal'd hut;)
O the strange fascination of these half-known half-impass-
         able swamps, infested by reptiles, resound-
         ing with the bellow of the alligator, the sad
         noises of the night-owl and the wild-cat,
         and the whirr of the rattlesnake,
The mocking-bird, the American mimic, singing all the fore-
         noon, singing through the moon-lit night,
The humming-bird, the wild turkey, the raccoon, the opossum;
A Kentucky corn-field, the tall, graceful, long-leav'd corn,
         slender, flapping, bright-green, with tassels,
         with beautiful ears each well-sheath'd in its
         husk;
O my heart! O tender and fierce pangs, I can stand them not,
         I will depart;
O to be a Virginian where I grew up! O to be a Carolinian!
O longings irrepressible! O I will go back to old Tennessee
         and never wander more.

MANNAHATTA

I was asking for something specific and perfect for my city,
Whereupon lo! upsprang the aboriginal name.

Now I see what there is in a name, a word, liquid, sane, unruly,
            musical, self-sufficient,
I see that the word of my city is that word from of old,
Because I see that word nested in nests of water-bays, superb,
Rich, hemm'd thick all around with sailships and steamships,
            an island sixteen miles long, solid-founded.
Numberless crowded streets, high growth of iron, slender,
            strong, light, splendidly uprising toward clear
            skies,
Tides swift and ample, well-loved by me, toward sundown,
The flowing sea-currents, the little islands, larger adjoining
            islands, the heights, the villas,
The countless masts, the white shore-steamers, the lighters,
            the ferry-boats, the black sea-streamers well-
            model'd,
The down-town streets, the jobbers' houses of business, the
            houses of business of the ship-merchants and
            money-brokers, the river-streets,
Immigrants arriving, fifteen or twenty thousand in a week,
The carts hauling goods, the manly race of drivers of horses,
            the brown-faced sailors,
The summer air, the bright sun shining, and the sailing clouds
            aloft,
The winter snows, the sleigh-bells, the broken ice in the river,
            passing along up or down with the flood-tide
            or ebb-tide,
The mechanics of the city, the masters, well-form'd, beauti-
            ful-faced, looking you straight in the eyes,
Trottoirs throng'd, vehicles, Broadway, the women, the shops
            and shows,
A million people—manners free and superb—open voices—
            hospitality—the most courgeous and friendly
            young men,
City of hurried and sparkling waters! city of spires and masts!
City nested in bays! my city!

ALL IS TRUTH

O me, man of slack faith so long,
Standing aloof, denying portions so long,
Only aware to-day of compact all-diffused truth,
Discovering to-day there is no lie or form of lie, and can be
            none, but grows as inevitably upon itself as
            the truth does upon itself,

Or as any law of the earth or any natural production of the
    earth does.

(This is curious and may not be realized immediately, but it
    must be realized,
I feel in myself that I represent falsehoods equally with the
    rest,
And that the universe does.)

Where has fail'd a perfect return indifferent of lies or the
    truth?
Is it upon the ground, or in water or fire? or in the spirit of
    man? or in the meat and blood?
Meditating among liars and retreating sternly into myself, I
    see that there are really no liars or lies after
    all,
And that nothing fails its perfect return, and that what are
    called lies are perfect returns,
And that each thing exactly represents itself and what has
    preceded it,
And that the truth includes all, and is compact just as much
    as space is compact,
And that there is no flaw or vacuum in the amount of the
    truth—but that all is truth without exception;
And henceforth I will go celebrate any thing I see or am,
And sing and laugh and deny nothing.

A RIDDLE SONG

That which eludes this verse and any verse,
Unheard by sharpest ear, unform'd in clearest eye or cun-
    ningest mind,
Nor lore nor fame, nor happiness nor wealth,
And yet the pulse of every heart and life throughout the world
    incessantly,
Which you and I and all pursuing ever ever miss,
Open but still a secret, the real of the real, an illusion,
Costless, vouchsafe to each, yet never man the owner,
Which poets vainly seek to put in rhyme, historians in prose,
Which sculptor never chisel'd yet, nor painter painted,
Which vocalist never sung, nor orator nor actor ever utter'd,
Invoking here and how I challenge for my song.

Indifferently, 'mid public, private haunts, in solitude,
Behind the mountain and the wood,
Companion of the city's business streets, through the assem-
    blage,
It and its radiations constantly glide.

In looks of fair unconscious babes,
Or strangely in the coffin'd dead,

Or show of breaking dawn or stars by night,
As some dissolving delicate film of dreams,
Hiding yet lingering.

Two little breaths of words comprising it,
Two words, yet all from first to last comprised in it.
How ardently for it!
How many ships have sail'd and sunk for it!
How many travelers started from their homes and ne'er return'd!
How much of genius boldly staked and lost for it!
What countless stores of beauty, love, ventur'd for it!
How all superbest deeds since Time began are traceable to it—
    and shall be to the end!
How all heroic martyrdoms to it!
How, justified by it, the horrors, evils, battles of the earth!
How the bright fascinating lambent flames of it, in every age
    and land, have drawn men's eyes,
Rich as a sunset on the Norway coast, the sky, the islands, and
    the cliffs,
Or midnight's silent glowing northern lights unreachable.

Haply God's riddle it, so vague and yet so certain,
The soul for it, and all the visible universe for it,
And heaven at last for it.

EXCELSIOR

Who has gone farthest? for I would go farther,
And who has been just? for I would be the most just person
    of the earth,
And who most cautious? for I would be more cautious,
And who has been happiest? O I think it is I—I think no one
    was ever happier than I,
And who has lavish'd all? for I lavish constantly the best I
    have,
And who proudest? for I think I have reason to be the proud-
    est son alive—for I am the son of the brawny
    and tall-topt city,
And who has been bold and true? for I would be the boldest
    and truest being of the universe,
And who benevolent? for I would show more benevolence
    than all the rest,
And who has receiv'd the love of the most friends? for I
    know what it is to receive the passionate love
    of many friends,
And who possesses a perfect and enamour'd body? for I do
    not believe any one possesses a more per-
    fect or enamour'd body than mine,

And who thinks the amplest thoughts? for I would surround
               those thoughts,
And who has made hymns fit for the earth? for I am mad with
               devouring ecstasy to make joyous hymns for
               the whole earth.

AH POVERTIES, WINCINGS, AND SULKY RETREATS

Ah poverties, wincings, and sulky retreats,
Ah you foes that in conflict have overcome me,
(For what is my life or any man's life but a conflict with foes,
               the old, the incessant war?)
You degradations, you tussle with passions and appetites,
You smarts from dissatisfied friendships, (ah wounds the
               sharpest of all!)
You toil of painful and choked articulations, you meannesses,
You shallow tongue-talks at tables, (my tongue the shallowest
               of any;)
You broken resolutions, you racking angers, you smother'd
               ennuis!
Ah think not you finally triumph, my real self has yet to come
               forth,
It shall yet march forth o'ermastering, till all lies beneath
               me,
It shall yet stand up the soldier of ultimate victory.

THOUGHTS

Of public opinion,
Of a calm and cool fiat sooner or later, (how impassive! how
               certain and final!)
Of the President with pale face asking secretly to himself,
               What will the people say at last?
Of the frivolous Judge—of the corrupt Congressman, Gover-
               nor, Mayor—of such as these standing help-
               less and exposed,
Of the mumbling and screaming priest, (soon, soon deserted,)
Of the lessening year by year of venerableness, and of the
               dicta of officers, statutes, pulpits, schools,
Of the rising forever taller and stronger and broader of the
               intuitions of men and women, and of Self-
               esteem and Personality;
Of the true New World—of the Democracies resplendent en-
               masse,
Of the conformity of politics, armies, navies, to them,
Of the shining sun by them—of the inherent light, greater
               than the rest,
Of the envelopment of all by them, and the effusion of all
               from them.

MEDIUMS

They shall arise in the States,
They shall report Nature, laws, physiology, and happiness,
They shall illustrate Democracy and the kosmos,
They shall be alimentive, amative, perceptive,
They shall be complete women and men, their pose brawny
    and supple, their drink water, their blood
    clean and clear,
They shall fully enjoy materialism and the sight of products,
    they shall enjoy the sight of the beef, lumber,
    bread-stuffs, of Chicago the great city,
They shall train themselves to go in public to become orators
    and oratresses,
Strong and sweet shall their tongues be, poems and materials
    of poems shall come from their lives, they
    shall be makers and finders,
Of them and of their works shall emerge divine conveyers, to
    convey gospels,
Characters, events, retrospections, shall be convey'd in gos-
    pels, trees, animals, waters, shall be convey'd,
Death, the future, the invisible faith, shall all be convey'd.

WEAVE IN, MY HARDY LIFE

Weave in, weave in, my hardy life,
Weave yet a soldier strong and full for great campaigns to
    come,
Weave in red blood, weave sinews in like ropes, the senses,
    sight weave in,
Weave lasting sure, weave day and night the weft, the warp,
    incessant weave, tire not,
(We know not what the use O life, nor know the aim, the
    end, nor really aught we know,
But know the work, the need goes on and shall go on, the
    death-envelop'd march of peace as well as
    war goes on,)
For great campaigns of peace the same the wiry threads to
    weave,
We know not why or what, yet weave, forever weave.

SPAIN, 1873-74

Out of the murk of heaviest clouds,
Out of the feudal wrecks and heap'd-up skeletons of kings,
Out of that old entire European debris, the shatter'd mum-
    meries,
Ruin'd cathedrals, crumble of palaces, tombs of priests,
Lo, Freedom's features fresh undimm'd look forth—the same
    immortal face looks forth;

(A glimpse as of thy Mother's face Columbia,
A flash significant as of a sword,
Beaming towards thee.)

Nor think we forget thee maternal;
Lag'd'st thou so long? shall the clouds close again upon thee?
Ah, but thou hast thyself now appear'd to us—we know thee,
Thou hast given us a sure proof, the glimpse of thyself,
Thou waitest there as everywhere thy time.

BY BROAD POTOMAC'S SHORE

By broad Potomac's shore, again old tongue,
(Still uttering, still ejaculating, canst never cease this babble?)
Again old heart so gay, again to you, your sense, the full flush
        spring returning,
Again the freshness and the odors, again Virginia's summer
        sky, pellucid blue and silver,
Again the forenoon purple of the hills,
Again the deathless grass, so noiseless soft and green,
Again the blood-red roses blooming.

Perfume this book of mine O blood-red roses!
Lave subtly with your waters every line Potomac!
Give me of you O spring, before I close, to put between its
        pages!
O forenoon purple of the hills, before I close, of you!
O deathless grass, of you!

FROM FAR DAKOTA'S CAÑONS

[June 25, 1876]

From far Dakota's cañons,
Lands of the wild ravine, the dusky Sioux, the lonesome
        stretch, the silence,
Haply to-day a mournful wail, haply a trumpet-note for heroes.

The battle-bulletin,
The Indian ambuscade, the craft, the fatal environment,
The cavalry companies fighting to the last in sternest heroism,
In the midst of their little circle, with their slaughter'd horses
        for breastworks,
The fall of Custer and all his officers and men.

Continues yet the old, old legend of our race,
The loftiest of life upheld by death,
The ancient banner perfectly maintain'd,
O lesson opportune, O how I welcome thee!

As sitting in dark days,
Lone, sulky, through the time's thick murk looking in vain
        for light, for hope,

From unsuspected parts a fierce and momentary proof,
(The sun there at the centre though conceal'd,
Electric life forever at the centre,)
Breaks forth a lightning flash.

Thou of the tawny flowing hair in battle,
I erewhile saw, with erect head, pressing ever in front, bearing
        a bright sword in thy hand,
Now ending well in death the splendid fever of thy deeds,
(I bring no dirge for it or thee, I bring a glad triumphal son-
        net,)
Desperate and glorious, aye in defeat most desperate, most
        glorious,
After thy many battles in which never yielding up a gun or
        a color,
Leaving behind thee a memory sweet to soldiers,
Thou yieldest up thyself.

OLD WAR-DREAMS

In midnight sleep of many a face of anguish,
Of the look at first of the mortally wounded, (of that in-
        describable look,)
Of the dead on their backs with arms extended wide,
        I dream, I dream, I dream.

Of scenes of Nature, fields and mountains,
Of skies so beauteous after a storm, and at night the moon so
        unearthly bright,
Shining sweetly, shining down, where we dig the trenches
        and gather the heaps,
        I dream, I dream, I dream.

Long have they pass'd, faces and trenches and fields,
Where through the carnage I moved with a callous compo-
        sure, or away from the fallen,
Onward I sped at the time—but now of their forms at night,
        I dream, I dream, I dream.

THICK-SPRINKLED BUNTING

Thick-sprinkled bunting! flag of stars!
Long yet your road, fateful flag—long yet your road, and
        lined with bloody death,
For the prize I see at issue at last is the world,
All its ships and shores I see interwoven with your threads
        greedy banner;
Dream'd again the flags of kings, highest borne, to flaunt
        unrival'd?
O hasten flag of man—O with sure and steady step, passing
        highest flags of kings,

Walk supreme to the heavens mighty symbol—run up above
      them all,
Flag of stars! thick-sprinkled bunting!

WHAT BEST I SEE IN THEE

[To U. S. G. return'd from his World's Tour]

What best I see in thee,
Is not that where thou mov'st down history's great highways,
Ever undimm'd by time shoots warlike victory's dazzle,
Or that thou sat'st where Washington sat, ruling the land in
      peace,
Or thou the man whom feudal Europe fêted, venerable Asia
      swarm'd upon,
Who walk'd with kings with even pace the round world's
      promenade;
But that in foreign lands, in all thy walks with kings,
Those prairie sovereigns of the West, Kansas, Missouri,
      Illinois,
Ohio's, Indiana's millions, comrades, farmers, soldiers, all to
      the front,
Invisibly with the walking with kings with even pace the
      round world's promenade,
Were all so justified.

SPIRIT THAT FORM'D THIS SCENE

[Written in Platte Canon, Colorado]

Spirit that form'd this scene,
These tumbled rock-piles grim and red,
These reckless heaven-ambitious peaks,
These gorges, turbulent-clear streams, this naked freshness,
These formless wild arrays, for reasons of their own,
I know thee, savage spirit—we have communed together,
Mine too such wild arrays, for reasons of their own;
Was't charged against my chants they had forgotten art?
To fuse within themselves its rules precise and delicatesse?
The lyrist's measur'd beat, the wrought-out temple's grace—
      column and polish'd arch forgot?
But thou that revelest here—spirit that form'd this scene,
They have remember'd thee.

AS I WALK THESE BROAD MAJESTIC DAYS

As I walk these broad majestic days of peace,
(For the war, the struggle of blood finish'd, wherein, O terrific
      Ideal,
Against vast odds erewhile having gloriously won,
Now thou stridest on, yet perhaps in time toward denser wars,

Perhaps to engage in time in still more dreadful contests,
          dangers,
Longer campaigns and crises, labors beyond all others,)
Around me I hear that eclat of the world, politics, produce,
The announcements of recognized things, science,
The approved growth of cities and the spread of inventions.

I see the ships, (they will last a few years,)
The vast factories with their foremen and workmen,
And hear the indorsement of all, and do not object to it.

But I too announce solid things,
Science, ships, politics, factories, are not nothing,
Like a grand procession to music of distant bugles pouring,
            triumphantly moving, and grander heaving
            in sight,
They stand for realities—all is as it should be.

Then my realties;
What else is so real as mine?
Libertad and the divine average, freedom to every slave on
          the face of the earth,
The rapt promises and luminè of seers, the spiritual world,
          these centuries-lasting songs,
And our visions, the visions of poets, the most solid an-
          nouncements of any.

A CLEAR MIDNIGHT

This is thy hour O Soul, thy free flight into the wordless,
Away from books, away from art, the day erased, the lesson
          done,
Thee fully forth emerging, silent, gazing, pondering the
          themes thou lovest best,
Night, sleep, death and the stars.

SONGS OF PARTING

AS THE TIME DRAWS NIGH

As the time draws nigh glooming a cloud,
A dread beyond of I know not what darkens me.

I shall go forth,
I shall traverse the States awhile, but I cannot tell whither
          or how long,

Perhaps soon some day or night while I am singing my voice
      will suddenly cease.

O book, O chants! must all then amount to but this?
Must we barely arrive at this beginning of us?—and yet it is
      enough, O soul;
O soul, we have positively appear'd—that is enough.

YEARS OF THE MODERN

Years of the modern! years of the unperform'd!
Your horizon rises, I see it parting away for more august
      dramas,
I see not America only, not only Liberty's nation but other
      nations preparing,
I see tremendous entrances and exits, new combinations, the
      solidarity of races,
I see that force advancing with irresistible power on the world's
      stage,
(Have the old forces, the old wars, played their parts? are the
      acts suitable to them closed?)
I see Freedom, completely arm'd and victorious and very
      haughty, with Law on one side and Peace on
      the other,
A stupendous trio all issuing forth against the idea of caste;
What historic denouements are these we so rapidly approach?
I see men marching and countermarching by swift millions,
I see the frontiers and boundaries of the old aristocracies
      broken,
I see the landmarks of European kings removed,
I see this day the People beginning their landmarks, (all others
      give way;)
Never were such sharp questions ask'd as this day,
Never was average man, his soul, more energetic, more like a
      God,
Lo, how he urges and urges, leaving the masses no rest!
His daring foot is on land and sea everywhere, he colonizes
      the Pacific, the archipelagoes,
With the steamship, the electric telegraph, the newspaper, the
      wholesale engines of war,
With these and the world-spreading factories he interlinks all
      geography, all lands;
What whispers are these O lands, running ahead of you, pass-
      ing under the seas?
Are all nations communing? is there going to be but one heart
      to the globe?
Is humanity forming en-masse? for lo, tyrants tremble, crowns
      grow dim,
The earth, restive, confronts a new era, perhaps a general
      divine war,

No one knows what will happen next, such portents fill the
    days and nights;
Years prophetical! the space ahead as I walk, as I vainly try
    to pierce it, is full of phantoms,
Unborn deeds, things soon to be, project their shapes around
    me,
This incredible rush and heat, this strange ecstatic fever of
    dreams O years!
Your dreams O years, how they penetrate through me! (I
    know not whether I sleep or wake;)
The perform'd America and Europe grow dim, retiring in
    shadow behind me,
The unperform'd, more gigantic than ever, advance, advance
    upon me.

ASHES OF SOLDIERS

Ashes of soldiers South or North,
As I muse retrospective murmuring a chant in thought,
The war resumes, again to my sense your shapes,
And again the advance of the armies.

Noiseless as mists and vapors,
From their graves in the trenches ascending,
From cemeteries all through Virginia and Tennessee,
From every point of the compass out of the countless graves,
In wafted clouds, in myriads large, or squads of twos or threes
    or single ones they come,
And silently gather round me.

Now sound no note O trumpeters,
Not at the head of my cavalry parading on spirited horses,
With sabres drawn and glistening, and carbines by their thighs,
    (ah my brave horsemen!
My handsome tan-faced horsemen! what life, what joy and
    pride,
With all the perils were yours.)

Nor you drummers, neither at reveillé at dawn,
Nor the long roll alarming the camp, nor even the muffled
    beat for a burial,
Nothing from you this time O drummers bearing my warlike
    drums.

But aside from these and the marts of wealth and the crowded
    promenade,
Admitting around me comrades close unseen by the rest and
    voiceless,
The slain elate and alive again, the dust and debris alive,
I chant this chant of my silent soul in the name of all dead
    soldiers.

Faces so pale with wondrous eyes, very dear, gather closer yet,
Draw close, but speak not.

Phantoms of countless lost,
Invisible to the rest henceforth become my companions,
Follow me ever—desert me not while I live.

Sweet are the blooming cheeks of the living—sweet are the
        musical voices sounding,
But sweet, ah sweet, are the dead with their silent eyes.

Dearest comrades, all is over and long gone,
But love is not over—and what love, O comrades
Perfume from battle-fields rising, up from the foetor arising.

Perfume therefore my chant, O love, immortal love,
Give me to bathe the memories of all dead soldiers,
Shroud them, embalm them, cover them all over with tender
        pride.

Perfume all—make all wholesome,
Make these ashes to nourish and blossom,
O love, solve all, fructify all with the last chemistry.

Give me exhaustless, make me a fountain,
That I exhale love from me wherever I go like a moist peren-
        nial dew,
For the ashes of all dead soldiers South or North.

THOUGHTS

1

Of these years I sing,
How they pass and have pass'd through convuls'd pains, as
        through parturitions,
How America illustrates birth, muscular youth, the promise,
        the sure fulfilment, the absolute success,
        despite of people—illustrates evil as well as
        good,
The vehement struggle so fierce for unity in one's-self;
How many hold despairingly yet to the models departed, caste,
        myths, obedience, compulsion, and to infidel-
        ity,
How few see the arrived models, the athletes, the Western
        States, see freedom or spirituality, or hold
        any faith in results,
(But I see the athletes, and I see the results of the war glorious
        and inevitable, and they again leading to
        other results.)

How the great cities appear—how the Democratic masses,
        turbulent, wilful, as I love them,

How the whirl, the contest, the wrestle of evil with good, the
        sounding and resounding, keep on and on,
How society waits unform'd, and is for a while between things
        ended and things begun,
How America is the continent of glories, and of the triumph
        of freedom and of the Democracies, and of
        the fruits of society, and of all that is begun,
And how the States are complete in themselves—and how all
        triumphs and glories are complete in them-
        selves, to lead onward,
And how these of mine and of the States will in their turn
        be convuls'd, and serve other parturitions
        and transitions,
And how all people, sights, combinations, the democratic
        masses too, serve—and how every fact, and
        war itself, with all its horrors, serves,
And how now or at any time each serves the exquisite transi-
        tion of death.

2

Of seeds dropping into the ground, of births,
Of the steady concentration of America, inland, upward, to
        impregnable and swarming places,
Of what Indiana, Kentucky, Arkansas, and the rest, are to be,
Of what a few years will show there in Nebraska, Colorado,
        Nevada, and the rest,
(Or afar, mounting the Northern Pacific to Sitka or Aliaska,)
Of what the feuillage of America is the preparation for—and
        of what all sights, North. South, East and
        West are,
Of this Union welded in blood, of the solemn price paid, of the
        unnamed lost ever present in my mind;
Of the temporary use of materials for identity's sake,
Of the present, passing, departing—of the growth of com-
        pleter men than any yet,
Of all sloping down there where the fresh free giver the
        mother, the Mississippi flows,
Of mighty inland cities yet unsurvey'd and unsuspected,
Of the new and good names, of the modern developments, of
        inalienable homesteads,
Of a free and original life there, of simple diet and clean and
        sweet blood,
Of litheness, majestic faces, clear eyes, and perfect physique
        there,
Of immense spiritual results future years far West, each side
        of the Anahuacs,
Of these songs, well understood there, (being made for that
        area,)

Of the native scorn of grossness and gain there,
(O it lurks in me night and day—what is gain after all to
     savageness and freedom?

SONG AT SUNSET

Splendor of ended day floating and filling me,
Hour prophetic, hour resuming the past,
Inflating my throat, you divine average,
You earth and life till the last ray gleams I sing.

Open mouth of my soul uttering gladness,
Eyes of my soul seeing perfection,
Natural life of me faithfully praising things,
Corroborating forever the triumph of things.

Illustrious every one!
Illustrious what we name space, sphere of unnumber'd spirits,
Illustrious the mystery of motion in all beings, even the tini-
     est insect,
Illustrious the attribute of speech, the senses, the body,
Illustrious the passing light—illustrious the pale reflection on
     the new moon in the western sky,
Illustrious whatever I see or hear or touch, to the last.

Good in all,
In the satisfaction and aplomb of animals,
In the annual return of the seasons,
In the hilarity of youth,
In the strength and flush of manhood,
In the grandeur and exquisiteness of old age,
In the superb vistas of death.

Wonderful to depart!
Wonderful to be here!
The heart, to jet the all-alike and innocent blood!
To breathe the air, how delicious!
To speak—to walk—to seize something by the hand!
To prepare for sleep, for bed, to look on my rose-color'd flesh!
To be conscious of my body, so satisfied, so large!
To be this incredible God I am!
To have gone forth among other Gods, these men and women
     I love.

Wonderful how I celebrate you and myself!
How my thoughts play subtly at the spectacles around!
How the clouds pass silently overhead!
How the earth darts on and on! and how the sun, moon, stars,
     dart on and on!
How the water sports and sings! (surely it is alive!)

How the trees rise and stand up, with strong trunks, with
    branches and leaves!
(Surely there is something more in each of the trees, some
    living soul.)

O amazement of things—even the least particle!
O spirituality of things!
O strain musical flowing through ages and continents, now
    reaching me and America!
I take your strong chords, intersperse them, and cheerfully
    pass them forward.

I too carol the sun, usher'd or at noon, or as now, setting,
I too throb to the brain and beauty of the earth and of all the
    growths of the earth,
I too have felt the resistless call of myself.

As I steam'd down the Mississippi,
As I wander'd over the prairies,
As I have lived, as I have look'd through my windows my eyes,
As I went forth in the morning, as I beheld the light breaking
    in the east,
As I bathed on the beach of the Eastern Sea, and again on the
    beach of Western Sea,
As I roam'd the streets of inland Chicago, whatever streets I
    have roam'd,
Or cities or silent woods, or even amid the sights of war,
Wherever I have been I have charged myself with contentment
    and triumph.

I sing to the last equalities modern or old,
I sing the endless finalés of things,
I say Nature continues, glory continues,
I praise with electric voice,
For I do not see one imperfection in the universe,
And I do not see one cause or result lamentable at last in the
    universe.

O setting sun! though the time has come,
I still warble under you, if none else does, unmitigated adora-
    tion.

AS AT THY PORTALS ALSO DEATH

As at thy portals also death,
Entering thy sovereign, dim, illimitable grounds,
To memories of my mother, to the divine blending, maternity,
To her, buried and gone, yet buried not, gone not from me,
(I see again the calm benignant face fresh and beautiful still,
I sit by the form in the coffin,

I kiss and kiss convulsively again the sweet old lips, the cheeks,
    the closed eyes in the coffin;)
To her, the ideal woman, practical, spiritual, of all of earth,
    life, love, to me the best,
I grave a monumental line, before I go, amid these songs,
And set a tombstone here.

MY LEGACY

The business man the acquirer vast,
After assiduous years surveying results, preparing for de-
    parture,
Devises houses and lands to his children, bequeaths stocks,
    goods, funds for a school or hospital,
Leaves money to certain companions to buy tokens, souvenirs
    of gems and gold.

But I, my life surveying, closing,
With nothing to show to devise from its idle years,
Nor houses nor lands, nor tokens of gems or gold for my
    friends,
Yet certain remembrances of the war for you, and after you,
And little souvenirs of camps and soldiers, with my love,
I bind together and bequeath in this bundle of songs.

PENSIVE ON HER DEAD GAZING

Pensive on her dead gazing I heard the Mother of All,
Desperate on the torn bodies, on the forms covering the battle-
    fields gazing,
(As the last gun ceased, but the scent of the powder-smoke
    linger'd,)
As she call'd to her earth with mournful voice while she stalk'd,
Absorb them well O my earth, she cried, I charge you lose not
    my sons, lose not an atom,
And you streams absorb them well, taking their dear blood,
And you local spots, and you airs that swim above lightly im-
    palpable,
And all you essences of soil and growth, and you my rivers'
    depths,
And you mountain sides, and the woods where my dear chil-
    dren's blood trickling redden'd,
And you trees down in your roots to bequeath to all future
    trees,
My dead absorb or South or North—my young men's bodies
    absorb, and their precious precious blood,
Which holding in trust for me faithfully back again give me
    many a year hence,
In unseen essence and odor of surface and grass, centuries
    hence,

In blowing airs from the fields back again give me my darlings,
    give my immortal heroes,
Exhale me them centuries hence, breathe me their breath, let
    not an atom be lost,
O years and graves! O air and soil! O my dead, an aroma
    sweet!
Exhale them perennial sweet death, years, centuries hence.

CAMPS OF GREEN

Not alone those camps of white, old comrades of the wars,
When as order'd forward, after a long march,
Footsore and weary, soon as the light lessens we halt for the
    night,
Some of us so fatigued carrying the gun and knapsack, drop-
    ping asleep in our tracks,
Others pitching the little tents, and the fires lit up begin to
    sparkle,
Outposts of pickets posted surrounding alert through the dark,
And a word provided for countersign, careful for safety,
Till to the call of the drummers at daybreak loudly beating
    the drums,
We rise up refresh'd, the night and sleep pass'd over, and
    resume our journey,
Or proceed to battle.

Lo, the camps of the tents of green,
Which the days of peace keep filling, and the days of war keep
    filling,
With a mystic army, (is it too order'd forward? is it too only
    halting awhile,
Till night and sleep pass over?)
Now in those camps of green, in their tents dotting the world,
In the parents, children, husbands, wives, in them, in the old
    and young,
Sleeping under the sunlight, sleeping under the moonlight,
    content and silent there at last,
Behold the mighty bivouac-field and waiting-camp of all,
Of the corps and generals all, and the President over the corps
    and generals all,
And of each of us O soldiers, and of each and all in the ranks
    we fought,
(There without hatred we all, all meet.)

For presently O soldiers, we too camp in our place in the
    bivouac-camps of green,
But we need not provide for outposts, nor word for the coun-
    ter-sign,
Nor drummer to beat the morning drum.

THE SOBBING OF THE BELLS

[Midnight, Sept. 19–20, 1881]

The sobbing of the bells, the sudden death-news everywhere,
The slumbers rouse, the rapport of the People,
(Full well they know that message in the darkness,
Full well return, respond within their breasts, their brains, the
     sad reverberations,)
The passionate toll and clang—city to city, joining, sounding,
     passing,
Those heart-beats of a Nation in the night.

AS THEY DRAW TO A CLOSE

As they draw to a close,
Of what underlies the precedent songs—of my aims in them,
Of the seed I have sought to plant in them,
Of joy, sweet joy, through many a year, in them,
(For them, for them have I lived, in them my work is done,)
Of many an aspiration fond, of many a dream and plan;
Through Space and Time fused in a chant, and the flowing
     eternal identity,
To Nature encompassing these, encompassing God—to the
     joyous, electric all,
To the sense of Death, and accepting exulting in Death in its
     turn the same as life,
The entrance of man to sing;
To compact you, ye parted, diverse lives,
To put rapport the mountains and rocks and streams,
And the winds of the north, and the forests of oak and pine,
With you O soul.

JOY, SHIPMATE, JOY!

Joy, shipmate, joy!
(Pleas'd to my soul at death I cry,)
Our life is closed, our life begins,
The long, long anchorage we leave,
The ship is clear at last, she leaps!
She swiftly courses from the shore,
Joy, shipmate, joy!

THE UNTOLD WANT

The untold want by life and land ne'er granted,
Now voyager sail thou forth to seek and find.

PORTALS

What are those of the known but to ascend and enter the Un-
     known?
And what are those of life but for Death?

THESE CAROLS

These carols sung to cheer my passage through the world I see,
For completion I dedicate to the Invisible World.

NOW FINALÈ TO THE SHORE

Now finalè to the shore,
Now land and life finalè and farewell,
Now Voyager depart, (much, much for thee is yet in store,)
Often enough hast thou adventur'd o'er the seas,
Cautiously cruising, studying the charts,
Duly again to port and hawser's tie returning;
But now obey thy cherish'd secret wish,
Embrace thy friends, leave all in order,
To port and hawser's tie no more returning,
Depart upon thy endless cruise old Sailor.

SO LONG!

To conclude, I announce what comes after me.

I remember I said before my leaves sprang at all,
I would raise my voice jocund and strong with reference to
        consummations.

When America does what was promis'd,
When through these States walk a hundred millions of superb
        persons,
When the rest part away for superb persons and contribute to
        them,
When breeds of the most perfect mothers denote America,
Then to me and mine our due fruition.

I have press'd through in my own right,
I have sung the body and the soul, war and peace have I sung,
        and the songs of life and death,
And the songs of birth, and shown that there are many births.

I have offer'd my style to every one, I have journey'd with con-
        fident step;
While my pleasure is yet at the full I whisper *So long!*
And take the young woman's hand and the young man's hand
        for the last time.

I announce natural persons to arise,
I announce justice triumphant,
I announce uncompromising liberty and equality,
I announce the justification of candor and the justification of
        pride.

I announce that the identity of these States is a single identity
only,
I announce the Union more and more compact, indissoluble,
I announce splendors and majesties to make all the previous
politics of the earth insignificant.
I announce adhesiveness, I say it shall be limitless, unloosen'd,
I say you shall yet find the friend you were looking for.

I announce a man or woman coming, perhaps you are the one,
(*So long!*)
I announce the great individual, fluid as Nature, chaste, affec-
tionate, compassionate, fully arm'd.

I announce a life that shall be copious, vehement, spiritual,
bold,
I announce an end that shall lightly and joyfully meet its trans-
lation.

I announce myriads of youths, beautiful, gigantic, sweet-
blooded,
I announce a race of splendid and savage old men.

O thicker and faster—(*So long!*)
O crowding too close upon me,
I foresee too much, it means more than I thought,
It appears to me I am dying.

Hasten throat and sound your last,
Salute me—salute the days once more. Peal the old cry once
more.

Screaming electric, the atmosphere using,
At random glancing, each as I notice absorbing,
Swiftly on, but a little while alighting,
Curious envelop'd messages delivering,
Sparkles hot, seed ethereal down in the dirt dropping,
Myself unknowing, my commission obeying, to question it
never daring,
To ages and ages yet the growth of the seed leaving,
To troops out of the war arising, they the task I have set
promulging,
To women certain whispers of myself bequeathing, their affec-
tion me more clearly explaining,
To young men my problems offering—no dallier I—I the
muscle of their brains crying,
So I pass, a little time vocal, visible, contrary,
Afterward a melodious echo, passionately bent for, (death
making me really undying,)
The best of me then when no longer visible, for toward that
I have been incessantly preparing.

What is there more, that I lag and pause and crouch extended
           with unshut mouth?
Is there a single final farewell?

My songs cease, I abandon them,
From behind the screen where I hid I advance personally
           solely to you.

Camerado, this is no book,
Who touches this touches a man,
(Is it night? are we here together alone?)
It is I you hold and who holds you,
I spring from the pages into your arms—decease calls me
           forth.

O how your fingers drowse me,
Your breath falls around me like dew, your pulse lulls the tym-
           pans of my ears,
I feel immerged from head to foot;
Delicious, enough.

Enough O deed impromptu and secret,
Enough O gliding present—enough O summ'd-up past.

Dear friend whoever you are take this kiss,
I give it especially to you, do not forget me,
I feel like one who has done work for the day to retire awhile,
I receive now again of my many translations, from my avataras
           ascending, while others doubtless await me,
An unknown sphere more real than I dream'd, more direct,
           darts awakening rays about me, *So long!*
Remember my words, I may again return,
I love you, I depart from materials,
I am as one disembodied, triumphant, dead.

FIRST ANNEX

SANDS AT SEVENTY

MANNAHATTA

My city's fit and noble name resumed,
Choice aboriginal name, with marvellous beauty, meaning,
*A rocky founded island—shores where ever gayly dash the
           coming, going, hurrying sea waves.*

PAUMANOK

Sea-beauty! stretch'd and basking!
One side thy inland ocean laving, broad, with copious com-
            merce, steamers, sails,
And one the Atlantic's wind caressing, fierce or gentle—
            mighty hulls dark-gliding in the distance.
Isle of sweet brooks of drinking-water—healthy air and soil!
Isle of the salty shore and breeze and brine!

FROM MONTAUK POINT

I stand as on some mighty eagle's beak,
Eastward the sea absorbing, viewing, (nothing but sea and
            sky,)
The tossing waves, the foam, the ships in the distance,
The wild unrest, the snowy, curling caps—that inbound urge
            and urge of waves,
Seeking the shores forever.

TO THOSE WHO'VE FAIL'D

To those who've fail'd, in aspirations vast,
To unnam'd soldiers fallen in front on the lead,
To calm, devoted engineers—to over-ardent travelers—to pi-
            lots on their ships,
To many a lofty song and picture without recognition—I'd
            rear a laurel-cover'd monument,
High, high, above the rest—To all cut off before their time,
Possess'd by some strange spirit of fire,
Quench'd by an early death.

A CAROL CLOSING SIXTY-NINE

A carol closing sixty-nine—*a résumé*—a repetition,
My lines in joy and hope continuing on the same,
Of ye, O God, Life, Nature, Freedom, Poetry;
Of you, my Land—your rivers, prairies, States—you, mottled
            Flag I love,
Your aggregate retain'd entire—Of north, south, east and west,
            your items all;
Of me myself—the jocund heart yet beating in my breast,
The body wreck'd, old, poor and paralyzed—the strange iner-
            tia falling pall-like round me,
The burning fires down in my sluggish blood not yet extinct,
The undiminish'd faith—the groups of loving friends.

THE BRAVEST SOLDIERS

Brave, brave were the soldiers (high named to-day) who lived
            through the fight;
But the bravest press'd to the front and fell, unnamed, un-
            known.

A FONT OF TYPE

This latent mine—these unlaunch'd voices—passionate pow-
        ers,
Wrath, argument, or praise, or comic leer, or prayer devout,
(Not nonpareil, brevier, bourgeois, long primer merely,)
These ocean waves arousable to fury and to death,
Or sooth'd to ease and sheeny sun and sleep,
Within the pallid slivers slumbering.

AS I SIT WRITING HERE

As I sit writing here, sick and grown old,
Not my least burden is that dullness of the years, querilities,
Ungracious glooms, aches, lethargy, constipation, whimpering
        ennui,
May filter in my daily songs.

MY CANARY BIRD

Did we count great, O soul, to penetrate the themes of mighty
        books,
Absorbing deep and full from thoughts, plays, speculations?
But now from thee to me, caged bird, to feel thy joyous warble,
Filling the air, the lonesome room, the long forenoon,
Is it not just as great, O soul?

QUERIES TO MY SEVENTIETH YEAR

Approaching, nearing, curious,
Thou dim, uncertain spectre—bringest thou life or death?
Strength, weakness, blindness, more paralysis and heavier?
Or placid skies and sun? Wilt stir the waters yet?
Or haply cut me short for good? Or leave me here as now,
Dull, parrot-like and old, with crack'd voice harping, screech-
        ing?

THE WALLABOUT MARTYRS

[In Brooklyn, in an old vault, mark'd by no special recognition, lie
huddled at this moment the undoubtedly authentic remains of the
stanchest and earliest Revolutionary patriots from the British prison
ships and prisons of the times of 1776–83, in and around New York,
and from all over Long Island; originally buried—many thousands of
them—in trenches in the Wallabout sands.]

Greater than memory of Achilles or Ulysses,
More, more by far to thee than tomb of Alexander,
Those cart loads of old charnel ashes, scales and splints of
        mouldy bones,
Once living men—once resolute courage, aspiration, strength,
The stepping stones to thee to-day and here, America.

THE FIRST DANDELION

Simple and fresh and fair from winter's close emerging,
As if no artifice of fashion, business, politics, had ever been,
Forth from its sunny nook of shelter'd grass—innocent,
golden, calm as the dawn,
The spring's first dandelion shows its trustful face.

AMERICA

Centre of equal daughters, equal sons,
All, all alike endear'd, grown, ungrown, young or old,
Strong, ample, fair, enduring, capable, rich,
Perennial with the Earth, with Freedom, Law and Love,
A grand, sane, towering, seated Mother,
Chair'd in the adamant of Time.

MEMORIES

How sweet the silent backward tracings!
The wanderings as in dreams—the meditation of old times
resumed—their loves, joys, persons, voyages.

TO-DAY AND THEE

The appointed winners in a long-stretch'd game;
The course of Time and nations—Egypt, India, Greece and
Rome;
The past entire, with all its heroes, histories, arts, experiments,
Its store of songs, inventions, voyages, teachers, books,
Garner'd for now and thee—To think of it!
The heirdom all converged in thee!

AFTER THE DAZZLE OF DAY

After the dazzle of day is gone,
Only the dark, dark night shows to my eyes the stars;
After the clangor of organ majestic, or chorus, or perfect band,
Silent, athwart my soul, moves the symphony true.

ABRAHAM LINCOLN, BORN FEB. 12, 1809

Publish'd Feb. 12, 1888

To-day, from each and all, a breath of prayer—a pulse of
thought,
To memory of Him—to birth of Him.

OUT OF MAY'S SHOWS SELECTED

Apple orchards, the trees all cover'd with blossoms;
Wheat fields carpeted far and near in vital emerald green;
The eternal, exhaustless freshness of each early morning;

The yellow, golden, transparent haze of the warm afternoon
    sun;
The aspiring lilac bushes with profuse purple or white flowers.

HALCYON DAYS

Not from successful love alone,
Nor wealth, nor honor'd middle age, nor victories of politics
    or war;
But as life wanes, and all the turbulent passions calm,
As gorgeous, vapory, silent hues cover the evening sky,
As softness, fullness, rest, suffuse the frame, like fresher,
    balmier air,
As the days take on a mellower light, and the apple at last
        hangs really finish'd and indolent-ripe on the
        tree,
Then for the teeming quietest, happiest days of all!
The brooding and blissful halcyon days!

FANCIES AT NAVESINK

THE PILOT IN THE MIST

Steaming the northern rapids—(an old St. Lawrence rem-
    ·iniscence,
A sudden memory-flash comes back, I know not why,
Here waiting for the sunrise, gazing from this hill;) *
Again 'tis just at morning—a heavy haze contends with day-
    break,
Again the trembling, laboring vessel veers me—I press through
        foam-dash'd rocks that almost touch me,
Again I mark where aft the small thin Indian helmsman
Looms in the mist, with brow elate and governing hand.

HAD I THE CHOICE

Had I the choice to tally greatest bards,
To limn their portraits, stately, beautiful, and emulate at will,
Homer with all his wars and warriors—Hector, Achilles, Ajax,
Or Shakspere's woe-entangled Hamlet, Lear, Othello—Ten-
    nyson's fair ladies,
Metre or wit the best, or choice conceit to wield in perfect
        rhyme, delight of singers;

* Navesink—a sea-side mountain, lower entrance of New York Bay.

These, these, O sea, all these I'd gladly barter,
Would you the undulation of one wave, its trick to me transfer,
Or breathe one breath of yours upon my verse,
And leave its odor there.

YOU TIDES WITH CEASELESS SWELL

You tides with ceaseless swell! you power that does this work!
You unseen force centripetal, centrifugal, through space's
  spread,
Rapport of sun, moon, earth, and all the constellations,
What are the messages by you from distant stars to us? what
  Sirius'? what Capella's?
What central heart—and you the pulse—vivifies all? what
  boundless aggregate of all?
What subtle indirection and significance in you? what clue to
  all in you? what fluid, vast identity,
Holding the universe with all its parts as one—as sailing in a
  ship?

LAST OF EBB, AND DAYLIGHT WANING

Last of ebb, and daylight waning,
Scented sea-cool landward making, smells of sedge and salt
  incoming,
With many a half-caught voice sent up from the eddies,
Many a muffled confession—many a sob and whisper'd word,
As of speakers far or hid.

How they sweep down and out! how they mutter!
Poets unnamed—artists greatest of any, with cherish'd lost
  designs,
Love's unresponse—a chorus of age's complaints—hope's last
  words,
Some suicide's despairing cry, *Away to the boundless waste,
  and never again return.*

On to oblivion then!
On, on, and do your part, ye burying, ebbing tide!
On for your time, ye furious debouché!

AND YET NOT YOU ALONE

And yet not you alone, twilight and burying ebb,
Nor you, ye lost designs alone—nor failures, aspirations;
I know, divine deceitful ones, your glamour's seeming;
Duly by you, from you, the tide and light again—duly the
  hinges turning,
Duly the needed discord-parts offsetting, blending,
Weaving from you, from Sleep, Night, Death itself,
The rhythmus of Birth eternal.

PROUDLY THE FLOOD COMES IN

Proudly the flood comes in, shouting, foaming, advancing,
Long it holds at the high, with bosom broad outswelling,
All throbs, dilates—the farms, woods, streets of cities—work-
men at work,
Mainsails, topsails, jibs, appear in the offing—steamers' pen-
nants of smoke—and under the forenoon
sun,
Freighted with human lives, gaily the outward bound, gaily the
inward bound,
Flaunting from many a spar the flag I love.

BY THAT LONG SCAN OF WAVES

By that long scan of waves, myself call'd back, resumed upon
myself,
In every crest some undulating light or shade—some retro-
spect,
Joys, travels, studies, silent panoramas—scenes, ephemeral,
The long past war, the battles, hospital sights, the wounded and
the dead,
Myself through every by-gone phase—my idle youth—old age
at hand,
My three-score years of life summ'd up, and more, and past,
By any grand ideal tried, intentionless, the whole a nothing,
And haply yet some drop within God's scheme's ensemble—
some wave, or part of wave,
Like one of yours, ye multitudinous ocean.

THEN LAST OF ALL

Then last of all, caught from these shores, this hill,
Of you O tides, the mystic human meaning:
Only by law of you, your swell and ebb, enclosing me the same,
The brain that shapes, the voice that chants this song.

ELECTION DAY, NOVEMBER, 1884

If I should need to name, O Western World, your powerfulest
scene and show,
'Twould not be you, Niagara—nor you, ye limitless prairies—
nor your huge rifts of canyons, Colorado,
Nor you, Yosemite—nor Yellowstone, with all its spasmic
geyser loops ascending to the skies, appearing
and disappearing,
Nor Oregon's white cones—nor Huron's belt of mighty lakes—
nor Mississippi's stream:

—This seething hemisphere's humanity, as now, I'd name—
        the still small voice vibrating—America's
        choosing day,
The heart of it not in the chosen—the act itself the main, the
        quadrennial choosing,)
The stretch of North and South arous'd—sea-board and inland
        —Texas to Maine—the Prairie States—Ver-
        mont, Virginia, California,
The final ballot-shower from East to West—the paradox and
        conflict,
The countless snow-flakes falling—(a swordless conflict,
Yet more than all Rome's wars of old, or modern Napoleon's:)
        the peaceful choice of all,
Or good or ill humanity—welcoming the darker odds, the
        dross:
—Foams and ferments the wine? it serves to purify—while the
        heart pants, life glows:
These stormy gusts and winds waft precious ships,
Swell'd Washington's, Jefferson's, Lincoln's sails.

WITH HUSKY-HAUGHTY LIPS, O SEA!

With husky-haughty lips, O sea!
Where day and night I wend thy surf-beat shore,
Imaging to my sense thy varied strange suggestions,
(I see and plainly list thy talk and conference here,)
Thy troops of white-maned racers racing to the goal,
Thy ample, smiling face, dash'd with the sparkling dimples of
        the sun,
Thy brooding scowl and murk—thy unloos'd hurricanes,
Thy unsubduedness, caprices, wilfulness;
Great as thou art above the rest, thy many tears—a lack from
        all eternity in thy content,
(Naught but the greatest struggles, wrongs, defeats, could
        make thee greatest—no less could make
        thee,)
Thy lonely state—something thou ever seek'st and seek'st, yet
        never gain'st,
Surely some right withheld—some voice, in huge monotonous
        rage, of freedom-lover pent,
Some vast heart, like a planet's, chain'd and chafing in those
        breakers,
By lengthen'd swell, and spasm, and panting breath,
And rhythmic rasping of thy sands and waves,
And serpent hiss, and savage peals of laughter,
And undertones of distant lion roar,
(Sounding, appealing to the sky's deaf ear—but now, rapport
        for once,
A phantom in the night thy confidant for once,)
The first and last confession of the globe,

Outsurging, muttering from thy soul's abysms,
The tale of cosmic elemental passion,
Thou tellest to a kindred soul.

DEATH OF GENERAL GRANT

As one by one withdraw the lofty actors,
From that great play on history's stage eterne,
That lurid, partial act of war and peace—of old and new
   contending,
Fought out through wrath, fears, dark dismays, and many a
   long suspense;
All past—and since, in countless graves receding, mellowing,
Victor's and vanquish'd—Lincoln's and Lee's—now thou with
   them,
Man of the mighty days—and equal to the days!
Thou from the prairies!—tangled and many-vein'd and hard
   has been thy part,
To admiration has it been enacted!

RED JACKET (FROM ALOFT)

[Impromptu on Buffalo City's monument to, and re-burial of the old
Iroquois orator, October 9, 1884]

Upon this scene, this show,
Yielded to-day by fashion, learning, wealth,
(Nor in caprice alone—some grains of deepest meaning,)
Haply, aloft, (who knows?) from distant sky-clouds' blended
   shapes,
As some old tree, or rock or cliff, thrill'd with its soul,
Product of Nature's sun, stars, earth direct—a towering human
   form,
In hunting-shirt of film, arm'd with the rifle, a half-ironical
   smile curving its phantom lips,
Like one of Ossian's ghosts looks down.

WASHINGTON'S MONUMENT, FEBRUARY, 1885

Ah, not this marble, dead and cold:
Far from its base and shaft expanding—the round zones cir-
   cling, comprehending,
Thou, Washington, art all the world's, the continents' entire—
   not yours alone, America,
Europe's as well, in every part, castle of lord or laborer's cot,
Or frozen North, or sultry South—the African's—the Arab's
   in his tent,
Old Asia's there with venerable smile, seated amid her ruins;
(Greets the antique the hero new? 'tis but the same—the heir
   legitimate, continued ever,
The indomitable heart and arm—proofs of the never-broken
   line,

Courage, alertness, patience, faith, the same—e'en in defeat
 defeated not, the same:)
Wherever sails a ship, or house is built on land, or day or
 night,
Through teeming cities' streets, indoors or out, factories or
 farms,
Now, or to come, or past—where patriot wills existed or exist,
Wherever Freedom, pois'd by Toleration, sway'd by Law,
Stands or is rising thy true monument.

OF THAT BLITHE THROAT OF THINE

[More than eighty-three degrees north—about a good day's steaming
distance to the Pole by one of our fast oceaners in clear water—Greely
the explorer heard the song of a single snow-bird merrily sounding
over the desolation.]

Of that blithe throat of thine from arctic bleak and blank,
I'll mind the lesson, solitary bird—let me too welcome chilling
 drifts,
E'en the profoundest chill, as now—a torpid pulse, a brain
 unnerv'd,
Old age land-lock'd within its winter bay—(cold, cold, O
 cold!)
These snowy hairs, my feeble arm, my frozen feet,
For them thy faith, thy rule I take, and grave it to the last;
Not summer's zones alone—not chants of youth, or south's
 warm tides alone,
But held by sluggish floes, pack'd in the northern ice, the
 cumulus of years,
These with gay heart I also sing.

BROADWAY

What hurrying human tides, or day or night!
What passions, winnings, losses, ardors, swim thy waters!
What whirls of evil, bliss and sorrow, stem thee!
What curious questioning glances—glints of love!
Leer, envy, scorn, contempt, hope, aspiration!
Thou portal—thou arena—thou of the myriad long-drawn
 lines and groups!
(Could but thy flagstones, curbs, façades, tell their inimitable
 tales;
Thy windows rich, and huge hotels—thy side-walks wide;)
Thou of the endless sliding, mincing, shuffling feet!
Thou, like the parti-colored world itself—like infinite, teem-
 ing, mocking life!
Thou visor'd, vast, unspeakable show and lesson!

TO GET THE FINAL LILT OF SONGS

To get the final lilt of songs,
To penetrate the inmost lore of poets—to know the mighty
    ones,
Job, Homer, Eschylus, Dante, Shakspere, Tennyson, Emerson;
To diagnose the shifting-delicate tints of love and pride and
    doubt—to truly understand,
To encompass these, the last keen faculty and entrance-price,
Old age, and what it brings from all its past experiences.

OLD SALT KOSSABONE

Far back, related on my mother's side,
Old Salt Kossabone, I'll tell you how he died:
(Had been a sailor all his life—was nearly 90—lived with his
    married grandchild, Jenny;
House on a hill, with view of bay at hand, and distant cape,
    and stretch to open sea;)
The last of afternoon, the evening hours, for many a year his
    regular custom,
In his great arm chair by the window seated,
(Sometimes, indeed, through half the day,)
Watching the coming, going of the vessels, he mutters to him-
    self—And now the close of all:
One struggling outbound brig, one day, baffled for long—cross-
    tides and much wrong going,
At last at nightfall strikes the breeze aright, her whole luck
    veering,
And swiftly bending round the cape, the darkness proudly en-
    tering, cleaving, as he watches,
"She's free—she's on her destination"—these the last words—
    when Jenny came, he sat there dead,
Dutch Kossabone, Old Salt, related on my mother's side, far
    back.

THE DEAD TENOR

As down the stage again,
With Spanish hat and plumes, and gait inimitable,
Back from the fading lessons of the past, I'd call, I'd tell and
    own,
How much from thee! the revelation of the singing voice from
    thee!
(So firm—so liquid-soft—again that tremulous, manly timbre!
The perfect singing voice—deepest of all to me the lesson—
    trial and test of all:)
How through those strains distill'd—how the rapt ears, the soul
    of me, absorbing

Fernando's heart, *Manrico's* passionate call, *Ernani's,* sweet
      Gennaro's,
I fold thenceforth, or seek to fold, within my chants transmut-
      ing,
Freedom's and Love's and Faith's unloos'd cantabile,
(As perfume's, color's, sunlight's correlation:)
From these, for these, with these, a hurried line, dead tenor,
A wafted autumn leaf, dropt in the closing grave, the shovel'd
      earth,
To memory of thee.

CONTINUITIES

[From a talk I had lately with a German spiritualist]

Nothing is ever really lost, or can be lost,
No birth, identity, form—no object of the world,
Nor life, nor force, nor any visible thing;
Appearance must not foil, nor shifted sphere confuse thy brain.
Ample are time and space—ample the fields of Nature.
The body, sluggish, aged, cold—the embers left from earlier
      fires,
The light in the eye grown dim, shall duly flame again;
The sun now low in the west rises for mornings and for noons
      continual;
To frozen clods ever the spring's invisible law returns,
With grass and flowers and summer fruits and corn.

YONNONDIO

[The sense of the word is *lament for the aborigines.* It is an Iroquois
term; and has been used for a personal name.]

A song, a poem of itself—the word itself a dirge,
Amid the wilds, the rocks, the storm and wintry night,
To me such misty, strange tableaux the syllables calling up;
Yonnondio—I see, far in the west or north, a limitless ravine,
      with plains and mountains dark,
I see swarms of stalwart chieftains, medicine-men, and war-
      riors,
As flitting by like clouds of ghosts, they pass and are gone in
      the twilight,
(Race of the woods, the landscapes free, and the falls!
No picture, poem, statement, passing them to the future:)
Yonnondio! Yonnondio!—unlimn'd they disappear;
To-day gives place, and fades—the cities, farms, factories
      fade;
A muffled sonorous sound, a wailing word is borne through the
      air for a moment,
Then blank and gone and still, and utterly lost.

LIFE

Ever the undiscouraged, resolute, struggling soul of man;
(Have former armies fail'd? then we send fresh armies—and
    fresh again;)
Ever the grappled mystery of all earth's ages old or new;
Ever the eager eyes, hurrahs, the welcome-clapping hands, the
    loud applause;
Ever the soul dissatisfied, curious, unconvinced at last;
Struggling to-day, the same—battling the same.

"GOING SOMEWHERE"

My science-friend, my noblest woman-friend,
(Now buried in an English grave—and this a memory-leaf for
    her dear sake,)
Ended our talk—"The sum, concluding all we know of old or
    modern learning, intuitions deep,
"Of all Geologies—Histories—of all Astronomy—of Evolu-
    tion, Metaphysics all,
"Is, that we all are onward, onward, speeding slowly, surely
    bettering,
"Life, life an endless march, an endless army, (no halt, but it is
    duly over,)
"The world, the race, the soul—in space and time the uni-
    verses,
"All bound as is befitting each—all surely going somewhere."

SMALL THE THEME OF MY CHANT
From the 1867 edition "L. of G."

Small the theme of my Chant, yet the greatest—namely, One's
    Self—a simple, separate person. That, for the
    use of the New World, I sing.
Man's physiology complete, from top to toe, I sing. Not physi-
    ognomy alone, nor brain alone, is worthy for
    the Muse;—I say the Form complete is
    worthier far. The Female equally with the
    Male, I sing.
Nor cease at the theme of One's-Self. I speak the word of the
    modern, the word En-Masse.
My Day I sing, and the Lands—with interstice I knew of hap-
    less War.
(O friend, whoe'er you are, at last arriving hither to com-
    mence, I feel through every leaf the pressure
    of your hand, which I return.
And thus upon our journey, footing the road, and more than
    once, and link'd together let us go.)

TRUE CONQUERORS

Old farmers, travelers, workmen (no matter how crippled or
        bent,)
Old sailors, out of many a perilous voyage, storm and wreck,
Old soldiers from campaigns, with all their wounds, defeats
        and scars;
Enough that they've survived at all—long life's unflinching
        ones!
Forth from their struggles, trials, fights, to have emerged at all
        —in that alone,
True conquerors, o'er all the rest.

THE UNITED STATES TO OLD WORLD CRITICS

Here first the duties of to-day, the lessons of the concrete,
Wealth, order, travel, shelter, products, plenty;
As of the building of some varied, vast, perpetual edifice,
Whence to arise inevitable in time, the towering roofs, the
        lamps,
The solid-planted spires tall shooting to the stars.

THE CALMING THOUGHT OF ALL

That coursing on, whate'er men's speculations,
Amid the changing schools, theologies, philosophies,
Amid the bawling presentations new and old,
The round earth's silent vital laws, facts, modes continue.

THANKS IN OLD AGE

Thanks in old age—thanks ere I go,
For health, the midday sun, the impalpable air—for life, mere
        life,
For precious ever-lingering memories, (of you my mother dear
        —you father—you, brothers, sisters, friends,)
For all my days—not those of peace alone—the days of war
        the same,
For gentle words, caresses, gifts from foreign lands,
For shelter, wine and meat—for sweet appreciation,
(You distant, dim unknown—or young or old—countless, un-
        specified, readers belov'd,
We never met, and ne'er shall meet—and yet our souls em-
        brace, long, close and long;)
For beings, groups, love, deeds, words, books—for colors,
        forms,
For all the brave strong men—devoted, hardy men—who've
        forward sprung in freedom's help, all fears,
        all lands,
For braver, stronger, more devoted men—(a special laurel
        ere I go, to life's war's chosen ones,

The cannoneers of song and thought—the great artillerists—
        the foremost leaders, captains of the soul:)
As soldier from an ended war return'd—As traveler out of
        myriads, to the long procession retrospective,
Thanks—joyful thanks!—a soldier's, traveler's thanks.

LIFE AND DEATH

The two old, simple problems ever intertwined,
Close home, elusive, present, baffled, grappled.
By each successive age insoluble, pass'd on,
To ours to-day—and we pass on the same.

THE VOICE OF THE RAIN

And who art thou? said I to the soft-falling shower,
Which, strange to tell, gave me an answer, as here translated:
I am the Poem of Earth, said the voice of the rain,
Eternal I rise impalpable out of the land and the bottomless
        sea,
Upward to heaven, whence, vaguely form'd, altogether
        changed, and yet the same,
I descend to lave the drouths, atomies, dust-layers of the globe,
And all that in them without me were seeds only, latent, un-
       born;
And forever, by day and night, I give back life to my own
       origin and make pure and beautify it;
(For song, issuing from its birth-place, after fulfilment, wan-
       dering,
Reck'd or unreck'd, duly with love returns.)

SOON SHALL THE WINTER'S FOIL BE HERE

Soon shall the winter's foil be here;
Soon shall these icy ligatures unbind and melt—A little while,
And air, soil, wave, suffused shall be in softness, bloom and
       growth—a thousand forms shall rise
From these dead clods and chills as from low burial graves.
Thine eyes, ears—all thy best attributes—all that takes cogni-
       zance of natural beauty,
Shall wake and fill. Thou shalt perceive the simple shows, the
       delicate miracles of earth,
Dandelions, clover, the emerald grass, the early scents and
       flowers,
The arbutus under foot, the willow's yellow-green, the blos-
       soming plum and cherry;
With these the robin, lark and thrush, singing their songs—
       the flitting bluebird;
For such the scenes the annual play brings on.

WHILE NOT THE PAST FORGETTING

Publish'd May 30, 1888

While not the past forgetting,
To-day, at least, contention sunk entire—peace, brotherhood
        uprisen;
For sign reciprocal our Northern, Southern hands,
Lay on the graves of all dead soldiers, North or South,
(Nor for the past alone—for meanings to the future,)
Wreaths of roses and branches of palm.

THE DYING VETERAN

[A Long Island incident—early part of the nineteenth century]

Amid these days of order, ease, prosperity,
Amid the current songs of beauty, peace, decorum,
I cast a reminiscence—(likely 'twill offend you,
I heard it in my boyhood;)—More than a generation since,
A queer old savage man, a fighter under Washington himself,
(Large, brave, cleanly, hot-blooded, no talker, rather spiritual-
        istic,
Had fought in the ranks—fought well—had been all through
        the Revolutionary war,)
Lay dying—sons, daughters, church-deacons, lovingly tend-
        ing him,
Sharping their sense, their ears, towards his murmuring, half-
        caught words:
"Let me return again to my war-days,
To the sights and scenes—to forming the line of battle,
To the scouts ahead reconnoitering,
To the cannons, the grim artillery,
To the galloping aids, carrying orders,
To the wounded, the fallen, the heat, the suspense,
The perfume strong, the smoke, the deafening noise;
Away with your life of peace!—your joys of peace!
Give me my old wild battle-life again!"

STRONGER LESSONS

Have you learn'd lessons only of those who admired you, and
        were tender with you, and stood aside for
        you?
Have you not learn'd great lessons from those who reject you,
        and brace themselves against you? or who
        treat you with contempt, or dispute the pas-
        sage with you?

A PRAIRIE SUNSET

Shot gold, maroon and violet, dazzling silver, emerald, fawn,
The earth's whole amplitude and Nature's multiform power
consign'd for once to colors;
The light, the general air possess'd by them—colors till now
unknown,
No limit, confine—not the Western sky alone—the high me-
ridian—North, South, all,
Pure luminous color fighting the silent shadows to the last.

TWENTY YEARS

Down on the ancient wharf, the sand, I sit, with a new-comer
chatting:
He shipp'd as green-hand boy, and sail'd away, (took some
sudden, vehement notion;)
Since, twenty years and more have circled round and round,
While he the globe was circling round and round,—and now
returns:
How changed the place—all the old land-marks gone—the
parents dead;
(Yes, he comes back *to lay in port for good—to settle*—has a
well-fill'd purse—no spot will do but this;)
The little boat that scull'd him from the sloop, now held in
leash I see,
I hear the slapping waves, the restless keel, the rocking in the
sand,
I see the sailor kit, the canvas bag, the great box bound with
brass,
I scan the face all berry-brown and bearded—the stout-strong
frame,
Dress'd in its russet suit of good Scotch cloth:
(Then what the told-out story of those twenty years? What of
the future?)

ORANGE BUDS BY MAIL FROM FLORIDA

[Voltaire closed a famous argument by claiming that a ship of war and
the grand opera were proofs enough of civilization's and France's
progress, in his day.]

A lesser proof than old Voltaire's, yet greater,
Proof of this present time, and thee, thy broad expanse, Amer-
ica,
To my plain Northern hut, in outside clouds and snow,
Brought safely for a thousand miles o'er land and tide,
Some three days since on their own soil live-sprouting,
Now here their sweetness through my room unfolding,
A bunch of orange buds by mail from Florida.

TWILIGHT

The soft voluptuous opiate shades,
The sun just gone, the eager light dispell'd—(I too will soon
                    be gone, dispell'd,)
A haze—nirwana—rest and night—oblivion.

YOU LINGERING SPARSE LEAVES OF ME

You lingering sparse leaves of me on winter-nearing boughs,
And I some well-shorn tree of field or orchard-row;
You tokens diminute and lorn—(not now the flush of May,
                    or July clover-bloom—no grain of August
                    now;)
You pallid banner-staves—you pennants valueless—you over-
                    stay'd of time,
Yet my soul-dearest leaves confirming, all the rest,
The faithfulest—hardiest—last.

NOT MEAGRE, LATENT BOUGHS ALONE

Not meagre, latent boughs alone, O songs! (scaly and bare, like
                    eagles' talons,)
But haply for some sunny day (who knows?) some future
                    spring, some summer—bursting forth,
To verdant leaves, or sheltering shade—to nourishing fruit,
Apples and grapes—the stalwart limbs of trees emerging—the
                    fresh, free, open air,
And love and faith, like scented roses blooming.

THE DEAD EMPEROR

Publish'd March 10, 1888

To-day, with bending head and eyes, thou, too, Columbia,
Less for the mighty crown laid low in sorrow—less for the
                    Emperor,
Thy true condolence breathest, sendest out o'er many a salt
                    sea mile,
Mourning a good old man—a faithful shepherd, patriot.

AS THE GREEK'S SIGNAL FLAME

[For Whittier's eightieth birthday, December 17, 1887]

As the Greek's signal flame, by antique records told,
Rose from the hill-top, like applause and glory,
Welcoming in fame some special veteran, hero,
With rosy tinge reddening the land he'd served,
So I aloft from Mannahatta's ship-fringed shore,
Lift high a kindled brand for thee, Old Poet.

THE DISMANTLED SHIP

In some unused lagoon, some nameless bay,
On sluggish, lonesome waters, anchor'd near the shore,
An old, dismasted, gray and batter'd ship, disabled, done,
After free voyages to all the seas of earth, haul'd up at last
    and hawser'd tight,
Lies rusting, mouldering.

NOW PRECEDENT SONGS, FAREWELL

Now precedent songs, farewell—by every name farewell,
(Trains of a staggering line in many a strong procession, wag-
    gons,
From ups and downs—with intervals—from elder years, mid-
    age, or youth,)
"In Cabin'd Ships," or "Thee Old Cause" or "Poets to Come"
Or "Paumanok," "Song of Myself," "Calamus," or "Adam,"
Or "Beat! Beat! Drums!" or "To the Leaven'd Soil they Trod,"
Or "Captain! My Captain!" "Kosmos," "Quicksand Years," or
    "Thoughts,"
"Thou Mother with thy Equal Brood," and many, many more
    unspecified,
From fibre heart of mine—from throat and tongue—(My life's
    hot pulsing blood,
The personal urge and form for me—not merely paper, auto-
    matic type and ink,)
Each song of mine—each utterance in the past—having its
    long, long history,
Of life or death, or soldier's wound, of country's loss or safety,
(O heaven! what flash and started endless train of all! com-
    pared indeed to that!
What wretched shred e'en at the best of all!)

AN EVENING LULL

After a week of physical anguish,
Unrest and pain, and feverish heat,
Toward the ending day a calm and lull comes on,
Three hours of peace and soothing rest of brain.*

  * The two songs on this page are eked out during an afternoon, June,
1888, in my seventieth year, at a critical spell of illness. Of course no reader
and probably no human being at any time will ever have such phases of
emotional and solemn action as these involve to me. I feel in them an end
and close of all. [*Whitman's note, referring to "Now Precedent Songs, Fare-
well" and "An Evening Lull."*]

OLD AGE'S LAMBENT PEAKS

The touch of flame—the illuminating fire—the loftiest look
    at last,
O'er city, passion, sea—o'er prairie, mountain, wood—the
    earth itself;
The airy, different, changing hues of all, in falling twilight,
Objects and groups, bearings, faces, reminiscences;
The calmer sight—the golden setting, clear and broad:
So much i' the atmosphere, the points of view, the situations
    whence we scan,
Bro't out by them alone—so much (perhaps the best) un-
    reck'd before;
The lights indeed from them—old age's lambent peaks.

AFTER THE SUPPER AND TALK

After the supper and talk—after the day is done,
As a friend from friends his final withdrawal prolonging,
Good-bye and Good-bye with emotional lips repeating,
(So hard for his hand to release those hands—no more will
    they meet,
No more for communion of sorrow and joy, of old and young,
A far-stretching journey awaits him, to return no more,)
Shunning, postponing severance—seeking to ward off the last
    word ever so little,
E'en at the exit-door turning—charges superfluous calling back
    —e'en as he descends the steps,
Something to eke out a minute additional—shadows of night-
    fall deepening,
Farewells, messages lessening—dimmer the forthgoer's visage
    and form,
Soon to be lost for aye in the darkness—loth, O so loth to
    depart!
Garrulous to the very last.

SECOND ANNEX

GOOD-BYE MY FANCY

SAIL OUT FOR GOOD, EIDÓLON YACHT!

Heave the anchor short!
Raise main-sail and jib—steer forth,
O little white-hull'd sloop, now speed on really deep waters,

(I will not call it our concluding voyage,
But outset and sure entrance to the truest, best, maturest;)
Depart, depart from solid earth—no more returning to these
        shores,
Now on for aye our infinite free venture wending,
Spurning all yet tried ports, seas, hawsers, densities, gravita-
        tion,
Sail out for good, eidólon yacht of me!

LINGERING LAST DROPS

And whence and why come you?

We know not whence, (was the answer,)
We only know that we drift here with the rest,
That we linger'd and lagg'd—but were wafted at last, and are
        now here,
To make the passing shower's concluding drops.

GOOD-BYE MY FANCY

Good-bye* my fancy—(I had a word to say,
But 'tis not quite the time—The best of any man's word or say,
Is when its proper place arrives—and for its meaning,
I keep mine till the last.)

ON, ON THE SAME, YE JOCUND TWAIN!

On, on the same, ye jocund twain!
My life and recitative, containing birth, youth, mid-age years,
Fitful as motley-tongues of flame, inseparably twined and
        merged in one—combining all,
My single soul—aims, confirmations, failures, joys—Nor sin-
        gle soul alone,
I chant my nation's crucial stage, (America's, haply human-
        ity's)—the trial great, the victory great,
A strange *elcaircissement* of all the masses past, the eastern
        world, the ancient, medieval,

* Behind a Good-bye there lurks much of the salutation of another be-
ginning—to me, Development, Continuity, Immortality, Transformation,
are the chiefest life-meanings of Nature and Humanity, and are the *sine
qua non* of all facts, and each fact.
    Why do folks dwell so fondly on the last words, advice, appearance, of
the departing? Those last words are not samples of the best, which involve
vitality at its full, and balance, and perfect control and scope. But they are
valuable beyond measure to confirm and endorse the varied train, facts,
theories and faith of the whole preceding life.

Here, here from wanderings, strayings, lessons, wars, defeats
——here at the west a voice triumphant——justi-
fying all,
A gladsome pealing cry——a song for once of utmost pride and
satisfaction;
I chant from it the common bulk, the general average horde,
(the best no sooner than the worst)——And
now I chant old age,
(My verses, written first for forenoon life, and for the sum-
mer's, autumn's spread,
I pass to snow-white hairs the same, and give to pulses winter-
cool'd the same;)
As here in careless trill, I and my recitatives, with faith and
love,
Wafting to other work, to unknown songs, conditions,
On, on, ye jocund twain! continue on the same!

MY 71ST YEAR

After surmounting three-score and ten,
With all their chances, changes, losses, sorrows,
My parents' deaths, the vagaries of my life, the many tearing
passions of me, the war of '63 and '4,
As some old broken soldier, after a long, hot, wearying march,
or haply after battle,
To-day at twilight, hobbling, answering company roll-call,
Here, with vital voice,
Reporting yet, saluting yet the Officer over all.

APPARITIONS

A vague mist hanging 'round half the pages:
(Sometimes how strange and clear to the soul,
That all these solid things are indeed but apparitions, concepts,
non-realities.)

THE PALLID WREATH

Somehow I cannot let it go yet, funeral though it is,
Let it remain back there on its nail suspended,
With pink, blue, yellow, all blanch'd, and the white now gray
and ashy,
One wither'd rose put years ago for thee, dear friend;
But I do not forget thee. Hast thou then faded?
Is the odor exhaled? Are the colors, vitalities, dead?
No, while memories subtly play——the past vivid as ever;
For but last night I woke, and in that spectral ring saw thee,
Thy smile, eyes, face, calm, silent, loving as ever;
So let the wreath hang still awhile within my eye-reach,
It is not yet dead to me, nor even pallid.

AN ENDED DAY

The soothing sanity and blitheness of completion,
The pomp and hurried contest-glare and rush are done;
Now triumph! transformation! jubilate!*

OLD AGE'S SHIP & CRAFTY DEATH'S

From east and west across the horizon's edge,
Two mighty masterful vessels sailers steal upon us:
But we'll make race a-time upon the seas—a battle-contest yet!
bear lively there!
(Our joys of strife and derring-do to the last!)
Put on the old ship all her power to-day!
Crowd top-sail, top-gallant and royal studding-sails,
Out challenge and defiance—flags and flaunting pennants
added,
As we take to the open! take to the deepest, freest waters.

TO THE PENDING YEAR

Have I no weapon-word for thee—some message brief and
fierce?
(Have I fought out and done indeed the battle? Is there no shot
left,

* NOTE.—*Summer country life.*—*Several years.*—In my rambles and ex-
plorations I found a woody place near the creek, where for some reason the
birds in happy mood seem'd to resort in unusual numbers. Especially at the
beginning of the day, and again at the ending, I was sure to get there the
most copious bird-concerts. I repair'd there frequently at sunrise—and also
at sunset, or just before. . . . Once the question arose in me: Which is the
best singing, the first or the lattermost? The first always exhilarated, and
perhaps seem'd more joyous and stronger; but I always felt the sunset or
late afternoon sounds more penetrating and sweeter—seem'd to touch the
soul- often the evening thrushes, two or three of them, responding and
perhaps blending. Though I miss'd some of the mornings, I found myself
getting to be quite strictly punctual at the evening utterances.

ANOTHER NOTE.- -"He went out with the tide and the sunset," was a
phrase I heard from a surgeon describing an old sailor's death under pecu-
liarly gentle conditions.

During the Secession War, 1863 and '4, visiting the Army Hospitals
around Washington, I form'd the habit, and continued it to the end, when-
ever the ebb or flood tide began the latter part of the day, of punctually
visiting those at that time populous wards of suffering men. Somehow (or
I thought so) the effect of the hour was palpable. The badly wounded would
get some ease, and would like to talk a little, or be talk'd to. Intellectual
and emotional natures would be at their best: Deaths were always easier;
medicines seem'd to have better effect when given then, and a lulling at-
mosphere would pervade the wards.

Similar influences, similar circumstances and hours, day-close, after great
battles, even with all their horrors. I had more than once the same experience
on the fields cover'd with fallen or dead.

For all thy affectation, lisps, scorns, manifold silliness?
Not for myself—my own rebellious self in thee?

Down, down, proud gorge!—though choking thee;
Thy bearded throat and high-borne forehead to the gutter;
Crouch low thy neck to eleemosynary gifts.

SHAKSPERE-BACON'S CIPHER

I doubt it not—then more, far more;
In each old song bequeath'd—in every noble page or text,
(Different—something unreck'd before—some unsuspected
        author,)
In every object, mountain, tree, and star—in every birth and
        life,
As part of each—evolv'd from each—meaning, behind the
        ostent,
A mystic cipher waits infolded.

LONG, LONG HENCE

After a long, long course, hundreds of years, denials,
Accumulations, rous'd love and joy and thought,
Hopes, wishes, aspirations, ponderings, victories, myriads of
        readers,
Coating, compassing, covering—after ages' and ages' encrus-
        tations,
Then only may these songs reach fruition.

BRAVO, PARIS EXPOSITION!

Add to your show, before you close it, France,
With all the rest, visible, concrete, temples, towers, goods,
        machines and ores,
Our sentiment wafted from many million heart-throbs, ethereal
        but solid,
(We grand-sons and great-grand-sons do not forget your
        grand-sires,)
From fifty Nations and nebulous Nations, compacted, sent
        oversea to-day,
America's applause, love, memories and good-will.

INTERPOLATION SOUNDS

[General Philip Sheridan was buried at the Cathedral, Washington,
D. C., August 1888, with all the pomp, music, and ceremonies of the
Roman Catholic service.]

Over and through the burial chant,
Organ and solemn service sermon. bending priests,
To me come interpolation sounds not in the show—plainly to
        me, crowding up the aisle and from the win-
        dow,

Of sudden battle's hurry and harsh noises—war's grim game
to sight and ear in earnest;
The scout call'd up and forward—the general mounted and his
aids around him—the new-brought word—
the instantaneous order issued;
The rifle crack—the cannon thud—the rushing forth of men
from their tents;
The clank of cavalry—the strange celerity of forming ranks—
the slender bugle note;
The sound of horses' hoofs departing—saddles, arms, ac-
coutrements.*

TO THE SUN-SET BREEZE

Ah, whispering, something again, unseen,
Where late this heated day thou enterest at my window, door,
Thou, laving, tempering all, cool-freshing, gently vitalizing
Me, old, alone. sick, weak-down, melted-worn with sweat;
Thou, nestling, folding close and firm yet soft, companion
better than talk, book, art;
(Thou hast, O Nature! elements! utterance to my heart be-
yond the rest—and this is of them,)
So sweet thy primitive taste to breathe within—thy soothing
fingers on my face and hands,
Thou, messenger-magical strange bringer to body and spirit of
me,
(Distances balk'd—occult medicines penetrating me from head
to foot,)
I feel the sky, the prairie vast—I feel the mighty northern
lakes,
I feel the ocean and the forest—somehow I feel the globe
itself swift-swimming in space;
Thou blown from lips so loved, now gone—haply from endless
store, God-sent,

* Note.—Camden, N. J., August 7, 1888.—Walt Whitman asks the *New York Herald* "to add his tribute to Sheridan":

"In the grand constellation of five or six names, under Lincoln's Presi-
dency, that history will bear for ages in her firmament as marking the last
life-throbs of secession, and beaming on its dying gasp, Sheridan's will be
bright. One consideration rising out of the now dead soldier's example as
it passes my mind, is worth taking notice of. If the war had continued any
long time these States, in my opinion, would have shown and proved the
most conclusive military talents ever evinced by any nation on earth. That
they possess'd a rank and file ahead of all other known in points of quality
and limitlessness of number are easily admitted. But we have, too, the eligi-
bility of organizing, handling and officering equal to the other. These two,
with modern arms, transportation, and inventive American genius, would
make the United States, with earnestness, not only able to stand the whole
world, but conquer that world united against us."

(For thou art spiritual, Godly, most of all known to my sense,)
Minister to speak to me, here and now, what word has never
       told, and cannot tell,
Art thou not universal concrete's distillation? Law's, all As-
       tronomy's last refinement?
Hast thou no soul? Can I not know, identify thee?

OLD CHANTS

An ancient song, reciting, ending,
Once gazing toward thee, Mother of All,
Musing, seeking themes fitted for thee,
Accept for me, thou saidst, *the elder ballads,*
And name for me before thou goest each ancient poet.

(Of many debts incalculable,
Haply our New World's chiefest debt is to old poems.)

Ever so far back, preluding thee, America,
Old chants, Egyptian priests, and those of Ethiopia,
The Hindu epics, the Grecian, Chinese, Persian,
The Biblic books and prophets, and deep idyls of the Naza-
       rene,
The Iliad, Odyssey, plots, doings, wanderings of Eneas,
Hesiod, Eschylus, Sophocles, Merlin, Arthur,
The Cid, Roland at Roncesvalles, the Nibelungen,
The troubadours, minstrels, minnesingers, skalds,
Chaucer, Dante, flocks of singing birds,
The Border Minstrelsy, the bye-gone ballads, feudal tales,
       essays, plays,
Shakspere, Schiller, Walter Scott, Tennyson,
As some vast wondrous weird dream-presences,
The great shadowy groups gathering around,
Darting their mighty masterful eyes forward at thee,
Thou! with as now thy bending neck and head, with courteous
       hand and word, ascending,
Thou! pausing a moment, drooping thine eyes upon them,
       blent with their music,
Well pleased, accepting all, curiously prepared for by them,
Thou enterest at thy entrance porch.

A CHRISTMAS GREETING

From a Northern Star-Group to a Southern, 1889–'90.

Welcome, Brazilian brother—thy ample place is ready;
A loving hand—a smile from the north—a sunny instant hail!
(Let the future care for itself, where it reveals its troubles, im-
       pedimentas,
Ours, ours the present throe, the democratic aim, the accept-
       ance and the faith;)

To thee to-day our reaching arm, our turning neck—to thee
    from us the expectant eye,
Thou cluster free! thou brilliant lustrous one! thou, learning
    well,
The true lesson of a nation's light in the sky,
(More shining than the Cross, more than the Crown,)
The height to be superb humanity.

SOUNDS OF THE WINTER

Sounds of the winter too,
Sunshine upon the mountains—many a distant strain
From cheery railroad train—from nearer field, barn, house,
The whispering air—even the mute crops, garner'd apples,
    corn,
Children's and women's tones—rhythm of many a farmer
    and of flail,
An old man's garrulous lips among the rest, *Think not we give
    out yet,*
Forth from these snowy hairs we keep up yet the lilt.

A TWILIGHT SONG

As I sit in twilight late alone by the flickering oak-flame,
Musing on long-pass'd war-scenes—of the countless buried un-
    known soldiers,
Of the vacant names, as unidentified air's and sea's—the un-
    return'd,
The brief truce after battle, with grim burial-squads, and the
    deep-fill'd trenches
Of gather'd dead from all America, North, South, East, West,
    whence they came up,
From wooded Maine, New-England's farms, from fertile Penn-
    sylvania, Illinois, Ohio,
From the measureless West, Virginia, the South, the Carolinas,
    Texas,
(Even here in my room-shadows and half-lights in the noise-
    less flickering flames,
Again I see the stalwart ranks on-filing, rising—I hear the
    rhythmic tramp of the armies;)
You million unwrit names all, all—you dark bequest from
    all the war,
A special verse for you—a flash of duty long neglected—your
    mystic roll strangely gather'd here,
Each name recall'd by me from out the darkness and death's
    ashes,
Henceforth to be, deep, deep within my heart recording, for
    many a future year,
Your mystic roll entire of unknown names, or North or South,
Embalm'd with love in this twilight song.

WHEN THE FULL-GROWN POET CAME

When the full-grown poet came,
Out spake pleased Nature (the round impassive globe, with
      all its shows of day and night,) saying, *He is
      mine;*
But out spake too the Soul of man, proud, jealous and un-
      reconciled, *Nay, he is mine alone;*
—Then the full-grown poet stood between the two, and took
      each by the hand;
And to-day and ever so stands, as blender, uniter, tightly hold-
      ing hands,
Which he will never release until he reconciles the two,
And wholly and joyously blends them.

OSCEOLA

[When I was nearly grown to manhood in Brooklyn, New York
(middle of 1838), I met one of the return'd U. S. Marines from Fort
Moultrie, S. C., and had long talks with him—learn'd the occurrence
below described—death of Osceola. The latter was a young, brave,
leading Seminole, in the Florida war of that time—was surrender'd to
our troops, imprison'd, and literally died of "a broken heart," at Fort
Moultrie. He sicken'd of his confinement—the doctor and officers made
every allowance and kindness possible for him; then the close:]

When his hour for death had come,
He slowly rais'd himself from the bed on the floor,
Drew on his war-dress, shirt, leggings, and girdled the belt
      around his waist,
Call'd for vermilion paint (his looking-glass was held before
      him,)
Painted half his face and neck, his wrists, and back-hands,
Put the scalp-knife carefully in his belt—then lying down,
      resting a moment,
Rose again, half sitting, smiled, gave in silence his extended
      hand to each and all,
Sank faintly low to the floor (tightly grasping the tomahawk
      handle,)
Fix'd his look on wife and little children—the last:
(And here a line in memory of his name and death.)

A VOICE FROM DEATH

[The Johnstown, Penn., cataclysm, May 31, 1889]

A voice from Death, solemn and strange, in all his sweep and
      power,
With sudden, indescribable blow—towns drown'd—humanity
      by thousands slain,
The vaunted work of thrift, goods, dwellings, forge, street,
      iron bridge,

Dash'd pell-mell by the blow—yet usher'd life continuing on,
(Amid the rest, amid the rushing, whirling, wild debris,
A suffering woman saved—a baby safely born!)

Although I come and unannounc'd, in horror and in pang,
In pouring flood and fire, and wholesale elemental crash, (this
      voice so solemn, strange,)
I too a minister of Deity.

Yea, Death, we bow our faces, veil our eyes to thee,
We mourn the old, the young untimely drawn to thee,
The fair, the strong, the good, the capable,
The household wreck'd, the husband and the wife, the engulf'd
      forger in his forge,
The corpses in the whelming waters and the mud,
The gather'd thousands to their funeral mounds, and thou-
      sands never found or gather'd.

Then after burying, mourning the dead,
(Faithful to them found or unfound, forgetting not, bearing
      the past, here new musing,)
A day—a passing moment or an hour—America itself bends
      low,
Silent, resign'd, submissive.

War, death, cataclysm like this, America.
Take deep to thy proud prosperous heart.

E'en as I chant, lo! out of death, and out of ooze and slime,
The blossoms rapidly blooming, sympathy, help, love,
From West and East, from South and North and over sea,
Its hot-spurr'd hearts and hands humanity to human aid
      moves on;
And from within a thought and lesson yet.

Thou ever-darting Globe! through Space and Air!
Thou waters that encompass us!
Thou that in all the life and death of us, in action or in sleep!
Thou laws invisible that permeate them and all,
Thou that in all, and over all, and through and under all, in-
      cessant!
Thou! thou! the vital, universal, giant force resistless, sleep-
      less, calm,
Holding Humanity as in thy open hand, as some ephemeral
      toy,
How ill to e'er forget thee!

For I too have forgotten,
(Wrapt in these little potencies of progress, politics, culture,
      wealth, inventions, civilization,)

Have lost my recognition of your silent ever-swaying power, ye
    mighty, elemental throes,
In which and upon which we float, and every one of us is
    buoy'd.

A PERSIAN LESSON

For his o'erarching and last lesson the greybeard sufi,
In the fresh scent of the morning in the open air,
On the slope of a teeming Persian rose-garden,
Under an ancient chestnut-tree wide spreading its branches,
Spoke to the young priests and students.

"Finally my children, to envelop each word, each part of the
    rest,
Allah is all, all, all—is immanent in every life and object,
May-be at many and many-a-more removes—yet Allah, Allah,
    Allah is there.

"Has the estray wander'd far? Is the reason-why strangely
    hidden?
Would you sound below the restless ocean of the entire world?
Would you know the dissatisfaction? the urge and spur of
    every life;
The something never still'd—never entirely gone? the invis-
    ible need of every seed?

"It is the central urge in every atom,
(Often unconscious, often evil, downfallen,)
To return to its divine source and origin, however distant,
Latent the same in subject and in object, without one ex-
    ception."

THE COMMONPLACE

The commonplace I sing;
How cheap is health! how cheap nobility!
Abstinence, no falsehood, no gluttony, lust;
The open air I sing, freedom, toleration,
(Take here the mainest lesson—less from books—less from
    the schools,)
The common day and night—the common earth and waters,
Your farm—your work, trade, occupation,
The democratic wisdom underneath, like solid ground for all.

"THE ROUNDED CATALOGUE DIVINE COMPLETE"

[Sunday—— — ——. —Went this forenoon to church. A college professor, Rev. Dr.——, gave us a fine sermon, during which I caught the above words; but the minister included in his "rounded catalogue" letter and spirit, only the esthetic things, and entirely ignored what I name in the following:]

The devilish and the dark, the dying and diseas'd,
The countless (nineteen-twentieths) low and evil, crude and
        savage,
The crazed, prisoners in jail, the horrible, rank, malignant,
Venom and filth, serpents, the ravenous sharks, liars, the dis-
        solute;
(What is the part the wicked and the loathsome bear within
        earth's orbic scheme?)
Newts, crawling things in slime and mud, poisons,
The barren soil, the evil men, the slag and hideous rot.

MIRAGES

[Noted verbatim after a supper-talk out doors in Nevada with two old miners]

More experiences and sights, stranger, than you'd think for;
Times again, now mostly just after sunrise or before sunset,
Sometimes in spring, oftener in autumn, perfectly clear
        weather, in plain sight,
Camps far or near, the crowded streets of cities and the shop-
        fronts,
(Account for it or not—credit or not—it is all true,
And my mate there could tell you the like—we have often
        confab'd about it,)
People and scenes, animals, trees, colors and lines, plain as
        could be,
Farms and dooryards of home, paths border'd with box, lilacs
        in corners,
Weddings in churches, thanksgiving dinners, returns of long-
        absent sons,
Glum funerals, the crape-veil'd mother and the daughters,
Trials in courts, jury and judge, the accused in the box,
Contestants, battles, crowds, bridges, wharves,
Now and then mark'd faces of sorrow or joy,
(I could pick them out this moment if I saw them again,)
Show'd to me just aloft to the right in the sky-edge,
Or plainly there to the left on the hill-tops.

L. OF G.'S PURPORT

Not to exclude or demarcate, or pick out evils from their for-
      midable masses (even to expose them,)
But add, fuse, complete, extend—and celebrate the immortal
      and the good.

Haughty this song, its words and scope,
To span vast realms of space and time,
Evolution—the cumulative—growths and generations.

Begun in ripen'd youth and steadily pursued,
Wandering, peering, dallying with all—war, peace, day and
      night absorbing,
Never even for one brief hour abandoning my task,
I end it here in sickness, poverty, and old age.

I sing of life, yet mind me well of death:
To-day shadowy Death dogs my steps, my seated shape, and
      has for years—
Draws sometimes close to me, as face to face.

THE UNEXPRESS'D

How dare one say it?
After the cycles, poems, singers, plays,
Vaunted Ionia's, India's—Homer, Shakspere—the long, long
      times, thick dotted roads, areas,
The shining clusters and the Milky Ways of stars—Nature's
      pulses reap'd,
All retrospective passions, heroes, war, love, adoration,
All ages' plummets dropt to their utmost depths,
All human lives, throats, wishes, brains—all experiences' ut-
      terance;
After the countless songs, or long or short, all tongues, all
      lands,
Still something not yet told in poesy's voice or print—some-
      thing lacking,
(Who knows? the best yet unexpress'd and lacking.)

GRAND IS THE SEEN

Grand is the seen, the light, to me—grand are the sky and
      stars,
Grand is the earth, and grand are lasting time and space,
And grand their laws, so multiform, puzzling, evolutionary;
But grander far the unseen soul of me, comprehending, en-
      dowing all those,
Lighting the light, the sky and stars, delving the earth, sailing
      the sea,

(What were all those, indeed, without thee, unseen soul? of
    what amount without thee?)
More evolutionary, vast, puzzling, O my soul!
More multiform far—more lasting thou than they.

UNSEEN BUDS

Unseen buds, infinite, hidden well,
Under the snow and ice, under the darkness, in every square or
    cubic inch,
Germinal, exquisite, in delicate lace, microscopic, unborn,
Like babes in wombs, latent, folded, compact, sleeping;
Billions of billions, and trillions of trillions of them waiting,
(On earth and in the sea—the universe—the stars there in the
    heavens,)
Urging slowly, surely forward, forming endless,
And waiting ever more, forever more behind.

GOOD-BYE MY FANCY!

Good-bye my Fancy!
Farewell dear mate, dear love!
I'm going away, I know not where,
Or to what fortune, or whether I may ever see you again,
So Good-bye my Fancy.

Now for my last—let me look back a moment;
The slower fainter ticking of the clock is in me,
Exit, nightfall, and soon the heart-thud stopping.

Long have we lived, joy'd, caress'd together;
Delightful!—now separation—Good-bye my Fancy.

Yet let me not be too hasty,
Long indeed have we lived, slept, filter'd, become really
    blended into one;
Then if we die together, (yes, we'll remain one,)
If we go anywhere we'll go together to meet what happens,
May-be we'll be better off and blither, and learn something,
May-be it is yourself now really ushering me to the true songs,
    (who knows?)
May-be it is you the mortal knob really undoing, turning—so
    now finally,
Good-bye—and hail! my Fancy.

INDEX OF TITLES

Aboard at the Ship's Helm, 218
Abraham Lincoln, Born Feb. 12, 1809, 387
Adieu to a Soldier, 263
After All, Not to Create, Only. *See* Song of the Exposition
After the Dazzle of Day, 387
After the Sea-Ship, 221
After the Supper and Talk, 403
Ages and Ages Returning at Intervals, 109
Ah, Poverties, Wincings, and Sulky Retreats, 367
All Is Truth, 364
America, 387
American Feuillage. *See* Our Old Feuillage
Among the Multitude, 126
And Yet Not You Alone (Fancies at Navesink), 389
Answerer, The. *See* Song of the Answerer
Apparitions, 405
Are You the New Person Drawn toward Me? 119
Army Corps on the March, An, 247
Army on the March, An. *See* Army Corps on the March, An
Artilleryman's Vision, The, 258
As Adam Early in the Morning, 112
As a Strong Bird on Pinions Free. *See* Thou Mother with Thy
    Equal Brood
As at Thy Portals Also Death, 378
As Consequent, *Etc.*, 285
As I Ebb'd with the Ocean of Life, 214
As I Lay with My Head in Your Lap Camerado, 261
As I Ponder'd in Silence, 31
As I Sat Alone by Blue Ontario's Shore. *See* By Blue Ontario's
    Shore
As I Sit Writing Here, 386
As I Walk Solitary, Unattended. *See* As I Walk These Broad
    Majestic Days
As I Walk These Broad Majestic Days, 371
As I Watch'd the Ploughman Ploughing, 350
As If a Phantom Caress'd Me, 346
As Nearing Departure. *See* As the Time Draws Nigh
As One by One Withdraw the Lofty Actors. *See* Death of
    General Grant

As the Greek's Signal Flame, 401
As the Time Draws Nigh, 372
As They Draw to a Close, 381
As Toilsome I Wander'd Virginia's Woods, 251
Ashes of Soldiers, 374
Assurances, 346
Autumn Rivulets, 285

Base of All Metaphysics, The, 118
Beat! Beat! Drums! 233
Beautiful Women, 229
Beginners, 36
Beginning My Studies, 36
Behold This Swarthy Face, 121
Birds of Passage, 195
Bivouac on a Mountain Side, 246
Boston Ballad, A, 222
Boston Ballad, the 78th Year of These States, A. *See* Boston
  Ballad, A
Bravest Soldiers, The, 385
Bravo, Paris Exposition! 407
Broad-Axe Poem. *See* Song of the Broad-Axe
Broadway, 393
Broadway Pageant, A, 206
Brother of All, with Generous Hand. *See* Outlines for a Tomb
Bunch Poem. *See* Spontaneous Me
Burial. *See* To Think of Time
Burial Poem. *See* To Think of Time
By Blue Ontario's Shore, 273
By Broad Potomac's Shore, 369
By That Long Scan of Waves (Fancies at Navesink), 390
By the Bivouac's Fitful Flame, 247
By the Roadside, 222

Calamus
  See Among the Multitude
        Are You the New Person Drawn toward Me?
        Behold This Swarthy Face
        City of Orgies
        Earth, My Likeness
        Fast-Anchor'd Eternal O Love!
        For you O Democracy, Over the Carnage Rose
          Prophetic a Voice
        Full of Life Now
        Glimpse, A
        Here the Frailest Leaves of Me
        I Dream'd in a Dream
        I Hear It Was Charged Against Me

     I Saw in Louisiana a Live-Oak Growing
     In Paths Untrodden
     Leaf for Hand in Hand, A
     No Labor-Saving Machine

Calamus
    See Not Heat Flames Up and Consumes
          Not Heaving from My Ribb'd Breast Only
          O Living Always, Always Dying
          O You Whom I Often and Silently Come
          Of Him I Love Day and Night
          Of the Terrible Doubt of Appearances
          Prairie-Grass Dividing, The
          Promise to California, A
          Recorders Ages Hence
          Roots and Leaves Themselves Alone
          Scented Herbage of My Breast
          Sometimes with One I Love
          That Music Always Round Me
          That Shadow My Likeness
          These I Singing in Spring
          This Moment Yearning and Thoughtful
          To a Stranger
          To a Western Boy
          To the East and to the West
          Trickle Drops
          We Two Boys Together Clinging
          What Place Is Besieged
          What Ship Puzzled at Sea
          What Think You I Take My Pen in Hand?
          When I Heard at the Close of the Day
          When I Peruse the Conquer'd Fame
          Whoever You Are Holding Me Now in Hand
Calming Thought of All, The, 397
Camps of Green, 380
Carol Closing Sixty-Nine, A, 385
Carol of Harvest, for 1867, A. *See* Return of the Heroes, The
Carol of Occupations. *See* Song for Occupations, A
Carol of Words. *See* Song of the Rolling Earth, A
Cavalry Crossing a Ford, 246
Centenarian's Story, The, 242
Chanting the Square Deific, 343
Chants Democratic
    See As I Walk These Broad Majestic Days
          By Blue Ontario's Shore
          Excelsior
          I Hear America Singing
          I Was Looking a Long Whil

     Laws for Creation
     Mediums
     Me Imperturbe
     On Journeys through the States
     Our Old Feuillage
     Poets to Come
     Song of the Broad-Axe
     Song for Occupations
     Song at Sunset
Chants Democratic
  See Thoughts (p. 375)
     To a Historian
     Vocalism
     With Antecedents
Children of Adam
  See Ages and Ages Returning at Intervals
     As Adam Early in the Morning
     Facing West from California's Shores
     From Pent-up Aching Rivers
     I Am He That Aches with Love
     I Sing the Body Electric
     Native Moments
     Oh Hymen! O Hymenee!
     Once I Pass'd through a Populous City
     One Hour to Madness and Joy
     Spontaneous Me
     To the Garden the World
     We Two, How Long We Were Fool'd
     Woman Waits for Me, A
Child's Amaze, A, 229
Christmas Greeting, A, 409
City Dead-House, The, 292
City of Orgies, 121
City of Ships, 242
Clear Midnight, A, 372
Clef Poem. *See* On the Beach at Night Alone
Come, I Will Make the Continent Indissoluble. *See* For You
  O Democracy
Come Up from the Fields Father, 247
Commonplace, The, 413
Continuities, 395
Crossing Brooklyn Ferry, 144

Dalliance of the Eagles, The, 228
Darest Thou Now O Soul, 342
Dead Emperor, The, 401
Dead Tenor, The, 394
Death of General Grant, 392

Delicate Cluster, 262
Did You Ask Dulcet Rhymes From Me? *See* To a Certain Civilian
Dirge for Two Veterans, 256
Dismantled Ship, The, 402
Dresser, The. *See* Wound-Dresser, The
Drum-Taps, 231
Dying Veteran, The, 399

Earth, My Likeness, 125
Eidólons, 33
Eighteen Sixty-One, 233
Election Day, November, 1884, 390
Elemental Drifts. *See* As I Ebbed with the Ocean of Life
Ended Day, An, 406
Ethiopia Saluting the Colors, 259
Europe, 223
Evening Lull, An, 402
Excelsior, 366

Faces, 356
Facing West from California's Shores, 111
Faith Poem. *See* Assurances
Fancies at Navesink, 388
Farm Picture, A, 229
Fast-Anchor'd Eternal O Love!, 126
First Dandelion, The, 387
First O Songs for a Prelude, 231
Flag of Stars, Thick-Sprinkled Bunting. *See* Thick-Sprinkled Bunting
Font of Type, A, 386
For Him I Sing, 35
For You O Democracy, 115
France, the 18th Year of These States, 202
From Far Dakota's Cañons, 369
From Montauk Point, 385
From Noon to Starry Night, 355
From Paumanok Starting I Fly Like a Bird, 234
From Pent-up Aching Rivers, 97
Full of Life Now, 127

Germs, 226
Give Me the Splendid Silent Sun, 255
Gliding O'er All, 230
Glimpse, A, 124
Gods, 225
"Going Somewhere", 396
Good-Bye My Fancy, 404

Good-Bye My Fancy!, 416
Grand Is the Seen, 415
Grant. *See* Death of General Grant

Had I the Choice (Fancies at Navesink), 388
Halcyon Days, 388
Hand-Mirror, A, 225
Hast Never Come to Thee an Hour, 230
Here Sailor. *See* What Ship Puzzled at Sea
Here the Frailest Leaves of Me, 124
How Solemn as One by One, 261
Hush'd Be the Camps To-day, 272
Hymn of Dead Soldiers. *See* Ashes of Soldiers

I Am He That Aches with Love, 110
I Dream'd in a Dream, 125
I Hear America Singing, 38
I Hear It was Charged against Me, 123
I Heard You Solemn-Sweet Pipes of the Organ, 111
I Saw in Louisiana a Live-Oak Growing, 121
I Saw Old General at Bay, 258
I Sing the Body Electric, 98
I Sit and Look Out, 227
I Was Looking a Long While, 307
If I Should Need to Name, O Western World. *See* Election
    Day, November, 1884
Imprisoned Soul, The. *See* Last Invocation, The
In Cabin'd Ships at Sea, 31
In Clouds Descending. In Midnight Sleep. *See* Old War-
    Dreams
In Midnight Sleep. *See* Old War-Dreams
In Paths Untrodden, 112
Indications, The. *See* Song of the Answerer
Inscription. *See* One's-Self I Sing
Inscriptions, 31
Interpolation Sounds, 407
Italian Music in Dakota, 315

Joy, Shipmate, Joy! 381

Kosmos, 310
L. of G.'s Purport, 415
Last Invocation, The, 350
Last of Ebb, and Daylight Waning (Fancies at Navesink), 389
Laws for Creations, 306
Leaf for Hand in Hand, A, 125
Leaf of Faces. *See* Faces
Leaves of Grass. *See* Beginners

Leaves of Grass
   See Aboard at the Ship's Helm
         All Is Truth
         As I Ebb'd with the Ocean of Life
         Assurances
         Germs
         I Sit and Look Out
         Laws for Creations
         Locations and Times
         Miracles
Leaves of Grass
   See Myself and Mine
         Night on the Prairies
         On the Beach Alone at Night
         So Long!
         Song of Prudence
         Song of the Answerer
         Tears
         There Was a Child Went Forth
         This Compost
         To You
         Unfolded Out of the Folds
         Vocalism
         What Am I After All
         Who Learns My Lesson Complete
         World Below the Brine, The
         You Felons on Trial in Courts
Lesson Poem. See Who Learns My Lesson Complete
Liberty Poem for Asia, Africa, Europe, America, Australia, Cuba, and the Archipelagoes of the Sea. See To a Foil'd European Revolutionaire
Life, 396
Life and Death, 398
Lingering Last Drops, 404
Locations and Times, 230
Longings for Home. See O Magnet-South
Long Long Hence, 407
Long, Too Long America, 254
Long, Too Long, O Land. See Long, Too Long America
Look Down Fair Moon, 260
Lo, Victress on the Peaks, 262

Mannahatta, 364
Mannahatta, 384
Mannahatta's Streets I Saunter'd, Pondering. See Song of Prudence
March in the Ranks Hard-Prest, and the Road Unknown, 250
Me Imperturbe, 37

Mediums, 368
Memories, 387
Memories of President Lincoln, 265
Miracles, 307
Mirages, 414
Mother and Babe, 229
My Canary Bird, 386
My Legacy, 379
My Picture-Gallery, 316
My 71st Year, 405
Myself and Mine, 203
Mystic Trumpeter, The, 359

Native Moments, 110
Night On the Prairies, 348
Night Poem. *See* Sleepers, The
Noiseless Patient Spider, A, 347
No Labor-Saving Machine, 124
Not Heat Flames Up and Consumes, 120
Not Heaving from My Ribb'd Breast Only, 117
Not Meagre, Latent Boughs Alone, 401
Not the Pilot, 252
Not Youth Pertains to Me, 259
Now Finalè to the Shore, 382
Not Heaving from My Ribb'd Breast Only, 117
  swerer
Now Precedent Songs Farewell, 402

O Captain! My Captain! 271
O Hymen! O Hymenee! 110
O Living Always, Always Dying, 348
O Magnet-South, 362
O Me! O Life! 227
O Star of France, 312
O Tan-Faced Prairie-Boy, 260
O You Whom I Often and Silently Come, 127
Of Him I Love Day and Night, 345
Of That Blithe Throat of Thine, 393
Of the Terrible Doubt of Appearances, 117
Offerings, 230
Old Age's Lambent Peaks, 403
Old Age's Ship and Crafty Death's, 406
Old Chants, 409
Old Ireland, 292
Old Man's Thought of School, An, 314
Old Salt Kossabone, 394
Old War-Dreams, 370
On the Beach at Night, 218
On the Beach at Night Alone, 219
424

On Journeys through the States, 36
On, On the Same, Ye Jocund Twain!, 404
Once I Pass'd through a Populous City, 111
One Hour to Madness and Joy, 108
One's Self I Sing, 31
Orange Buds by Mail from Florida, 400
Osceola, 411
Others May Praise What They Like, 310
Our Old Feuillage, 153
Out from Behind This Mask, 303
Out of the Cradle Endlessly Rocking, 209
Out of the Rolling Ocean the Crowd, 109
Out of May's Shows Selected, 387
Outlines for a Tomb, 302
Over the Carnage Rose Prophetic a Voice, 257
Ox-Tamer, The, 313

Pallid Wreath, The, 405
Passage to India, 321
Patroling Barnegat, 221
Paumanok, 385
Paumanok Picture, A, 355
Pensive and Faltering, 350
Pensive on Her Dead Gazing, 379
Perfections, 227
Persian Lesson, A, 413
Picture. See Offerings
Pilot in the Mist, The (Fancies at Navesink), 388
Pioneers! O Pioneers! 196
Poem of Apparitions in Boston, the 78th Year of These States.
    See Boston Ballad, A
Poem of Faces. See Faces
Poem of Joys. See Song of Joys, A
Poem of Perfect Miracles. See Miracles
Poem of Procreation. See Woman Waits for Me, A
Poem of Salutation. See Salut au Monde!
Poem of the Body. See I Sing the Body Electric
Poem of the Child That Went Forth, and Always Goes Forth,
    Forever and Forever. See There Was a Child Went Forth
Poem of the Daily Work of the Workmen and Workwomen of
    the States. See Song for Occupations, A
Poem of the Heart of the Song of Manhattan Island. See Ex-
    celsior
Poem of the Last Explanation of Prudence. See Song of Pru-
    dence
Poem of Many in One. See by Blue Ontario's Shore
Poem of the Dead Young Men of Europe, the 72d and 73d

Years of These States. *See* Europe, the 72d and 73d Years of These States

Poem of the Poet. *See* Song of the Answerer.

Poem of the Propositions of Nakedness. *See* Transpositions, *and* Reversals

Poem of the Road. *See* Song of the Open Road

Poem of the Sayers of Words of the Earth. *See* Song of Rolling Earth, A

Poem of the Singers, and of the Words of Poems. *See* Song of the Answerer

Poem of Walt Whitman, an American, A. *See* Song of Myself

Poem of Women. *See* Unfolded Out of the Folds

Poem of Wonder at the Resurrection of the Wheat. *See* This Compost

Poem of You, Whoever You Are. *See* To You (p. 200)

Poems of Joy. *See* Song of Joys, A

Poets to Come,   39

Portals,   381

Prairie-Grass Dividing, The   123

Prairie States, The,   316

Prairie Sunset, A,   400

Prayer of Columbus,   328

Promise to California, A,   124

Proto-Leaf. *See* Starting from Paumanok

Proudly the Flood Comes In (Fancies at Navesink),   390

Proud Music of the Storm,   316

Queries to My Seventieth Year,   386

Quicksand Years,   347

Quicksand Years That Whirl Me I Know Not Whither. *See* Quicksand Years

Race of Veterans,   260

Reconciliation,   260

Recorders Ages Hence,   118

Red Jacket (from Aloft),   392

Respondez. *See* Transpositions

Resurgemus. *See* Europe

Return of the Heroes, The,   286

Reversals,   285

Riddle Song, A,   365

Rise O Days from Your Fathomless Deeps,   240

Roaming in Thought,   228

Roots and Leaves Themselves Alone,   120

"Rounded Catalogue Divine Complete, The",   414

Runner, The,   229

Sail Out for Good, Eidólon Yacht,   403

Salut au Monde!   127

Sands at Seventy, 384
Savantism, 37
Scented Herbage of My Breast, 112
Sea-Drift, 209
Shakspere-Bacon's Cipher, 407
Ship Starting, The, 38
Shut Not Your Doors, 38
Shut Not Your Doors to Me Proud Libraries. *See* Shut Not
Your Doors
Sight in Camp in the Daybreak Gray and Dim, 251
Singer in the Prison, The, 299
Sleep-Chasings. *See* Sleepers, The
Sleepers, The, 330
Small the Theme of My Chant, 396
So Long! 382
Sobbing of the Bells, The, 381
Sometimes with One I Love, 126
Song, A. *See* For You O Democracy
Song at Sunset, 377
Song for All Seas, All Ships, 220
Song for Occupations, A, 183
Song of Joy, A, 158
Song of Myself, 49
Song of Prudence, 297
Song of the Answerer, 149
Song of the Banner at Daybreak, 235
Song of the Broad-Axe, 163
Song of the Exposition, 172
Song of the Open Road, 136
Song of the Redwood-Tree, 180
Song of the Rolling Earth, A, 190
Song of the Universal, 195
Songs of Parting, 372
Soon Shall the Winter's Foil Be Here, 398
Sounds of the Winter, 410
Spain, 1873–74, 368
Sparkles from the Wheel, 308
Spirit That Form'd This Scene, 371
Spirit Whose Work Is Done, 262
Spontaneous Me, 106
Starting from Paumanok, 39
Still Though the One I Sing, 38
Stronger Lessons, 399
Sun-Down Poem. *See* Crossing Brooklyn Ferry

Tears, 217
Tests, 312
Thanks in Old Age, 397

That Music Always Round Me, 347
That Shadow My Likeness, 127
Then Last of All (Fancies at Navesink), 390
There Was a Child Went Forth, 290
These Carols, 382
These I Singing in Spring, 116
Thick-Sprinkled Bunting, 370
This Compost, 293
This Dust Was Once the Man, 272
This Moment Yearning and Thoughtful, 122
Thou Mother with Thy Equal Brood, 350
Thou Orb Aloft Full-Dazzling, 355
Thou Reader, 39
Thou Vast Rondure, Swimming in Space. *See* Passage to India
Thought, 229
Thought, 229
Thought, 230
Thought, 349
Thought. *See* As They Draw Close to Me
Thoughts, 226
Thoughts, 307
Thoughts, 367
Thoughts, 375
To a Cantatrice. *See* To a Certain Cantatrice
To a Certain Cantatrice, 37
To a Certain Civilian, 262
To a Common Prostitute, 306
To a Foil'd European Revolutionaire, 295
To a Foil'd Revolter or Revoltress. *See* To a Foil'd European
    Revolutionaire
To a Historian, 32
To a Locomotive in Winter, 362
To a President, 227
To a Pupil, 309
To a Stranger, 122
To a Western Boy, 126
To Foreign Lands, 32
To Get Betimes in Boston Town. *See* Boston Ballad, A
To Get the Final Lilt of Songs, 394
To Him That Was Crucified, 305
To My Soul. *See* As the Time Draws Nigh
To Old Age, 230
To One Shortly to Die, 348
To Oratists. *See* Vocalism
To Other Lands. *See* To Foreign Lands
To Rich Givers, 228
To the East and to the West, 126
To the Garden the World, 96

To the Leaven'd Soil They Trod,   264
To the Man-of-War-Bird,   217
To the Old Cause,   33
To the Pending Year,   406
To the Prevailing Bards. *See* That Shadow My Likeness
To the Sayers of Words. *See* Song of the Rolling Earth, A
To the States,   36
To the States, To Identify the 16th, 17th, or 18th Presidentiad,
   230
To the Sunset Breeze,   408
To the Year 1889. *See* To the Pending Year
To Think of Time,   337
To Those Who've Fail'd,   385
To Workingmen. *See* Song for Occupations, A
To You,   39
To You, Whoever You Are,   200
To-day and Thee,   387
Torch, The,   312
Transpositions,   337
Trickle Drops,   121
True Conquerors,   397
Turn O Libertad,   264
Twenty Years,   400
Twilight,   401
Twilight Song, A,   410
Unexpress'd, The,   415
Unfolded Out of the Folds,   309
United States to Old World Critics, The,   397
Unnamed Lands,   296
Unseen Buds,   416
Untold Want, The,   381

Veteran's Vision, The. *See* Artilleryman's Vision, The
Vigil Strange I Kept on the Field One Night,   249
Virginia—The West,   241
Visor'd,   229
Vocalism,   304
Voice from Death, A,   411
Voice of the Rain, The,   398
Voices. *See* Vocalism

Wallabout Martyrs, The,   386
Walt Whitman. *See* Song of Myself
Walt Whitman's Caution. *See* To the States
Wandering at Morn,   315
Warble for Lilac-Time,   301
Washington's Monument, February, 1885,   392
We Two Boys Together Clinging,   124

We Two, How Long We Were Fool'd,   109
Weave In, My Hardy Life,   368
What Am I After All,   310
What Best I See in Thee,   371
What Place Is Besieged?,   38
What Ship Puzzled at Sea,   347
What Think You I Take My Pen in Hand?,   125
When I Heard At the Close of the Day,   119
When I Heard the Learn'd Astronomer,   226
When I Peruse the Conquer'd Fame,   123
When I Read the Book,   35
When Lilacs Last in the Dooryard Bloom'd,   265
When the Full-Grown Poet Came,   411
While Not the Past Forgetting,   399
Whispers of Heavenly Death,   343
Who Learns My Lesson Complete?   311
Whoever You Are Holding Me Now in Hand,   114
With All Thy Gifts,   315
With Antecedents,   205
With Husky-Haughty Lips, O Sea,   391
Woman Waits for Me, A,   105
Word Out of the Sea, A. *See* Out of the Cradle Endlessly
    Rocking
World Below the Brine, The,   219
World Take Good Notice,   260
Wound-Dresser, The   252

Year That Trembled and Reel'd Beneath Me,   252
Years of Meteors,   204
Years of the Modern,   373
Years of the Unperform'd. *See* Years of the Modern
Yet, Yet, Ye Downcast Hours,   345
Yonnondio,   395
You Felons on Trial in Courts,   305
You Lingering Sparse Leaves of Me,   401
You Tides with Ceaseless Swell (Fancies at Navesink),   389
Youth, Day, Old Age and Night,   194

SELECTED BIBLIOGRAPHY

Other Works by Walt Whitman

Drum-Taps, 1865   Poems
Democratic Vistas, 1871   Prose
Passage to India, 1871   Poem
Two Rivulets, 1876   Poems
Specimen Days, 1882   Autobiographical Narrative

Collect, 1882   Prose
November Boughs, 1888   Poems
Good-Bye, My Fancy, 1891   Poems

Selected Biography and Criticism

Allen, Gay Wilson. *Walt Whitman Handbook.* Chicago: Packard & Company, 1946.

————. *The Solitary Singer: A Critical Biography of Walt Whitman.* New York: The Macmillan Company, 1955.

Brooks, Van Wyck. *The Times of Melville and Whitman.* New York: E. P. Dutton & Company, Inc., 1947.

Canby, Henry Seidel. *Walt Whitman, an American.* Boston: Houghton Mifflin Company, 1943.

Chase, Richard. *Walt Whitman Reconsidered.* New York: William Sloane Associates, Inc.; London: Victor Gollancz, Ltd., 1955.

de Selincourt, Basil. *Walt Whitman: A Critical Study.* New York: Mitchell Kennerley, 1914.

Fausset, Hugh l'Anson. *Walt Whitman: Poet of Democracy.* New Haven: Yale University Press, 1942.

Holloway, Emory. *Whitman: An Interpretation in Narrative.* New York: Alfred A. Knopf, Inc., 1926.

Matthiessen, F. O. *American Renaissance: Art and Expression in the Age of Emerson and Whitman.* New York: Oxford University Press, 1941.

Perry, Bliss. *Walt Whitman, His Life and His Work.* Boston: Houghton Mifflin Company, 1906.

Rodgers, Cleveland, and John Black (eds.). *The Gathering of the Forces* [Whitman's Contributions to the Brooklyn *Eagle*]. New York: G. P. Putnam's Sons, 1920.

Schyberg, Frederik. *Walt Whitman.* Translated by E. A. Allen. New York: Columbia University Press; London: Oxford University Press, 1951.

Shephard, E. *Walt Whitman's Pose.* New York: Harcourt, Brace and Company, Inc.; London: George G. Harrap & Co., Ltd., 1938.

Willard, Charles B. *Whitman's American Fame: The Growth of His Reputation in America after 1892.* Providence, R. I.: Brown University Press, 1950.

𝓒

SIGNET CLASSICS by American Authors